To Run Be

Copyright © 2020 Michael Rothery

All rights reserved

United Kingdom Licence Notes
The right of Michael Rothery to be identified as the
Author of this work has been asserted by him in
accordance with the Copyrights, Designs and Patents
Act 1988

All rights reserved. Apart from any use permitted
under UK copyright law no part of this publication
may be reproduced, stored in a retrieval system, or
transmitted, in any form or by any means, without the
prior permission of the publisher.

This is a work of fiction. Names, characters, places,
events, and incidents are either the products of the
author's imagination or used in a fictitious manner.
Any resemblance to actual persons, living or dead, or
actual events is purely coincidental and not intended
by the author.

ISBN: 9798673685426
Imprint: Independently published

To Run Before the Sea

Michael Rothery

Paperback Edition
First Revision: October 2020

Weatherdeck Books

CONTENTS

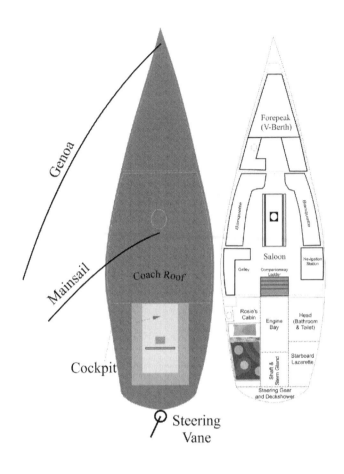

Pasha's Layout

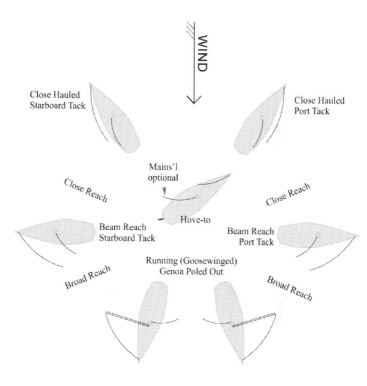

WIND

Close Hauled
Starboard Tack

Close Hauled
Port Tack

Close Reach

Mains'l
optional

Close Reach

Beam Reach
Starboard Tack

Hove-to

Beam Reach
Port Tack

Broad Reach

Running (Goosewinged)
Genoa Poled Out

Broad Reach

Points of Sail

Poppy Day Edition

We Will Remember Them

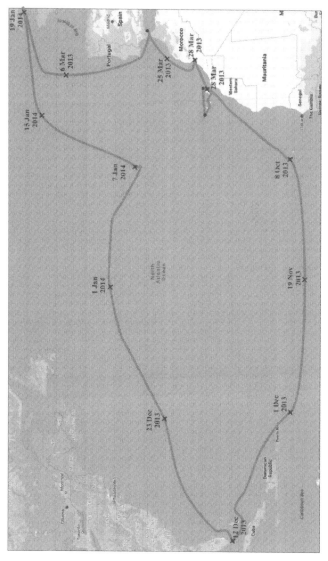

Rosie & Pasha's Atlantic Track

Voices in a Lonely Mind

Although my yacht speaks not, she conjures words
from the complexity of simple sounds:
the whisper-rush of water on the hull;
the sighing sough of wind upon the sail;
the groan of straining sheet around the drum;
the clacking of a halyard on the mast.

Oft times she gives a chiding, scolding start,
admonishing some error on my part;
or bracing words when nerve and sinew strain
to shorten sail in storm and stinging rain.

Through all the raw complexity of noise
I simply hear her calm, ethereal voice;
such haunting, such tranquillity of tone;
a mate imagined, voyaging quite alone.

EPISODE ONE

The Fall

1/1

Shipmates

As I drove past Portsmouth naval barracks, the rain that had harried me since Winchester grew torrential as if trying to drown my resolve. Nose up to the windscreen, I peered through overwhelmed wipers at the river that was Queen Street as my old jeep sweeshed her way down towards the dockyard gate. The armed plod opened the barrier and waved me through without leaving the shelter of the gatehouse: a mere glance at my blue dockyard pass inside the windscreen. The Threat Level was still 'Substantial', but they all knew my old white Suzuki.

At Southwest Wall, I parked as close to the ship as possible. I grabbed my bag and ran for it, splashing across the jetty and up the gangway with rain thundering on my jacket hood and bouncing off the flight deck like peas on a drum. The bosun's mate gave me a thumbs up from inside the hangar to let me know he'd checked me on-board – I waved my thanks then hurried down the starboard side and unclipped the screen door. I took off my jacket in the lobby and shook it, then swung down the ladder into the ionised air of Eton Walkway – the wide thoroughfare running down the centre of Two Deck.

The squeak of my trainers on the polished tiles merged with the hum of ventilation fans and the murmur of amorphous sounds that filled a busy destroyer's working day. I felt back where I belonged, but the sympathetic glances I collected on my way aft portended to what lay ahead, and I dreaded it. It was just after ten: Stand Easy, when everyone would be in the Mess on tea break – fucking perfect.

At Echo Section, I swung down the ladder to our cross passage and listened at the door – I could hear talking, a wave of laughter, gossipy chit-chat. So, was I prepared to be the bereaved messmate: expected to endure the condolences, the mumbled platitudes, the embarrassing silences? No, I fucking well wasn't! Not going to happen. I took a deep breath, pushed open the door, and strode in.

It looked like I'd scored a full house: HMS *Windsor Castle's* entire complement of female junior rates were there: all twenty-three of them. As faces turned up, the chatter died. Doc Halliday, my best friend, gave me a somewhat surprised and wary look. Every eye watched as I hung up my jacket, unlaced and stepped out of my soaked trainers. Every eye tracked me across the mess square. I dropped my holdall onto the carpet and poured myself a mug of tea – concentrating on holding it together. I set my drink on the table and shuffled down between beefy Weapons Technician, Karen

Pitman, and the always perfectly groomed Wardroom Steward, Yvonne Taylor.

'So, how are you, Rosie,' Yvonne crooned, bringing a chain reaction as in droned all the soothing voices. I hid behind a bland mask until the murmuring subsided. I was Meryl Streep playing *The Iron Lady* in her new movie – I was out for an Oscar. When silence reigned, I paused a moment longer for effect, then laughed. Only instead of Meryl's haughty chuckle, what came out was an unhinged giggle.

'Shit happens, eh?' I added rather stupidly.

I keened around at their stunned faces, felt my eyes beginning to pool and my resolve melting in a crucible of self-doubt. 'I'm over it,' I wailed. 'It's history, okay?' Abandoning all hope of a grand homecoming, I made for the safety of the bunk-spaces. Reaching my locker, I realised I'd left my holdall in the mess square. Oh, God, I was going to have to face them again.

That was when Doc followed me in and dropped the bag at my feet.

'Thanks,' I mumbled.

'What the fuck was that all about?' she demanded.

I brushed savagely at my eyes. 'Just— just being a dick, that's all.' Then I grinned at my friend through blurry pools, 'Full marks for effort though, eh?'

'Now you're just a smart-arse,' she snapped. She gave me that funny squint of hers through her rimless glasses. Made her look quite the nerd, despite her pale prettiness. 'Trust me, Girl, the way you're handling this—'

'You think I'm handling it?'

She saw I was close to cracking up again; her face softened, and she laid a hand on my shoulder. 'You should go home, Rosie, you've come back before you're ready.'

For some unfathomable reason, her words angered me, and I shrugged her hand off me. 'You finished, Doc?'

With a tired sigh, she slumped down on the bottom bunk and watched me change into my No 4 working dress.

'Why are you back so soon?' she said, eventually.

So I told her why. Told her how it felt: stuck alone at home, not knowing a soul in the village, getting out of my skull every night on Dad's whisky collection. And gradually turning into an alcoholic. Then I stopped blubbing, blew my nose, checked myself in the mirror and pulled on my beret.

'Where are you going now?' she asked.

'Up to see Redfern,' I said with a resolute sniff. 'Tell her I'm back.'

'Well don't,' she said, standing up and grabbing my shoulders. 'You need to get your head out of your arse, Girl. So go home and get your bike out, or take a short break to the Algarve, or fuck off to Wales and climb a fucking mountain. Anything. Just don't sail with us while you're feeling like this. Trust me, Sweetie—'

'OUT PIPES,' the tannoy interrupted her. 'HANDS CARRY ON WITH YOUR WORK'

'Go on then,' I told her. 'Toddle off back to your office and give me a break.'

She stared at me a moment longer, then sighed and shook her head, 'Don't know why I fucking bothered.'

Left alone in the bunk space, I listened as everybody filed out of the mess and back to their workplaces. Only when I heard the mess door slam shut on silence did I come out of hiding. I stepped out into the cross passage and zipped up the three ladders to where my Divisional Officer, Lieutenant Redfern, had her cabin. I found her typing on her laptop with her door open. She looked up when I knocked – her brow furrowed.

'Rosie, what are you doing back? You've got another—'

'I've had enough wallowing at home, Ma'am,' I said briskly. 'Time I was back at work.'

She pulled around a chair from behind her. 'Come in and take a seat. You don't think you've come back too early?'

'What makes you say that, Ma'am?' I said, stepping sideways into the cramped cabin.

She stared at me a moment, then gave a sigh and closed the lid of her laptop.

'Well, let's see, it's only been what, five days since you buried your mother? You've got another week's leave, more if you need it. And your father's still in hospital – don't you think you should be home, supporting him?'

'There's nothing for me to support,' I argued. 'My Dad's unresponsive and might never wake up.'

She looked down at her computer and scattered paperwork as if for inspiration. Sensing my advantage, I pressed on. 'There's nothing for me at home, Ma'am. Reckon I'm better off on-board with people I know.'

'Don't you have friends at home? There seemed to be a lot of people there last week for the funeral.'

I shook my head, 'My parents moved to the village after I joined up – they had different lives. Apart from Lester Granville and Father Donahue, the only people I knew were you and Leading Writer Halliday – thanks for coming, by the way, appreciated.'

'Rosie, are you sure—'

'Look at it this way, Ma'am, we're sailing for SAT's and Workup on Friday, I've got my Board coming up next month that I need to pass to transfer to commissioned rank. How would it look if I wimped out now?'

She gave me a look of infinite tolerance, 'I'm sure the Board will be sympathetic—'

'Besides,' I interrupted, 'you know what the blokes will say if I skip this trip – that "girls can't hack it" crap. You've been there, Ma'am, you know what it's like.'

That won a silent stare – she didn't like to admit she'd come to her commission from the Lower Deck – as I intended to do.

'Please, Ma'am, I *need* to be on-board.'

She had the patience of a saint, my DO, but no bottle.

I went to find 'Dinger' Bell next – he was my PO on the Fo'c'sle, and I needed him on-side. I found him in the Ops Room yarning with his pal, CPO Reg Gardiner, the ship's Air Controller, over a cup of tea. When he saw me, he took me to one side.

'Rosie, what're you doing back already?'

'I've been cleared to come back to work, PO.' A small deception – I didn't say who had 'cleared' me.

He paused a moment, not sure he believed me. 'You sure you're ready?' he said. 'Only—'

'Yes, PO, I need to be here, and my DO agrees.' I was trying not to let my lower lip tremble.

He could have checked with Redfern, but like everyone else, he was too busy getting ready for Friday to bother, so he let it ride like I knew he would.

Morale got a significant boost from the lads that afternoon – it was big Pincher Martin who spoke for the fo'c'slemens' delegation:

'Rosie, we're all *really* sorry— about, you know, your Mum, and that—'

The others quickly rallied to his rescue, and a chorus of supportive murmurs broke out amid shy shuffling of steaming-boots. I was touched by their clumsy efforts, until that mutinous opportunist, Tony Rawlidge, stepped forward.

'Aww, shipmate's hug?' he cooed, coming at me like a Dalek.

'Get off me you silly sod!' I said, sidestepping his illicit embrace. 'But thanks, Guys. Now back to work, the lot of you.'

A little later, the chaplain found me and invited me for tea in his office. God, at this rate, I'd need an appointment book. But at least I could tell the vicar about Dad, knowing it wouldn't go any further – how I felt about him being four times over the limit when he'd crashed the car. When I finished, he offered no comment, no advice, no urging me to forgive. Just aimed those sympathetic brown eyes at me for a few moments, and then asked if I was sure I was ready to come back to work. I assured him I was.

That's when he changed tactics. 'Tell me about your Mum, Rosie. The good, happy things you remember about her.'

I had to think about that for a moment. If the vicar had asked me to recall happy things about Dad, I would have had no hesitation in raving on about our sailing weekends. Mum never sailed. There were, of course, plenty of lovely memories of her, but I hadn't given them much thought over the years, believing she'd always be there. So, now I was being forced to acknowledge my loss, a kaleidoscope of random recollections appeared out of nowhere. It was when I began narrating them for the chaplain that I realised something bizarre had happened to my memory.

The date still raw, of course, was Sunday the 17th of June, 2012, Father's Day, just ten days ago – the Day of the Accident. But now all my childhood memories came flooding back with a date stamp. I knew that the three of us had climbed Snowdon on June the 19th, 1999, and that it was a Saturday. I knew Mum had let go of me on my bike without stabilizers on 7th May 1991, a Tuesday.

'I became "Rose" on Sunday, the 7th of June 1992,' I told him. 'That was the day my grandmother took me in the garden and showed me her rosemary bush. I was five, and I bawled my eyes out. Mum took me on her knee and told me I was a beautiful rose, and I was Rose from then on - Rosie after I joined up.

Now it's only my Dad that calls me Rosemary—' I stopped talking and stared at the vicar who was looking quite startled.

'Sorry,' I said. 'I was rambling, wasn't I?'

'Um, that's quite alright, Rosie. Is there—'

'I need to get back to work, Padre. Thanks for the tea.'

I almost ran from his office, mortified by this strange new ability I seemed to have acquired. My exceptional memory was something I was never comfortable with, especially in the close confines of a warship where it was essential to fit in, to appear normal. This thing with dates was a whole new source of potential embarrassment.

In hindsight, they were right, of course: Doc, Redfern, Dinger Bell, and the chaplain – I had no business being on-board in my state of mind. But everyone that could have intervened, from the Captain downwards, was focussed on getting us into shape for Sea Acceptance Trials and Workup. Like a glass-eel slipping in under cover of night, I infiltrated my sane and sober shipmates.

1/2

Boarding Stations

I woke up to the lights flickering on, followed by the blarting of the Action Alarm. I looked up at the clock and groaned; twenty-past seven in the morning, barely an hour since I'd turned in after my six-hour defence watch. I flumped over onto my side and watched Doc and Yvonne hauling out their action kits.

Noticing I hadn't got up, Doc said, 'You not playing?'

I shrugged. 'Can't be arsed.'

'Rosie, don't sod about, you need to—'

> 'HANDS TO BOARDING —'

At the word 'Boarding', I swung out of my bunk and opened my locker.

> '—STATIONS, HANDS TO BOARDING STATIONS. BOARDING PARTY MUSTER OUTSIDE THE ARMOURY.'

'Do you suppose she's got a boat to drive?' Doc quipped to Yvonne.

'Beats fires and floods any day,' I said, spilling the foul-weather gear and lifejacket from my locker onto the deck. I didn't rush into my kit. With the ship still rumbling along at twenty-odd knots, there'd be plenty of time yet.

I was last to arrive at the armoury lobby down on Five Deck, which won me a sour glance from Dinger Bell. My PO was standing in for the Royal Marine Colour Sergeant, who usually led the boarding party.

I signed for my Glock and holstered it, then stood back with my crew as the six boarders checked their assault rifles under the supervision of the PO. The officer in nominal command was Sub Lieutenant Francis – a pimply twenty-two-year-old barely out of Naval College.

In boots and helmets, armed and not very dangerous, we clattered up seven ladders to the boat deck, while the officer went to the Bridge for our orders. Reaching the lobby first, I unclipped the door and swung it open, catching a face-full of cold spindrift. The Watch-on-Deck were already out there removing the seaboat's covers and lashings. Helen Redhead was Leading Hand of the Watch and grinned when I stepped out and staggered against the sudden gust. I sneered at her briefly then turned to assess the sea conditions. Relentless waves rolled in from starboard like charging cavalry, their breaking manes ripped away by the near-gale-force wind. The *Pacific* seaboat, hanging there on its davits, looked mean and purposeful. I revelled in anticipation of driving her again, the thrill and the fear.

Maybe too rough for our novice boarding party, though. Our Royal Marine Detachment – currently rolling in the snows of Norway – would have been chomping at the bit. This shambling lot loitered nervously around the deck with worried glances at the boat then at each other, their unfamiliar weapons carried with feigned nonchalance. I exchanged grins with my boat crew: Tony Briggs and Andy Rice.

'Okay everybody,' shouted the officer, joining us from his briefing, 'gather round.'

As we shuffled into a loose semi-circle around him, the Watch-on-Deck crowded in behind us. The subby looked uncertainly at his swollen audience, then at Dinger Bell for guidance.

'Right, listen up, you lot, ' the PO growled, hinting to the young officer that curious bystanders were not something he should worry about and to just get on with it.

The officer checked his notes once more and cleared his throat.

'The trawler, *MV Brownlea,* is suspected of running guns from Libya to Northern Ireland. *Windsor Castle's* orders are to intercept her, board and search. She's now six miles ahead, making twelve knots on a northerly heading. Our Estimated Time of Arrival alongside her is in one hour. Any questions?'

'Yes sir,' I piped up, glancing out at the burgeoning seas. 'How big is this trawler – if she is a trawler – and do we know how much freeboard she has?'

'That's an unknown, Winterbourne,' he said dismissively.

'It's a bit lively out there, Sir,' I prompted. 'Best we have a plan of where and how to board.'

He should have asked about that at his briefing on the Bridge. Basic question.

'We'll have to assess her when we see her,' he blustered. 'Then I'll tell you what's required.'

'Dickhead,' muttered Andy from behind me, echoing my thoughts. I turned and gave him a warning glance.

'Anything else?' asked the officer, a little flushed I thought – perhaps he'd heard Andy's comment. When nobody answered he rubbed his hands together and said, 'Right then, Winterbourne, get the boat ready to slip and—'

'Sir!' I interrupted, angered at how he addressed me and feeling he needed a reality check. 'I know my job, just make sure you know yours— Sir!'

Some of the guys were smirking, and the officer reddened visibly. I hadn't meant to sound quite so sharp.

'Right, okay then—' he floundered, trying to recover his authority. 'Right then, carry on, Cox'n.'

Which is what he should have called me in the first place, the twat. He turned and walked briskly to where his Boarding Party sat huddled against the bulkhead. Fuck! I'd screwed up – any officer worth his stripe would have called me out for that. I turned and came face to face with Dinger. His face was thunder.

'You crossed a line there, Leading Seaman Winterbourne.'

I didn't answer, just glared back defiantly.

He pursed his lips and shook his head. 'Not like you to gob off at officers, Rosie.'

'Sorry, PO, but he's out of his depth, he sh—'

'Steady!' he growled. 'Come over here.' He led me out of earshot then turned to me, stony-faced. 'I know what you've been through, Rosie, and you shouldn't have been allowed to come back so soon after – it wasn't my decision. But while you're on-board this ship, you'll maintain good order and discipline and show the leadership expected of a senior leading hand. And you don't fuck off junior officers in front of the troops, understood?'

'PO,' I said. Despite the cold wind, I could feel my face heating up.

He glanced around, then softened his tone and said, 'A word to the wise, Rosie. I want you to make Dartmouth and I've supported you all the way. But you're not an officer yet, and you can't afford lapses of judgement like that. So get yourself back on track and don't let me down, okay?'

I chewed my lip and nodded.

'Right, let's have no more of it. I'll have a quiet word with young Mr Francis later and persuade him not to press charges.'

An hour later, the target came into view on the starboard bow, and we all crowded to the guardrail for a look. She was an old steel-hulled motor fishing vessel requisitioned by the navy in the sixties. She was making heavy weather of it, battering into the troughs – green water breaking over the bow – then pointing skywards to show off her red-painted bottom. I could see there was no way we would be able to board her – not even the Bootnecks would risk that. Nevertheless, I felt a pang of disappointment when a short time later, the pipe came over the Tannoy:

> 'D'YA HEAR THERE. REVERT
> TO DEFENCE STATIONS.
> BOARDING PARTY STAND
> DOWN – EXERCISE
> CANCELLED DUE TO
> ADVERSE CONDITIONS.'

Waiting in line back down in the armoury lobby I unholstered my Glock to return it, thinking perhaps it was just as well we had no ammo. Afterwards, I went and crawled back into my pit. I was on watch in three hours, but couldn't sleep; beating myself up, feeling like an idiot, but also aware that I had little defence against it happening again.

1/3

Talking to Dad

It was Saturday. *Windy C* was back in Pompey for the weekend, and I'd finally summoned up the courage to come and see Dad.

They'd moved him out of ICU into a private room; open windows to let in the summer, chintzy curtains billowing in the breeze. It was good to see him unhooked from life-support: just a feeding tube up his nose, a cannula in his forearm, and a catheter tube sneaking discretely from under his bedclothes. He looked at peace.

I didn't say much about Workup – Dad had done his twenty-two and had been in a real war at sea – he didn't need any reminders. I wanted to tell him about my disciplinary issues at work, feeling a need for some of his fatherly wisdom. Dad could always find a handy aphorism or two to set my world to rights. But even if he had been able to comfort me, I was still far too angry with him.

I gave his limp hand a shake as if he would wake up. It was hard to pretend he was awake and listening, harder still to act the devoted daughter. Touching his lank hair, I made a note to ask the nurses when they'd last washed it. I gave his forelock a little tug, gripped it tighter, feeling my temper rise. It was all I could do not to yank it out by the roots. I released his hair and watched his blank face. Not a flicker. I took a breath, counted slowly to ten, then popped a grape into my mouth.

'Mm. Nice grapes. Those big seedless ones from Sainsbury's, sweet and juicy. Sorry, Dad, you'll just have to take my word for it.'

I studied his face more closely. He was sixty-seven but had always looked so much younger than his age. Now he looked eighty. I used to worship this man.

And now I— what, despised him?

'Mm, met a couple of your mates in the Dragon last night: Er, Don and Eddie? — Yeah, those two. I was with Doc – you remember my friend, Doc Halliday? Yeah, the Leading Writer. She's staying with me at the house. I reckon your mates think we're an item.'

That happened a lot, I reflected. Life on-board tended to erode a girl's coyness in favour of mannish manners and flavoursome language. We both wore our hair short. Doc was petite and pretty, while I, with my five-foot-nine athletic frame and gamine looks, was usually taken for the dominant partner. In truth, both of us were drawn exclusively to the male gender – we were simply too career-focused at that time to be distracted by romance.

'Too polite to say so, of course,' I continued. 'You know, those funny old-fashioned looks? My generation, they'd just ask. Yeah, I know. Anyway, Dad, they all send their best.'

I paused my rambling and picked up his big floppy hand again.

'Hey, Dad, twitch a finger if you can hear me—'

Oh well, worth a try. According to Dad's bedside chart, he had a GCS of seven. Glasgow Coma Scale, I'd looked it up online: three was brain-dead, and fifteen was fully awake and healthy. So seven was, what? I'd asked the nurse about it earlier.

'Julie tells me Mister Murchison – that's your quack by the way – reckons your latest brain scan shows a faint glimmer of activity. So, hey, Dad,' I tapped an index finger on his brow, 'looks like something's going on in that brain after all.'

I sat back and studied the ceiling, waiting for calm to return. But in the end, I just surrendered to my fury and hissed, 'So, if you can hear me in there—' I leaned in close to whisper something horrible, then stopped myself. Instead, I sat back, watching his face. One day, he was going to wake up. I hoped so because I wanted to ask him what the fuck he was thinking, getting behind the wheel drunk.

'I've asked Lester about Power of Attorney.' I snorted. 'Doc calls it Power of Eternity. So I can raid your bank account to pay the bills. Of course, Dad. That's what Power of Attorney means, dur. But he said it might take months to sort out. Until then, well, I'm in Limbo.' I looked around, then leaned into him, speaking softly, and just let it go: 'If you were properly brain-dead I'd just tell them to turn you off.'

I drove home, hating myself.

1/4

Pasha

The next day, Sunday, I cycled the thirty miles down to Mullhaven Boatyard to take a look at our old boat, maybe bring back some pleasanter memories. I was locking the bike to a railing when I was startled by a voice behind me:

'Can I help you, my love?'

I turned and recognised the speaker. 'Gary Palmer?' I asked.

'That's right, what can I do for you?'

'Rosie Winterbourne, I emailed you.'

'Ah yes, Peter's daughter.' We shook hands. 'Haven't seen him in years, how's he getting on?'

Gary Palmer had taken over as Boatyard Manager shortly before I joined the Navy more than seven years ago. He was a heavily-built man, relatively tall, but looked less in-shape than I recalled – middle-age spread held in check by too-tight dungarees – but the same salt 'n pepper beard and raddled hair.

'Er, how well do you know my dad?'

He shrugged. 'Ooh, you know, knew him to speak to. Had a pint with him sometimes over in the *Chandler's Arms*. Why do you ask?'

'Okay, well it's not great news, I'm afraid. There was an accident back in June; my mum died, and Dad's in a coma in hospital.'

Gary seemed speechless, staring at me as if I'd just landed from Zog. Concerned, I asked if he was okay. He shook his head as if to clear it, then seemed to recover.

'Sorry,' he said, 'I'm not good with stuff like that.'

'Well, me neither, actually, but—'

'Rosemary,' he interrupted hastily, 'I should've said first off – I'm so sorry for your loss— that's er, how are you coping yourself?'

He maybe had trouble with empathy. I smiled at him to ease his discomfort and said offhandedly, 'Oh, I'm okay now – it's been two months. I miss Mum, of course, I always will. It's just my Dad, you know, not knowing? Oh, and I prefer Rosie, by the way, so that you know.'

I turned from him and scanned the forest of masts down in the yard. 'So, where is she, our old *Pasha*, then?'

'Come by the office, we'll grab the key, and I'll walk you down.'

I followed him into the building, where he introduced me to Sandra, his Admin Assistant. She gave me a gleaming corporate smile for two seconds while her sparkly nails hovered above her keyboard, then resumed her typing.

Gary walked me down the yard through an assortment of chocked and cradled boats: a few shiny gin palaces, project vessels waiting for attention, and sad, festering hulls that had sat there neglected for years. I began to get a bad feeling.

'So, how is he, your Dad?'

'Oh, you know, comfortable enough. The staff there reckon he'll come round, but when?' I shrugged, 'Nobody knows.' I flashed him an encouraging smile, 'Thanks for asking, by the way.'

'I hope he pulls through,' he said gruffly.

'Yeah, me too.'

We walked on in silence – me trying to guess which of the better-looking yachts ahead was the one I had known and loved.

Gary stopped walking, and half turned to me. 'So, what're you going to do about her? Do you know yet?'

'*Pasha?*' I shook my head. 'Not sure, I want to take a good look at her first.'

He looked surprised. 'Well, here she is.' He was looking at a shabby old tub sitting on a set of rusting props. I didn't understand.

'Want me to put the ladder up for you?' Without waiting for a reply, he stooped under the hull of the boat and dragged out a long metal ladder. Then, to my astonishment, leaned it up against the same shabby old boat.

I gaped at the tired hulk that had been Dad's pride and joy, unable at first to reconcile it with my fond memories. 'That's *Pasha?*'

'Ah, she ain't in the best condition, right enough,'

While he secured the ladder, I took a walk around her hull. I'd never seen her out of the water and wondered if I'd been expecting too much. She was in a dreadful state: the bare gelcoat, riddled with fine cracks, lumps of rust had erupted on the keel, and part of the rudder exposed down to splintered plywood where an old repair had fallen away.

I stood back and studied her as Gary came back down the ladder.

'All secured, my love, safe to go up now.'

He looked at me, looking at the boat and nodded wisely. 'Bit o work needed,' he said, reading my thoughts. He walked aft and tapped the damaged rudder with a knuckle, causing another lump of filler to fall out. 'Don't think you'll want to be repairing this again, better off replacing it – unless you plan to sell the boat. Then it'll be somebody else's problem.'

He checked his watch. 'When you're done here swing by the office, and we'll talk options. And be careful up there, it's a long way to fall.'

I gave him a smile to cover the empty pit where my hopes had been. My gloom deepened when I climbed the ladder and got my first look at *Pasha's* uppers. The lovely teak decks I remembered skipping barefoot on, buried beneath years of accumulated grey filth. The cockpit was a mess; green moss and dried seagull shit over everything, stinking of decay and neglect.

Down below was better; a few patches of black mildew on the seat covers, but the smell was of dusty abandonment, no damp odours, no sign of leaking windows or hatches. The sails were all bagged up neatly in the forepeak, along with the bedding in taped-up polythene bags. A tiny ray of hope twinkled. Maybe not quite so bad.

I blew a layer of sneezy dust off the chart table to reveal an Admiralty paper chart: *English Channel, Central Part.* With a pencilled track – I recognised my hand: Weymouth Bay to St Catherine's Point to Mullhaven Harbour. My thoughts drifted back seven years – Sunday the 7th of August, 2005.

'Right, young lady,' Dad had announced after breakfast, 'Take us home.'

'Righty Ho, Skipper,' I chirped, starting the engine and expecting him at least to help me slip the lines as he usually did. But when I looked back, he'd disappeared below. Thinking no more of it, I stepped over the guardrail onto the floating pontoon. I took off the bowline, throwing it onto the foredeck, then went aft and took off the stern line. I stepped smartly back aboard just as the boat started to drift away. I put her into gear, then eased on the revs, slowly wheeling over into the channel. Dad still hadn't reappeared. I heard him rattling pots and assumed he was washing up the breakfast things.

'Okay Dad,' I called, 'I've got this, don't worry.'

No response.

I shrugged and motored on out of the harbour, still feeling confident, proud of his trust in me. Clearing the high ramparts of Nothe Fort, I unfurled the genoa to the brisk sou'wester, killed the engine, and aimed for the open Channel and the distant cliffs of Purbeck. Beyond, stood the hazy outline of the Isle of Wight. Weird. Dad would typically be up checking on me by now.

'North or south of the Island?' I shouted down the companionway.

Dad's face appeared. He had a cup of tea in his hand but did not attempt to come up the ladder. 'Dunno,' he said. 'You're the skipper.' He turned away and picked up the Sunday paper he'd bought this morning – I glimpsed the headline announcing:

ROBIN COOK DIES

'Who's Robin Cook?' I called.

He looked back up. 'Labour MP, good bloke, resigned over the Gulf War.'

'You coming up, Dad, or what?'

He glanced up once more, shook his head, and disappeared back inside to read the paper. For a horrible moment, everything I knew just floated away on a terrifying tide of uncertainty.

I grinned at the memory of that day-long, virtually solo, passage; Dad's faking seasickness and pretending to barf over the side, then disappearing below again, groaning. It was an Oscar-winning performance, but later, when I went down to make myself a cuppa, he was sitting comfortably on the banquette reading his paper.

He looked up as I mounted the ladder with my tea.

'Er, what will you be cooking us for lunch, Rosemary? Only I'm getting a bit peckish.'

He looked mildly shocked at my response – wasn't used to such expletives from his daughter. That was the last time we sailed *Pasha*. Two weeks later, I went down to Plymouth to start my naval training.

In the chart drawer, I found a sheet of polished plywood with painted squares, which started a movie running in my head; Dad and I huddled over it in the cockpit like two chess masters. With a nostalgic sigh, I slipped the Uckers Board back under the pile of charts, making a note to rescue it before I sold the boat – if I sold her.

I stepped back up the ladder and handed my way carefully along to the foredeck. First I lowered the bagged up dinghy to the concrete below, so there was room to move. I then flipped open the chain locker and groaned. The anchor chain lay there in a heap of rust. Then, grabbing a shroud on my way back aft, a wire splinter ripped open my middle finger.

—unless you plan to sell the boat. Then it'll be somebody else's problem.

I sighed heavily. Could I sell *Pasha*, along with all the memories? Sucking my bleeding digit, I swung down into the saloon to consult the first-aid kit.

1/5

Obsession

For the next few weekends after Workup, Doc came with me up to Cobbingden. She told me it was because she preferred the village ambience over London where her Mum lived, but I suspected it was to keep on eye on me in case I wobbled. I wasn't complaining, for she was the perfect housemate.

There was another reason I was grateful for Doc's company. For it seemed I had acquired a stalker – I called him Range Rover Man. When I'd first seen him, a few days after Mum's funeral, he'd been walking up and down our street, looking at every house but ours, and I guessed he might be a local newshound. But then I saw him get into his green Range Rover (L205 NPP) and drive away. I'd seen him again once or twice, same vehicle, same registration, each time parked in a different part of the street. The last time was when Doc first came home with me, and he drove away the moment I pulled into our drive.

For a while, our regular girly weekend worked well for both of us – until that Friday night, when Doc met Ron. After that, she spent more time at Ron's flat, and I spent more time working on the boat. At some point, my ambition to get her into shape became a kind of obsession – *Pasha* became a living thing that was sucking up all my unspent affection. Doc's romantic distraction left me free to drive straight to Mullhaven on Fridays and sleep on-board *Pasha* Friday and Saturday. I'd then pick up Doc on Sunday after my weekly visit with Dad.

And so the work on *Pasha* progressed, and by the end of August, her hull was ready for antifoul.

'You'll need ten litres,' Gary told me in the *Chandler's Arms* beer garden one Saturday night. 'Two good coats and I wouldn't skimp on the quality – you'll want self-polishing copper oxide-based antifoul.'

'How much will that cost, do you think?' I asked, thinking maybe I could stretch to a fiver a litre.

'About ninety quid for a two-and-a-half litre tin.'

'Jesus! That's nearly four-hundred pounds.'

He nodded sagely, 'Yachting's an expensive hobby, another reason people lose interest. What about that standing rigging, any ideas yet?'

I had begun to resent Gary's so-called reality checks – it felt like he was rubbing my nose into my financial doo-doo. After ripping my finger open, I'd asked a rigger to come and inspect all my shrouds and stays. He'd universally condemned them as unsafe, pointing out rusty sections and more wire splinters. Not surprising really; *Pasha's* standing rigging was over thirty years old. This morning I'd been online looking at 7mm inox wire rope and was shocked to discover that seventy-five metres came to nearly a grand. And that was before the rigger's bill for swaging on the end fittings.

I put my head in my hands. 'What am I gonna do?'

'You could still sell her,' Gary suggested, for the umpteenth time.

'Fuck off, Gary,' I told him, 'not an option. One way or another she's going back in the water, and I'm going to sail her again.'

He was silent for a long while, then grunted to get my attention. He leaned across and murmured sneakily, 'I shouldn't say this, Rosie, and if anybody asks, I'll deny it, but the Navy own sailing yachts, don't they?'

I sat back and stared at him, stunned. He looked away and studied the ivy growing up the wall.

'Can I bum a roll-up?' I said, reaching for his tobacco. Set against the sordid temptation to try what Gary was implying, going back to smoking no longer felt like a big deal.

1/6

Dockyard Scam

I'm going home this weekend,' I told Doc, meeting her at the mess door after my six-hour morning on the gangway. 'So I can give you a lift, save your train fare.'

It was now mid-September and, aside from the antifouling and standing rigging, I'd run out of things to do on the boat.

'Yeah, great,' Doc said, with a heroic grin, 'let's have a girly weekend, I'll buy some wine. I'm on leave next week, so I'll go straight up to Mum's on Sunday from yours. Got to dash, I'm already adrift.'

I followed her out into the cross-passage and stopped her.

'Hey, no way, Doc, don't let me cramp your style.'

'Actually, I was planning to go straight to London on Friday. I'm on leave, remember?'

'What about Ron, big romance over?'

'Yup, he's history, I'll tell you later. Gotta go.'

She put a foot on the ladder, half-turned and said, 'And deffo *Yes* to the weekend.'

'Did you just say "deffo"? – what're you, twelve?'

She grinned back then scurried up to Eton Walkway where her office was.

After breakfast and a quick shower, I went forward to the Paint Shop. As I neared the bow, the sharp stink of chemical solvents told me that the painter was already at work preparing for the daily rush. I found him stirring a 20-litre drum of something with a sawn-off broom handle.

'Morning, Dicky,' I said breezily, 'how's it hanging?'

'Ah, you know?' he murmured in his soft Dublin brogue, 'slack and happy, as always. Got the side party coming soon for their boot topping, horrible stuff this.'

He raised the stick vertically, and we both watched transfixed as the black goo oozed back into the can with satisfying slurpy noises. 'Underwater paint,' he said, 'but if it gets under your fingernails, you can kiss goodbye to your Royal Garden Party invitation.' He wiped the stick clean with a rag and replaced the lid on the drum.

'Right, what can I get you, Madam?' he said. 'The yellow chromate primer's on offer this week,' he flourished an unopened paint-can, 'and it's a cracking vintage – Chateau d'Admiralty 1983, lovely bucket, like primroses in spring.'

But I wasn't here to listen to Dicky's blarney – I was more interested in the rumour I'd heard of his dodgy civilian contacts in the Dockyard.

Graeme, the Scottish NAAFI Manager, raised an eyebrow and said, 'Smoking again are we, Rosie?' when I went to buy my ration of two-hundred Bensons. He knew I'd stopped smoking a year back, even though I was still officially registered as one of the few remaining puffing pariahs. With favours called in from elsewhere, I now had the requisite one-thousand duty free cigarettes with which to bargain.

But for what I wanted, I needed more than just ciggies.

At morning Stand Easy, I went ashore with my holdall and drove through the dockyard. I parked by the pedestrian gate to HMS Nelson – the admin and accommodation site for the Naval Base – and walked through the entrance to the nearby Cash Clothing Store with my shopping list. The matronly CPO gave me a funny look when I ordered all men's items, then glanced at my stick-like figure when I asked for them all in XL sizes.

'They're for some of the lads on-board, Chief,' I explained, feeling the sweat break out on my brow. 'We've got a six-month deployment coming up.'

She didn't question my purchases, just swiped my debit card and watched me suspiciously as I crammed the woollen seamen's jerseys into my holdall.

Returning to the car, I drove to my final stop in the Dockyard: the 'Valuable & Attractive' warehouse. Dicky had told me I was to ask for a civilian storekeeper called Bunny Warren. By now, my heart was shuttling like a demented road-drill.

1/7

Guilt

I met Doc at the gangway, glad-rags and lippy on, holdalls packed, ready for a chillout weekend – it was summer, the sky was kingfisher blue, the breeze was silky warm. What could go wrong?

Everything!

I'd never smuggled anything before and imagined all eyes watching, accusing. While crossing the jetty to the car, my legs seemed to have forgotten how to walk. The fear I felt overwhelmed the logic that I'd never once been stopped and searched on leaving a dockyard.

'You okay?' Doc asked after I recovered my dropped key from the footwell and fumbled it into the ignition.

'Yeah, fine,' I lied, 'just keen to be away.'

Crawling along in the Friday afternoon queue to leave the dockyard fed my paranoia. The driver in front kept on looking at me, even adjusting his mirror at one point for a better look. Christ! He must have seen me loading up the jeep last night. He was

going to tip off the plod on his way through. Oh shit!
I thought about pulling out of the queue.

'Look at that twat in front,' said Doc, 'ogling us in
his mirror.' She reached over to toot my horn at him.
Luckily, I dashed her hand away in time.

'Spoilsport!' she said to me, grinning. Then to my
horror, she shouted out of her open window, 'Seen
enough, Pal? Eyes front, Dude!'

He readjusted his mirror and didn't look back
again. The MoD-plod barely looked at us as we went
through the gate – gunning the jeep up Queen Street,
it was all I could do to keep the delight off my face.

We stopped at the Sainsbury's in Liphook for Doc
to go and forage for our weekend food and drink. I
stayed in the jeep and rolled a ciggy. Twenty
minutes later she returned with two bulging carrier-
bags, two bottles of Rioja poking out of one of them.

'Sorry, big queue at the checkout.'

'Don't put them in the back,' I told her, 'just wedge
them on the deck behind the seats.'

She sniffed the air as she got in. 'You started
smoking again?'

I didn't reply, just blasted the air on full.

The trouble began when we got home, and Doc got
to the boot hatch before me and lifted out our two
holdalls.

'Ooh! What's under the blanket?'

Before I could stop her, she whipped the rug off my
goodies.

'You shouldn't have done that, Doc,' I said. 'Now
I'll have to kill you.'

For a withering moment, she stared at the incriminating tins of paint and the shiny coil of wire rope. I could almost hear her brain processing.

Finally, she blew out a sigh. 'Jesus, Rosie!'

'Oh, cool it, Girl,' I told her. 'It's just a few bits and bobs for the boat.'

'Why didn't you tell me?'

I could tell by her rising flush this wasn't going to end well.

'What,' I said, 'and have *both* of us crapping ourselves going through the gate?'

'No! Because I wouldn't have been there. What the fuck were you thinking?'

I shrugged, deciding to roll with it. 'That I might float my boat?'

'Not funny! You might have given up on *your* career, Rosie, but you'd no right to risk mine.'

Without waiting for my response, she picked up her bag and straight-legged it up to the house. I replaced the blanket and closed the boot then followed her up to the front door, thinking: *given up on my career? What a scary idea.*

'Sorry,' I said, as she moved aside to let me unlock the door. 'You were right; I wasn't thinking.'

There was a stinging retort ready on her lips, but she just glared at me instead.

For once, Doc didn't feel like cooking, so I got us a takeaway from the Indian in the village, and we ate it watching the usual Friday night drivel on the box. Despite the bottle of red we demolished - and my attempts to lighten things up - my friend stayed cold and distant and went to bed early, leaving me feeling like shit.

Coming downstairs at sparrow-fart next morning I found her in the hall, dressed and packed to go.

'Taking the train up to London,' she explained, 'about time I visited my Mum – been neglecting her lately.'

'I thought you were seeing her on Sunday – on leave, you said.'

She just shrugged, gave me a hard stare and turned to open the door.

'Alright,' I said, 'if that's how you feel, I'll drive you to the station.'

'No thanks, I'd rather get the bus.'

'Listen, Doc,' I began, reaching to touch her shoulder.

'Don't!' she slapped my hand away.

We stared at each other for a moment. Doc's bespectacled brown eyes were darkly unforgiving. At the bottom of the drive, she stopped and half-turned.

'See you a week on Monday, Rosie. Have fun.'

'Yeah,' I murmured. 'Bye, then.'

1/8

Lift In

When Doc had gone, I went back inside and called Gary on his mobile, asked him if we could lift *Pasha* in tomorrow.

'What, without antifoul?'

'No, Gary. *With* antifoul. I'm coming down to do it today. I'll work as long as it takes.'

'Okay. Well, you're lucky, the lads don't normally work on Sundays, but they're hauling a couple of boats out tomorrow. Otherwise, I'd need to charge premium rates.'

'That's great, Gary, thanks. And will the rigger's shop be open?'

'What, you got the wire as—'

'Yes, I got that as well. Will the shop be open?'

'Yup, the riggers'll be there Saturday, but not Sunday. I'll warn them you're coming. So why all the rush?'

'I can't afford your outrageous storage fees any longer, Gary, so I'm mooring her out in the harbour.'

I didn't tell him I just wanted to be rid of the evidence. Doc's pissed-off reaction had brought home the significance of what I'd done. I didn't regret the theft – that was wholly necessary for my overarching need to get *Pasha* on the water. It was the realisation of the consequences of getting caught, and Doc's discovery of my crimes had increased the risks. I would need to be far more careful in my future acquisitions, of which I planned quite a few more now I'd taken the first plunge.

An hour later I arrived at the boatyard and drove straight down to park next to *Pasha*. I needed a scaffold to work on, and seeing nobody around, walked back up to the office to find Gary. That's when I noticed the police car up in the car park – and a uniformed copper talking to Gary sent a slow chill up my spine. I stepped into the office and found Sandra leafing through her desk draw. She looked up and flashed me her thousand-pound smile.

'Hi, Rosie. Gary said you'd be in this morning. He won't be long. Can I get you a coffee?'

'No thanks,' I said. 'I just saw Gary with a policeman, is everything okay?'

The corporate smile faded, and I saw something else creep into her eyes. 'Oh, yes. They're talking to everyone right now about the murder – still looking for witnesses. The killer must be miles away by now. He wouldn't hang around, would he? Not after—'

'Murder! What murder?'

'Oh, hadn't you heard? Been all the talk this last week. Of course, you don't live local, do you?' She picked up a newspaper from her desk and handed it to me. 'Here, read for yourself.'

The paper was the Mullhaven Echo, dated yesterday.

MURDERED WOMAN WAS 'SEXUALLY ASSAULTED' SAY POLICE!

It was confirmed last night that the body of the woman found in Mill Street on Monday morning had been sexually assaulted before being strangled. Sources close to the investigation revealed a connection with several previous attacks going back almost twenty years.

I handed the paper back to her, shaking my head. 'Christ, Sandra, you must be terrified.'

She nodded gravely. 'My Dad brings me to work now and picks me up when I finish. And it's only ten minutes walk.'

She looked suddenly younger – beneath that business-like veneer was the face of a frightened young woman. Had I not been so preoccupied with concealing my own lesser crimes, I might have paid more attention to that story and shared her fears.

Gary's face, when he saw what I had in the back of the jeep, was a picture; a mixture of awe and guilt.

'Nothing to do with me, remember, not a word to anyone.' He looked furtively around, then picked up one of the MoD paint tins and read the label.

'Quality stuff! But you'll need to decant it – I'll bring you an empty drum down, then I'll get rid of these for you.'

I worked all that Saturday and long into the evening, slapping the glutinous blue mess onto the rudder, keel and hull, not to mention my hair and overalls. It was late in the afternoon - while I was starting the second coat - that the riggers came down to replace *Pasha's* rusted stays and shrouds. The master rigger told me he'd take the twenty-five metres of leftover wire rope in lieu of payment.

I got home around ten that night and took a long soak in the bath, feeling relieved that I'd got away with it, and looking forward to *Pasha's* Big Day tomorrow.

It was late on Sunday afternoon that I watched with pride as the handlers adjusted the two slings around *Pasha's* glistening belly. When she was clear of the steel supports, I moved in with a pot of leftover antifoul to touch up where they'd been. Then she was moving toward the dock to the sound of the traveller's warning bleeper. I followed behind with the stern line in hand.

I held my breath as the driver carefully manoeuvred the crane's wheels either side of the dock until she hung suspended over the murky water. He now began to lower *Pasha,* and as the deck drew level with the dockside, I jumped aboard. My heart did a little flip when I felt her settle on the water, rocking slightly as the weight eased off the slings. Grinning proudly I went below to open the sea-cocks and check for leaks.

Thanks to the new starter battery the engine cranked up at the third attempt; an eruption of acrid smoke at the stern before the old diesel settled down to an uneven rumble. I looked over the starboard quarter to check that cooling-water was pulsing from the exhaust. It was. There was a spontaneous round of applause from the guys on the dockside – Gary with a smiling thumbs up. I gave her a spurt of revs to make sure the prop turned, then went back below to check the stern gland.

As I motored out into the sun-sparkled bay with my dinghy in tow, I chuckled as the sound of the engine exhaust triggered a childhood memory:

'It goes giggle-gurgle, Daddy,' I'd declared when I heard it for the first time at age six.

When Dad later told Mum what I'd said she had smiled proudly.

'Onomatopoeia,' she said. 'We'll make a poet of you yet, Rose.'

'No,' insisted Dad, 'she definitely said "giggle-gurgle".'

Mum had patted his cheek indulgently.

That was the thirteenth of June 1992, I recalled, a Saturday.

I headed out to where five other yachts lay in a line, and dropped anchor, letting out twenty-five metres of my shiny new anchor chain.

There was still much to do, but I took a moment to roll a ciggy and soak up the freedom of being on the water, at last, no more mooring fees, all essential work completed. I tried not to think about the risks I'd taken to get *Pasha* here.

I spent the early evening reassembling the bunk in my cabin and making the saloon comfortable. Later I made a sandwich and drank a glass of wine listening to music on the radio, then turned in and drifted off to *Pasha's* gentle rocking and the comforting caress of wavelets lapping the hull.

I woke to the sound of spraying water drumming on the wet duvet, splashing cold on my face. In a wild panic, I struggled to free myself from the tangle of bedding. Try as I might I could not move the cover off me – the duvet seemed tightly wound around me as if I'd rolled over and over in it. Water began slopping over the bunk sill, seeping into the mattress and bedding. I screamed with frustration at my helplessness, but no sound came, just the slop and splash of rising water. I gave a mighty heave to free myself, to no avail.

Then, suddenly I was free, just like that. The duvet lay loose over me, and I was perfectly dry. I got up and put my feet down on the dry carpet of my cabin. Morning sunlight from the cabin window threw watery reflections onto the deckhead. Confused, I listened to the slapping and sucking of water on the freshly painted hull and the cries of gulls in the harbour. Everything was normal. I tumbled backwards onto my bunk, a hand clutching my brow in amazement. I let out a snigger, then stopped.

What the fuck just happened?

1/9

Aunt Georgie

'Now I've got a fridgeful of food,' I informed Dad. 'And you know me and cooking – it's an oxymoron.'

It was the weekend after *Pasha's* lift in, and I was telling Dad about what happened with Doc after she discovered I wasn't the goodie-two-shoes she thought I was. Without thinking, I had let on to Dad about the stolen goodies. I was now wondering whether he, in his unutterable thoughts, would be condemning or approving. Assuming he could hear me at all – I was still sceptical about this locked-in theory.

They'd given him a haircut, and his jim-jams smelled laundry-fresh. I stood and went to the bottom of the bed, lifting the cover to check his feet.

'Ooh, nasty!'

He'd been getting sores on his heels, and they'd put a rolled-up towel under his ankles to lift them clear.

'Still, nurse reckons those pie-crusts will drop off soon?' I replaced the covers and resumed my seat.

'Guess what, dear Papa, our old *Pasha's* back in the water. Hardly cost me a penny, thanks to, well, you know.

'Ooh, and that reminds me, my Power of Attorney came through.' I patted his cheek, 'Turns out you're as broke as me. No insurance for Mum, just you. Very gallant, but you didn't die, did you?'

I bit my tongue; I'd come here determined to start again with Dad and put the bitterness behind me. Some hope.

There was not quite five thousand pounds in his current account, his accumulated monthly pensions from Navy and State. No savings, so that was that. Even the wrecked car had only been third-party insured. I'd had no idea how financially challenged M & D had been in their retirement. Mum's assets were still undergoing probate, but our solicitor, Lester Granville, didn't think there'd be much left after fees and Mum's funeral expenses.

For something to do, I slipped Dad's patient record clipboard from the bed end and perused it for a while, put it back, then paused. The chart I'd just been looking at flashed before me like an afterglow zoomed in on the Blood Group box. I picked the clipboard up again.

No, that can't be right.

'They must have made a mistake with your blood group,' I told Dad, 'and just so's you know, sweet Papa—'

I looked up as the door swung open, expecting to see the nurse on her hourly checks.

Instead, I saw a ghost.

I jumped to my feet, knocking over the chair, head swimming, legs like willow-twigs. I staggered back until I felt the warm radiator against the backs of my legs. I saw the thing coming towards me, the apparition that was Mum but couldn't be Mum. The spectre shimmered suddenly, coloured feathers sprouting from its outspread arms. The kind face I once knew so well morphed into something predatory, eyes growing inscrutably cruel – the eyes of a raptor. The delicate nose curved into a hawk's bill, which opened, emitted a scream; strange and terrible. The stretching limbs that were now powerful, multi-hued wings spread wide, and the creature, a rising phoenix, soared overhead. Suddenly the world slipped sideways, and my cheek slapped onto cold floor tiles.

I wanted to scream, but my vocal cords refused to constrict. I tried to get up, but the muscles would not respond. Disorientated – reality drifting away.

I was disembodied, floating in nothingness. A sound drifted in, music, strangely familiar; a Wurlitzer organ playing a waltz. And there before me, a stunning image materialised; turning together on the night among the stars, M & D, smiling into each other's eyes. They looked like a couple in an old movie that Mum used to watch repeatedly. Except that old classic was in black and white. Here the colours were as improbable as the scene itself; ineffably beautiful, the music, surreal. A lurid sunrise drew my omnipotent senses briefly away from the scene. And then, turning back to where my parents had been dancing, I saw a pair of silhouettes on the wing, flying towards the dying purple of the night.

I opened my eyes on overhead strip-lights and heard the squeak of a nurse's crocks. A face appeared above me; Julie, the daytime Staff Nurse.

'Ah, Rosie, you're awake.' A hand cupped my brow. 'How are you feeling?'

I began to tell her about my fantastic dream – but no sound came. My mouth remained closed; my tongue was a dead thing. I started to panic.

Julie frowned. 'Rosie. Blink for me?'

I blinked.

Did Locked-in run in families, like breast cancer and diabetes?

But I blinked, didn't I?

I blinked again, closed my eyes for longer, then reopened them. Julie must have seen the anxiety there. She stroked my brow and, smiling reassurance, said, 'Don't worry, Rosie, I expect it's just temporary. I'm sure you'll be fine in a few minutes, then we'll have a nice cuppa, okay?'

I focussed on an image of that nice cuppa and must have drifted off to sleep.

'So Margie never mentioned me, eh?' the woman that looked like Mum said over her teacup.

I looked around me. I couldn't recall coming down to the Hospital Coffee Shop. Did this person come with me, or did we meet here?

I shook my head, 'I'm sorry, what did you say?'

'Your mother, my sister, Margie, she never told you about me?'

'Er No. No, she didn't. Weird – you sound American. When did you last see Mum?'

'Ah, not for twenty-five years. We kind of separated. I emigrated to the States shortly after you were born. Gosh, Rosemary, you don't half remind me of Margie, you've certainly got her looks.'

I laughed shakily. 'So have you. Er, sorry, what did you say your name was?'

Her hand came across and stroked mine – she had hands just like Mum's.

'I'm sorry, Sweetie, you're still in shock. My name's Georgina; I'm your aunt, your Mum's twin sister. I should have been a bit more cautious, I guess, instead of just barging in on you like that.'

I tried to grin through my anxiety and said, 'Why didn't I know?'

She stared at me, thoughtful, sad.

'It's a long story, Rosemary,' she said at last, 'can we leave it for another time, d'ya mind?'

'Okay. And it's Rosie, by the way. So, you came here alone?'

'Yeah, my partner and I run a business, no way both of us could come.'

I looked at her in silence, thinking, wondering. There was something off about this whole situation. How had this stranger popped into my life from nowhere?

Eventually, I said, 'Any American cousins I should know about?'

She reddened slightly and shook her head. 'Would have been nice to have a kid, but not possible, I'm afraid.'

I suddenly realised what she was trying to tell me.

'Mum was such a prude,' I said. 'Your partner is—'

'Anna.'

I smiled, 'Thought so. Don't worry. I'm not Mum.'

She gave me a crooked grin. 'Talking of which, I fly home tomorrow, and I'd like to visit Margie's grave. Do think you could take me?'

'Course, we can go right now if you like. It's not far.'

The next thing I knew, I was alone outside the hospital entrance. My hands were shaking so badly I could barely roll my ciggy as I recalled an odd incident on my sixth birthday that had faded into the years. Our doctor at the time, Doctor Lambert, had assured Mum it was only a childhood aberration. But now, after twenty years, it appeared my narcolepsy was back. And then there was this enigmatic woman calling herself Aunt Georgina that had appeared out of nowhere. A long lost sister? What the fuck was that all about?

And talking of which, where had she gone now?

As that thought occurred, I reflected on the oddness of events since my seizure in Dad's room: like a series of snapshots with no recollection of the transition from one scenario to the next. All I did know was that someone new and essential had entered my life, and we were going to see Mum.

1/10

Remembrance

After my smoke, I went back into the hospital, to the florist, and bought a bunch of white lilies, then went to the car park and brought the jeep around to the entrance. Aunt Georgina was there, on her phone. She gave me a little wave, so I sat with the engine running until she'd finished.

'So, that was Anna,' she explained, climbing into the jeep. 'Wanted my flight details. Says hello, by the way, she's delighted I caught up with you.'

I wound down my window – the lilies on the back seat were getting overpowering.

'So how did you find me,' I said, pulling away from the kerb, 'I mean, how did you even know which hospital?'

'Honey, you wrote me,' she said. 'Though it was pretty obvious you didn't know who I was – so impersonal. Anna thought it was quite rude.'

I scrolled through my memory for all the people I'd written to – the list from Mum's address book. Was one of the addresses in America? I would surely have remembered.

'I swung by your house this morning. Nobody home so I came to see Peter, and there you were.'

'I was down at Mullhaven,' I told her, 'working on the boat. Didn't get back till noon, then I came straight here.'

She went quiet, and when I glanced her way, she was staring ahead.

'What?' I said.

'Just thinking about old *Pasha*.'

'You know my boat?'

'Your boat? She was—' She broke off and looked out of her window.

'Go on,' I said.

'I used to sail her,' she finished, still looking away.

And then it suddenly dawned. A picture I'd seen looking through Mum's stuff. An old photograph with writing on the back. A Florida address. I stopped for traffic lights, then turned to her and clicked my fingers.

'GA? Miami?'

She chuckled. 'Our little cryptic code – stood for Georgie Anna. People weren't so liberal-minded back in the eighties.' She smiled sadly. 'Peter was an exception – sailors generally are.'

'Mum kept a photo,' I said, 'a blonde woman at the helm on *Pasha*. Would that be Anna?'

She nodded. 'That would be Anna.'

Silence, until the lights changed, and I pulled away.

'You used to sail with Dad as well?'

'Sure. When Anna was working, Peter stepped in to crew for me.'

'That's why you wanted to talk to him.'

She nodded. 'We were good friends. Such a shame to see him like that.'

I concentrated on turning in through the narrow gap into the churchyard and parked. Switching off the engine, I turned and looked at my aunt pointedly.

'*How* good friends?'

She stared at me nonplussed, then snorted and swung open her door.

'Ha! The very thought!' she chimed, climbing out.

She waited until I'd locked the jeep and joined her, then said, 'It was just Anna and me, always was, always will be. Peter was our casual crew; that's all. Besides, he was besotted with Margie by then and would never have done anything to hurt her.'

I smiled brightly and hooked my arm into hers. 'Come on. Mum's down this way.'

We walked slowly down the cobbled footpath – lined with the withered remains of Spring's daffodils. Arriving at Mum's grave, we stood contemplating the black headstone, Aunt Georgina weeping silent tears, my throat working furiously. Then my arm was under hers again, and she pulled me in close, rubbing my hand.

'All those wasted years,' she murmured, dabbing her eyes with a tissue.

After a time, I disengaged myself and began tidying around the headstone.

'Hi, Mum— Dad's still dozing in the hospital, the lazy sod.' I spluttered a laugh and my vision blurred. 'He'll wake up— one day, don't worry, he's not gonna come and annoy you just yet.'

I pulled out the dried flowers from my last visit then began arranging the new ones – their heady perfume swam around me. When I was satisfied, I stood back next to Aunt Georgina. She looked at my face and handed me a tissue. We stood for a moment in silent contemplation of the crisp white lilies, proud and sombre against the black marble, like swans sleeping in the night.

I squeezed her hand. 'Take some time. I'll wait for you.'

Alone, I wandered up the slope to where two yew trees stood like sentinels and turned to watch my aunt – she reminded me of someone lost. After a moment I strolled back to the jeep.

1/11

Spaghetti and Scotch

We drove back to mine, where I squeaked the cork on Doc's remaining bottle of Rioja.

'So, Aunt Georgina,' I said, handing her a glass of wine, 'tell me about *Pasha*.'

'Please, darling, just Georgie. "Aunt Georgina" sounds so formal, don't you think?'

I flopped down beside her on the sofa, 'Okay, Georgie.' I took a slurp of wine. Georgie sipped hers, then set the glass carefully down on the coffee table, but not before I'd noticed the slight wrinkling of her nose.

'You don't like Rioja,' I said, 'sorry, I should have asked.'

She gave a sly grin, 'I seem to remember Peter kept a fine stock of whisky—'

I laughed, standing up, 'Highland or Island? We've got both.'

'Got a Laphroig, by any chance?'

'Och Aye. The Islay's were Mum's favourite.'

Adding water to her scotch the way Mum had liked it, it struck me once again how alike, and yet, how different the two women were. Georgie was the basic model – Mum without the conservative straightjacket. Mum could ramble on about art and literature till the poles melted. But anything about personal feeling would bring instant shutdown. My aunt, as I was learning, was transparent and open-hearted in a way Mum could never have been.

She took a generous gulp of the spirit and gave a deep, contented sigh. 'Ooh, that's better. Now, you ready for some Brenton family history?'

I shuffled back comfortably into the sofa.

'You might know some of this, but I'll tell it anyway. My Dad,' she began, 'your Grandpa, whom you never knew because he died two years before you were born, left a covenant to make sure Mum, Granny Bee, would be okay in her old age. In it, Margie and Peter were given a half share in the house in Guildford, on the proviso they moved in with Mum. You with me so far?'

I nodded, 'I knew it was something like that. But nobody ever mentioned that Mum had a sister. So you weren't part of this covenant?'

'Oh, I was looked after well enough. I got *Spectre*, your grandad's old boat, and a chunk of cash. It was easier for Anna and me living aboard, especially back then.'

She sipped her scotch and continued. 'But *Spectre* was a shabby old boat, and we ended up selling her for a song. Then we used some of Dad's money to buy a brand new boat – a modern racer in her day.'

'Why the name *Pasha?* Dad was always vague when I asked him.'

'It was our secret, mine and Anna's. In the Florida Gay community, it's a pet name for an adopted child. Because it's non-gender specific, we heard it a lot while we were on holiday there in '79. We felt it appropriate.

'So, that was what, 1985, when you bought her?'

'Yes, dear, the year before you were born.'

'And my Dad, you say he was around then?'

'Oh yes, we'd known him for years. He used to skipper the Royal Navy's yacht, *Planet Mars*, for the Round the Island Race. One year we entered *Spectre* and met him at the Yacht Club in Cowes. He crewed for us a few times after that, so when we got *Pasha,* he was the logical choice to help us get her commissioned.

I chuckled, 'You know, I think there was a big painting of *Planet Mars* in Granny Bee's house, at the top landing.'

'That's right, one of your Dad's pals from the navy painted her.'

'I loved growing up in that old house,' I said. 'All those wonky passageways and creaky floorboards, and the huge garden with its orchard. And the cellar where Granny Bee made her wine – it always used to smell of apples and fermenting fruit, all those huge jars bubbling away—'

'—Brenton's Damson Wine,' Georgie chimed in, 'Brenton's Raspberry Jam. Do you remember Brenton's Ye Old Strong Cyder, spelt with a Y? People used to come to buy it at the door.'

Memories of Granny Bee's old house roiled in my head like a kaleidoscope.

'I was pretty pissed off when they sold it after I joined up,' I complained, 'they didn't even consult me.'

She studied the ceiling. 'Probably did you a favour with your inheritance. The upkeep of that old listed building was hideous even when I was growing up.'

The room was getting dark, so I jumped up and flicked on a light.

'You hungry?' I asked.

'Mm, I could manage a bite. What you got?'

I realised I hadn't a clue. Whatever Doc had loaded the fridge with before she'd thrown one and deserted me. I was sorting through the various packets, wondering what I could make them into, when Georgie slipped into the kitchen behind me.

'I thought maybe a sandwich?' I said, 'we've got ham, and tomatoes, salad stuff—' I turned to her, 'what do you think?'

'You don't cook, do you?' she said, surveying the assortment of chilled packages piled randomly on the worktop.

'Never was my thing,' I admitted, reddening, 'we could go to the pub?'

We didn't go to the pub. Georgie took charge while I watched her peeling and slicing and chopping and grating, and listened to her talking about her life in Florida. At last, the delicious aroma of frying onions and minced beef reminded me I hadn't eaten since breakfast.

'So you're a computer boffin?' I said.

She scoffed, 'Anna's the geek in the partnership, she runs the technical team – I just count the beans.'

I watched her smear garlic butter onto slices of French bread and made a mental note to give Doc some money for the food and wine. Georgie slid the reconstructed French stick into the oven, then fed a bunch of dried spaghetti sticks into a pan of boiling water.

'There,' Georgie said, after checking the simmering meat sauce, 'we eat in fifteen minutes.' She waggled her empty glass, 'Any chance of another nippy-sweetie? And then you can tell me all about life in the British Navy, and this friend of yours who buys a shedload of food and doesn't stay to eat it.'

1/12

Corvus corvix

The following Friday afternoon, I skipped work early and drove straight to Mullhaven, devoting the whole weekend to *Pasha*. It was late Sunday afternoon when I drove home. Despite being badly in need of a bath, I went to see Dad first because it would be my last chance till Christmas.

The duty staff nurse intercepted me at his door and handed me a jar of aqueous gel. 'For his feet,' she explained, smiling. 'Use plenty.'

At his bedside, I drew up the bedcover. 'Oh, good. Those heels look much better. Just going to smear some nice moisturiser on, Dad, so don't go walkabout for a while, okay? We don't want you skidding all over the ward, eh?'

Dad still had good feet for his age, I mused, as I unscrewed the jar and began work. After a few moments, I could contain it no longer and blurted out what I wanted to say to him.

'Dad! Do you realise how pissed off I am that nobody ever told me Mum had a sister?'

I looked over at his blank face.

'Nothing to say, huh? Well, here's the thing: remember when I told you last year that after the Caribbean Hurricane Season we'd be visiting Port Everglades and Mayport? Wouldn't that have been a good time to tell me I had an aunt in Florida?'

His maddening silence was too much to bear. With a tightening knot in my stomach, I walked up and knocked on his forehead with my knuckles, hard enough to hurt. 'Hello!' I called wildly, 'Anybody home?'

I breathed in sharply and bit my lip – shouldn't have done that. Flushed with guilt, I covered Dad's feet and walked outside, stood for a minute, taking deep breaths then went downstairs for a smoke.

Ten minutes later, I breezed back in and returned to his bedside. Calmer, but not feeling any better disposed towards him, not really – scary thing was, I could easily imagine smothering him with his pillow. Instead, I resumed rehydrating his feet.

'Some news to cheer you up, Dad,' I said as I worked the gel between his toes. 'I took *Pasha* for a quick sail around the harbour this morning – she's wonderful. Can't wait to take her out into the Channel.'

I took another dollop of gel and started on the other foot – use plenty, she'd said, so I did.

'But that won't be till December,' I continued, 'Cos we sail tomorrow on a three-month deployment. Yeah, I know. You want to know who's looking after *Pasha*. Well, Gary's men are going to check her once a week, run the engine, keep the batteries charged etcetera. And he won't bill us unless they have to move her. Result, eh?'

I finished his feet and re-covered them, put the jar on his bedside table, and sat down. I rubbed his forehead where the hint of a bruise had appeared.

Without warning, a wave of remorse shuddered through me. 'Oh, Dad—'

'Everything alright in here, Rosie?'

I started guiltily – it was the Staff Nurse, standing at the door, looking worried. She walked over.

'What's that on his brow?' she said sharply.

I drew my thumb over the treacherous giveaway that had darkened on his forehead. 'I'm afraid that was me, sorry. That jar slipped out of my hand.'

The nurse moved me aside and leant down to examined the bruise, then turned to me with frosty eyes, 'Maybe you should go now, Rosie. Let him rest.'

It wasn't my ripe body odour that made me drive with the jeep's windows wide open – but the stench of remorse that followed me out of the hospital. I wasn't going to see him again for three months, how could I have been such a vicious bitch? And now to my astonishment, all the accumulated resentment of the past weeks evaporated. He was my Dad, and I wanted him back.

And it was in that filial spirit that, as I arrived home, I finally addressed the question I'd left hanging for the past week. My long-overdue bath would have to wait a little longer. I ran upstairs to the spare room and opened the filing cabinet where

Dad kept the family documents, including both their Medical Cards.

I stared at their cards, first one, then the other, willing my eyes to see something different. Mum's blood group was 'A' Negative, as I'd thought. Dad's was 'O', the same as I'd read on his Hospital Care Chart. Mine was AB Negative, and I was sure that couldn't be right.

Back downstairs in the Dining Room, I flashed-up my laptop and logged on to Google. After a moment's thought, I typed: 'blood group genotypes'. The first offering was on the NHS web site. I chose it, then held my breath. When the page came up, I scrolled down to the parents/offspring chart, then stared at the monitor. Dad was, well, that's just it – he wasn't.

Suddenly the computer lid snapped shut with a deep resonance like the closing door of a vault. I tried to stand, but my knees buckled, and I collapsed back onto the dining chair; the room rotated, and the back of my head hit the thick pile of the carpet. I felt wide awake – aware of being still seated on the tipped-over chair with its carved wooden back digging uncomfortably into my pliant one – but unable to move. That was my last sensible deduction before everything got unhinged. For there above me, my laptop was strangely transformed; animated and airborne, flapping around the room like a mechanical bird. My surroundings became ever more unreal, dreamlike – reality fading, fading.

Trapped in the room with me was a hooded crow. I recognised its species: *Corvus cornix*, as illustrated in the 1998 Collins' Guide, page 209 – *why did I know that?* The bird flapped its wings against the window, talons tearing at the blinds. As the shards of plastic fell away, the beast began pecking at the glass – tap, tap, tap – until the window shattered soundlessly in a shower of silver raindrops. But before it could make its escape, the crow exploded in a spray of black lilies, floating outwards and trailing their stems behind them. Now the black petals morphed into demonic heads sprouting slender tongues. And the flower-stems began to wriggle, like grinning tadpoles. Grey clouds folded around me.

I came awake suddenly. Everything was back to normal in the room. There was pain along my spine, and the backs of my knees ached where they hung over the upended seat. It had been daylight when I'd collapsed, but now the room was illuminated only by the dim glow from the laptop monitor.

While I waited for the recovery that must surely come soon, I distracted myself with the less pressing problem of my parentage. What could it mean? Had Mum had an affair that had got her pregnant? Did Dad know I wasn't his daughter? Or was I adopted?

And did it matter?

My thoughts turned inevitably back to what did matter right now: paralysed in an empty house with no chance of help coming anytime soon. I was due back on-board on Monday morning. Was it already Monday?

I had no idea what time it was or what day.

I closed my eyes and tried to sleep, tried to escape the conclusion that my life was turning to shit, and there wasn't a thing I could do about it. But sleep eluded me as panic and pain vied for dominance. Useless torment. Mum's wise words on Granny Bee's passing (16th of May 1999, a Sunday) came to me: *'No point lamenting what you can't change, Rose, just try to think positive thoughts.'*

But they were scant comfort – positive thoughts eluded me – I saw only my once-promising career lying broken in a trail of wreckage. The only thing I could think of was remotely upbeat was that I hadn't started to run the bath. I startled myself with a vision of the ceiling under a ton of water collapsing on me. To bring on sleep, I began to count animals in my head: sheep, llamas, three-toed sloths, it didn't matter.

1, 2, 3, 4, 5—

I woke up when my left leg twitched violently, and I rolled off the chair groaning in agony. I opened my eyes to the first grey light of dawn filtering through the window blinds.

1/13

Sailing Orders

I made it on-board just in time, not adrift as I'd feared – which carried extra penalties with the ship under Sailing Orders. Doc was back from her week's leave that morning, and I found her getting dressed in our bunk space.

We were alone, so I charged straight in, 'Doc, I'm sorry about putting you—'

She silenced me with a slender index finger held up theatrically like someone just struck by a bright idea. 'Let's not go there again. Far as I'm concerned, we're unconditional. Now shut the fuck up and get a shower, cuz, Girl – you stink!'

We both turned as somebody walked in on us. 'Hiya, sorry to interrupt. Where am I?'

'Oh, hello, Donna,' Doc said. 'You may as well take Martha's old bunk,' she indicated the bunk space adjacent to ours. 'It's the middle one on the left. Your locker's the one with the key in it.'

'Hi, Donna,' I said grinning. 'Welcome back – hope you've got your sea legs on.'

Donna was our usual Naval Nurse Practitioner, seconded to us for operational deployments. There was no spare cabin for her, so she had to slum it with us in the Women's Mess. I think she preferred our company anyway – Donna was a consummate socialite and loved her runs ashore with the girls.

'There might be another free bunk here soon,' Doc said with a sly grin when Donna had drawn out of earshot to unpack her holdall.

I gaped at her, 'Your B13 came through! Congratulations, *Petty Officer*.' I gave her a quick hug. 'When did you find out?'

'Before I went on leave when I opened the Captain's mail that Friday morning – perks of being Ship's Writer. I was going to tell you over that weekend, but—' she shrugged, 'you know, didn't work out as planned.'

'Sorry,' I grimaced. 'So, is anyone else's B13 in?' I gave her the eyebrow.

She shook her head sadly, 'What can I say, Rosie?'

A non-comital answer – she wouldn't tell me even if mine *had* come through.

'So when's it gonna be official?' I asked her.

'The next Skippers is a week on Wednesday, so keep shtum till then.'

An hour later, freshly showered and in uniform, I stood at ease in line on the cable deck with the rest of the Fo'c'sle Party as we left the harbour. We were off on a three-month tour to the Eastern Mediterranean in support of NATO. After a tedious few months in Pompey, we were all looking forward to doing the job for which we'd trained.

The usual crowd of friends and relatives had gathered on Southsea Castle to see us off. Some of the Fo'c'sle Party waved at their loved ones gliding past, triggering in me a wave of sadness – M & D should have been out there on those battlements today.

My thoughts turned to Dad. Yes, he was still my Dad, even if not biologically. If he didn't know, I certainly wasn't going to tell him. But curiosity had me wondering; just who *was* my birth father? I wasn't adopted, I'd decided – apart from being taller, I looked too much like Mum. Even Georgie had said so. And Georgie must have known anyway – just how deep *was* the conspiracy?

I couldn't get out of my head what I'd done at the hospital on my last visit. I no longer blamed Dad for what happened. I just wanted him to wake up and hug me. I wanted to say sorry for how I'd treated him since the accident. Too late now – I wouldn't see him till Christmas.

I missed Mum too, but somehow that burned less fiercely; an intangible void that left only a dull ache whenever I thought of her. But strangely, it was a void that had begun to fill with Georgie; was that why my grief felt so oddly diminished?

As we drew past Spitbank Fort and all the yacht sails in the Solent came into view, my thought's drifted to *Pasha*. Doc had been wrong about me losing interest in my naval career. It was true I'd sooner have been slicing silently through the water under sail than thundering along on a dirty great destroyer. But I could easily endure the camaraderie of shipboard life, at least for a few more years. Once

I became an officer of significant rank, I would have more career choices.

As we cleared the ship channel, we were fallen out to stow ropes and fenders and secure for sea. The ship would remain on heightened alert during our transit of the busy Channel and then revert to the more relaxed Cruising Watches until Gibraltar.

Wednesday night was Inter-mess Quiz night. As it got started, I tucked myself into my usual out-of-the-way corner of the mess with my Kindle.

'Not doing the quiz, Rosie?'

I looked up from my reading. It was Freddie, the new Leading Cook who'd only joined the ship last week. She'd decided I was lonely and needed company. I wasn't, and I didn't.

'Mess Rule 106:' I told her, 'Leading Seaman Winterbourne recuses herself from quiz night.'

I grinned at her bewilderment. I'd hardly spoken to Freddie but knew she'd been having difficulty settling into shipboard life. I guessed her career thus far had been shore-based.

'*You* should join in though, Freddie, help you get to know everybody, you know, get down and dirty with the girls?'

'What are you reading?' she asked, not taking the hint.

I let out a sigh and snapped the Kindle shut. 'Reading's not a spectator sport, but never mind.' I turned and gave her my undivided attention. 'Tell me, Freddie, how are you settling in with the galley heavies?'

Before she could answer, Karen, who was writing down the quiz answers, shouted across to me, 'Rosie, what's the capital of Tuvalu?'

'Has anyone had a guess?' I shouted back.

'You're joking. We don't even know where it is.'

'Funafuti,' I told her, 'it's in the Pacific, you numpties.'

I turned back to Freddie, who was giving me a weird look. I put a finger to my lips. 'What you just heard comes under Mess Rule 101,' I told her. 'So, you're settling in okay in the galley?'

She wrinkled her nose. She was relatively young for a killick chef, and if she was not used to the cut and thrust of a male-dominated ship's galley, I could see it being quite tricky for her.

'My advice?' I said. 'Forget the hook on your arm for the first few weeks; just look and listen and give a hand where needed. Don't flirt, and don't let anyone touch you, and if you get any abuse, verbal or otherwise, take it straight to your boss, don't let it fester.'

She smiled, looked relieved – I wondered if anyone in her department was mentoring her. She was quite pretty, which could be a help or a hindrance, depending on how strategic she was. I gave her a happy face. 'Don't worry, Freddie, once you've joined the team you can start to exert—'

'Hey, Google, which Athenian General led the Syracuse Expedition in 415BC?'

'Cheeky bint!' I retorted. 'Any of you masterminds got a clue?'

'Lynda thinks it's Pericles.'

'That's right.' I called. 'Well done, Lynda.'

I grinned at Freddie and winked.

'That wasn't true, was it?' she said.

'Nah. It was Alcibiades. Teach 'em to take the piss. Besides, it doesn't look good if we win all the time.'

The Weapons Electrical Mess won the cake that night.

And so life settled down to sea routine. Soon the days just rolled past each other, the time marked not by days of the week but by our waypoints of Quiz night, Tombola night, Film night, Sunday Prayers, Clean Ship Day, Evening Drills etcetera. We could have done the passage down to Gib in three days, but this was the navy, and the navy never went anywhere in straight lines. We were heading out into the open ocean for a few days of weapons training with live firings.

Everything went swimmingly for a week.

And then it didn't.

1/14

Goblins & Blue Meanies

The quarterdeck after dark. Against the moonless black velvet the Milky Way gave a display so sharp and brilliant it watered the eyes. It was a calm evening, getting perceptibly warmer as our latitude decreased. I had relieved the Lifebuoy Sentry for the last half hour of his watch to be alone for a while.

It was Wednesday again – Quiz Night. It was also my 26th Birthday. The Quiz would be over before I came off watch, but it would still be my Birthday. And that was a worry because the emotional stuff was what seemed to trigger those narcoleptic seizures and having one on board would almost certainly get me CASEVAC-ed ashore. So far I'd gotten away with it – even Doc seemed to have overlooked the auspicious day.

My relief showed up at five-past-eight.

'Sorry, Hooky' he mumbled.

I handed him the binoculars and glared at him in the starlight but said nothing. I went inside and sauntered along the full length of Eton Walkway, and down the ladder at Echo Section to our cross-passage. I reached the mess door and listened. All quiet. Good. I pushed open the door and stepped over the sill – and knew something was up because it was dark. There was just a faint glow through the heavy inner curtain. The mess-square lights were never switched off at sea because of watchkeepers coming and going. That should have been my cue to flee and hide somewhere.

But I didn't. In a flash of recklessness, I closed the door behind me and threw the curtain aside, and saw a sea of dimly flickering faces in the light of a single candle. All at once the lights came on, accompanied by a cacophony of wild cheering, faces grinning and laughing – so many faces, not just the girls, but blokes as well, those I considered mates: Tony Briggs, and Andy Rice; big Pincher Martin and a bunch of other lads from the fo'c'sle, even Graeme, the NAAFI Manager.

Men were banned from the female mess at sea – not just a Mess Rule but a Queen's Regulation. Despite my earlier worries, I was delighted. I grinned deliriously to see them all there for me – but as Doc funnelled the noise into a ragged chorus of Happy Birthday, I felt a familiar shipwreck coming on.

As the scene dissolved into chaos, I heard a shout of 'Oh my God!' the syllables drawn-out like a slowed-down recording. The faces around me were leering caricatures of the people I knew, prehensile fingers like talons, reaching towards me, growing longer. Goblins! I saw only goblins all around me now: vile snickering faces, blackened teeth, evil grins; they hissed and slurped and drooled, and drew purple, wormlike tongues over their cracked, bloodstained lips.

Sudden shards of intense light pierced my eyes, and the nightmarish creatures vanished. Everything was gone. A sensation of floating, floating towards a sky of unearthly splendour, a million rainbows of impossible hues. Someone's voice in my ear, Doc. But I could not make out her words; she might have been speaking Martian. Her strident calling gradually faded into the background.

Silence.

I was in another world, a world of incredible beauty, a world of stunning jewels that wanted to pull me up into their midst. Weightless now, I rose with astonishing speed into the spangled night. I passed Mars, red and silent. I wheeled past Jupiter, her daughters, chattering and fizzing as they danced around their giant parent. Then I penetrated Saturn's silvery rings. Finally, deep space: empty, frozen silence.

After an eternity, I began to notice the mundane world around me once more. I saw a strip-light and the perforated soundproofing in the deckhead, bodies moving in and out of view, a gabble of voices against the faint humming of fans.

'Her eyes just opened!' somebody yelled.

A face came into my line of vision, Donna, our seconded Nurse Practitioner. I felt my hand taken hold of and lifted.

'Can you hear me, Rosie?'

Even though I'd been through this before and knew it would pass eventually, I felt a rising panic. I was encased in solid rock, held in stasis when all my senses screamed for movement, for escape – in terror of suffocation. My fear must have been plain to Donna.

'Stay with her, Doc, I'll be back in a jiffy.'

She slipped out of view and another face swam in – Doc with a furrowed brow. I calmed a little as my best friend smiled down at me, 'You okay, Rosie? You gave me quite a fright there.'

I blinked.

'Oh! Rosie, blink twice if you can hear me.'

I blinked twice.

'Er, wow! Okay, blink once for yes, twice for no, okay?'

I blinked.

'Are you in any pain?'

I blinked, paused, waited for her frown, then blinked again.

Doc's grinning face withdrew, replaced by fat Karen's.

'She must be okay,' I heard Doc announce. 'She's taking the piss.'

Karen grinned. 'That right, Rosie?'

My left leg twitched.

'What's that, Donna?' I heard Doc ask.

'Just a shot of Valium, to ease her anxiety. Then I'll get my boss to look at her.'

Karen moved aside, and Donna's head reappeared over me. I saw the syringe in her hand and shook my head.

I shook my head!

'No!' I shouted, pushing her away. I sat up and dropped my feet to the deck.

'S'okay,' I said to the stunned medic, 'I'm okay now. Just give me a minute.'

Donna put the hypo on the table and sat down beside me. Doc's arm came around my shoulders from the other side, and she pulled me in protectively. I looked around at the concerned faces of messmates and male visitors. The mess clock said quarter past eight. I'd only been out of it for a few minutes. It had seemed like years.

Shaking off Doc's arm, I laughed. 'Had you all there for a minute, eh? Just so's you know, I hate surprise parties.'

I leaned over and blew out the single candle on the cake.

No one clapped or cheered. Nobody even spoke.

I was climbing into my pit after my shower, when Doc, already turned in, asked, 'What the fuck happened to you tonight?'

'Just a funny turn,' I told her. 'Probably overtired.'

'Bollocks!'

'Look, I'm okay now so let's drop it, eh? And remember Mess Rule 101.'

A poster in the mess square reminded everyone of the sacred mantra:

MESS RULE 101

What you do here

What you see here

What you hear here

Let it stay here

When you leave here!

'And the blokes won't say anything,' I added, 'because they weren't supposed to be there.'

'Okay,' Doc said doubtfully, 'but I should have a word with the NP before she goes up to sickbay in the morning. She's bound to mention it to the Quack.'

'Don't worry about Donna. I had a quiet word earlier. She won't blab.'

In truth, it had been Donna who'd cornered *me*. She'd followed me down the ladder when I went for my shower.

'Has that ever happened to you before?' she asked.

Turning, I'd looked the medic in the eye and lied. 'Never. And please, keep this to yourself, okay?'

'We should get you checked over, Rosie,' she insisted. 'You could have a form of epilepsy.'

'Trust me on this, Donna, it's not epilepsy. If it happens again, I'll go and see the Quack myself. Meanwhile, just do me a favour and keep shtum, alright?'

She shook her head, pursing her lips, unwilling to let it go. So I added an incentive. 'Otherwise,' I told her, 'I might have to mention a beach party in Tobago: August 26th, 2011 – which was a Friday by the way. A party involving a certain NP and some banned substances.'

I know! It was horrible. I'd made an enemy, but at least saved my career – for now.

1/15

Bottle-walk

The Angry Friar, Friday evening – first night in Gib:

'Gangway, coming through,' I warned, clutching my bottle of Moet & Chandon and a fan of flute glasses.

A familiar voice rose above the din: 'Shampoo, Rosie? What's the occasion?'

I paused as Pincher Martin came shuffling through, head and shoulders above the melee. I liked Pincher, but I think he liked me back a bit too much. It doesn't do to get too close to shipmates.

'Celebrating Doc's promotion,' I told him. 'Her B13 for PO came through.'

He shrugged, 'Send her my congrats, but I'll stay with the lad's coz we're in a round.'

'I never offered,' I grinned. 'It's a girlie night.'

Freddie Symmonds caught my eye as I shuffled past her by the doorway.

'Hello, Rosie, where are you sitting?'

She was with a bunch of male chefs, and I was pleased she seemed to be fitting in at last. I nodded to one of the outside tables where Doc and the others were waiting for their bubbly.

'Come on over and say hi to the new PO Writer – she'll be moving out of the mess tomorrow.'

Freddie eyed the Champaign. 'I'll come and find you in a bit.'

At our table, they all helped unload me, then Helen popped the cork and poured the bubbly. I proposed the toast:

'To my Best Oppo, *Petty Officer* Writer Joanna Halliday, Cheers Doc, and congrats. And – wait a minute, not yet – before anyone asks: No, Doc, I ain't jealous that you got yours before me.'

We chinked glasses. I paused until they were all drinking, before adding, 'Jammy bitch!'

Snorts of laughter, Yvonne was discharging snotty bubbly back into her glass. I guess we got quite loud and giggly after that, and as the Champaign expired, we moved back on the Pinot Grigio.

'This sounds fun, mind if I join you?'

'Course not, Freddie' I said, moving along the bench to make room. 'Champagne's all gone, I'm afraid.'

'S'okay,' she held up her glass, 'I'll stick to the red. Well done on your PO's, Doc. Deserved I'm sure.'

We left the Angry Friar when the tuneless singing got too loud, and the bobbies started eying us from across the road. Karen and Helen declared for the night went back on-board, while the remaining four of us walked up the hill to The Hole in the Wall.

Freddie told us she found the chefs a bit too wild ashore – she didn't like getting drunk and thought we'd be better company for her. Yvonne was also new in our company, and I was surprised when she'd tagged along. Curvaceous and leggy in high heels and a skimpy green dress, she'd unfastened her blonde hair to fall luxuriously around her bare shoulders. Freddie, by contrast, was dressed for comfort in tee-shirt, pedal-pushers and trainers – cutely attractive without a trace of makeup.

Reaching the bar in the crowded downstairs cellar, Doc demanded a round of tequila slammers with a panache I'd rarely seen in her. She had taken off her specs and spent some time on her face – a sure sign she was going for it. My best friend looked her willowy best: a silky white top that exposed her tanned midriff and denim shorts. I especially loved her leather sandals, which were decorated with coloured beads.

For me, it was a grey shirt hanging loose over pink shorts and flip flops, a flick of mascara and a press of lippy – all I'd had time for after securing the Fo'c'sle.

We had a couple more shots in Casemates Square, then headed for the Frontier. A warm, blustery breeze buffeted us across the expanse of the runway. Doc, with her arms linked between Freddie and me, was trying to lead us in some half-remembered smutty sailor's song. Yvonne tottered alongside in her heels, attempting to make banal conversation that we ignored.

As the Frontier approached, we shushed each other, then lapsed into muted giggling. The Spanish border guard waved us through with barely a glance at our passports, seemingly more interested in the surreptitious study of Yvonne's shapely, if slightly unsteady legs.

Noisy people packed the *La Casa de la Esquina.* The place zinged with delicious aromas, the baristas miraculously keeping up with orders shouted randomly from all sides. We ate at the bar and shared a bottle of Ribera. For Doc and me the tapas-house was a favourite on previous visits, and Freddie too seemed to enjoy its anarchic noise and bustle. But it was soon clear Yvonne was not impressed.

'This place sucks,' she announced. She necked her wine and belched, then said 'Come on, Girls, let's find some fucking life.'

Wall-to-wall people packed Molly Bloom's Irish Pub, live rock music blasting from its flashing interior; the crowds spilling out onto the plaza, many of them from our ship. Yvonne volunteered to brave the crush to get our drinks while we three grabbed an outside table. After an age, Yvonne returned with a tray of beers. It was then I noticed a commotion out in the plaza involving some of our guys, and I spotted Pincher Martin amongst them. Leaving Yvonne and Freddie to guard our table, Doc and I wandered over to investigate.

It turned out a bottle-walk challenge was underway between a bunch of our lads and some of the local honchos. Pincher Martin, an athletic six-foot-two, was limbering up to beat the long reach of an equally tall Spaniard. Shouts of encouragement from our lot – darkened by the inevitable anti-Spanish jingoism - mingled with the good-natured jeering from the home opposition. Though much of the Spanish went over our guys' heads, the taunting sentiments were straightforward enough: this contest was serious stuff – for National Pride was at stake.

It was a long reach, and though I'd seen Pincher do better, I thought he looked a little unsteady tonight. A triumphant cheer went up from our lads when his bottle outreached the other by a hair, followed by silence as it wobbled and clinked against the opposition's bottle. Then a collective groan as both bottles fell over and our champion collapsed in a heap of laughter and disappointment.

The Spaniards' cheering was frenzied, but their man, with a surprising show of chivalry, walked over and helped Pincher to his feet, patting his back in commiseration. It was then that Pincher spotted me across the crowd. His eyes lit up.

'C'mon,' I told Doc, urgently, 'let's get back to the table.'

'Huh-uh,' she grinned, slowly shaking her head and barring my escape.

The inevitable chanting began, accompanied by a slow hand-clap, led by Pincher, and seconded now by Doc, who stood away to let me know she'd joined the conspiracy.

'Rosie, Rosie, Rosie—' went the relentless chorus of my shipmates, until I had no choice but step up to the hockey. As the ridiculous chanting grew louder and faster, the Spaniard eyed me with a puzzled, mildly amused expression. Tall, fit-looking and handsome, with an unruly mop of black, curly hair, this guy, I thought, was fit in both senses of the word.

'Technically,' I shouted above the noise, 'you've won. But my *amigos* want me to have a go. Do you mind?'

'Please, *Señora*,' he said, beckoning me forward with a dramatic sweep of his arm, 'if you win, I buy you champagne.'

'Done!' I said.

I reached down with my legs straight and settled my palms over the two empty Guinness bottles – wishing I'd worn jeans instead of skimpy shorts. I began walking the bottles out to the mark. While Pincher had had a five-inch height advantage, my lighter build and strength gave me greater lateral reach. Though now at my age, I thought the game rather childish and was particularly conscious of my bottom stuck up in undignified fashion.

The chants of 'Easy!' became deafening, a brief hiatus as one of my wrists wobbled, then I was out at full stretch with only my toes and my baggy shirt touching the ground. It all went quiet – the moment of truth. Transferring all my weight gingerly onto the bottle in my left hand, I reached out with my right, placing the other a good two inches beyond the Spaniard's bottle. I then snatched up the Spaniard's bottle and walked myself safely back to the hockey.

The cheering, as I stood up, was noisy and ecstatic; mates were gathering round with much back-slapping and hearty congratulations. But my Spanish opponent was nowhere to be seen, which kind of spoiled my moment.

'He fucked off right after you won,' Doc shouted, slurring and laughing deliriously, 'getting beaten by a mere girl was too much for his ego. A bit dishy, though, wasn't he?'

'Bit of a dickhead, more like,' I said.

We found Yvonne chatting up the band members who'd come out to our table on their break. They were young, long-haired and greasy-looking, and it was clear Yvonne's drunken charms were of little interest. Freddie had moved a cautious distance away and looked relieved to see us. We dragged up two more chairs.

'These are the boys from the band,' Yvonne confided loudly. 'Forgotten all their names, but they're going back in for another session in—' she stopped, and her mouth fell open as a big shiny ice-bucket arrived on the table in front of me.

'Ooh, hello!' she cooed huskily, looking up doe-eyed at my defeated bottle-walk opponent.

'I apologise for it take so long,' said the man, with a smile that was just for me, placing two champagne glasses on the table, 'It is only cava, I am afraid.'

'No need to be afraid, Pedro,' slurred Yvonne, grabbing the bottle out of the ice and unwiring the cork, 'all contributions gratefully accepted.'

Freddie looked shocked. Doc too was outraged, and the poor guy who brought me the promised gift just gave me a helpless grimace, and said, 'This not the time, but I see you again, perhaps?'

Just then we were all startled by the sudden roar of a motorbike a couple of streets away, and when I looked back, he was gone.

'He left this,' Doc said, picking a card out of one of the champagne glasses.

'Whose your admirer?' Freddie asked me, then gave Yvonne a meaningful look.

'Mateo Galindez,' supplied Doc, squinting at the card, 'his mobile and email. Aww, how romantic is *that?*'

I snatched the card from her.

Just then Yvonne popped the cork on the cava, on her feet and off her head, whooping crazily and showering the band boys with the sticky fizz, hastening their retreat inside.

'That got rid of them losers,' she slurred, sitting down with a silly smirk on her face. 'Now, where's that gorgeous waiter gone?'

Freddie made to point out her misreading of the situation, but I stopped her. 'No, it's okay, Freddie, just leave it, yeah?'

Shortly afterwards Pincher Martin came over to say he was heading back with some of the lads and did we want to come?

'Yvonne!' said Doc assertively. 'You want to go with them?'

Yvonne got up, swaying a little so Pincher had to steady her. She peered down at us. 'You three coming?'

'Nah,' I said, catching Doc's microscopic head shake, 'we'll hang on a bit longer, still got our drinks to finish.'

'Actually,' said Freddie, 'I'm on breakfast tomorrow, so I think I'll tag along with them.'

Yvonne took a defiant swig from the cava bottle which then fizzed over and all down her lovely party frock.

'You two going to be okay?' Pincher said.

'We're big girls now,' Doc grinned up at him. 'Go on, off you toddle.'

'Hey, Pincher,' I called as he walked away with Yvonne.

He turned back, and I gave him my kindly face, 'Thanks for caring, Shipmate.'

He returned a grinning thumbs-up, then just managed to grab Yvonne before she veered out of control, and steered her firmly across the plaza behind the dozen or so other returning guys.

Doc and I exchanged looks, then spluttered simultaneously into giggles. Freddie grinned back at us before following them at a discrete distance.

1/16

Smuggler

Doc and I headed back half an hour later, picking up a couple of kebabs to eat on the hoof. Chatting away cosily, we took little notice of the growl of yet another motorbike from the direction of the yacht marina opposite.

'Well?' said Doc, linking arms with me, a wicked smirk spreading on her face. 'Are you going to get in touch with your cute Spanish beau?'

'Behave yourself,' I said. 'You'd better sober up before we hit the Frontier.'

'Come on, Winterbourne, admit it, you do have the hots for him, don't you?'

'Okay, probably,' I allowed.

'Probably? *Probably?* What kind of—'

Suddenly she released me and gave a terrified scream, backing away from a cockroach the size of a bus that was scuttling across the sidewalk. Doc had a morbid phobia of giant creepy-crawlies.

Then I got distracted by two motorbikes gunning out of the trees opposite – they shot away with flashing blue lights towards the roundabout ahead of us. I saw then who they were after. Another motorbike emerged at speed from the marina approach road, one of the frequent cigarette smugglers – two big cardboard boxes lashed to the pillion.

Doc was still freaking out at the oversized insect that seemed to be stalking her. She'd backed up against a big concrete planter that stood between her and the road. I glanced worriedly at the roundabout, where the first guy had gone the wrong way around to escape the pursuing *Guardia Civil*. Now they were all three racing back towards us – a lot was suddenly happening at once, and I started to get a bad feeling.

'Doc, it's only a fucking cocky, you daft bint. Come back here. There's a—'

Before I got further, she stepped around the planter to get away from the insect, and suddenly she was in the road.

'Doc!' I shrieked, 'get off the fucking road!'

The fleeing smuggler would have seen her in time if he hadn't been looking back at the cops. When he spotted her, he swerved and lost it; the bike went over onto its side, spilled its rider, bounced on the road then flipped, barrelling over and over, striking a cascade of sparks in its wake.

In the garish yellow light from the streetlamps, I saw it all in horrifying slow-motion. My best friend stared in frozen terror at the motorbike tumbling towards her. Cigarette cartons flew behind the careering machine like a flock of maddened gulls.

I screamed as the heavy motorcycle bowled into her with a sickening crump, slamming her onto the bike's frame. There was a spurt of blood and a dreadful pop as a pedal pierced her eye socket. Thus impaled, my friend journeyed on with the bike as it skidded another twenty metres or more before screeching to a halt.

My scream turned abruptly silent as if someone had muted the volume. For there in front of me – amid the chaos of scattered cigarette cartons – lay a severed foot with painted toenails, twitching and bloody in its pretty, beaded sandal.

My world tipped sideways, and foliage came up to meet me, obscuring the terrible scene – I felt the side of my face settle among fresh, fragrant flowers. The last thing I saw was flashing blue lights filtered through a profusion of leaves.

1/17

Reflections

The windows of the airport departure hall were like giant two-way mirrors. The Rock of Gibraltar filled the view, north face vertical and unvegetated. A perfectly lenticular cloud was stationed upon its ridge – a craggy-faced soldier wearing a white beret. In contrast, my reflection: a transparent figure in jeans and grey top, a bulging holdall at her feet. My mirror image stared forlornly back into the terminal, as if not sure whether it really existed or was merely a reflection of misery. A reflection of the past two ghastly days, days of confusing visions and sudden flashbacks: of all the savagery of that dreadful night, the image of Doc's severed foot would haunt me always.

It had all seemed so real. Then the shock of waking up, once again in total paralysis, bewildered by the worried face of my best friend looking down at me, unharmed and pouring soothing words into my disbelieving mind.

My secret was finally out – public knowledge. If only I'd come out of it before the ambulance arrived to take me to Gib Hospital.

Doc had tried, bless her, all the way back across the frontier; 'She'll be okay in a minute, you'll see,' she told the medics repeatedly. 'Look, see? She blinked.'

Doc and I had said our goodbyes this morning, promising to stay in touch. It felt peculiar to stand and watch my ship sail away without me, my shipmates lining the decks, blue collars fluttering in the breeze. In that moment I felt so empty and abandoned I could have just stepped off the quayside and let my holdall drag me down.

I shifted my focus onto the airfield. Over on the RAF side a huge C17 transporter – doubtless on its way back from supporting those same operations – dwarfed the two Tornado fighters parked beside it. The EasyJet Airbus that would soon fly me away stood on the apron beneath the window disembarking its arrivals.

I registered dully the reflection of my escorting officer approaching from behind with our coffees, sensible heels clopping on the shiny tiles. She was a sub-lieutenant from the Naval Base, drawn the short straw because she was flying home on leave, saving *Windy C's* travel budget. She looked about twenty and was unhappy to be put in charge of a traumatised and possibly psychotic rating.

They'd booked us into cattle-class, but the check-in clerk, aware of my circumstances, upgraded us to Business. Despite the added comfort, I slept fitfully for most of the three-hour flight. I woke up feeling groggy as the announcement came to fasten seatbelts for our final approach. We were met in the Arrivals Hall by a uniformed QARNNS Officer holding up a card with my name on it. My prior escort wished me all the best and scuttled off to her leave.

I'd assumed we'd travel up by train, but Baxter, the Nursing Officer, walked me out onto the bus stand where a black BMW awaited us. No expense spared, it seemed, for little wibbly-wobbly me.

It was a damp, drizzly afternoon as our car filtered into the motorway traffic. Nobody had spoken since we'd left the airport. Once or twice, I caught the driver watching me in his mirror. The NO, next to me in the back, seemed content to travel in silence.

'So, what happens now?' I asked eventually.

She half-turned in her seat to face me, her thin face drawn into a tight smile. I got a fleeting image of Cruella De Vil.

'Today, nothing much. The first thing is to get you settled into RCDM.'

'RCDM? What's that?'

Her hard features softened, she chuckled gently. 'Royal Centre for Defence Medicine. Tomorrow we'll admit you to the Neurology and Mental Care Ward, where Professor Hardy's team will assess you. We're all quite civilized, so don't worry. Tomorrow you'll meet the Professor himself for your initial—'

'Are they going to kick me out?' I blurted.

She gave a tolerant sigh, 'Our job is to assess your fitness for active service, to get you back to your unit as soon as possible. My advice is to just focus on that and stay in the moment.'

My room was on the third floor – and was surprisingly unmilitary. From its powder blue carpet with matching curtains to the Ikea-style pine bed with a sprung mattress under crisp, white sheets, it was a pleasant little home from home. There was even a small writing desk, complete with Internet socket – and the en-suite had a bath as well as a shower. It would have all delighted me if only I hadn't felt so wretched.

The window looked out onto the Birmingham University Campus. I tried the opener, and it yielded to let in faint traffic sounds; at least they didn't have me down as a jumper.

My home for the next—ooh! Who knew?

After unpacking, I plugged in my laptop, logged into Facebook, then sat staring at my profile picture, Doc's grinning bespectacled face pressed close to mine. Tears dripped onto the keyboard.

1/18

Assessment

Why do you think you're here, Rosie?'
A hawkish-looking man with reddish hair turning silver at the sides, Professor John Hardy spoke with a soft Caledonian accent. But his most striking feature was his pale blue eyes, the kind of eyes that pierced one's soul.

'I was hoping you could tell *me*,' I said.

I expected a rebuke, but he was unfazed. He seemed to have all the time in the world. And he was silent, a silence I soon began to find excruciating. I let it go on, defiant, waiting for him to crack and say something. But finally, it was me who gave way.

'Okay, look. Three nights ago, I saw my best mate mashed up by a motorbike. It was horrible – I saw her foot chopped off in the middle of the road, bleeding and twitching. The thing is, Professor, it never happened, it was all in my head – like a nightmare but, you know, more real?

'Then, when I woke up, I couldn't move a muscle, I couldn't even speak. The ambulance took me to the hospital in Gib, and I stayed paralyzed for about three hours. When I recovered, I got discharged back on-board, and our ship's doc sent me here. That's it, no more to tell, really.'

Now he spoke. 'You make it sound like that experience had never happened to you before. Is that what you want me to believe?'

I stared at him a moment. He seemed omnipotent – a psychologist's trick. But how much did he know?

I shrugged. 'There were similar— once or twice. But I was dealing with it, until—'

'—until your secret was out, eh? Mm, and how, exactly, have you been you dealing with it?'

'I just kept a lid on my emotions,' I said, carelessly. 'Seemed to work, most of the time; as long as I keep it cool, I'm okay.'

'But when your colleagues threw you a surprise party last week? What happened to keeping a lid on it then?'

'Oh! You know about that. Who—? Oh, never mind, I think I know. Yeah, well—'

'And tell me, Rosie, when you thought your friend was about to be struck by a motorcycle, was that you, keeping it cool?'

I said nothing. This wasn't fair – I wasn't here to be bullied.

'Tell me, Rosie, did you at any stage consider the danger of you suffering a seizure during action in an active warzone? The danger to yourself and colleagues who rely on you?'

I had no answer. Was this what it was going to be like – piling on the guilt?

The Professor let the silence drift around us while I fidgeted and avoided his gaze; those pale eyes that seemed to know everything.

'Is that how you dealt with your mother's death,' he said eventually, 'by keeping your emotions under control?'

I didn't reply. A defensive wall had arisen around me. Once again, that long spate of silence. I realised my right knee was trammelling under the Professor's intent gaze; he sat motionless, like a spider watching for an insect to snag in its web.

With a determined effort, I got my knee under control. Then, when I least expected it, I began crying.

'Yes, of course, I knew I was an idiot not reporting those— those seizures,' I blubbered. 'How did I deal with Mum's death? Fucking awful – excuse my language. I wailed when the surgeon told me he hadn't been able to save her.' I expelled a big sigh and sniffed. 'It was only later when I had to identify her— when I saw her lying there her face all gashed open, a sh-sheet up to her chin but I could see that underneath she was, well, broken, you know?

'I just felt cold then, numb. I didn't want to see my Mum like that. I tried to remember her how she was, but I couldn't picture her any more. I was terrified that this damaged body was all I would ever remember.

'And I wanted to talk to Dad, but he was somewhere upstairs in ITU being brain-scanned or something, and I had no idea if I would ever see him again either.'

I stopped talking and waited for him to say something, anything. He said nothing, just drilled me with that relentless stare.

'What else do you want from me, Professor? I want to go now.'

He nodded slowly. 'We're nearly finished, Rosie. We'll explore more of those feelings about your mother over the next days. Now, tell me about your father – he remains in a coma, I understand.'

Stabbing guilt suddenly waded in, pricking the backs of my eyes.

'You find it painful to talk about him?'

I tried to organise a response. 'No, no, not really. Sorry. It's just that—' I trailed off, not knowing where I was going with it, not knowing where to start.

'It's complicated,' I said, finally.

'Alright, Rosie,' he said. 'We'll deal with all that in due course. For now, let me tell you what will be happening in the coming weeks. You'll be on a journey, a journey of self-discovery. It's a journey I'll be coming along with you on. There's going to be a lot of pain, a lot of emotional upset. You need to learn to trust me, which at the moment you don't. We'll work on that.

'But first, we need to find out precisely what is going on neurologically. So over the next few days, we're going to do some tests. We'll test for epilepsy and other neurological disorders, and we'll be looking at your sleep patterns. We'll monitor your brain activity and other vital signs during natural sleep.

'Our primary concern here is to get you back to fitness for duty, back to your ship. But we must also face the possibility that we might not achieve our objective, and the service may have to let you go. If that happens, then we will do all we can to ensure you a safe and orderly transition into the care of our colleagues in the NHS and ultimately, into civilian life.'

He stopped there, abruptly, so that his doom-laden words seemed to roll around each other, like an ever-repeating echo charging the very air of the room. The full implications of my illness had finally sunk in. He continued to watch me, assessing, analysing. The silence once more grew unbearable.

'Are we done?' I said at last.

'Almost. How well do you sleep, normally?'

I shrugged. 'As well as anybody. Maybe five hours most nights – that's usually enough. I read a lot – I get through two or three books a week.'

'Do you dream, or should I say, do you remember your dreams in normal sleep?'

I shook my head. 'No, not really. Never have.'

He looked thoughtful, then seemed to come to a decision. 'I just want to try something if you'll bear with me. Tell me about a random day in your life, for example, 24th February 1997.'

'Mm, that was a Monday. I was eleven and four months. Let's see. Biology with Mister Atkins in the lab was excellent – we did a thing with cell-division and mitochondria. Erika Jenkins fell over in the playground and sprained her ankle— what?'

For the first time, Professor Hardy was smiling.

I shook my head. 'Weird how I remember stuff like that – it just comes to me.'

He unfolded from his chair, motioned me to rise and moved towards the door. 'Try to relax for the rest of the day, Rosie,' he said, suddenly business-like. 'Read a book, use the common room, meet some of the other patients. Take a walk but stay on the campus. No alcohol. I'll see you again at ten am tomorrow.' He opened the door.

'Thanks,' I mumbled, fleeing past him.

1/19

Diagnosis

I was in the place for only three weeks, but it felt like forever. There were tests and more tests, stuff I'd never heard of: Polysomnographic Testing, Hypocretin Testing – testing this, testing that. The brain-technicians triggered a couple of my weird seizures and sometimes made me sleep overnight in a small room with electrodes on my head. There were sessions where I got hypnotised during which I recalled everything that went on. Or so I believed at the time.

None of it was unpleasant. I made friends with a few army veterans, some with amputations, most with some kind of mental issues – some with whom you had to be a bit careful. The 'walking wounded' could go out in the local area – I mostly stayed around the University campus – no alcohol and curfew at nine pm. I developed a happy camaraderie with the staff and especially the professor, whom I learned to trust more than I would have believed possible. If I'm honest, I found the routine and the restrictions quite cathartic.

The day finally came for my meeting with the Prof to hear the verdict. From what I'd already gleaned from the various specialists I'd seen and talking to my fellow patients, I thought I was ready to hear the worst. For it was a stark fact that few people leaving here ever returned to active service.

'So, Rosie, how would you sum up your time here with us?'

'Looking for a five-star review on TripAdvisor, Prof?' A flippant response to cover my anxiety.

He smiled back. 'Very well, let us go with that hypothetical: What would you say in your review?'

Typical of the Prof to turn my joke back on me.

'Okay. Well, I'd give the accommodation four stars, the food is, well, what can I say. There's a chippy and a gastropub out on the Bristol Road, and the Student Union Bar if you prefer vegetarian. The staff are generally harmless. But if you want to keep your private life private, avoid the mad guy in the kilt and tam-o-shanter because he'll waterboard you to get to your darkest secrets. How am I doing, Prof?'

'Kilt I'll allow in extremis, but Tam-o-shanter?' He shook his head in mock despair. 'I believe these reviews are a two-way process?'

I swallowed. 'So, spill the beans, Prof. How much of a looney am I?'

Even expected, the news pulled at my gut. I stared unseeingly at my feet, then looked up into the Prof's kindly countenance. He kept a supportive silence, in tune as ever to my emotions as they moved from heart-breaking disappointment, through pointless anger to eventual acceptance. I had conjured up a contingency plan for the immediate future, but right then I couldn't bring myself to reach out for its consolation. There was simply no room in that dreadful wave of regret for the question 'now what?' All I saw was the bright shiny future I had worked so hard at hanging dull and withered on the tree.

With a trembling sigh, I pulled the corners of my mouth up into some sort of smile. 'So, too loony for the navy, now what?'

'Well, that's mostly up to you. For my part, I believe that in most civilian occupations, you will not present a danger to yourself or anyone else. Consequently, the Centre will not be seeking an order under Section 5 of the Mental Health Act.'

I nodded to hide my shock – I hadn't even realised that was a possibility.

'I am convinced,' the Prof continued, 'that Rosie Winterbourne is strong enough to get through this. With, of course, a little counselling to begin with. I see her in a couple of years finding a new path to follow and putting all this behind her.'

The Professor's words registered as sincere and heartfelt but still sounded hollow to my defeated mind. I pulled out a tissue, wiped my eyes and blew my nose. 'So, bottom line, Prof, what exactly do you think is wrong with me.'

He pursed his lips. 'I can summarise what's in your discharge notes, but it's pretty dry and technical – I don't want you falling asleep on me again.'

I guffawed through once again pooling tears – he was referring to one of our hypnosis sessions, where

I nodded off – actually snoring if I was to believe the Professor. Embarrassing. I wiped my eyes again and sniffed. 'Fire away, Prof, I might as well know it all.'

Committing all those fancy clinical terms to my perfect memory made me no more the wiser. For all their knowledge and professionalism, I realised, I still understood my condition at least as well as they did. It was just that now I knew what to call it, should anyone have the nerve to ask me. The only other thing I left there with was a mild crush on Professor John Hardy.

Back in my room, with my bag packed, I looked through my discharge instructions. I was to report myself at Defence Medical Services Reception at Aldershot Health Centre next Monday morning to get my weekly rehab appointment schedule. Apart from that, I was on sick leave, a free agent. I slumped on my bed and sighed. So the Prof was handing me over to a new shrink – I wasn't his problem anymore. I felt betrayed. He might not have let me down so lightly if he'd known about my Plan B.

EPISODE TWO

The Contingency Plan

2/1

Telling Dad

Even though the nurse had warned me before I went in, it was shocking to see Dad with his eyes open, just staring ahead. He couldn't even blink; eye-drops every hour. And they closed them at night, like window shutters.

They'd moved a TV on a trolley into his line of sight; some nature programme was on; bats in Borneo, the sound turned down but audible. I switched it off and pulled a chair to his bedside.

'Hi, Dad, s' mee.' I kissed his forehead, 'back from the Funny Farm.'

His bed was different, too – high tech: electronic controls to change position, and a feature to set it slowly undulating to prevent bedsores. His eyes disturbed me, made him look even more dead than with them closed.

I told him everything, haltingly, chokingly, sobbingly; longing to see those lifeless eyes turn to me and soften. I wanted him to say to me it would be alright. I wanted a hug.

I *know*, wallowing in self-pity, feeling about ten.

But somehow, spilling it all out like that calmed my screwed-up emotions – or let them ride out, or whatever; I felt suddenly chirpier.

'Good news is, they've moved me to a rehab centre in Aldershot. Quite a laidback place, really – I go to counselling sessions once a week, and the rest of the time I'm home on sick leave.'

I sighed – time to break his heart. 'Sorry Dad, but I'm for the chop. Three months rehab, then a medical discharge with a part pension and a resettlement grant. Then they want to hand me over to some NHS day clinic in Guildford.'

For some reason, I was expecting him to sit up, right there. It just felt like that's what should happen in a fair and just world. Some hope, eh? So now was the time for me to show Dad I was still his feisty daughter, to make him proud of me again.

'Well, sod that for a game of soldiers,' I gushed. 'Shrinks and Neuro-specialists are all useless – want to hear my cunning plan?'

I imagined him saying: 'Go on then, Baldrick, let's hear it.'

Perhaps it was cruel to tell him about my intention to sail away, far away from here. But how much crueller to stop visiting him without explanation? I pictured his reaction – calmly but firmly guiding me out of it. Because the furthest I'd ever sailed was Alderney, and that was with him ten years ago; I'd *never* sailed single-handed.

Until yesterday, that is. On a whim, I'd taken *Pasha* out into the Channel, and then decided to spend the night at sea. Out there on the black water, alone under the vast, spangled universe, the epiphany came to me with an almost physical bang. Plan B was not going to be just moving on-board and sailing around the UK as I originally envisaged. A long solo cruise, I realised, was what I needed. To cross an ocean, to take huge risks, to take control of my destiny would do for me what all the shrinks and neuro boffins could not.

It was almost dark when I left the hospital, but still light enough to notice a vehicle I recognised pull out and drive away. It was a Range Rover, registration L205 NPP. My stalker was back. I wondered if he knew where I'd spent the last three weeks – if he did, maybe he'd fuck off and leave me alone.

2/2

Disaster

The following Saturday, the first weekend in December, I drove back down to Mullhaven to take *Pasha* out for her final sea-trial. I was preparing for what I had started calling my Big Adventure.

Gary intercepted me in the car park. 'Got a minute, Rosie, something to show you.'

I followed him into the boatshed behind his office.

'There,' he said, stopping in front of a pile of junk, 'came off an old wooden ketch – if you're still set on this big adventure, that is.'

I stared bewildered at the heap of rusty metal struts and wire cables.

'Oh, and this,' he said, adding a wooden paddle, 'the business end o things.'

'Ah, let me guess. Er, part of a self-steering vane, maybe?'

He looked hurt. 'Actually, that's the whole thing. A bit weatherworn, granted, but strong and serviceable, and this rig will fit your boat without too much modification.'

'How much, Gary?' I'd looked at self-steering gear online and decided even second-hand ones were way beyond my budget.

'Two-hundred, fitted and set up.'

I whistled. 'Okay, what's the catch?'

A mischievous twinkle came into his eye. 'Didn't your old man tell you never look a gift-horse in the mouth?'

I pretended to think a moment, then shook my head, 'No, Dad would be more likely to say: "always check astern before you start a turn". Very apt in the circumstances I would say.'

He chuckled. 'Nah, trust me, this one's all kosher. Cost me nothing, so I'm just charging you labour.'

We shook hands on the deal, with the caveat that it worked. I agreed to bring *Pasha* to the floating pontoon after my sail, so he could get to work on it next week.

'Oh, and I dug you out a set of charts and pilotage guides. They're a few years out of date, but I'm letting you have them for free – better than spending a grand on new ones, eh?'

'Thanks, Gary, what would I do without you?'

He blushed and grinned. He seemed to thrive on pleasing me, which I have to admit, I rather exploited.

The sky, as I paddled the dinghy out to *Pasha*, was grey and overcast. A fresh westerly breeze was whipping up whitecaps from the waves beyond the harbour entrance. The forecast promised a dry day with clouds clearing in the afternoon. It was just the sort of day for a good workout under sail. The kind of day that would have had Dad rubbing his hands with anticipation.

I'd shaken the reef out of the mainsail from my previous trip because today I wanted a full load trial, her first serious work with the new rigging. Likewise, I let out the genoa to its maximum extent. I gave an involuntary whoop as she heeled over sharply to leeward, the wind at ninety degrees on the starboard beam: a beam reach.

Clearing the harbour entrance, I killed the engine, then just sat there; transported by the sensation of racing along in relative silence. *Pasha's* sleek hull sliced effortlessly through the short, choppy sea. I imagined I could hear her rejoice in that blissful whisper of wind and water.

I eased her gradually downwind, knowing I'd have a challenging beat upwind to get back. Because that was the plan; I'd been a bit slow on changing tack on previous trips and wanted to up my game before the passage south. Meanwhile, it was time to practice the downwind sailing techniques I would need.

Eventually, after much trial and error, I got the 'Goosewing' rig (one sail on either side, with the wind behind) deploying like a dream. The sun came out, and I sat rolling a congratulatory ciggy as we coasted past spectacular white cliffs at a blistering ten knots.

After lunch, I unrigged the pole holding out the genoa and began the long beat back to Mullhaven. This involved zigzagging upwind, turning through the wind at the end of each leg. The solo-sailor has to set the boat in a turn while letting go the one genoa sheet and hauling in on the other. Get it right, and it goes like clockwork. Get it wrong, and it's a mad, exhausting scramble. This solo-sailor discovered she needed the practice.

Four hours and a gruelling sixteen tacks later, with the sun lowering over the port bow, I was within sight of the harbour entrance. Switching to autopilot, I sat down to roll a ciggy.

It must have been the delight of a successful trip, the euphoria of achievement, that distracted me in those critical minutes, not to mention rotten luck. Nevertheless, I should have been more alert to my surroundings.

First, there came a furious cry of *'Leeeewaaard!'*, which gave me a real fright for my sanity. I stood up, casting around for the source of that terrible cry, when a dreadful shiver ran through the boat, an ominous crunch from the bow. I was slammed against the wheel as we slewed violently to port. I grabbed onto the backstay as *Pasha* tacked and settled beam to wind, dipping her port rail deep into the waves – a swirl of cold green water filled the cockpit. There was a shriek of tortured fibreglass and rumbling vibrations as a massive cylindrical mooring buoy disengaged from *Pasha*'s shattered bow, scraping along the hull before bobbing clear astern.

2/3

Damage Control

Miraculously *Pasha* had hove-to, heeled over to port, so the damaged starboard bow was mostly clear of the water. With a prayer and a sinking heart, I rushed below.

Water welled up through the saloon sole and slopped from side to side as the boat wallowed on the swell. I opened the forepeak door and stared horrified at the wreckage that had been the v-berth cabin. Bed-cushions dislodged and torn among a melee of shattered woodwork, pushed away from the impact on the starboard side, where daylight alternated with the inrush of green water through a ragged, football-sized hole.

I dragged a pillow from the wreckage and stuffed it into the hole. That stemmed the inflow of water for the time being, but I could see it wouldn't last long – that sodden pillow would wash out as soon as I tried to get underway.

What would Dad do? I didn't know – we'd never had a collision.

I looked across the saloon at the VHF radio – it had an emergency button. If I pressed it, an automatic distress signal would go out with my position. The coastguard would respond immediately, take me off the boat and try to tow her in. I imagined her slowly sinking, and finally being abandoned.

'We're so sorry. We couldn't save your boat.'

No way!

I had been well trained in ship damage control and knew the principles of repairing a breached hull. But I would need to improvise.

I began by clearing away the wreckage from the forepeak; I needed room to work, and time to think. A sheet of wood was required, something robust but bendy enough to fit into the curvature of the hull. While I worked an image popped up; a sunny day in East Cowes, Dad teaching me to play Uckers in the cockpit.

Dad's Uckers Board! A sixty-centimetre square sheet of polished marine-ply, together with a piece of old carpet I had should make a snug and watertight cofferdam. I pulled two lengths of timber from the port lazarette to use as shores and got to work with the wood-saw cutting them to size. The fitting of the improvised cofferdam was straightforward, and the result looked entirely professional.

But no time for preening. I'd shipped enough water to make the boat wallow heavily; it was over my ankles in the saloon and spilling over the sill of the engine bay. First I started the engine, realising if saltwater got into the battery, I'd be fucked.

Then, soaked and shivering, I set to work cranking the hand pump. It took three exhausting hours to eject the worst of the water – including frequent breaks to check our position and look out for shipping – before I could call it a day. There was still a fair amount slapping under the sole boards, but we were okay now to enter harbour safely.

The red and green lights of the entrance winked on the starboard quarter. The wind had dropped to a light breeze, the sea black and calm. I released the genoa sheet and furled it, allowing *Pasha* to sail off on a starboard tack. Once she had way on, I tacked and pointed at the harbour entrance. With the damaged section now underwater, I went down to check my cofferdam. There was a little seepage around the carpet seal, but nothing that gave me concern. I returned to the cockpit and flipped the engine into gear, then turned upwind and dropped the mains'l.

At last, I had time to refresh myself. I sank onto the seating, and I drank some water, and by now weak and shivering, chewed greedily on a cereal bar.

I have to confess to being full of myself in that euphoric moment. I was, of course, in denial of the complacency and poor seamanship that had got me into this mess. For the entirely avoidable error had probably wrecked my plans for the Big Adventure. Those recriminations would come later. For now, I congratulated myself on a disaster averted by prompt and effective action.

But then, rolling a ciggy, I was sobered by the recollection of that strange voice I'd heard just before we'd hit the buoy. Was it some kind of spooky premonition? Or was I really on the verge of madness?

2/4

For Auld Lang Syne

Gary's attitude towards me had changed since my amateurish error in the Channel. He seemed no longer so eager to please me for a start.

'Six grand!' I said. 'Really?'

Sandra was tapping away at her keyboard, but I could see her sympathetic frown. She'd warned me that Gary was not opposed to loading up the costs if an owner were over a barrel. I had a choice – find the money somehow, or put poor *Pasha* up for sale with the unique selling point of a holed bow. Since my obsession with the old girl was carved in stone, only one of those choices was acceptable.

'Plus VAT,' he reminded me. 'That includes haul out and lift in, a full repair of the hull, v-berth rebuilt and reupholstered – all work guaranteed. Don't worry. We'll charge it directly to your insurance company.'

'She's only insured Third Party,' I told him.

I heard Sandra's sharp intake of breath.

Gary sucked in softly, shaking his head. 'Sorry, Rosie, not my problem – not much else I can say.'

Yes, Gary had me over that fucking barrel, and he knew it.

'And supposing I found the cash, how long would it take?'

He did that sucking thing through his teeth. 'We're quite busy just now, what with Christmas, and all the—'

'Gary! How long?'

His brow darkened; he sat smouldering a moment, then grunted, 'End of January. Best I can do.'

It was evening, three days after my collision, when I emailed Aunt Georgina. I didn't exactly ask her for the money, just told her what happened, trying to make it a funny story. But I secretly hoped she'd come through for me. I hated doing it, but I had nowhere else to turn. The reply came back immediately – she must have been already in her emails. The screen blurred.

> Don't worry – everything will
> come good.
> Much Love
> Georgie xx

I spent Christmas Day with Dad. The nurses had arranged a dinner party in his room with Santa hats, balloons and crackers, and a miniature Christmas tree. And, of course, I told him all about my mishap in the Channel. I imagined Dad wincing, then giving me a lecture about keeping lookout, and much later, telling a joke about it to his mates in the pub.

The nurses all listened goggle-eyed, a different kind of Christmas story for them.

The ward staff's devotion to my catatonic father reassured me: I felt Dad would be in good hands during my long absence.

Supposing, of course, I managed to get *Pasha* repaired. *Everything will come good.* What the fuck does that mean? Georgie could be so cryptic sometimes. I wished she'd just say whether she was going to help me or not. I had about fifteen hundred pounds in my bank account. I needed five thousand more to get Gary started on the work. At least he'd hauled her out of the water, so I didn't need to worry about her sinking at anchor.

On New Year's Eve – after swapping festive emails with Pincher Martin – I drove down to Pompey to catch up with some of my old shipmates. *Windy C.* had got back from her deployment in mid-December. Most of the girls were on leave, including Doc. We'd exchanged a few emails, and she had promised to drop by at the house for a weekend catch-up early in the New Year. But some of the Ship's Company were still around: those who were detailed, or had volunteered, to stay on-board during the leave period, and those sad old farts like Dicky Doyle. He simply had nowhere else to go.

I got there just after seven, checked into the Royal Home Club, then walked down to The Hard to meet up in the Ship Anson. A cheer went up when I walked in. They found me a seat, and a pint quickly arrived in front of me.

I knew Pincher Martin would be there, of course, and I was pleased to see Freddie Symmonds, whom I'd only just started getting to know when the brown stuff hit. And fo'c'sle wag Tony Rawlidge, who was currently holding court with a selection of his latest smutty jokes. It was fabulous to be there, among those familiar faces, and for a few short hours, I was one of them again.

When some of us went out for a smoke, Freddie sidled up to me and asked for a roll-up.

'So, Freddie, how's it going?' I said, trying not to watch her fumbling the paper and baccy.

'Very well, thanks. Your advice that time came just when I needed it.'

'You're not a roller, are you,' I said, rescuing the makings from her and finishing the job.

She took a few drags then stamped it out and went back inside – too cold, she said. Then Dicky Doyle – the ship's painter who'd helped me purloin the stuff I'd needed for *Pasha* – came over and called me aside.

'MoD plod been on-board, asking questions,' he murmured, looking furtively around, 'apparently, one of the dockyard stores bods got arrested. Could be something to do with the stuff you er, acquired, shall we say.'

'Shit! How much do they know?'

'Not much. Don't think it's anything to worry about.'

So why tell me, you idiot? I thought. 'So, they questioned you?'

He chuckled. 'Yeah, put on me best cherubic visage. Look, don't worry, your name didn't come up.'

When I went back in, I sensed I'd been the topic of conversation.

'What!' I said, giving Dicky my suspicious face.

But it was Tony Rawlidge who spoke up. 'Freddie here says you'd win *Who Wants to be A Millionaire* hands down – reckons you'd answer every question without seeing the three choices. Is that right, Rosie, or is she bullshitting?'

I gave Freddie a hard stare and waggled a finger. 'Mess Rule 101, Freddie, you just blew it.'

I drained my beer, then stood up and said, 'My shout, so who wants what?'

But once they scented blood, this pack was not going to be bribed – they just had to test my memory, and questions began firing at me from all directions. I answered the first few to humour them but then held up my hand.

'Stop! Look, I have a thing called hyperthymesia – it's not funny, and it's not as cool as you might think. It's not that I remember stuff, it's that I can't forget anything – and that's fucking horrible. Now can we get on with New Year's Eve? Because that's what I came down here for.'

'You mean you want us to forget it?' cracked Tony, to sniggers all round.

I gave him a crooked grin, but I got no more trouble, and Freddie looked suitably abashed for her indiscretion.

At 1130 we all trailed back into the dockyard, to *Windy C's* berth on Southwest Wall. They dragged me along to witness - for old times sake - the ringing of Sixteen Bells for New Year: eight for the Old, eight for the New. As the youngest dark-haired person present, Freddie was the nominated bellringer, an honour she performed with undue glee. Afterwards, we all tumbled down the ladders to the Seaman's Mess, where much beer and other beverages where waiting.

At some point, Pincher Martin, when it suddenly dawned on him that I was no longer under the constraints of the 'No Touching Rule' held up a piece of mistletoe and kissed me. Somehow that turned into a full-blown snog, with him pushing me up against the bulkhead so I could feel his two years of restrained desire.

'Come round to my bunk space, Rosie,' he breathed in my ear. 'I need to show you something.'

There came a moment of alcohol-induced libido when I wavered; but then, aware they were all watching us, I pushed him away, laughing. 'Sorry, Pincher. You're a gorgeous hunk, and I love you – but I'm afraid you're just not in my league, sunshine.'

'Aww fuck,' he said, sitting down again and picking forlornly at his sprig of mistletoe. 'Story of my life.'

2/5

Windfall

Back home on the following Wednesday, there was an email from Lester Granville, our solicitor, asking me to call at his office at my earliest convenience. Intrigued, I drove to Guildford early the next morning, arriving just after nine. The office was in the High Street, a short walk from Tesco's car park; the modest door hemmed between a barbershop and a florist. A small brass plaque read simply: Granville & Finningwold, Solicitors.

Lester Granville, seventy-something, tall, urbane and immaculate as always in his three-piece pinstripe, was stood talking to Charlene, the firm's receptionist.

'Rose, my dear!' he said, peering over antique half-moon spectacles, 'come on through.'

Lester had been the family's solicitor for as long as anyone could remember. He had been a close friend of Granny Bee's when we'd all lived in her old house in Guildford. His office was as genteel and old-fashioned as the man himself. Oak panels adorned with paintings – mainly of racehorses – a sprawling walnut desk fronted by two comfortable chairs upholstered in shiny red leather.

'Take a seat, dear. Tea?'

'Thanks, but no,' I said, eager to know why I was here and hoping for something miraculous.

'Jolly good, let's get down to business. We've now completed probate for your late mother's estate. These are the documents.' He handed me a thin buff folder. 'Read them at your leisure, but please keep them in a safe place – we have to charge you if you ever need duplicates.'

Was that it, a folder he could just have posted?

'There's something else we need to discuss, but first, there's this.' He slid a cheque across his desk to me. 'The balance of your mother's estate, minus our fee and the outstanding bills and invoices.'

I looked at the cheque; £879.69p. That wouldn't even buy the fibreglass for *Pasha*'s repair.

'You'll find a full financial breakdown in your copy.'

He turned a page of the file in front of him, and then paused, looking down. I thought for a moment he'd nodded off, but then he looked up and smiled apologetically.

'Rose, first let me say, I have no idea why we didn't pick this up earlier, but I think Margaret may have been trying to conceal it for some reason.'

I gave him a puzzled frown, 'Sorry, I'm not with you, Mr Granville. Concealed what?'

'Ahem. You weren't aware of your mother's Private Equity Trust Fund?'

I shook my head.

'No, I thought not. So you'll be delighted to learn you've inherited a sum of money.'

'But I thought they were broke.'

'It wasn't money they had access to.'

'Then where did it come from?'

'From the sale of a yacht in 1986. The donor wished to remain anonymous, but they bequeathed the proceeds to your mother. She invested it in a trust fund for you – it has accrued a fair amount of interest, so the balance is relatively substantial.'

My throat went dry. 'How much?'

'Something in the region of thirty-five thousand pounds.'

I phoned Gary as soon as I left Lester's, then took myself out for some long-delayed retail therapy. After dropping the jeep home, I spent a boozy evening in the Dragon to celebrate progress at last on *Pasha's* repairs.

I awoke the following morning excited, but also frustrated. Because, despite now having all the money I needed and more, it would still take weeks to get *Pasha* back in the water. These were weeks that I didn't have if I was to make an Atlantic crossing before the Hurricane season.

Today was a beautiful if somewhat chilly January day. To take my mind off *Pasha,* I went out for a vigorous bike ride along the cross-country trails. I headed north initially, along a path that followed the River Wey, then branched east along the Tillingbourne River to Abinger. I bought lunch in the Hammer pub where Mum and I had often stopped, then cycled home again, a round trip of some forty miles.

And then there was the email from Doc. She was coming to stay for the weekend, which reminded me of the closeness we'd always shared – an instinctive knowing when one of us sorely needed the other's company. She was coming on the train from Plymouth and would I pick her up from Guildford? An unexpected windfall, an exhilarating day's cycling, and now my best friend was coming for the weekend. I was walking on air.

The following Monday, after dropping Doc at the station, I went down to Mullhaven to check progress on *Pasha's* repairs. Locking up the car in the boatyard car park, I again noticed a police car by the office, nobody inside. I wouldn't usually have given it another thought, but Dicky's news had left me edgy.

They'd un-stepped *Pasha*'s mast and moved her into the boatshed. There was scaffolding around the bow; they had cut the damaged section out, leaving a square hole through which I could have climbed.

'What's happening, Gary? I'd have thought they'd have at least started on the fibreglass by now.'

'Got staff problems,' he said. He saw my glum look and softened his tone. 'Look, Paul will be back from his hols tomorrow, and then we'll get started. She'll be ready end of the month, promise.'

If he kept to that, I'd have time to get down to the Canaries by the end of February, which was early enough to make the crossing.

'So what do the cops want?' I said.

'Oh, them—' He took a big sniff as if he were about to reveal a pearl of wisdom. 'They're still trawling for witnesses for that murder back in September. They're talking to some of the younger lads that might've been out on the town the night it happened.' He sniffed again before adding, 'A bit late if you ask me.'

He must have noticed my relief. 'Don't worry, Rosie, you ain't on their radar.'

As far as you know, I thought. The sooner I sailed away from here, the better.

2/6

Ground Rules

G ary was true to his word. By the beginning of February, *Pasha* was back in the water, restored to her beautiful self. However, the self-steering vane bolted onto the transom kind of spoiled her clean lines.

I spent the following week ferrying bags of food and clothing from home down to Mullhaven. By Sunday the 10th, with every nook and cranny filled with tinned food and bottles of water, with *Pasha* fuelled-up and me fired-up, I was ready to go.

On my final drive home, I popped in to say goodbye to Dad, promised him I'd email whenever I could and held his hand until my tears dried up.

I locked the jeep up in the garage and secured the house. It was a cold and crisp February afternoon, but dry and sunny, perfect for the thirty-mile ride down to Mullhaven. It would be useful to have the bike where I was going, and with the wheels taken off it would fit nicely in the starboard lazarette.

Coming up to the cockpit next morning I was grateful for my heavy-duty salopette and seaboots. There was little wind as yet. Still, it was a chilly, overcast morning and looked like snow. I was just preparing to slip from the pontoon when Gary Palmer came running along the jetty. He was carrying a large holdall.

'Look, Rosie, I been thinking. You've never used a steering vane before, right? They can be a mite tricky if you don't know how to set 'em up. So why don't I come with you as far as Lisbon, and I'll teach you how it works?'

The out-of-the-blue offer stunned me – he'd had all the past week to mention this, and anyway, I felt more than a little put out by his assumption that I'd even want him along. It also felt patronising – the vane gear didn't look complicated; it couldn't be rocket-science – I knew the principles involved. Besides, I wanted to do this alone.

'I don't know, Gary, I'm not really prepared for a two-hander. You know, food, water; and I've only got one lifejacket, one set of foul-weather gear.'

He gave me a worried frown.

'I got all me own gear,' he said, 'and we can always pop in at La Corunna if we get short of provisions.' He nodded at the vane on the stern, 'That stuff ain't as simple as it looks, you know, and getting it wrong could get you in all sorts o trouble. Now, you got a nice new bunk in the v-berth, what say I break it in for you, eh?'

'But what about your work? Aren't you needed here?'

'Oh, Sandra can manage without me for a couple o weeks, she practically runs the place anyway. I been thinking about a holiday; a nice cruise and a week in the Algarve sounds just perfect.'

I tried to find other objections, but in the end, I caved in and threw him a happy face.

'All right, Gary, you're on. Climb aboard.'

There was an odd moment after he swung his bag over the rail and made to grab the shroud – the boat suddenly healed over away from him, and he almost lost his balance. He got safely aboard, however, and grinned sheepishly.

'Whew, that could've ended badly, must've been a bit o groundswell.'

I looked out onto the estuary – it was a millpond. Weird.

After we cleared the entrance, a light easterly breeze sprang up. We set full sails to run before it and killed the engine.

'Cup of tea?' I asked Gary, who'd taken the helm while I'd trimmed the sails.

'Lovely!'

While I was waiting for the kettle, I started the log with the initial entry:

Friday 8th February 2013
Rosie Winterbourne (Capt), Gary Palmer (Crew)
0745: Departed Mullhaven bound for Lisbon,
Portugal.

From now on, I would log our Position, Course & Speed every four hours. When I came back up to the cockpit, the wind had risen and brought sporadic flurries of snow. Gary, who'd pulled on his foul-weather jacket, flicked on the autopilot, sat down and took a slurp of his tea.

'Ah, that's just what I needed,' he said, which for some reason I found irritating.

He'd seemed quite tense as we'd crossed the harbour but now appeared more relaxed. Like me, I thought; most at home out on the water. We both began rolling cigarettes. I'd made a New Year Resolution to only smoke with a drink. Tea counted.

I noticed the mains'l billowing at the luff and inched in the sheet a little to trim it out. Our speed climbed a fraction. 7 knots. A smooth sail and a good start.

'Nice easterly,' I said. 'We should make Ushant by midnight tomorrow.'

Gary didn't reply. I looked around at him and saw he was doing something with his phone.

'You'll be out of range soon, Gary, so I should text all your fans now, while you can.'

He looked up and grinned. 'Sorry, just a bit of business, all done now.'

He put the phone away, drank his tea, and flicked his cigarette butt away over the side. I was going to have to have a word. Maybe later, though. Pick my moment.

'Right,' he said, putting down his empty mug, 'let's have a go at that steering vane.' He hitched himself up onto the stern counter and patted a seat beside him. 'Hop up here, sweetheart, and we'll get started.'

Biting my tongue, I joined him on the counter.

'Now, this is—'

'Just two things, Gary, before we start—' I waited until he looked at me, then said firmly, 'On my boat, we don't flick cigarette filters into the sea. And while I'm on the subject, that goes for plastics, bits of rope, and fishing line. Paper and food waste, glass and metals, is all we ditch overboard. Is that clear?'

He stared at me, and for a horrible moment, I thought he was going to challenge me. Then he said, 'Fair enough. And the second thing?'

'Lose the "sweetheart", okay? "Rosie" or "Skipper" works just fine.'

'Okay, okay, got the message. Your boat, your rules.'

'Good, let's keep this civilized and respectful.' I twisted round to face the steering rig, hitching a leg up onto the counter. 'So, start at the top, what's this bit?'

He took half an hour to explain, but I got it at once – not rocket science.

'One last thing,' Gary said, 'and this is a refinement of me own.'

He took a coil of dayglow line from his pocket and tied it around the pendulum's universal joint, led the line outboard and over the guardrails, and dropped the remaining coil onto the banquette.

'When you're on your own at night, just chuck it overboard and let it trail,' he explained. 'If you go over just grab the line and pull the pendulum out of kilter, stop the boat sailing off without you, see?'

I examined the bright yellow line, uncoiling it, running it through my hands to gauge its length. The rope was braided polypropylene, about thirty metres long with a monkey's fist at the end. I did a rough mental calculation and smiled grimly.

'At five knots that's about ten seconds before it's out of reach. And, as I recall you telling me once, you can't swim, so unless you go over the stern, you'd be lucky to catch it.'

Gary shrugged, 'Better than no chance at all though, eh?'

'We won't be needing it,' I told him, dropping the coil into the cockpit well. 'My policy during night watches: always wear your harness and clip-on. That's a red line, Gary, understood?'

He glared at me, and I got an awful feeling right there.

'You've got the watch,' I told him. I pointed to his yellow line, 'I'll leave you to remove this and stow it before it causes an accident. I'll relieve you at four.'

2/7

Mutiny

I spent the afternoon reading and dozing in the saloon, and took the watch at 1600, leaving Gary free to cook us a meal. By 1730 it was fully dark; the clouds had cleared away leaving a faint panoply of stars, outshone by a near-full moon swinging high on the starboard bow.

'Right, I'm going to get some shuteye,' Gary declared after dinner. 'Call me when you want relieving.'

'That'll be five to eight then, Gary,' I told him. 'Standard four-hour watch routine, at least until we clear Ushant. *If* that's alright with you?'

He paused at the top of the ladder, looked round at me bull-faced.

'Too bad if it ain't by the sounds of it,' he growled, then stomped below.

'Just remember who's skipper here,' I yelled after him, 'and we'll get along fine.'

'Doubt it,' he muttered, slamming the forepeak cabin door behind him.

Fuck this! A fortnight at sea with this idiot? Time for a change of plan.

Fifteen miles to the northwest was Portland Bill, its loom visible over the horizon. In the morning, I decided right then. I would drop him off somewhere convenient for the train.

The east-south-easterly wind of this afternoon had gradually backed towards the north, and soon I was forced to gybe – and that decided it; I set a new course for Torbay. I would need to tell Gary tonight of my change of plan.

1945: 50 28.3N 02 31.7W Co 275M Sp 5.
Wind NNE 14 kts Px 1014MB
Main (2 Reefs) + Full Genoa.
Heading for Brixham to drop off crewman.

After writing up the log, I returned to the cockpit. We had passed a small fishing fleet earlier – their green masthead lights indicating they were trawling – and I was wary of meeting more. Trawlers needed a wide berth. I brought my phone back up with me and switched it on, hoping to be in range of the Portland telecom beacons. I could at least check the train times from Brixham for Gary. The phone beeped, four bars, and almost immediately, an incoming text. It was from Sandra at the Mullhaven Marina office.

> Hi Rosie, just to let you know,
> police have been round
> asking for Gary, he's gone
> missing, and they want to talk

> to him again. Did you see him
> this morning before you left?

What the fuck! Had he not told his Admin Assistant he was going away for a fortnight? I checked the time she sent it: 1234 this afternoon.

—they want to talk to him again.

My mouth went dry. I noticed there was another text from Sandra. And five missed calls, two from her, and three more from a withheld number.

Sandra had sent her second text at 1457.

> Rosie, please tell me Gary's
> not with you? Because I think
> he might be a suspect for that
> murdered girl. Ring me if you
> can.

No! The guy was an idiot, and a lousy crewmate, and probably a closet misogynist. But a murderer and rapist? No way. I hit the call-back icon and held the phone to my ear—nothing for a long time, then a beep. I looked at the phone.

No Service.

Fuck! I tried to think, through increasing alarm, as doubts began to trickle into my mind. Why had he been so keen to get away, almost begging me to take him? He'd seemed jittery on the way out and had only seemed to relax when we lost sight of the Purbeck coast. That was when he showed me how to work the steering vane, once out of sight of land.

I should call the coastguard, at least check-in, let them know where I was – just in case. I got up to go below, but my left foot snagged in something. I lifted my boot and saw it was Gary's emergency line that I'd said we wouldn't be needing. Despite my instructions, the moron had left it there in a mess in the cockpit sole. I hurriedly untangled my foot and swung down to the saloon.

I had a moment of indecision with a finger hovering over the VHF transmit button, reluctant to make the call because I wasn't sure – it could all be a misunderstanding. I looked at the phone in my other hand. Three bars, now. I hung up the mic and hit redial on the phone, then held it to my ear. The forepeak door opened and Gary stepped out. He saw the phone and frowned. There was still no ring tone, so I checked the screen.

No Service

'Who were you calling?'

'Oh, n-nobody. It was just a friend wishing me bon voyage. You okay?'

'Surprised you got a signal this far—' he glanced at the chartplotter, did a double-take, then leaned over and looked more closely at the screen.

'Rosie, why are we in Lyme Bay?'

I sighed, trying for assertiveness but it came out shaky, 'This isn't working, Gary, for either of us. I'm going to drop you in Brixham.'

He stared, his expression wolf-like. 'Not gonna happen, my dear.'

'Sorry, Gary, I'm not arguing about it. I'm very grateful for—'

He slapped the phone out of my hand, sending it skittering along the sole boards,

'You're not listening, darling. This boat goes to Portugal.'

2/8

'Man Overboard!'

I took a step backwards, fighting for clear thoughts, glanced back at the VHF – at the Distress Button. Clocking my intention, he pushed me away, turned off the radio, then swung around.

In desperation, I heaved off a straight-arm punch as hard as I could at his face. It could have worked, but he turned his head, and my best shot glanced off his cheekbone and sent a sharp pain up my arm. As swift as a snake, he grabbed my wrist and held it in an iron grip.

'Left-hander, eh?' He rubbed his cheek, scowling.

I glared at him, trying to step back but was held there firmly by the wrist, angry and terrified.

'It *was* you, wasn't it?' I accused. 'That girl in Mullhaven?'

He snorted, leering cruelly. A sheen of sweat had broken out on his ruddy face, madness in his eyes; such a shocking transformation that I didn't see the blow that sent me sprawling into the galley space. I lay there stunned and not fully comprehending what had just happened, until Gary's furious face descended towards me, banana fingers groping for my throat.

Somehow I got my legs up and catch him on my feet - with a strength fuelled by terror, I catapulted him across the saloon. With a timely lurch from *Pasha*, the big man tumbled into the narrow gap between the seating and the table.

Sweeping up my phone, I flew up the ladder into the cockpit. The phone had four bars again. In a fever of fumbling in the moonlight, I tried to get the dial-pad up on the screen, hitting all the wrong keys as Gary's huge shadow rose out of the companionway. Too late, he was on me; he dashed the phone out of my hands and sent spinning overboard. The man was quick as a cobra. Before I knew it, he had pinned my wrists while arching me painfully back over the cockpit table.

'Feisty girl, ain'tcha?' he grunted in my ear, his coarse beard crushed against my bruised cheek. It wasn't until I felt my zipper jerking that I grasped his intention. Still, all I could do was beat feebly at his greasy mat of hair as his hand began to explore inside my salopette.

Suddenly, my thoughts cleared. I stopped resisting, reaching my free arm backwards, feigning submission.

'That's right my dear,' he breathed into my ear, then drew his head back to look at me, his lustful stare ghostly in the reflected moonlight, stale breath, hot and urgent.

His hand was now inside my pants. Fighting revulsion, I concentrated on my task – willing my

arm to stretch, to grow longer, reaching, reaching –
blocking out what was going on below. At last, my
fingertips brushed the canvass pocket. I shuffled my
body upwards for a better reach, which must have
felt to Gary like an invitation. He drooled as his
fingers found my most sensitive spot, even as my
fingers were closing around the cold steel of the
winch handle. My revulsion gave strength to the
swing of the tool, hitting the side of his head with a
sickening crack. As Gary slumped forward over me,
I felt a splash of his warm blood on my face.

Hitching further up onto the table I lifted my legs
and with a furious shunt, propelled his slack carcase
away from me. I quickly rezipped my salopette to
the neck, then stepped up onto the starboard counter,
clinging to the bimini frame with one hand while
clutching the winch handle in the other. I stared
fearfully at my attacker, acutely aware of the rush of
moon-spangled water three feet beneath me.

Gary sat with his lowered head shaking slowly
from side to side like a dazed mule. In the bright
moonlight, I could see the damage to his left temple;
hair glistened black, dark lines of blood ran down
his cheek and jaw. But I couldn't bring myself to
finish the job, not in cold blood. Justifiable homicide
– was that even a thing?

Think, girl. How to call for help? My phone was
gone. The radio? Switched off – it would need thirty
seconds to warm up. Then I remembered the EPIRB
– the emergency beacon clipped to the bulkhead at
the bottom of the ladder. Yes! All I had to do was
pull the pin to activate it and send out a distress
signal.

I edged gingerly toward the companionway, but then my left foot snagged, something caught around my seaboot – that fucking line again. I stooped to free it. But oh fucking hell, I was too late. Gary staggered to his feet and propped himself up in the companionway, black eyes glinting with profound hatred.

I fought for calm. 'Let me call the coastguard, Gary, and I promise I won't mention any of this. I'll say you had a fall, let them take you ashore, eh? Get you fixed up?'

He stood there snorting like a bull, then with a snarl, he sprang at me. There was nowhere left to go, so I swung the winch handle, which he blocked with his forearm, a resounding thunk on flesh and bone – he seemed oblivious to pain. But at that moment, unaccountably, *Pasha* lurched heavily to starboard as the wind dropped away. Thrown off-balance, Gary wavered there for a moment, grabbing frantically at the air, then toppled over the guardrail with an anguished cry. For a nanosecond, I thought it was over. But I was suddenly jerked backwards: to my horror, Gary had somehow caught the rescue strop on the back of my salopette. Worse, his legs were dragging in the water, causing him to twist and jerk on the webbing strap. Under that combined momentum, I could hold on no longer and was carried over the rail. The last thing I heard before I hit the water was Gary's howl of despair as the bastard released his death-grip and was swept away astern.

A roar of crashing waves, then frigid silence, down, down, the icy sea quickly soaking through to my skin, muscles stunned and debilitated by the sudden chill. Disorientated and weightless, I searched for any point of reference. And there, floating around me in the wobbly, watery moonlight, a swirl of the bright yellow line, still tangled around my left seaboot. I made a grab and caught it just as the line tautened. I kicked my foot free of the bight and tried to take a grip on the line. The polypropylene cordage slipped through my hands until cold-enfeebled fingers snagged the monkey's fist at the end. *Pasha* dragged me through the water a few feet until I could hold on no longer. The golf-ball-sized knot zipped away in a trail of bubbles. And then it was gone, taking with it all hope of survival.

2/9

Survival

A big wobbly moon beckoned me upwards through the swirling confusion. I broke surface gasping with cold-shock. My water-filled seaboots were trying to drag me back down. I was dimly aware of Gary somewhere close by, spluttering and crying out incoherently.

I took a deep breath and slipped under, wrestling with ridding myself of those leaden seaboots. Surfacing at last, bootless and buoyant, I calmed myself and considered my predicament. The waves were still a couple of metres high but weren't breaking, so at least I could catch my breath without swallowing water. I'd practised sea-survival countless times in the Navy and knew the rules, knew my chances. Estimated survival time in these waters, good swimmer without a lifejacket?

Ten minutes.

Lifted on a wave, I glimpsed *Pasha*'s stern-light as she self-piloted away into the night. Gary's safety-line idea hadn't worked. His final betrayal, I thought. But no, he had one more; falling back into the trough, a desperate grunt as hands grasped onto my shoulders from behind. Swimming clear, I surfaced to see Gary flailing hopelessly, glugging and spluttering.

'I can't— swim,' Gary gasped pleadingly. 'Please— help me.'

He lunged out for me again, but I kicked away, continued until I lost him from sight in the churning darkness, his desperate cries growing weak and distant. After a short while, I couldn't hear him anymore.

I felt no jubilation for Gary's passing, and oddly, no fear for my own. Just a weird kind of dislocation and a calm acceptance of the fate that had determined that this madness of tumbling water and silver moonlight, was to be my demise. Deep regret that my Big Adventure should come to such an ignominious end, but most of all, profound sadness that I wouldn't be there to greet Dad out of his long sleep.

Minutes passed as memories of childhood romped in the waves. I was heaved up on a crest, plunged into a trough, then slewed sideways down the slope, hypnotic motion, swinging up, sliding down – getting sleepy, comfortable in my iced cocoon.

Then, as another wave lifted me, out of the dappled silver of surging seas came a brief flare of green. My numbed brain tried to focus on the significance of what I thought I had seen. It seemed important, but why? I shook my head wildly from side to side as the next wave lifted me. There it was, a steady green light. How far? It could have been close, or it could be a mile away – I had no idea. Up, up – I kicked my frozen feet, willing my neck to grow. Yes, there! Maybe not too far to swim – and gone again. I pictured a trawler hauling nets. Hoping against hope, I reached out and began to pull my numbed body towards where I thought I saw the light. I imagined grabbing onto a trawler's nets, hauling myself up, strong hands reaching to help me aboard.

Swimming in that short, choppy sea was sluggish and desperate. The cold had penetrated my joints, making them ache, weakening my efforts. Once it got to my core that would be it, game over. But hope pushed me on, slow, steady strokes; don't overwork, conserve energy. Timeless, mindless slogging through the waves, losing sight of that green light in the troughs, hope fading until the next crest when the tantalising green beckoned me onwards once more.

Arms flailing desperately now, slow, uneven strokes, barely making headway, cold thighs scissoring to paddle feet that had long since lost any sensation. Hope followed despair, despair followed promise. But I slogged on through that moonlit mayhem, adjusting direction with each enticing glimpse of green, my focus on one simple objective – to reach that green light - to survive.

But inevitably, the deadly cold seeping through to my core and the drag of my waterlogged salopette took their toll on frozen limbs. I lost track of time; everything became dreamlike in the dim realisation

that I hadn't seen the light for some time now. Numb
and exhausted, my strokes slowed as hope finally
faded. I hung there, reserves spent. I rolled onto my
back, eyes open as the waves washed over me, and
looked through the water at that big, wobbly,
silvery-green moon for the last time. I held on to that
last lungful of air, waiting for the moment when I
could hold it no longer; the moment I would be
overcome by the primordial urge to breathe.

I thought about Dad, wondered if he'd forgive the
things I'd said. I should have been more supportive,
a better daughter. He'd been a good father, after all.
I wondered what would happen on the Other Side.
Was there an 'Other Side'? Buddhists monks
thought death was merely waking up from a bad
dream – a curious but compelling concept.

For the second time I was drifting comfortably
away, the silvery moon had acquired a green tint.
Strange, I thought, that the moon should turn green
like that. Green cheese, that was the old trope.

Then, just as I was about to welcome cold, soothing
seawater into my tortured lungs, something hard
butted against my head. I struggled upright and
sucked in a humungous lungful of air. I ran my
hands disbelievingly over the smooth white surface
of the vessel. A green glow surrounded me – it was
the light I'd been swimming for, I realised,
somewhere above me. I tried to shout out for help,
but it came out a feeble croak. I banged a fist weakly
on the hull – a dull thunk. No, not a trawler –
fibreglass. My dulled brain failed to register the
truth, but from somewhere, I found the strength to
grope along the hull to find a way to climb aboard.

Reaching the stern, I saw the name on the transom and thought I must have died after all. And there was my way aboard; my beautiful, fantastic, life-saving self-steering rig.

2/10

Mayday

My epic climb up the wind vane was slow and
incremental. And utterly exhausting. I finally
flopped onto the stern counter and allowed my frail
body to slide down into the cockpit. I was desperate
to sleep right there but to do so in the freezing night
air in sodden clothing would be fatal. Somehow I
found reserves to stumble below, strip off my
waterlogged salopette and boil a kettle. I sat for a
while, numbed, semi-unconscious, wrapped in my
thick duvet, shivering so violently I couldn't hold
the mug of coffee without it spilling. Somehow I
must have found the presence of mind to switch on
the VHF radio – but passed out without making a
call or even activating the Distress button.

  When I woke, I was flat out on the banquette rolled
into my duvet. The ship's clock read 2205. I felt
deliriously comfortable and wanted to sleep some
more, to not move out of my warm nest, but my
fuzzy brain knew there were things I had to do. So I

shuffled to my cabin, pulled dry clothes from my locker, dressed, then made coffee and slumped down again, exhausted by the effort of even those simple tasks.

I sat there for ages, weeping, in an emotional backspin – reliving the relentless pushing and shoving and heaving and dropping of my helpless body in that lonely moonlit sea. I felt again the hopelessness, the terminal thoughts, and most tearfully astonishing of all, the miracle of my survival.

Gary's wind vane idea had, after all, worked when I had tugged on the line – the green light I saw had been *Pasha's* starboard running light after she hove-to. It would remain a constant mystery to me how I ever made that lifesaving swim.

So what to do now?

'Call it in, Rosemary.'

I sat up, suddenly alert, and a little scared.

'Who said that?' I said, feeling immediately stupid for having done so. Okay, so I was hallucinating, hearing voices. That was understandable for someone in hypothermic shock. Wasn't it?

But whether imagined or otherwise I should call in a Mayday. Someone had just died, after all. I struggled to my feet, stiff and creaking like an old crone, and activated the VHF Distress button. I checked our position on the chartplotter, paused to assemble what I wanted to say, then opened the mic.

'Mayday, Mayday, Mayday
This is sailing yacht *Pasha*,

My position, three-one miles east of Berry Head, I say again, three-one miles east of Berry Head.
I have a man overboard, I say again, man overboard.
Have been unable to locate my lost crewmember. Please send assistance.
This is sailing yacht *Pasha*, over.'

The reply came instantly.

'Pasha, this is Falmouth Coastguard,
Copied your Mayday. Rescue services are being alerted.
Please report the time of your man overboard and your best estimate of the datum position?'

I thought a moment, then opened the mic.

'This is *Pasha*,
He went overboard within the past two hours, and my best estimate is within one mile of me, possibly to the north, over.'

'Thank you, Pasha, now please report the size of your vessel, and the number of souls remaining on-board.'

'I am a thirty-eight-foot sloop, with one person remaining on-board, over.'

'Falmouth Coastguard, Roger that, Pasha. Please remain in your current location. Helicopter, callsign Rescue 56 has been scrambled and should be with you shortly. Out.'

Then:

'All Stations, All Stations, All Stations. This is Falmouth Coastguard, Search and Rescue operations in progress in Lyme Bay West. One person reported missing. All vessels in the area are requested to keep a good lookout and report any sightings. Stations not involved are requested to minimise traffic on Channel Sixteen until further notice, Falmouth Coastguard, out.'

I slumped back down and rolled a ciggy. Twenty minutes later, Rescue 56 came on the radio, ordering me to sail to Dartmouth and await further instructions. It was some hours later when the report came through that the helicopter had recovered a body and rescue services were ordered to stand down.

The long night passed as if in a dream. I kept myself conscious with endless cups of tea and cereal bars; fixing on the light to starboard, Berry Head, as it drifted slowly astern. As the new day dawned, I reached the Dart Estuary weary beyond words. I started the engine and furled in the genoa. A pilot boat was waiting in the river and invited me by radio to follow. The pilot led me to a berth at the town's Harbour Office, where a woman in a Coastguard sweater took my lines.

'My word!' she said when we were all secured. 'You look all in, my dear. Moind if I steps aboard?'

She was a large woman in her fifties, short black hair, weathered, slab-like cheeks – the look of a seafarer.

'Yes, of course,' I said, come aboard. 'But I have to warn you, I won't be good company, I'm knackered.'

She stepped over the rail. 'S'okay my dear, I won't keep you from your bunk longer'n I have to. Just we need to have a little chat so's you know what's gonna happen next. Let's go below and get out o this wind, shall we?'

She followed me down the ladder and sat herself down on the starboard banquette. I offered her tea, but she shook her head. 'As I said, I won't k— Oh, what happened to your face?'

I touched the bruising on my left cheek and winced, but didn't answer, just sat down opposite and stifled a jaw-breaking yawn.

'Okay, not my business,' she said, looking worried. 'Now, my dear, my name is Doreen Lister, and I'm Duty Officer for the Maritime and Coastguard Agency. You'll know that your crewman sadly didn't survive, so first, can I ask what relation the deceased gentleman was to you?'

'His name was Gary Palmer. He was the Boatyard Manager at Mullhaven, and he offered to crew for me at the last moment.'

'And would you say Mr Palmer was a friend?'

I shook my head. 'I thought so once. But now? Well, put it this way, I won't be shedding any tears for him, because the bastard tried to kill me.'

The woman's rough complexion paled. 'Oh, oh, my dear. Well, I shouldn't say any more about that to me. The police have taken charge. You might find one of 'em here standing sentry when you wakes up – that's standard procedure when there's been a fatality. I just wanted to let you know that a Marine Accident Investigator is on his way over from Falmouth. He'll want to talk to you and take your statement – but from what you've told me the police might want first dibs. In the meantime, you've got to stay on your boat, and you mustn't try to move her till the police say you can, is that clear?'

I nodded, too exhausted to argue.'

'You get some sleep now, Rosie. I'll see myself ashore, and we'll talk again later when hopefully things become a bit clearer.'

2/11

Interview

I awoke to a knocking on the side of the boat.
'Hello, anyone aboard?' A man's voice.
'Just a minute,' I croaked, climbing stiffly out of
my bunk. The side of my face throbbed painfully. I
glanced in the mirror at the colourful bruise on my
left cheekbone from Gary's club of a hand. I
checked the ship's clock; quarter-past eleven. I'd
been asleep for less than three hours. They knocked
again, obviously hadn't heard me.

I shouted up the hatch, 'Hold your horses, I'll be up
in a minute.'

Pulling on jeans and sweater, I poked my head out
of the companionway. The blue sky of early this
morning now looked pale and dirty, like somebody
had dragged a greasy cloth across it. I peered at the
three figures standing on the quayside. Doreen stood
there with an apologetic smile. Beside the
coastguard officer stood a smartly-dressed man in
suit and tie, briefcase and a grim face. Standing apart
from them was a uniformed female copper.

'Hi,' I said, climbing out into the cockpit. Hugging myself in the chill wind I took a quick sweep of the river and the surrounding town, re-establishing my bearings. Following the Pilot upriver this morning had felt unreal, but then I'd been almost crying with fatigue.

It was Doreen who spoke. 'Hello again, Rosie. Sorry to wake you so soon. This gentleman is Mark Bland, from the Marine Accident Investigation Branch.'

Bland stepped forward. 'May we come aboard?'

I looked at the copper. 'Is that okay or do I talk to your lot first?'

'No, that's okay,' she smiled. 'DS Yardley hasn't arrived yet. He's driving round from Brixham. Mr Bland can take your statement first.'

Despite the city outfit, the man stepped confidently over the guardrail, and Doreen followed. I led them down below where they declined the tea I offered them. Doreen gave me a grin and shuffled in next to me on the banquette. The man remained aloof as if wanting to distance himself from Doreen's natural affability. He took a seat opposite and lifted his briefcase onto the table in front of him.

'I'm sorry for your loss, Ms Winterbourne,' he said.

I nodded, not sure how to react. Rejoicing wouldn't look great.

'Was he a relative?' he said.

I looked at Doreen, who just smiled her apologetic smile – she hadn't briefed him.

I shook my head. 'Gary joined me in Mullhaven yesterday. I'd intended to go solo, but he stepped in at the last moment and offered to crew for me as far as Portugal.'

He gave a slow nod, relieved probably, that he wasn't dealing with a grieving relative or spouse. 'And how are you feeling, now, Ms Winterbourne?' he said. 'Are you up to answering a few questions?'

'Fire away,' I said, a little more cheerfully than was appropriate under the circumstances. 'And please, call me Rosie.'

He lifted his briefcase onto the seat next to him, leaving two pre-printed forms and an A4 notepad on the table. He took a pen from his inside pocket, and clicked it, efficient and business-like – a no-nonsense Civil Servant.

'Now, Ms Winterbourne – er, Rosie' he said, 'I'm here to investigate a fatality at sea – a standard procedure, and nothing sinister. My job is not to apportion blame or responsibility, but to determine the facts of the accident and submit them for Branch Review. After the necessary paperwork, I'll need to see your boat registration, ship's log and take photographs of your current navigation chart, or a take a copy of your GPS record, as appropriate. Then you'll need to show me exactly what happened last night. I'll take a look around the boat and may snap off a few photos—'

I was almost nodding off when I heard voices on the quay. I felt someone step aboard.

'Excuse me, Doreen,' I said, nudging her as I stood up. 'I need to see who that is.'

She moved out of my way, and I stepped on the ladder, then stepped back again as a pair of heavy-duty boots clumped down.

'Sorry, Mark, but I need you to stop this interview,' said the big man lumbering into the saloon. 'This ain't no straightforward case, and the witness needs to be interviewed by us under caution.'

'Oh!' Bland said, giving me a curious eyebrow. 'Well now, Rosie, I suppose we'll be seeing you later at some point.'

The civil servant scooped his documents back into his briefcase and shuffled his way awkwardly in my suddenly crowded saloon to the ladder. He turned and smiled at me. 'I'll leave you in the capable hands of Detective Sergeant Yardley, then.' He clapped a hand on the detective's beefy shoulder. 'All yours Jago. Give us a call when you're finished, yeah?'

2/12

Suspicion

Rosemary Winterbourne is it?' said the detective, in soft west-country tones that belied his daunting physic. He was big and square, bald and bullnecked, and his lower lip protruded aggressively; more like a nightclub bouncer than a detective.

'That's right, but I go by Rosie,' I said, in no mood to be intimidated and wondering just how much longer before I could crawl back into my bunk and die.

'I'm Detective Sergeant Yardley, Rosie. You lost a crew member last night.'

'Funnily enough,' I said, 'that's what we were just getting round to talking about. I did ask the constable on the quay if the police wanted to do me first, so to speak.'

Yardley stared at me a moment, assessing me, I assumed, and probably wondering at my flippancy in the light of circumstances. Not a lot of humour in this guy.

'Yes, well,' he said at last. 'Ordinarily, it'd make no difference whether you gave your AIB statement first or second, but there are certain aspects to this case that are raising questions. So I'd like you now to grab a coat and come with us to the police station for a formal interview.'

'Okay,' I said with forced levity. Reaching into my cabin to take my warm fleece from its hook, I paused for a longing look at my bunk that seemed to be beckoning to me.

I followed the detective up the ladder, slotted in the two washboards and locked them and shrugged into my fleece. The female uniform was still there, but she was now joined by two male colleagues, one standing by her, the other next to a police car.

Yardley waited for me to step ashore then said, 'Rosemary Winterbourne, I'm obliged to caution you. You do not have to say anything. But it may harm your defence if you do not mention when questioned something which you later rely on in Court. Anything you do say may be given in evidence. Do you understand?'

I stared astonished. 'Am I under arrest, then?'

'No, Rosie, I'm not arresting you,' he said, looking carefully at my face. 'Bearing in mind the caution I just gave you, is there any reason to think that I should?'

'Certainly not,' I said, quite haughtily.

'Glad to hear it. Now, Constable Davies here will stay with your boat,' Yardley explained, 'while we pop along to Flavel Road and have a nice little chat.'

I shrugged and said nothing, still feeling weary and dull of thought, despite the frightful caution. The uniformed woman moved to the car and opened the rear door, inviting me to climb in ahead of her. Yardley got in next to the driver. Nobody spoke during the short drive, and for a second or two, I dozed off in the car.

The police station was a drab, three-story building from the sixties, huddled in a quiet backstreet next to a library and an arts centre. Yardley showed me to a dreary interview room – a whiff of disinfectant and a hint of whatever it was meant to cover up. A table stood against one wall, four moulded plastic chairs, and a recording machine. The light came from a pair of large frosted windows – the grey-painted bars on the inside a sobering reminder of the room's purpose.

Yardley followed me in and invited me to take a seat facing away from the door, then took one of the two opposite, slapping a buff file cover onto the table. A woman in an olive plaid suit entered and closed the door. Her heels clonked on the concrete floor; the ground-floor room had an oddly hallow acoustic, and there were faint voices and creaking movements from the rooms above. She placed a plastic cup in front of me before taking the seat next to Yardley.

I picked up the cup and studied the grey solution half-filling it.

'It's tea,' she explained helpfully. 'No sugar I'm afraid – we're out.' She smiled a perfunctory apology.

I grimaced and moved the cup out of my line of sight. 'Don't worry,' I said. 'I'm sweet enough.'

Yardley switched on the recorder. 'Interview with Rosemary, er— Rosie Winterbourne on Tuesday twelfth of February 2013, officers present: Detective Sergeant Jago Yardley and Detective Constable June Agutter. The time now is 1536.'

He turned his big face to me. 'Now, Rosie, we're investigating the death of Gary Palmer. Before we begin, I have to remind you you're still under caution. Please state your name and home address for the record.'

'Do I need a lawyer?'

'Only if you intend to lie to us, in which case, tell us now, and I'll arrange someone.' Yardley said, deadpan, holding my stare.

I snorted, then spoke carefully into the machine, 'My name is Rosie Winterbourne, and I live at Juniper Cottage, Cobbingden, Surrey.'

'Just relax, Rosie,' said the woman kindly. 'You're not being accused of anything. We have to investigate fatalities at sea.'

'So, take your time,' Yardley cut in smoothly, 'and tell us how Mr Palmer ended up going overboard.'

I told the whole story, exactly how it all happened. When I got to the part where I whacked Gary with the winch handle, they exchanged glances, Yardley nodding to his constable, and she smiling grimly back.

When I'd finished, they looked at me in silence for a moment, then Yardley laid a photograph in front of me. It was of Gary's pallid face, eyes closed, turned slightly away to expose the washed-out gash in his right temple. The sprocket marks from the winch handle were unmistakable.

He said, 'Constable Agutter recognised the marks from a winch handle, she being a sailor herself.'

'You must have given him one hell of a whack,' said Agutter, 'it left quite a crack in his skull.'

'Yeah, I didn't hold back,' I told her. 'Because the moron had his hand stuffed into my pants at the time. What would you have done, Constable?'

She had the grace to blush but said nothing.

Yardley cleared his throat. 'Here's the thing, Rosie. We only have your word that Mr Palmer attacked you, while the evidence and your own admission point clearly to you attacking him. Can you see our problem here?'

'Not really,' I said, 'I told you what happened, and why I had to hit him to save myself.' I pointed to my bruised left cheek. 'How do you think I got this?'

'Ah, well you see, a dead man can't argue his side, so I've got to try and do that for him. Now, you may well be telling the truth. Still, where there is room for doubt, we have to explore the possibility of an alternative explanation.

I shook my head, overwhelmed by tiredness and sick of this dogged dispute of what was so patently a straightforward case of self-defence. I couldn't be bothered to argue. Eventually, I said, 'Look, I think Sussex Police are looking for Gary in connection with something in Mullhaven.'

That made them both sit up.

'Sandra from the marina there texted me yesterday about it,' I continued. 'So why don't you just phone them? Then maybe you'll understand what kind of monster we're dealing with here.'

'Okay, we'll do that.' He nodded to the woman, who stood up and left. 'Detective Constable Agutter is leaving the room,' he said into the recorder.

'Now, Rosie, I noticed you locked your boat when we left, so please could I have the keys?'

'Why?' I said.

He looked surprised that I asked. 'Because your vessel is a possible crime scene, and we'll need to search it for evidence.'

'Well, yes, it's a crime scene alright, no 'possible' about it – an attempted rape with probably worse to follow if I hadn't defended myself. What evidence do you expect to find? And if I'm not under arrest, why should I hand over my keys? And anyway, don't you need a warrant or something?'

'Well, Rosie, yes, if you refuse to cooperate, then we can apply for a warrant. But is that the attitude for an innocent person to take?'

I let out a long sigh. 'Look, you can search my boat, but I want to be there. And if it's alright with you, I'll hang on to my keys. Okay?'

He cocked his head to one side. 'Alright, Rosie, we'll let that ride for now. But bear in mind if I decide to arrest you then I won't need a war—'

Just then, the door opened behind me. 'Sarge, could I have a word?'

It was Agutter. Yardley let out a sigh, then spoke into the recorder: 'Interview suspended at 1614.' He switched it off and rose to his feet. As he left the room, a male constable shuffled in and closed the door behind him, then stood there at ease.

Ignoring him, I turned my chair, so its back was against the wall, then sat, leaned back and closed my eyes. My thoughts jumbled, became nonsensical, and I quickly drifted off.

'Rosie? Please wake up.'

I came to with a start, utterly disorientated for several seconds. I scrubbed my eyes and shook my head. Yardley was back in his seat, looking at me with a bland expression. Agutter took her place next to him.

'Sorry—' I gave another massive yawn. 'Uh, I'm a bit knackered. Did you speak to Sussex Police?'

'Yes, we did. And our colleagues there confirmed they want to speak to a Gary Palmer in connection with a murder investigation.'

'That's great. So can I go now?'

'I don't think so, Rosie,' said Yardley, grim-faced. 'As well as the unlawful killing of Mr Palmer, there's now an additional charge to consider. Namely that of "Aiding an Offender"'

'*Aiding an Offender?* What the f— What the hell does that mean?'

'It means, Rosie, that if Palmer turns out to be the killer Sussex Police are looking for, then you could be charged with helping him to escape.'

I was suddenly out of my stupor, and looking at him, horrified. How could this be happening?

I said, 'If I'd known he was an offender, I wouldn't have taken up his offer to crew for me.'

'That's as maybe. But according to the staff at Mullhaven boatyard, you were quite close with Mr Palmer and could well have been aware of his alleged crimes. Also, we have—'

'But—,'

Yardley held up a dinner plate-sized hand and pressed doggedly on, '—been asked to provide a DNA sample from Palmer's body so they can match it to samples from the victim. If Palmer turns out not to be the perpetrator, that again calls into question your claim that he attacked you. Until we know more, I'm afraid you need to stay here with us.'

I jumped to my feet. 'But you can't keep me here if—'

Yardley's enormous mass rose from his chair. 'Rosemary Winterbourne, I'm arresting you on suspicion of the unlawful killing of Gary Palmer. You remain under caution, and you will be held in custody while we carry out further investigations. Now, I'll have those keys, please.'

2/13

Custody

Amazing! The cell they put me in was almost as comfortable as my cabin on *Pasha*. Apart from being four-times the size, it had a proper single bed with a decent mattress. No bedsheets, but a folded grey blanket and pillow – both looked reasonably clean.

A straight wooden bench stretched the width of the cell beneath the small barred window – no doubt the intended prisoner's bed. Clearly, some enlightened soul had decreed a more caring confinement for the un-convicted. Against the wall opposite the bed stood a table and chair, which seemed an odd addition for a holding cell. Perhaps South Devon had a more genteel class of detainee who liked to spend their time in confinement writing their memoirs. Made sense, I thought – this was, after all, Agatha Christie country. It was certainly quiet enough down here in the basement.

An opening in the wall led to a tiny ablution: a stainless-steel loo and matching washbasin, all clean and shiny and stinking of strong detergent. So I wasn't too disturbed about taking a pee – there was even a square of soap and a roll of paper towels above the basin. Afterwards, I wasted no time disparaging my fate – I shrugged out of my fleece, wrapped the blanket around me, and crashed out. I was asleep in seconds.

I woke up in darkness, and it took a scary moment to recall where I was until I discerned the faint moonglow spilling between the bars of the small window. I was thirsty, and my tummy was grumbling. Kicking aside the rough blanket I got up and banged the flat of my hand on the steel door.

'Hello, can anybody hear me?'

A light came on in the cell. Down the corridor, a door opened. Footsteps were approaching, slow, methodical. They stopped outside my door. The inspection flap slid open, and a face peered in.

'Woke up then? Thought you were out for the night.'

I tried on an endearing smile. 'Any chance of a bottle of water, and some food?'

'Yeah, I'll see what I can do. DS Yardley wants a word anyway – I'll tell him you're awake.'

As the flap slid closed, it occurred to me for the first time that I might be in serious trouble. When the constable had put me in here, all I could focus on was the bed and sleep. I trusted then that although the system was currently skewed, justice was bound to prevail and they would let me out, perhaps with an apology for my appalling treatment. Now I was not so sure. I wondered why they hadn't offered me a legal brief when they charged me – isn't that what happens? Damn! How could they be charging me with, what did he say? Unlawful killing – what the fuck?

I was sitting on the bed contemplating possible futures when I heard footsteps coming back, more than one person this time, indistinct voices. The flap slid back, and the same face as before appeared, then the door clunked and swung open, the doorway filled by the bulk of Detective Sergeant Yardley.

'Now then, Rosie, I trust you had a good sleep?' For the first time, there was the beginning of a smile lifting the corners of the Detective Sergeant's bulldog mouth.

'This can't be right,' I said. 'I've done nothing wrong. Shouldn't I have a solicitor if you're charging me?'

He lumbered into the cell and pulled out the chair to sit facing me. He didn't speak, just handed me a bottle of water and put a shop-bought sandwich on the table. I glared at him a moment, then broke the seal on the bottle and drank deeply.

'I've been having a long chat with my colleagues from Sussex,' he said at last. 'Apparently, someone on a boat that was near yours in Mullhaven overheard your conversation with Palmer yesterday morning. We've subsequently agreed that you probably didn't know Sussex Police were investigating him.'

I reached for my fleece. 'Okay, so now I can—'

'Now hang on, Rosie, don't get too excited. We've searched your vessel, and we found a holdall, presumably belonging to Mr Palmer, in the forepeak.'

'So, you went ahead and searched my boat anyway,' I snapped.

'We had no choice, I'm afraid. Otherwise, we only had your word that Palmer had ever been on your vessel, and that simply would not be good enough for the Coroner. As well as the holdall, we took some DNA samples that proved he slept in your forepeak. So I have to ask you, were you at any point aware that Palmer was carrying a large quantity of cash in his holdall?'

'Jesus!' I breathed, then let out a grim laugh. 'Almost makes me wish I hadn't called it in.'

'I'll take that as a no, then. The mayday call brings me nicely to my next point. The fact that you made it works in your favour. If you'd been colluding with Palmer, there was nothing to stop you just sailing away with all the money.'

'Until the body washed up on a beach somewhere— No, forget I said that. How much was there anyway?'

He grinned, then shook his head. 'There wouldn't have been a body – it's a gruesome fact that the crabs in Lyme Bay are quite voracious.'

'How nice?' I grimaced, then nodded at the sandwich he'd brought me. 'That's not crab, is it?'

'So, I've spoken to my Chief Super. Since there's no real evidence that foul play was a factor in Palmer's death we've agreed that your account of events is the most plausible scenario.'

'Very big of you. So now I can go?'

He nodded. 'We've decided to drop the charge against you and will not be seeking any further prosecution – you're free to go.' He handed me my boat keys with a kindly smile. 'But I would ask you to come back to the station tomorrow morning to sign a formal statement once we've transcribed it from this afternoon's interview. Shall we say after ten?'

'Thanks,' I said. I prodded the bed. 'At least you've got comfy cells.'

He stood and grinned. 'Don't forget your egg sandwich.'

2/14

Inquest

After I signed my statement for the police the next morning, I moved *Pasha* across the river to take a berth in the marina at Kingswear. The MAIB were no longer interested in me now that it was a police matter, so there was nothing to keep me at the very public town berth.

I was to attend a coroner's inquest on Gary's death a week on Monday in Totnes, so I was stuck here for eight more days. But at least at the marina, I could get an electric hook-up with internet and shoreside bathroom facilities. First thing I did was email Georgina and told her what happened.

I spent the days walking the cold winter clifftops and feeding myself up in the tourists-starved local pubs. In the evenings, I curled up in the saloon with the fan heater and read back-to-back crime novels on my Kindle. By Saturday night there was still no reply from Georgina.

On Sunday I motored up the Dart, winding my careful way on the incoming tide up the picture-book river to Totnes. There I found a space to tie up for up to forty-eight hours on the Steamer Quay.

The inquest was at ten-o-clock next morning at the Civic Hall. I got there early and took a seat at the back. Yardley was already there, stood talking to a couple of uniformed officers up near the raised bench; he nodded to me as I entered but didn't come over. Press photographers and reporters milled around in little groups. There were a few curious glances as I took my seat, but I avoided eye contact. They would know who I was soon enough.

The detective sergeant was first to give evidence, quietly and matter-of-factly telling what happened. After prompting from the clerk, he read out the transcribed statement I'd signed last week. I was then called and asked if the account was accurate if there was anything I wished to add.

I was about to answer when I was distracted by a face I recognised in the audience. It took me a moment to realise it was the man I'd seen hanging around outside my house shortly after Mum's funeral – Range Rover Man.

'Miss Winterbourne,' the coroner snapped rather fiercely. 'Is there anything you wish to add or correct in your statement?'

I turned back to him. 'Er, sorry, no, no, it's all correct.'

'Thank you, Miss Winterbourne, you may step down.'

When I looked back, Range Rover Man had left his seat and was disappearing out of the door.

Some bloke from the Crown Prosecution was called next. He told the court there was compelling evidence, confirmed by a DNA sample, that Palmer had been the prime suspect of a brutal murder in Mullhaven. Plus the rape of several young women over the past twenty years. He had been about to be apprehended by West Sussex Police when he made his escape, deceiving Ms Winterbourne into helping him abscond abroad. He also mentioned that Gary's holdall had contained a large quantity of cash which he'd embezzled from the Boatyard.

The cause of death was drowning. The pathologist did not consider the blow to the head a contributing factor. The verdict was Death by Misadventure. When it was over the press made an untidy exit, and I was about to follow when Yardley intercepted me.

'Not that way, Rosie, unless you want those morons to be firing questions and flashbulbs in your face.'

He led me to a door in the back of the hall, down a corridor to a side entrance.

'Can I give you a lift down to Dartmouth?' he said as we emerged onto a small car park at the back.

'Thanks, but my boat's here. I motored up yesterday.'

'Oh, okay then. I'd keep your head down for a few days. You'll be front-page headlines tomorrow, my dear. Then the world and his brother'll be after you for interviews and pictures.'

I thanked him and scurried away back to *Pasha*. The press could take a running jump – I was going back downriver on tomorrow morning's ebb tide and then out to sea. I planned to be in the Western Approaches by midnight tomorrow and in Gibraltar ten days from now.

2/15

Gotcha

I emerged early next morning ready to slip and found two men on the quay looking at the boat, and then looking at me as I stepped out into the cockpit. They both wore suits and ties.

'Can I help you?' I said.

'Er, Miss Winterbourne?'

'If you're journalists, I'm not—'

'Nothing like that, Miss. Can you confirm that you are Rosemary Winterbourne?'

The speaker was around thirty, short-cropped hair and shiny brown shoes.

'*Rosie* Winterbourne,' I said warily. 'So, who are you?'

'Detective Sergeant Walker,' he flashed me an ID card, 'Ministry of Defence Police, and this is my colleague, Detective Sergeant Trimble.'

As I stared blankly back at him, I felt my face reddening. How the fuck—? I resisted the urge to glance up guiltily at my wire rigging. Walker was watching me with studied blandness, as if not letting on that he knew that I knew why they were here. At last, I found words. 'I'm not in the Navy anymore.' I told him. 'I was officially discharged two weeks ago.' *Shit! Why did I say that?*

'We know that, Miss,' said the second man, sauntering up from where he'd been studying *Pasha*'s bow, and particularly, I suspected, her anchor chain.

'We'd like to ask you some questions. Would you mind stepping ashore?'

I stayed where I was. 'Why, what's this about?'

'Look, Miss,' said the first man, Walker, 'just step ashore and come quietly with us to the Police Station. Otherwise, we'll have you arrested by the local plod. I'm sure you don't want that.'

My heart pounded furiously. 'Just give me a minute, I'll get a coat.' I stepped down to the saloon, mind in a flat spin. For a brief second, I wondered what I came down for, then snatched my fleece from its hook and a light waterproof from my locker. And, as if trying to cover my guilt and desperation, I pulled on my beany hat.

I paused a moment on the ladder, trying to breathe normally, then stepped up into the cockpit. I slotted in the washboards and locked them, then stepped ashore.

The interview room was starker and more intimidating than the one in Dartmouth. The table and chairs were in the centre of the room and bolted down. There were no windows. Only the smell was similar. They didn't seem to care where I sat, so I took a seat facing the door.

'I'll come straight to the point, Ms Winterbourne,' said Walker, taking a seat opposite. At the same time, his colleague remained standing.

'We're investigating the theft of certain naval stores items from Portsmouth Naval Base in September last year. We have reason to suspect your involvement while serving on-board HMS *Windsor Castle*.'

I kept quiet, looking him in the eye but conscious of the other staring from over his shoulder.

'As you may be aware, we have no powers of arrest away from Crown Property. At this stage, we are merely fact-finding. You are not under caution, and anything you tell us will be strictly between us. If there is sufficient *prima facie* evidence implicating you, then we will be obliged to hand the matter over to the appropriate authorities. Do you understand?'

'So, I don't have to speak, I'm not under arrest, and you can't detain me. Why don't I just walk?'

'In theory, that's true,' conceded Walker, 'but I advise against it until you've heard what we have to say. It's in your interests to know how much evidence we already have. And I would add that the local police are co-operating closely with our investigation, hence the use of this facility.'

'And these er, "appropriate authorities" you mentioned?'

'That would be the Royal Hampshire Constabulary.'

I slumped back and blew out a breath. 'Okay—'

He pulled a brown envelope from an inside pocket and shook out several photographs face down onto the desk. He shuffled through them and selected one, which he placed in front of me.

'During a search of the work-premises of Gary Palmer in Mullhaven boatyard, West Sussex Police came across these four items in a boatshed and brought them to our attention. Do you know what they are?'

'Obviously,' I said, 'empty paint cans.' The pusser's antifoul cans Gary had promised to incinerate. Huh, revenge from beyond the grave, or what?

'Interesting that you know they're empty.' Walker said, a gleam in his eye. 'Anything else special about them, the markings?'

I picked up the photo and made a show of studying it.

'It says, "Antifoul, Yacht, Ocean Blue, Self-polishing "'

Walker sighed. 'And underneath that?'

'"MoD Property"'

'Ministry of Defence Property. And what do you suppose they were doing in a civilian boatyard, Rosemary?'

'It's *Rosie*. How should I know?'

'Well, *Rosie*, I can tell you that these four tins were in the category V&A, Valuable and Attractive. Every item is barcoded and subject to random checks. During a routine audit in October last year, these serialised items from a stores manifesto could not be accounted for. Ring any bells?'

I shook my head.

'You were working on your boat in Mullhaven around then, is that right?'

'That doesn't mean—'

'A witness we interviewed in the boatyard and is willing to testify in court claims he saw you applying antifoul paint to your vessel on the fifteenth of September.'

For a moment, I felt defeated, but then pulled myself together.

'Doesn't prove anything. Did your witness *see* the cans?'

He didn't reply to that, just nodded slowly then selected another picture and put it on top of the first.

'This picture, taken on 12th of September, is from a security camera outside the V&A Store from where the paint went missing. Can you explain why your vehicle was there on that day?'

I picked up the picture of my Suzuki Jeep – the registration number was legible.

'I was collecting paint for the ship, doing a favour for a friend, really.'

'And that friend would be Able Seaman Doyle, is that correct?'

'The ship's painter, yes.' I said. It felt like I was driving downhill with no brakes.

'Doyle has corroborated that you collected a waiting order of paint for the ship. But that paint came from the Inflammable Paint Store, not the V&A Store, so I ask again, what was your vehicle doing parked outside the V&A store?'

I kept silence, just glared defiantly.

'Earlier that same day,' he continued, 'you went to the Cash Clothing Store in HMS Nelson and purchased six woollen jersey's, size, extra-large.

Now, I would guess your size as medium, Rosie. Is that about right?'

My headlong rush downhill increased, a brick wall coming up ahead.

'Yes,' I whispered.

'Oh, and these are all male pattern jersey's, according to the receipt. Who were they for?'

I didn't say anything.

'Were they for the dockyard storeman, Rosie, Mr Warren? To exchange for the antifoul paint that you later smuggled out of the dockyard?'

I pressed my lips together to stop my chin wobbling – I wanted to crawl into a hole and die.

Walker looked up at Trimble.

Trimble nodded. 'Yeah, I'm happy if you are.'

Walker gathered up the pictures and stood to leave.

'What, that's it?' I said.

'Unless there's any more you want to tell us, Rosie?' said Trimble.

I started to shake my head, then a thought occurred. 'Er, just a question. Is it just you two, or is there another one, tall man, athletic-looking, short brown hair? He was at the inquest.'

They glanced at each other, and then Walker shook his head. 'No, it's just the two of us.'

I believed them because when I thought about it, Range Rover Man had started stalking me before my Dockyard misdemeanours.

They filed out of the room. No thank you or goodbyes, not even a backward glance. They left the door open, and as I stood to go, a uniformed policeman stepped in, and behind him, a female officer. It was she who spoke.

'Rosemary Winterbourne, I am Inspector Connelly from the Royal Hampshire Constabulary. I'm arresting you on suspicion of theft of Crown property from Her Majesty's Naval Base, Portsmouth. You don't have to say anything but—etcetera, etcetera, etcetera.'

EPISODE THREE

The Indictment

3/1

Legal Advice

There was a newspaper on Lester Granville's desk, one of the national broadsheets, folded on a page with my picture, the same sketch they'd shown on TV last night.

SAILING HEROINE FOILS
MULLHAVEN MAULER

Lester saw me looking and turned the paper over.

'Rather disconcerting, I imagine,' he said, 'seeing yourself in newsprint. No photos though, so you've managed to slip their net, eh?'

'So far,' I said, 'until somebody who knows me tips them off.'

'And how are you, Rose. Can't imagine what you went through last week. Must have been terrifying.'

I nodded, biting my lip to stop it quivering. Charlene came through with two coffees, softly touched my shoulder, and left again without speaking.

'Want to talk about it?' he said when she'd closed the door.

I shook my head, gulped, and pulled myself together. 'Lester, I'm in big trouble.'

He leaned back and took off his spectacles, pursed his lips. 'If this is about you leaving that animal to drown, I don't think—'

'No, no, nothing like that.'

I paused, took a sip of my coffee. I was wondering how much I could safely tell my solicitor without prejudicing my case and putting him in an awkward position. It all hung on whether I was going to come clean or try to wing it on a denial, a decision with which I was still struggling.

'I've been charged with stealing some stuff from the dockyard, back in September. I have to appear at Portsmouth Crown Court tomorrow.'

He started forward, made an O with his mouth.

'And did you?' he held up a hand. 'No, don't answer that. For now, just tell me whether you intend to deny the charge.'

'I haven't said anything, at least, not officially.'

'What does that mean, exactly, not officially?'

I told him about the two MoD plods talking to me off the record, what they'd shown me, telling me what they knew.

'But you made no admission of guilt, Rose? Think carefully. You said nothing by way of admission to either the police or the MoD detectives?'

I shook my head. 'I'm sure I didn't.'

'Good. Now, as you're aware, I'm not a criminal lawyer. I'll have to hand you off to one of my colleagues, a barrister. If you're happy for me to appoint him, I'll call him right now.'

I nodded, and he pressed the buzzer on his intercom:

'Charlene, get me Mr O'Sullivan on the phone, please.'

'Yes, Mr Granville.'

I sipped my coffee. My hand was shaking, and I wanted a ciggy.

'So, Rose, how's your Dad?'

I'd been thinking a lot about Dad. Should I go and see him? If I did, I'd only end up blurting out the whole sorry mess. Would that be fair on him?

'I haven't seen him since Sunday before last,' I said, 'but they tell me he's comfortable.'

'No sign of him coming out of this Locked-in thing?'

I shook my head. 'No change. He just sits watching telly all day— Oh shit! Sorry, I've got to go.'

I ran furiously to the car park, cursing my stupidity. Arriving at the hospital in eye-watering time, I left the jeep unlocked and badly parked, sprinted through reception and up the stairs to Dad's ward.

'Rosie?' said the nurse at the desk, 'We thought—'

'Has my Dad been watching telly? Has he seen the news?'

'No, Rosie, he hasn't,' she came around to the front and put her hands on my shoulders. 'We all heard about that— what you went through. We didn't open his eyes this morning, and we took his television away.'

'Thank you,' I gushed, 'Oh God, thank you!' I took her hands from my shoulders and held them, 'Thank you, I mean it.'

I went in to see Dad, not to talk, just to look at him. I stood quietly by his bed, wanting desperately to take his hand, to say I loved him.

The doorbell rang promptly at two-o-clock.

'Rosie, is it? I'm Kieran O'Sullivan.'

The barrister was audibly Irish, mid-forties with a holiday-tan and carried an old-style leather briefcase that bulged at the sides. I showed him into the dining-room where I had a fresh pot of tea waiting.

'Now, Rosie,' he began, taking an A4 pad from his case and placing it in front of him. 'The first thing to say is that I've talked to the Clerk of the Court and managed to get a time for your hearing – ten-thirty tomorrow morning, okay?'

'Oh, that's better,' I said, pouring the tea.

'They invariably run a little late, but we should be out well before noon, anyway.'

'You reckon it'll be that quick? Surely not.'

'Ah! You thought you had your trial tomorrow. Well, no, Rosie. Tomorrow's only the plea and trial-preparation hearing – what's called an Arraignment. The clerk will read the charges out to you and ask whether you plead Guilty, or Not Guilty. Depending on your plea, you'll be sent either for trial or sentencing.'

'And how long before that happens, either way?'

'In the case of a Not Guilty plea, it'll be up to the Crown prosecutors, based on how long they need to complete their investigations. Most likely they'll give you a fixed date within two weeks of the Hearing. Should we decide to plead guilty, then the Court will decide on a date for sentencing.'

I bit my lip as the implications finally sank in. Kieran watched me a moment, and his brown eyes softened.

'It's all a bit daunting, I know. But try not to get too anxious. Okay?'

I nodded.

'Let's start with what happened in Totnes when the MoD detectives first questioned you about these allegations. You say they didn't caution you, is that right?'

That first session with Kieran took the whole afternoon, exploring avenues for mitigation and whether or not a guilty plea would or would not be my best option. I ended up enumerating everything I'd acquired from the dockyards stores. I must confess to being startled by my audacity when I saw the list written out like that. Having opened up to him, I was now committed to a guilty plea.

'And that's it, Rosie? You're sure there's nothing else?'

'Nah, that's the lot. Seemed a good idea at the time. Stupid, now, looking back. So what will I get?'

He pursed his lips. 'Recent military service, no previous, lay it on thick, a saint who slipped by the wayside— we've got a reasonable judge who's usually reluctant to send people down. Victor Mumbles.'

I couldn't help a grin. 'Does he, really?'

He ignored the quip, probably heard it a hundred times.

Thursday morning. Kieran was right. We were in court for about twenty minutes. They read the charges, I pled Guilty, with other offences taken into account. Kieran handed the Judge and Prosecution a list of all the stuff I'd illegally procured during August and September last year:

> **Antifoul (10 litres),**
> **Batteries, AGM 120Ah (4)**
> **8mm Anchor Chain (50 metres)**
> **7mm Inox Wire Rope (75 metres)**
> **Swage-fittings (various) (16).**

The case was referred for sentencing the following Friday. My bail application was not opposed.

Kieran, still in his silks and wig, caught up with me as I left the Courts.

'Rosie, we need a chat. Give me five minutes; then I'll meet you in the café across the square. That okay?'

By the time I'd rolled and smoked my ciggy, he joined me, and we went in together. I found a table in a quiet corner while Kieran went for the coffees.

'I managed to find out about your boat,' he said, placing two lurid green coffee mugs on the table, 'she arrived in Gosport this morning, and they'll lift her out this afternoon.'

'Oh, that's all right then,' I said, 'any more good news?'

He looked hurt but smiled, anyway. 'It's always better to know the worst early, more opportunity to prepare a defence.'

'Ha! That shouldn't take long. And what was all that stuff the Judge rattled on about Disclosure? Confused the hell out of me.'

'I'll be straight with you, Rosie, it doesn't look good. The best we can try for is mitigating circumstances for a lenient sentence. Anything I plan to bring up in the way of evidence to support a case for leniency must be shared with the Prosecution beforehand. That's what the Judge meant by Disclosure.'

'Mitigating circumstances? What mitigating circumstances?'

He sighed. 'That's up to you, Rosie, whatever you can tell me; your state of mind when you did it, anyone who might have encouraged you to do it. Though I realise it might be difficult for you to implicate a friend.'

I sat thinking a moment, then shook my head.

'You're sure there's nothing? Nothing at all I can use?'

I gave him my earnest face and shook my head again. I didn't intend to discuss my state of mind with anyone. And saying that a dead man had sparked the original idea seemed too convenient, such an obvious scapegoat.

'Okay, fair enough.' He pushed a business card across the table. 'If you think of anything, give me a call, or email. There's still another angle we can look at, but I'll need to do some research.'

'Another angle?'

He leaned forward and spoke quietly. 'Corruption in dockyard services that make these crimes so easy, tempting otherwise honest people to break the law.'

'Now I can see why barristers get paid so much.'

'Rosie, just one more thing.' He checked over his shoulder for eavesdroppers, then leaned in, 'there was at least one press reporter in court today. Normally a case like this wouldn't arouse much interest, but sooner or later someone is bound to make the connection with, you know, what happened to you? It might harm our case if you talk to them, so best say nothing, no matter what they offer for your story – just until it's concluded. Agreed?'

'Suits me fine,' I said.

3/2

Paparazzi

I saw them as soon as I turned into our street – I pulled into the kerb and sat with the engine running. Half a dozen paparazzi, men and women, loitering outside our drive, some with cameras, others wired up with microphones, looking up at the house for signs of life. The street was full of their parked cars. I toyed with the idea of turning around, maybe drive up to Islington and stay with Ivy, Doc's mum, for a while.

But no. I had to be at home for Georgie; she could show up anytime. Besides, I wasn't going to let them drive me from my own home.

Oh, fuck it!

I slammed into gear and gunned it, and with horn blaring, spun recklessly into the drive, scattering the panicked paparazzi, and squealed to a stop inches from the garage door.

A flash went off in my face as I threw open the jeep's door, a barrage of shouted questions, more camera flashes. Someone barred my way to the door, a young woman.

'Just an interview, Rosemary, five minutes, that's all. We'll make it—'

'Get out of my fucking way!' I snarled in her face.

She paled and stepped aside, but others were now crowding in behind, clicking away, firing questions. I unlocked the door and slammed it behind me, leaning against it, breathing hard.

The clamour outside continued, like some zombie movie. Someone pushed in the letterbox flap, 'Just a few words, Miss Winterbourne, please?'

I snapped it down with the heel of my hand, rewarded with a yelp of pain from beyond the door. They didn't try it again.

I went around pulling closed all the downstairs curtains, then made a sandwich and settled down to watch TV – with the volume turned up to drown out the wheedling from outside. An hour later, it was quiet, and when I twitched aside the sitting-room curtain, the street was empty. It wasn't until darkness fell, and the newshounds hadn't returned, that I finally began to relax.

Aunt Georgie turned up shortly after seven.

I cooked us a meal, much to Georgie's approval. She hovered in the kitchen, watching me work, but didn't interfere; just chatted on about the difficulties of getting a last-minute flight in the high season.

'Not the recommended way of doing it, but shit, Sweetie, I was desperate. You shouldn't have to go through this nightmare alone.'

'There's something else I have to tell you,' I said, 'and you're not going to like it.'

Georgie listened grim-faced as I told her what I'd done to get *Pasha* to sea, her eyes growing wider with each new revelation. I told her about my arrest, and afterwards, she just sat staring at me in disbelief.

'Well, say something,' I said at last.

'What do you want me to say, Rosie? *You're a stupid bloody fool?* But I guess you already know that. *I'm sure things'll work out?* But that'd be a bloody lie. The truth is that the only thing that'll work out is a spell in gaol.'

'I— I thought you'd understand why—'

'Understand? *Understand?* What I understand is: you turned yourself into a damned criminal.'

'It was only bad luck I got caught. If Gary had got rid of those tins like he was supposed—'

'Rosie, can you hear yourself? You stole from your government. That's like, like treason, for Christ's sake. A crime against taxpayers. In the States, that'd get you—'

But I couldn't listen to any more. Stung by my aunt's betrayal, I dashed into the kitchen, grabbed my makings, and went out into the garden. I was shaking so badly I couldn't roll my ciggy.

The kitchen door creaked open behind me.

'Here, let me,' Georgie said, taking the train-crash of paper and tobacco from my fingers. In seconds she handed me back a perfectly-made cigarette.

I spluttered a laugh. 'Where did you learn to do that? I didn't know you even smoked.'

'Ah, there's a lot you don't know about your Aunt Georgie,' her eyes glinted through the dark chill of night.

I lit up and took a deep drag, blowing smoke into the bare branches of the old apple tree. After a while, I said, 'I've let you down, Georgie, I know that. After everything you've done for me. I'm so sorry.'

'Well, sweetie, to be fair, you didn't even know I existed when you did that stuff. So it wasn't me you let down—' She left the rest unsaid.

Next morning there was an email from Kieran; could he come to see me on Wednesday morning to discuss our defence. I agreed.

Around mid-morning a couple of yesterday's newshounds reappeared; one came up to the door and tried the bell, but I'd disconnected it. When one of them started hammering at the door, Georgie stuck her head out of the window.

'She's got nothing to say, so fuck off and stop harassing her.'

She slammed the window on his protested 'rights to represent the Public Interest'. Next time I looked out, they were both gone.

'They'll be back, I know it.' I grumbled.

'Then why don't we both take off somewhere?' Georgie suggested.

The thought of venturing out gave me the collywobbles. Maybe I was paranoid, but I feared anyone recognising me from pictures taken during yesterday's paparazzi frenzy. And for once in my life, I didn't want to be by the sea. As if it were somehow to blame for, or at least, a constant reminder of, all my woes.

3/3

To the Hills

We must have driven to Great Malvern, though I have no recollection of the hundred-odd-mile drive it would have taken to get there – like in a movie: just a sudden change from one scene to the next. It was late afternoon, and we whiled away the remainder of the day walking around the quaint little town.

Georgie bought a jade bracelet and matching earrings to take home for Anna. They were beautiful and looked expensive, and I thought how sweet it was to be still buying romantic gifts for each other after all these years.

'How long will you stay?'

'Fed up with me already?'

'Course not,' I hooked my arm into hers. 'Just want to know how long I've got you for.'

She patted my hand. 'Let's just get next Friday over, then we'll see.'

We paused outside the Festival Theatre.

'I love Greek Tragedy,' Georgie said. She looked at my face for a moment, then decided. 'C'mon, let's get tickets, broaden your education. You'll love The Medea, Sweetie,' she screwed up her face, 'Lots of murder and revenge.'

'Lovely!' I said. 'Oh, go on then, you've won me over.'

Then we were in a pub for dinner – crowded, but we found a free table.

'Didn't she kill her children?' I said as we sat down with our drinks.

Georgie looked impressed, then a little disappointed. 'I thought you hadn't seen it?'

'I read it at Uni. It's a story that sticks in your craw.'

'You went to University? I didn't know that.'

'No, I know, how would you? I signed up for Humanities at Bristol, dropped out of year two to join the Navy.'

She studied my face intently.

'Best thing I ever did,' I said, 'I loved the Mob, loved the travel, loved being at—'

It crept up out of nowhere. One second I was chatting happily, the next, I was weeping like a kid after someone kicked his toys away. And people were looking.

Georgie took my hands in hers. 'C'mon, Sweetie, let's pop outside for a minute, you can have a smoke and tell your Aunt Georgie all about it.'

I gave an involuntary laugh through snuffles and nodded.

We were in a beer garden – a few bench-tables on weed-pocked flag-stones – the only ones braving the sharp evening air. Georgie had brought along our coats, which we shuffled into before sitting down. I took out my makings.

'This time last year,' I said, 'I was in the Caribbean – West Indies Guardship, you know? I was having the time of my life: stopping off for days at a time at these amazing islands, beach parties, swimming and snorkelling. All that stuff most civvies only ever see in their dreams. At sea, we used to intercept drug-runners and rescue yachts and motorboats that had got into trouble. There was so much to do, so much to keep us busy.'

Georgie watched me with an intensity I hadn't seen before. She didn't say a word, just waited for me to go on.

'I had the best mates in the world, comrades, you know? We put our lives on the line for each other. Not for Queen and Country, or any of that bullshit – we were there to watch each other's backs, and we did.

'I was on a roll, back then, a good career ahead. A PO's Course coming up in August, a great service record, and looking forward to my Officer's Board and at least another fifteen years.'

I paused to light my ciggy, then looked at the glowing end.

'Didn't smoke then, either.' I had done for a short while but packed up after the previous Christmas.

'What I'm trying to say, Georgie, in the frame of mind I was then, I would never have dreamt of doing what I did, nicking all that gear. I would probably have shopped anyone I caught doing it. What a hypocrite!'

She raised her eyebrows and nodded agreement. 'We're all of us hypocrites at one time or other, Sweetie, me included.'

'It all started to unravel after Mum— you know, after the accident. At first, I thought I had it all under control. Get over it, I kept telling myself, these things happen, but you're still in control. Do you know what I'm saying? I was in control, alright; in control of what though? Stealing from the Navy I loved, and piling the guilt on my helpless Dad for killing Mum?'

I noticed Georgie was shivering, and it dawned on me that twenty-four hours ago she'd been in the tropics. I stubbed out and stood to leave.

'You okay, my love?'

I hadn't noticed the man standing in the shadows having a smoke.

'Yeah, fine,' I assured him, hurrying inside.

Despite its dark and disturbing plot, I loved The Medea. In this production, an American tourist falls asleep amid the ruins of ancient Corinth. As the haunting voices of the chorus grew, and grey shapes closed around the sleeping form, I felt transported to the time of legend, and the gods. For three hours, I was in another place, where magic was real and jealousy invariably lethal. My knowledge of the conclusion did nothing to lessen its shocking impact.

We were walking the ridgeway footpath on the Malvern Hills, warmed by our exertions and undeterred by the occasional flurries of wintery rain. It was strange to see Georgie in Mum's walking gear, and once, I almost called her 'Mum'. Our walk culminated in an iron-age fort. We reached it just as the sun made its first appearance of the day, low on the horizon, winking goodnight from beneath a huddle of crimson cloud.

3/4

The Judge

Wednesday morning: we'd just cleared away the breakfast things when Kieran showed up.

'I got a look at the Prosecution's evidence this morning, Rosie. The evidence they recovered from your boat.'

Georgie came through and perched herself at the head of the table.

'Just pretend I'm not here,' she said.

'But why do they need evidence if I've already pled Guilty?'

'Costs, I expect,' Georgie said.

I turned and glared at her.

'Sorry, dear. Just ignore me.'

'Costs,' Kieran said. 'They need to know the value of the goods so they can ask for the appropriate sentence. But more importantly, from the Prosecution's point of view, they'll be immediately ready for trial if you change your plea at any time.'

He leaned in. 'Now, Rosie, is there anything, anything at all I can use to mitigate your case? Think carefully; this might be our last chance, our only chance, to avoid you going to prison.'

I shook my head.

'Of course there is!' Georgie chimed in, 'go on, Rosie, tell him.'

I ignored her. 'No, Kieran, as I said, nothing I can think of.'

Georgie was red-faced and livid, 'If you think I'm going to sit here quietly while you throw away a chance to stay out of gaol, my girl, you can think again. Now pull yourself together and don't be so fucking spineless. Tell him!'

'Okay,' said Kieran, standing up, 'I'm sure there's something you're holding back, Rosie, and if you decide you do want to use it in mitigation, just give me a call, alright.'

I said, 'Kieran, please sit down a minute. Alright, there is something – something I need to tell you about me.'

Sentencing Day. Kieran met me at the entrance. Once through Security, he led me to a table in the big hall under the lawcourts. All around us people sat in huddled conversation with their briefs, indistinct whisperings echoing in the high vaulted ceiling.

'Last day of freedom,' I murmured, looking around the crowded hall.

'Not necessarily, Rosie. Victor can be a bit of a tyrant, but he's always fair, and doesn't like sending people down if he can avoid it.'

'Doesn't he have to follow certain rules, I mean, sentencing guidelines?'

'Only if the case is straightforward. From what you told me on Wednesday, and what I've discovered since I think we've got a good case for a non-custodial.'

I sat up straight. 'Discovered! What have you discovered?'

He reached into his battered briefcase and pulled out a blue folder.

'I've managed to acquire a copy of your Service Record.'

I stared at him. 'Really? How on earth—?'

'Let's just say, from someone who wants to help. The original will be sent to you anyway, in due course.'

I leaned in. 'You know, Kieran, stealing from the Navy can get you into big trouble.'

My flippancy won a hard stare as my barrister held up the folder. 'What I read in here is interesting, Rosie. Why didn't you tell me about your break in Good Conduct in August last year, about your, let's see,' he flipped the file open and read, '"Often erratic behaviour and lack of concentration at work" and, "A disappointing lapse after six years of sparkling performance."'

He raised a quizzical eyebrow.

'I'm not exactly proud of it.'

'Depression is not something to be ashamed of, Rosie. It's well understood these days and goes a long way to explain why you acted out of character in doing what you did. Listen to what your Captain wrote about your promotion to Petty Officer: "Stood over for six months pending improvement in conduct. This otherwise *exemplary* rating recently

- 221 -

lost her mother in an accident which left her father in a semi-comatose state. Since she has declined the offer of indefinite compassionate leave, we should expect her to settle down again in due course. In the meantime, we should handle her with some sensitivity."'

'You're asking me to say I was having a breakdown, and that's why I stole the stuff for my boat?'

'Not quite, Rosie. All I want you to do is stand in the witness box and answer my questions. I won't ask you to give an opinion about your state of mind, I promise, just the facts. The important thing is, just answer openly and truthfully. You'll be cross-examined by the Prosecution, almost certainly. Still, it's nothing to worry about, just stay calm and answer the questions. If you don't lie or try to cover up, they can't trap you.'

Our case went into session in Court Three at ten-thirty, and I waited alone in the corridor for another anxious half-hour after that. Then I was through those imposing double doors, being led by the Usher. The room felt crowded and confused; the only face I saw in focus was Georgie's, smiling encouragement from the Public Gallery. Once up in the dock, I felt less exposed and began to match my surroundings to what Kieran had briefed me about the court setup. There was a surprising lot of chatter, mostly from the dozen or so people up where Georgie was. I wondered who they all were; when I looked the question at my aunt, she just shrugged and gave a little shake of her head.

I focussed on one face staring at me, and suddenly realised she was the reporter I'd pissed off last week outside the house. My heart sank when I realised the truth; they were all probably newshounds hoping for a bit of drama. But no. There was one other I recognised. I'd once thought he was press, but now I knew better. He was my stalker: Range Rover Man. For a brief moment, our eyes met across the court. He smiled, the cheeky bastard. I ignored him.

Kieran sat alone at a table just below me. He turned and nodded to me with a half-grin that looked distinctly nervous, then went back to flicking through his paperwork, grey wig bobbing up and down as he read. He reminded me of an actor unsure of his lines as the play was about to start.

In contrast, the Prosecutor, a slinky creature in a pristine robe, faultless wig and professionally applied make-up, stood calmly chatting and chuckling with a couple of male colleagues. Her name, Kieran had told me, was Leonora Markham and I shouldn't be taken in by her softly-spoken appeal. She was as ruthless as she was stunningly gorgeous.

Then came a resounding 'Silence in Court, all rise.'. A hush descended, a door opened behind the bench, and through it walked Judge Victor Mumbles, QC.

He strolled to his seat and slumped down: an elderly man with heavy jowls that framed his double chin and seemed to drag his eyes into a houndlike expression. This image was heightened by the flaps of a prehistoric grey wig.

He glanced glumly around the room, studied me briefly over his glasses, then said, 'Please, sit down everybody.'

He nodded down at the Clerk, who stood and turned to face me.

'The Defendant will stand.'

I stood.

'State your name, and address, for the court.'

As I did, I caught Georgie's eye. She gave me a wink that transported me for a moment back to our walk the Malvern Hills. I then noticed Range Rover Man had gone. My thoughts drifted to my stalker and what his purpose might be in following me everywhere. I became aware of someone talking down at the front, and everyone but me listening. I tuned in and realised it was the clerk, reading my charges.

'Do you understand the charges?'

'Y— yes.'

'And do you stand by your plea of Guilty?'

'Yes, Yes, I do.'

'The defendant may sit,' said Judge Victor Mumbles, QC.

I sank onto the bench.

'Ms Markham,' said Judge Victor Mumbles, QC, 'I understand you wish to oppose the Pre-sentencing Report.'

The woman stood up, flashed a pointed glance at Kieran, then answered the judge, 'Yes, My Lord. The plaintiff is concerned that the Basis of Plea if allowed, would suggest that the Ministry of Defence had failed in its duty of care to Miss Winterbourne during part of her active service, an allegation it strongly refutes.'

She plonked herself down, and Kieran immediately bobbed up.

'My Lord, my client has admitted her crimes and stands by her plea of Guilty. My Learned Friend's only motive for contesting Basis of Plea is to avoid future claims against the MoD by my client. Protection against possible future litigation cannot be valid grounds for—'

A furious-looking Markham jumped up, 'My Lord, if my Learned Friend is sugg—'

'Enough!' said an irritated Judge Victor Mumbles, QC, holding out a palm to each of the pair and then beckoning them forward, 'Counsels will approach the Bench.'

A good start, I thought.

3/5

The Officer

I watched the two lawyers arguing their points *sotto voce* amid much head-shaking and gesticulating. At the same time, Judge Victor Mumbles, QC, looked from one to the other with what looked like an avuncular indulgence. He finally shut the squabble down with a gesture, gave his ruling, and sent them back to their respective places. I hadn't heard a word of the exchange, but the self-satisfied smirk on the woman's face, and Kieran's grimace as he glanced up at me, gave me scant confidence.

Once both had taken their seats, Judge Victor Mumbles, QC, beamed his rheumy eyes around the court before they finally came to rest on me.

'Now, Ms Winterbourne, the remainder of these proceedings will take the form of a Newton hearing. Your counsel will call witnesses who may then be cross-examined by the counsel for the prosecution. You must understand this is not a trial, though it may at times feel like one, merely a hearing to petition the court for a more lenient sentence. The final decision is mine, and mine alone, and though it might not be the result you may have wished for, my conclusion will be fair and unbiased. Do you understand?'

I nodded. 'Y-yes,' and gave the judge my sweetest little-girl smile.

He lowered his gaze to Kieran.

'Mr O'Sullivan, are all your witnesses present?'

Kieran bobbed up, 'They are, My Lord.'

'Ms Markham?'

'We are ready to proceed, My Lord.'

'Very well, let us get started. Mr O'Sullivan?'

'I call Megan Redfern.'

My former DO entered and walked smartly to the witness box, sat down and removed her cap and placed it tidily in her lap.

The clerk swore her in, and Kieran took the floor.

'Good morning Lieutenant, would you please start by confirming your name, and telling the Court your role concerning my client, Rosemary Winterbourne while she served aboard HMS *Windsor Castle*.'

'My name is Megan Redfern, Lieutenant, Royal Navy. I was Leading Seaman Winterbourne's Divisional Officer, responsible for all aspects of her welfare and conduct, the maintenance of her Service Record, and, in consultation with her line manager, oversight of her work performance.'

'And how long were you Ms Winterbourne's Divisional Officer?'

'From when she first joined the ship in January 2010 until she left us in October 2012 in Gibraltar.'

'So you knew Ms Winterbourne for almost two years. And would I be right in assuming you had a unique knowledge of both her career development and personal circumstances?'

'Yes.'

'And how would you summarise *Leading Seaman* Winterbourne's professional conduct during the period you first became acquainted until the summer of last year?'

'I would say she was exemplary, as she had been, according to her Service Record, on her two previous ships. She showed herself a skilled and dedicated seaman, often outperforming many of her male colleagues, and setting a fine example to junior members of her Part-of-Ship.'

Jesus, she was laying it on a bit thick.

'And I understand she was due for promotion, is that right?'

Redfern nodded. 'Yes. She was recommended for Petty Officer early in 2012. Unfortunately, the ship was too operationally committed at the time to release her. Still, she eventually sat her PO's Board in August. She passed with better than average points, which was surprising, considering what she'd recently been through.' She glanced up at me for the first time, wearing a worried frown.

'I assume you mean the events of the seventeenth of June. Would you please tell the court what happened?'

'Yes, of course. At around half-past midnight on Sunday morning when I received a phone call at home from the Duty Officer on-board. He told me there had been a road traffic accident involving

- 229 -

Leading Seaman Winterbourne's parents. No details were available, except that they had been taken to a hospital near Cobbingden. Winterbourne herself had been on duty over the weekend, so she was on-board. The Duty Officer told me he had informed her of the accident and released her from duty, whereupon she had driven straight to the hospital.'

Redfern cleared her throat before continuing. I felt her pain in telling the tale, and my own eyes began to fill as I relived that dreadful night.

'The Duty Officer called me at home to brief me on events. The following morning, I received a call from Leading Seaman Winterbourne. She told me her mother had died and her father was in the ICU, apparently in a coma.'

She paused and took a shaky breath before continuing, and I took the opportunity to blow my nose.

'I granted her compassionate leave for two weeks and told her to call if she needed longer.'

Kieran looked over at me, then up at the bench.

'We'll take a fifteen-minute recess,' rumbled Judge Victor Mumbles, QC.

'Kind of brought it all home to me,' Georgie said, as we met in the corridor outside the Courtroom, 'what you went through that night.'

I was desperate for a smoke, but there wasn't time to get through Security and back again.

'Where's Kieran,' she said, casting around at the milling groups outside the other courtrooms. The other witnesses were sitting together on a bench down the corridor, Redfern now with them. My brief had warned me to stay away from them until afterwards. No problem there – a friendly chat with my old DO and my ex-Shrink was the last thing I needed right now. I looked up and down the corridor for Range Rover Man but couldn't see him. For a stalker, he was quite elusive.

'The judge called them both to his chambers,' I said. 'Chummy drinks and a chat, I expect.'

Georgie laughed. 'You watch too many courtroom dramas, Sweetie. Mind you, that lady on the other side could be straight out of *The Good Wife*. No, it'll be some technical issue, maybe the old duffer wants to speed things up. That lieutenant of yours was a pretty good character witness. Made me wonder why they didn't try harder to keep you in.'

I gave her a sour grin, 'I expect you're about to find out.'

'Now, Lieutenant,' Kieran began after we'd resumed our places, 'how did Ms Winterbourne's performance and attitude hold up after this tragic accident?'

'Well, to be frank, it didn't. Rosie came back from leave only a few days after her mother's funeral. I urged her to go home and stay away for at least another week.'

'Oh? Why was that?'

'I thought her unusually cold and distant, uncommunicative. I'd always found her a gregarious and cheerful rating. Now she seemed sullen, like a different person. I knew she wasn't ready to come back. I felt she needed more time to get herself together, so to speak.'

'You told her you thought she wasn't ready to come back?'

'I did. But Rosie wouldn't hear of it, insisted she would be better off among her friends on-board. Under the circumstances, it would have been inappropriate to order her ashore. I did, however, review her case with the Captain and the ship's Chaplain. We concluded it would be best she returned to her duties, her friends and colleagues, and relative normality, and where we could keep a close eye on her.'

'And during those first few days after her return, did anyone else in authority talk to her concerning her bereavement and personal circumstances?'

'Yes, I understand the Chaplain spoke to her, although of course, any conversation between them would have been in strict confidence.'

'Yes, of course. Now, Lieutenant, was Ms Winterbourne at any point in the days following her return, offered bereavement counselling?'

'Objection, My Lord,' said Markham, jumping to her feet, 'witness has already explained she could not know what advice the Chaplain had offered.'

Before the Judge could intervene, Kieran said, 'Very well, I'll rephrase the question. Lieutenant, to the best of your knowledge, was Ms Winterbourne at any point in the days following her return, offered bereavement counselling?'

'To the best of my knowledge, no.'

'And as her Divisional Officer, and I quote from your own testimony, "responsible for all aspects of her welfare", would it have been within your terms

of reference to seek bereavement counselling for
Leading Seaman Winterbourne?'

'Well, yes, of course. But it's a matter of
judgement. Everyone reacts differently to a family
bereavement, and some ratings see it as interference
in their private affairs.'

'And in your judgement at the time, an offer of
counselling was not justified in my client's case?'

'At the time, no. With the benefit of hindsight?
Well, it was probably the wrong call.'

She glanced up at me again, looking a little
beleaguered, I thought. I was beginning to feel sorry
for her and wished Kieran would back off a little.
She'd done her best for me, after all.

'Probably the wrong call,' echoed Kieran,
unnecessarily. 'Let us now turn to—'

Markham was on her feet again. 'My Lord, I object
to counsel's tone. His witness has provided open and
frank testimony on behalf of the Plaintiff, and, I
would remind the court, is not the guilty party here
and should not be badgered in this way.'

'I agree,' growled Judge Victor Mumbles, QC, 'Mr
O'Sullivan, turn down the rhetoric. This session is a
mitigation hearing, not a jury trial.'

'Very well, My Lord,' said Kieran, his holiday tan
turning puce. 'Lieutenant Redfern, let us now turn to
the period late June to early October 2012. I
understand the ship remained in Portsmouth during
that time?'

'There were five days at sea, twenty-fifth to
thirtieth of June, in support of ships on Operational
Workup. But after that, yes, we were in DED,

preparing for a deployment to the Eastern Mediterranean in the Autumn.'

'DED?'

'Sorry. Docking and Essential Defects. We spent a week in dry dock in late July, then returned to Northwest Wall until early October, when we sailed for the Med.'

'And the five days at sea, what was the ship doing during that week?'

'It was pretty intensive. Three warships and a Fleet Auxiliary were working up in the Western Approaches in preparation for a Deployment to the Middle East. We were part of a five-ship Task Group in support of their training.'

'Thank you. Now, I realise much of your work is classified, but can you give the Court an idea of what kind of operations took place?'

'Broadly speaking, yes. There were Anti-aircraft and anti-submarine operations, replenishments at sea, refuelling at sea, helicopter transfers, naval gunfire support and support of amphibious operations.'

'And what duties would the then Leading Seaman Winterbourne be expected to perform during these operations?'

'Mainly seamanship and replenishment evolutions, coxswain of the seaboat when required, as well as watch on deck duties throughout night watches. Her main day duty was Leading Hand of the Forecastle Part of Ship where she supervised maintenance, anchoring and berthing operations.'

'Quite a full and varied list of roles. And how well did my client perform during that week, would you say?'

'Generally, Rosie performed her duties adequately. But I have to say, there were one or two problems, several adverse reports that gave me some concern. Rosie's attitude to superiors was frequently described as surly and uncooperative, bordering at times on insubordination.'

'And what action, if any, was taken to correct this lapse in Ms Winterbourne's good conduct?'

'Allowances were made. Rosie was given a warning.'

'Allowances were made, presumably because she'd only buried her mother the previous week, and her father lay in a hospital in a —'

'Objection!' cried Markham, on her feet and furious, 'Counsel is once again attempting to badger the witness into implied criticism of her employers.'

'Overruled,' rumbled Judge Victor Mumbles, QC, 'I find the question pertinent. The witness will answer it. And I remind you, Ms Markham, there is no jury here. I am quite capable of reaching my judicial conclusions without your assistance.'

The beauteous barrister blushed prettily, nodded and sat down.

'Well, Lieutenant?' said Kieran.

'Yes.'

'And just one final question: in the three months following that week at sea, was there any marked improvement in Ms Winterbourne's performance and behaviour?'

'Well, yes, and no. Rosie worked hard at her PO's Board, and as I pointed out earlier, passed with unusually high points. But I'm afraid that wasn't reflected in her work on-board subsequently. She became sloppy and careless, argumentative with superiors, and seemed to lose her motivation for advancement. I was deeply disappointed, especially since she was earmarked for Officer Selection, and reprimanded her several times.'

'So she worked hard for her promotion, excelled with flying colours, even expressed a wish to become an officer, then, inexplicably, seemed to just, what, lose interest?'

'To be frank, she seemed more interested in working on her father's boat and spent all her free weekends there. When her Form B13 (that is, her promotion to PO) arrived in September, the Captain declined to endorse it on several recommendations. He ordered it returned: Not Approved.'

'Thank you, Lieutenant. No further questions, but please remain seated.'

'Ms Markham?' rumbled Judge Victor Mumbles, QC, 'do you wish to redirect?'

'Yes, My Lord, just a couple of questions.' She smiled sweetly at Redfern. 'Lieutenant, how long have you been carrying out the duties of Divisional Officer?'

'Oh, about Six and a half years now, on *Windsor Castle* and two previous ships.'

'Presumably, you had both men and women in your division?'

'Yes. The navy treats men and women equally.'

'And during your time as a Divisional Officer, roughly speaking, how many of your junior ratings have suffered a family bereavement, would you say?'

Her head jigged minutely from side to side, and she did a mental recount.

'Around eight, I would say, maybe more.'

'Around eight. And of those eight ratings, how many would you say had their naval careers blighted in the way you've just described?'

'Well, none that I can recall. Most go through a rough patch for a day or two, sometimes a week or two, but then bounce right back into normal shipboard life.'

Kieran, at his table below me, stared down at his notes, shaking his head as he listened to the beauteous barrister win back his hard-fought points.

'So, in general, ratings suffering bereavement are not offered counselling; indeed, don't need it.'

'I would go further and say that many would actively resent it.'

Markham glanced across at my brief, the gleam of victory in her eyes.

'Thank you, Lieutenant. You may leave the court.'

So, first I was the bee's knees – then in the next breath, I was a sulky insubordinate who couldn't take orders. And now a sad spineless wimp, to boot.

I hope this is worth it, Kieran.

Redfern didn't look up as she walked stiffly out of court, her face shielded from me by the peak of her cap.

3/6

The Professor

'Thank you for coming, Professor Hardy,' said Kieran, 'please introduce yourself to the court?'

My old shrink looked characteristically calm and relaxed; open-necked shirt, tweed jacket unbuttoned. I'd been terrified at my first consultation with the Prof, but in later sessions had begun to find him quite pleasant, and even entertaining.

'My name is John Hardy, and I'm the Senior Clinical Neurologist at The Royal Centre for Defence Medicine in Birmingham. I work primarily with service personnel psychologically affected by exposure to battlefield-trauma. We assess their capacity for continued active service, and, where necessary, triage them for the most appropriate treatment to aid their recovery.'

A withering look from Judge Victor Mumbles, QC quickly silenced the curious flutter among the press.

I conjured up tonight's headlines:

MENTAL MARITIME MAID
MASTERMINDS
DOCKYARD HEIST

Okay, maybe not that lurid, but still.

'Thank you, Professor. Now, my client, then Leading Seaman Rosemary Winterbourne, was referred to you in October 2012, is that correct?'

'Yes, it is. The eleventh of October, to be precise.'

'And could you outline for us the circumstances of that referral?'

'Ahem. While serving on-board her ship in Gibraltar, the patient, Rosie Winterbourne, suffered a psychotic seizure which presented with an unusual form of narcolepsy. This prompted the ship's Medical Officer to set up a conference call with staff at RCDM. During this online meeting, the Centre's Clinical Director summoned me to advise on the case because of my specialist knowledge on sleep disorders.'

Judge Victor Mumbles, QC, harrumphed and leaned over towards the witness box. 'Assuming that narcolepsy is not a common occurrence in the Royal Navy, Professor, can you elaborate on what you mean by "unusual"?'

'Certainly, My Lord. The subject suffered a hallucinatory seizure while on evening shore leave from her ship. On waking, she underwent severe and prolonged cataplexy. Put simply, she suffered vivid sensory delusions, went to sleep, and woke up paralysed, a condition which persisted for some three hours.'

Judge Victor Mumbles, QC, turned his rheumy eyes on me, 'How dreadful!'

I absorbed his gruff sympathy with a chin-wobble.

'So,' Kieran said, 'there was a video conference to decide what to do. What was the conclusion?'

'First indications suggested a straightforward case of narcolepsy with associative hallucinations and sleep paralysis. I suspected a neurological cause and recommended the patient's immediate evacuation to RCDM for investigation.'

'You used the word "straightforward" just now. Am I to take it this is a common disorder?'

'The condition affects about one in two-thousand of the general population at some time in their lives and can be a chronic recurring disorder in a small minority of cases. As this case had presented several times in the recent past, the latter was a distinct possibility.'

'You say this had happened before, Professor. Why was it only after this last event that anyone took action?'

'A good question, and an internal matter for the ship concerned. Rosie was resourceful in concealing her condition.'

'But your subsequent sessions with my client did reveal to you the history of her illness, is that correct?'

'Yes.'

'And would you be willing to share your discoveries and clinical analysis with the court? And you can take it as read that my client has given her consent.'

'With Rosie's consent, I would.'

Kieran glanced up at the Bench.

'Ms Winterbourne,' boomed Judge Victor Mumbles, QC, 'has your counsel discussed this with you?'

I nodded, 'Yes, Sir.'

'Nevertheless, we'll have privacy for the remainder of this witness's testimony. Clear the public gallery!'

The disgruntled paparazzi filed out, leaving a defiant Georgie sitting there alone. Oddly, nobody challenged her.

'Mr O'Sullivan, you may proceed.'

'Thank you, My Lord. Professor Hardy, how long was my client under your care?'

'About three weeks, during which we had once-, sometimes twice-daily sessions.'

'And could you, in lay terms, describe what occurred during these sessions?'

'Several different approaches were used. First, there was Polysomnographic Testing, a method for analysing sleep patterns – the patient is allowed to fall into normal sleep. We record brain waves, blood oxygen levels, heart rate and breathing, as well as eye and leg movements. Then there was Hypocretin Testing, where we test for Orexin levels. Reduced or absent levels of Orexin is an important indicator of narcolepsy and the inability to sleep effectively. Normal levels are 200 picograms per millilitre or higher. Rosie's levels were below 50. Aside from that, there were psychoanalysis interviews by myself and selected members of my staff. And, of course, I used clinical hypnosis on several occasions to verify certain of Rosie's recollections and deeper thought processes.'

'You hypnotised her, Professor?'

'I did, and to beneficial effect. By allowing Rosie to express her anger for her father's role in the death of her mother, we were able to help her overcome her guilt over her abusive treatment of him since the accident. This was a factor in her clinical depression. Hypnoanalysis also gave us better insight into the nature of her narcoleptic episodes.'

'And what did you finally conclude about her condition, Professor?'

'My conclusion is that Rosie suffers from a form Post Traumatic Stress brought about by a sense of sudden and devastating loss and suppressed grief. This is further complicated by a pre-existing psychosis. The physiological cause of this underlying condition is a chemical imbalance occurring during moments of extreme emotional reaction to external events. Put simply; she has an allergy to some naturally produced hormones such as serotonin and endorphins combined with low orexin levels.

'The effects of the condition can be quite terrifying. When something triggers in Rosie a strong emotional reaction, she enters a hypnagogic hallucinatory state, where bizarre and improbable images manifest as real. At the same time, she suffers catastrophic cataplexy, an almost total loss of muscle control. Sleep soon follows, during which vivid dreams often continue. On waking, she invariably remains in cataplexy, which can last minutes or even hours.'

'My research assistant managed to unearth Rosie's early medical records when she was under the care of a Doctor Charles Lambert of Guildford, now long retired. Lambert noted several similar episodes in her early childhood when the condition was less well understood. The seizures seem to have ceased after the age of seven, however.

'What does seem to have persisted from childhood, is an unusually precocious memory – noted with a degree of scepticism by Lambert at the time. The condition is consistent with this exotic form of the illness. The inability to forget, a syndrome called hyperthymesia, is linked to sleep disorders. The hippocampus - the structure of the brain that deals with memory and learning - requires a particular mode of sleep we call Slow Wave Sleep. We believe this organises temporal experience into long- and short-term memories. Narcoleptics like Rosie do not enter this mode of sleep. Chronologically separated events stay as fresh as the moment they happened.' He looked up at me and smiled. 'For example, if I were to ask Rosie what day of the week was, say, the 14th of May 1992, she would tell me without thinking—'

'Thursday,' I mouthed silently back at him.

'— and could go on to tell me everything she experienced on that day.'

'Extraordinary!' declared Judge Victor Mumbles QC, surveying me over his spectacles.

What is puzzling, however,' continued the Prof, 'is that Rosie presents few of the symptoms usually associated with this disorder, such as persistent tiredness. And her sleep events are not strictly spontaneous as in most cases – rather they are triggered by external events. And this is perhaps why she was able to conceal it from, well, virtually everyone.'

'Thank you, Professor. Now, aside from those early manifestations as a child, when did her condition first reappear in the adult?' Kieran glanced at the beauteous barrister who'd jumped up to intervene, and quickly added, 'As far as you could ascertain, that is.'

She sat down again, disappointed.

'As far as I could ascertain, the first event coincided with the appearance at her father's hospital bedside of someone who closely resembled her recently deceased mother. And this brings me to the most bizarre element of Rosie's illness. She had on occasions what we might call, an imaginary friend, in this case, an Aunt who closely resembled her mother.'

'No!' I said, standing up. I stared at Georgina, sitting there large as life in the otherwise empty public gallery. She smiled and gave a little wave. 'No!' I screamed again, pointing at my aunt. 'She's there look! She's sitting right there. *Are you all blind?*'

Judge Victor Mumbles, QC, banged his gavel and said, 'The offender will SIT DOWN!'

I remained rigid, unable to comply if I'd wanted to. The Professor was looking stunned at my outburst. Kieran, the beauteous barrister, the court officials all stared on in total shock.

But something very odd was going on with Judge Victor Mumbles, QC. His facial features were growing outwards, and what had been mild liver spots on his cheeks were expanding into dark patches, dappling his face brown and white even at it changed shape. My hand flew to my mouth as an ominous, but familiar shadow rose inside me. I was fixated on the judge's strangely elongating face that was looking increasingly canine, his jowls drooping like melting wax. In slow motion, he raised his gavel and struck it down with reverberating thunder. I felt my legs giving way, and then things got properly unreal.

A leering bloodhound was bounding over the bench towards me, silvery strings of saliva streaming from his flapping jowls. His droopy, watery eyes glistered with evil intent, closer, closer – so close I could smell his doggy breath in my face. The fur on his nose wrinkled as the vast jaws opened and swallowed me up into a toothless, pink maw. I was helpless to stop myself tumbling towards the dark cavern opening before me. I sank into a smooth gullet – I was suddenly blind. I smelled something familiar as my wet cheek slid down a cold, hard surface. What was that smell? I wondered. Suddenly I had it. My last sensation before oblivion was the smell of Johnson's furniture polish.

Paralysis lasted only minutes. The court usher kneeled in to put a cushion under my head. Then Professor Hardy appeared, beaming reassurance into my face then taking charge and calming everyone down.

When I recovered the Prof and Kieran ushered me down into the Jury room, where a cup of strong coffee appeared.

'Sorry about that, Rosie,' said the Prof. 'But I thought we'd dealt with Aunt Georgina before you left my care – I had no idea she was back on the scene.' He looked accusingly across the table at Kieran.

'Okay,' said Kieran, 'It was my idea to bring that up, but the Judge had to see the whole picture to get onside.'

'What are you both talking about? She was there,' I said, not understanding anything. 'You must have seen her.'

'There was nobody in the gallery, Rosie,' the Prof said gently. 'We've been through this many times, haven't we. Aunt Georgina is in your mind, Rosie. Your mother never had a sister – we agreed that, remember?'

I let out a big sigh – I was going to have to suck it up again. 'Okay, sorry. You're right, of course. When do we start again, Kieran?'

My brief looked taken aback by what he supposed was my sudden U-turn. The Prof just looked suspicious.

Kieran said, 'Finish your coffee, Rosie, and I'll tell the Judge we're ready to reconvene.'

3/7

Don't Worry...

Two hours later, I walked downstairs to the big hall with Professor John Hardy, a grin on my face that was beginning to make my jaws ache. We found a free table to wait for Kieran – John went to get us tea. I looked around at the still crowded hall, feeling elation that my ordeal was over. At the same time, most of these people wore the anxious frowns of uncertainty as they listened to their briefs.

'When I get back to my office,' John Hardy said, setting my tea down, 'I'll email you a list of suitable practitioners in your area.'

I grinned at him. 'Can't I stay with you, Prof?'

He leaned down and spoke quietly, 'I wid take ye on like a shot, Hen, but I've got more'n enough loonies on ma lest.'

I grinned, then noticed he'd only brought one tea. 'Aren't you having one?'

'Got to fly, I'm afraid, needed back at the coalface.' He leaned down and surprised me with a peck on the cheek. 'Glad it went well for you, Rosie.

Now, remember what the judge said – you need to make that appointment as soon as next week, or they'll be coming after you with a Section Five Order.'

He made to leave, then turned back. 'By the way, is Aunt Georgina with you right now?'

I forced a smile. 'Prof, you're such a wag.'

'Jesus!' said Georgie, after he'd gone, 'when the judge said he was giving you three years I nearly had kittens. Was it my imagination, or did he leave it hanging in the air just a little longer than necessary?'

'What, before he said—' I dropped my voice to a growl, '"The sentence shall be suspended for five years with specific conditions. You may go, young lady, and offend no more."'

Georgie guffawed and said, 'Sounds more like Winston Churchill, don't give up your day job, Sweetie.'

Kieran joined us, all brisk and business-like.

'Right,' he said, 'I've got three pieces of good news. First up, the Prosecution has agreed to waive costs. Second, the MoD isn't interested in claiming damages because the sums involved aren't sufficient to cover the paperwork. So, there's nothing to pay.'

'Except for your fee.' I said.

'Except for my fee,' he agreed with a wry grin. 'Our bill will go to Lester Granville for payment, so there'll be no rush to settle. Lester's quite laid back with money.'

'And the third thing?' I asked.

He slid a brown envelope across the table, 'Your passport and the Order of Release for your boat, you can go over and sail her away anytime you like. But don't go far, Rosie – you still have conditions on your suspension remember. You need to let the court know next week who you're seeing, okay?'

I nodded meekly.

My first sight of *Pasha* made me feel physically sick. The MoD might have dropped their damages claim, but they'd certainly made sure I wouldn't benefit from my crime.

Gloomily, I surveyed the disorder of equipment piled on the greasy concrete, noticing first the missing wire rigging, then the QRC anchor without its chain. I had no doubt there would be no batteries in the boat either, so taking her away today would be out of the question.

'At least they didn't scrape off the antifoul,' Georgie observed dryly.

'I wouldn't've put it past them,' I said, 'vindictive bastards!'

Georgie touched her shoe against the un-stepped mast, 'and at least you've got the chance to change the bulb in the anchor-light.'

We locked eyes for a second; then both spluttered into hysterical giggling.

'Something funny, my dear?'

We turned and straightened our faces, or at least I did, Georgie's attempt was still in progress. It was the Yard Superintendent who'd let us in; a short, square man, blue work-coat and wellies.

'Private joke,' said Georgie.

'When yer moving her out? I need this space.'

'You haven't exactly made it easy for us,' said Georgie, nodding at the chaotic jumble.

When he ignored her, I added, 'Ever heard of Duty of Care?'

'Nothing to do with me, love, blame the filth. You've got till Wednesday to get her out of here, after that, it's an 'undred quid a day.'

With that, he turned and stumped off.

I bought a recondition battery at a garage to crank the engine. The yard crew lifted her in for us on Monday morning with the mast and boom lashed down along the coach-roof. We stuffed all the other gear into the two lazarettes. We motored down the creek to the nearby commercial marina and boatyard.

'Now what?' I said after we'd tied up at a finger-pontoon.

'What a silly question!' said Georgie. 'Now, we talk to the boatyard and see what deal we can do to get the old girl back on her feet inside a week. Then you can sail away before they drag you off to the funny farm.'

She studied my face a moment, then smiled and patted my cheek.

'As de man said, don't worry, 'bout a ting, cos every little ting's going to be alright.'

EPISODE FOUR

The Big Adventure

4/1

Under Pressure

Wednesday 6th March 2013
0105 48 55.4N 009 27.3W Course 185 Speed 6.5 kts
Wind: North Speed 22 Px: 1026mb (rising)
Main (1 Reef) + Full Genoa
Sailing on Windvane

I awoke to a shift in the familiar sounds and motions of my universe. I lay for a moment listening to the rattle of loose blocks; the rumple of lazy sails, the sucking of water on a stationary hull, and realised *Pasha* had become unfettered. A racehorse without her rider. With an effort of will, I unzipped and rolled out, shivering in my undies, and crossed the saloon to the chart table. The barometer read 1029: a rise of three millibars in two hours. *Fuck!*

Feeling as sluggish as the weather, I donned salopette, seaboots, and foul-weather jacket. Climbing the ladder to the cockpit, I blinked to clear my bleary eyes. The wind had dropped to a gnat's fart; I looked out on an ocean of gently rolling mercury – a monochrome masterpiece with rippling smears of silver. *Pasha's* masthead was tracing circles around a cradle moon set in a frozen sky.

Cursing the unseasonable high pressure, I fired up the engine, and furled-in the genoa. With twenty-seven horses grumbling us southwards, I sat in a chilled stupor, too furious and numbed by inertia to drag myself back below to my warm cocoon.

The sixty vigilant hours transiting the Channel had left me mentally exhausted. Rather than joining the convoy of shipping crossing the Bay of Biscay, I'd stood on out into the Atlantic to find empty seas where I could sleep in relative safety. There was always a risk, of course, because nowhere is entirely traffic-free. But now I had a little helper. I had invested some of Mum's money in an AIS system. This piece of wizardry displayed shipping on the chartplotter and gave warning of potential collisions. Yeah okay, just call me Gadget-Girl.

I gazed eastwards where a faint luminosity sharpened the horizon – a harbinger of approaching dawn. In a frozen moment, I saw my aunt: wrapped in Mum's old winter overcoat, waving from the jetty as I motored *Pasha* out of the Gosport marina. I had just managed to avoid getting hauled away for missing my appointment with the new shrink in Guildford.

With a resigned sigh, I scanned the cobalt horizon once more, then took myself back to bed, hoping for the returning wind. If this high-pressure system – unusual for March – stayed with us, we could be chugging along like this for days and would need to call in somewhere in Portugal for fuel. Not that I was in any hurry – it was too late in the year to attempt a crossing now – it was just the noise and stink, not to mention the expense, that pissed me off.

I planned now to sail to Gibraltar, stay a week or so there, then head on down to the Canaries where I would wait for the trade winds in November. Next Christmas in Florida was the revised objective.

The calm continued into the morning. After breakfast, I sat in the cockpit reading. I was already sick of the monotonous grind of the engine, the giggle-gurgle from the exhaust, and the acrid taste of diesel fumes wafted into the cockpit by the slipstream of our windless passage. The sea was a rolling sheet of stippled glass; the calm westerly swell rocked us relentlessly from side to side as we rumbled southwards. The sky remained obstinately clear throughout the morning with no sign of the returning wind.

The change began mid-afternoon, starting with mare-tails of wispy cirrus high in the western sky, slight darkening on the margin of the sea. A front was approaching.

By 1600 a battalion of grey cumulus clouds had risen above the horizon. Despite having wished for it, an approaching front always made me uneasy. As that familiar anxiety now came on, concentration on reading became impossible.

'Time for a cuppa,' I said aloud, getting up from where I'd been lounging lazily since lunch.

'No, Rosemary, time to shorten sail.'

Startled, I froze where I was, half out of my seat, gripping the console. Hearing voices wasn't so unusual, especially when the engine was running. But this voice was no giggle-gurgle illusion, no flight of fancy conjured up by tiredness and prolonged solitude – this was a real voice, close and intimate and strangely familiar. I'd heard it a couple of times before and put it down to a symptom of my depression. But now I wasn't so dismissive.

Was *Pasha* talking to me?

I seized that magical notion, almost willing it to be true. The voice had reminded me of one of Dad's favourite aphorisms: 'If you watch and wait, it'll be too late.'

'Okay—' I said, feeling faintly ridiculous, 'you win, whoever you are.'

I went below to change.

By the time I returned on deck with my harness on a faint breeze had sprung up from the southwest and the clouds had gathered, towering dark and ominous and lumbering our way. Working quickly now, I loosened off the mainsheet and dropped the mainsail down to the second reef. Snapping my harness onto the jackstay, I handed my way gingerly along the rolling deck to the mast.

Hooking on the two reef toggles was straightforward, but back in the cockpit, I struggled with the reefing lines that had become snagged. It took longer than expected because I needed to fold back the bimini frame to reach the tangle of rope at the end of the boom. With increasing urgency, I fought to loosen the fouled lines while clinging to the dangerously swinging boom. Finally, I got both lines hauled taught on the winch and the surplus sail stowed into the lazy-bag. I sagged down onto the banquette. *Fuck it!* I should've been ready for that, instead of sitting on my arse reading.

By the time I had unfurled the genoa to the third reef marker – about one-third of its full size – the wind was up to fifteen knots from the starboard bow, a close reach, and we were making seven knots. I killed the engine, waited for the speed to stabilize, then trimmed the sails. Still fuming at myself I went below to put the kettle on.

An hour later the wind was gusting twenty-five, and we were creaming along at eight knots with the wind vane now in charge of our steering. I was relearning the hard way that preparation is everything and delayed precautions can be fatal. Without Dad there to kick my arse, I had become lazy. I would need to sharpen up before the Big One.

4/2

La Linea

Friday 15th March 2013
1056 36 07.6N 005 33.1W Course 060 Speed 7 kts
Crossing Algeciras Bay to Gibraltar
Wind: Southwest Speed 14 Px: 1015mb

I took one look at Gibraltar's busy Marina Bay and changed my plan. Seeing the boats packed in like sardines and recalling the night-time noise of the place, I decided instead to motor around the corner to La Linea, on the Spanish side of the Frontier. Alcaidesa marina was quieter, roomier, cheaper, and had floating pontoons – a combination that made it a no-brainer.

After my first shower in two weeks, I felt like just falling into my bunk and sleeping for a week. But I had things to do. I took my laptop up to the marina bar, chose a shaded table outside, and ordered a beer from a handsome young barista.

My first email was to Dad's hospital ward, asking for an update and adding a few newsy lines about my trip to be read to him. Next, I composed one to Doc, whom I hadn't seen since the weekend before my ill-fated trip with Gary in February, though we'd kept in touch. (*Windy C.* was back in the Caribbean on a three-month stint as Belize Guardship.) And finally, I squirted a note off to Georgie to tell her of my safe arrival.

'Mind if we join you, bonny lass?'

I looked up, closing the lid of my laptop, and was surprised to see the place had filled up around me. The guy who'd spoken in a Geordie accent was a bearded grey-hair, around fifty; his partner looked a little younger, skinny with an open face and blonde frizz.

'Please do,' I said, slipping the laptop into its sleeve.

'Saw you come in.' the woman said, pulling up a chair as the man went off to get drinks. 'Welcome to Spain. I'm Kate.'

'Hi Kate, I'm Rosie.' We shook hands – she had rings on every finger. 'So where are *you?*'

'Blue-hulled sloop, three berths in from you. You're a single-hander, yeah?' Her accent was pure Estuary – vowels as long as her smile was wide.

'Oh yeah, the Moody,' I said. 'Nice looking boat.'

Kate nodded. 'Bill takes good care of her – more'n he does o me. I'm only his fuckin' missus.' The wicked glint in her eye spoiled the deadpan delivery.

'Tak no notice of her, lass' said Bill, putting down three beers and passing one to me. 'If I didn't look after her, Kate'd be first to complain. Besides, I've got bugger all else to do all day.'

'When did *you* arrive?'

'About seven years ago,' Kate replied.

'We liked it here, so we stayed,' Bill said.

'It's a good life,' Kate confirmed.

'If you don't weaken,' Bill added.

'I work in Gib,' Kate explained. 'The money's good, 'specially if you live over this side. Bill does odd jobs for boats in transit.'

'For me beer money,' Bill explained. 'Kate's the one who keeps us from the breadline.'

I'd intended an early night but found myself recharged by the pair and their hilarious counterpoint. I was still there as the sun dipped behind the Andalusian hills. It was after I'd shared a meal with them that I felt myself wilting and apologised amid stifled yawns. Crawling onto my bunk a little later, I realised I hadn't paid for anything and made a sleepy note to settle with them tomorrow when I'd got myself some Euros.

Surprisingly, I was up at first light, feeling refreshed and alive with no ill-effects from what had been a reasonably boozy night. But after nearly two weeks at sea, my body screamed for exercise, so I quickly donned jogging kit to begin my run before the full heat of the day.

Even from this side of the frontier, the Rock dominated the eastern skyline, blocking out the risen sun whose hidden corona painted the cloudless sky a dull duck-egg grey. Over the lip of the high massif, the *Levante* chucked up whispery streams of moisture that would by mid-morning form a perfect white discus, brooding on the rocky ridge until early evening. For Gibraltarians on the west side, that

Levantine cloud spelt a damp day in the shade. Still, from over here in sunlit Spain, the phenomenon provided a unique and iconic spectacle.

I began with a gentle jog – shaking out my atrophied leg muscles – then speeded up as I left the marina gates. I worked up to a heart-punching sprint to the frontier then slowed through passport control, opening up the pace again across the runway. Relishing the stress pains in my leg muscles and the sustained load on my heart and lungs, I sprinted effortlessly past Victoria Stadium and into Casemates Square. Here, soaking with sweat and huffing like a steam train, I bought a bottle of water and sank on a bench, my UK winter body prematurely sapped by the sultry heat.

Gibraltar was the ideal place to replace the phone that Gary had sent spinning into the English Channel; I got a duty-free bargain on a dual SIM Motorola.

While passing the duty-free tobacco kiosk, an associative craving hit me from the last time I'd bought tobacco here. To fight the demon addiction, I broke into a desperate sprint for the Frontier, slowing only to show my passport. Never to smoke again was only one of a raft of vows I'd taken in my determination for a fresh start and hopefully an end to those ridiculous seizures.

In La Linea I called at an ATM and drew out two-hundred Euros, then found a phone shop where I bought a SIM card with 10 Euros of credit. Somehow, having a phone again seemed a sign that my life was coming back together.

Back on *Pasha*, I toyed with the new phone – in my other hand was a card I'd been fidgeting with nervously. It had been in the back of my purse since the last time I'd been here. In a burst of brio, I thumbed the number into the phone and selected the Spanish SIM, then paused, once again undecided. Would he even remember me? The encounter had been so short-lived, and the circumstances far from pleasant. My finger must have brushed the screen; for suddenly, it was dialling. I heard it ringing out and tried to cancel, but too late:

'Sí, Mateo aquí, quién es este?'

I put the phone to my ear, but couldn't speak – I didn't know what to say.

'Hablame!'

I ended the call and sat fuming at myself. The phone buzzed in my hand, then rang – the same number calling back. Damn!

I swiped to answer.

'Dime, quién es?'

'Hi, Mateo, you probably don't remember me, but my name is Rosie. We met briefly last October. I was—'

'Ah! Rosey! Rosey! Rosey!' he chanted.

'Yes, *that* Rosie,' I said, laughing, hugely relieved.

'Of course, I remember you – I was hope for call but no call. Estaba decepcionado – I— disappointed.'

'I'm sorry. I would have called, but something happened. I had to go home.'

'You have Spanish number, yes?'

'I'm here in La Linea, I just wondered if—'

'Estupendo! You want we meet, Rosie?'

'Sí, Mateo,' I laughed, 'I want we meet.'

4/3

Mateo

Anxiety began to gnaw at my bowels almost as soon as I ended my call with Mateo. Those therapy sessions with Professor Hardy had conditioned me to caution:

'You need to learn to control your body's production of serotonin, Rosie, that means avoid excitement – **any** kind of excitement.'

Since then, I'd been terrified of the emotional high of an orgasm or even the anticipation of it. How would it play tonight with a guy to whom I felt so strongly attracted? But hell, I had to start somewhere, sometime. I wasn't going to live life like some celibate nun. In the meantime, I busied myself with my laundry, stowing the mainsail, hosing down the decks and rigging, and cleaning up below.

We'd agreed to meet at seven at a small café on Calle Caboneros in the centre of town. I got a little lost and found him sitting alone at an outside table under a large parasol, spooning sugar into his espresso. He wore coral-pink chinos, white canvas shoes, white shirt and cream linen jacket. He looked good enough to eat. And that mop of curly, jet-black hair – phew!

'Hi Mateo,' I said breathlessly, 'sorry I'm late.'

He looked up, a momentary hesitation, then a broad smile and a flash in his deep-brown eyes that took me back to our all-too-brief encounter almost six months ago.

'Rosie,' he said, standing up. 'It is so good to see you.'

He was taller than I recalled – a good six-foot-two, I thought. I got a scent of sharp, musky shower gel as he bent to give me an Andalusian greeting. I responded awkwardly and then worried he might think I'd been going for an early lip-lock.

He stood back, grinning, and gave me the briefest of up-and-down inspections. Last time he'd seen me I was in shorts and string sandals. Tonight, it was a light blue cotton dress, high-heeled shoes with ankle-straps, and a little more makeup than just the usual press of lippy. I'd even put on my dangly earrings and matching necklace which I hadn't worn in years.

'You look— nice,' Mateo said, flustered. And then – as if realising his English might not adequately express his admiration – added, *'Muy hermosa!'*

Which was just as well – dressing girly isn't easy on a boat, and this was my only outfit. My chivalrous date peeled his eyes off me and pulled out a chair, 'Please, Rosie, you sit. You grow your hair?'

'Yes,' I said, taking the seat and hooking my bag over the chair back, 'I left the navy – now I can wear it how I like.'

'It suits you longer. What can I get you for drink?'

'Er— *gracias, vino tinto, por favor*.' It was about time I at least *tried* to speak his language.

We spent the next hour chatting, me doing most of it, him asking the questions: how come I left the navy? Which I managed to hedge around; what I was doing now? Which gave me the opportunity to steer the topic to *Pasha* and my plans to cross the Atlantic. It was apparent he wasn't a sailor and had little idea of what that meant, but seemed genuinely interested. I began to relax. Whether, under his charm, or the wine, or both, I found myself opening up about my recent past. My deeds and misfortunes seemed to astonish him, and while he empathised in all the right places, I began to realise we had little of substance in common. Mateo seemed charming and considerate, but our relationship was likely to be more brief than beautiful.

With the café getting ready to close and darkness settling over the town, we moved up the street to a charming little taverna where Mateo seemed to know all the waiters. We ordered more wine and talked. A waiter brought a basket of bread, and before long small plates of tapas began to arrive at our table, unordered but very welcome. Each time a dish was emptied, a waiter came to replace it with a different delicacy.

'So, Mateo,' I said in a pause in the conversation, 'you know all about me, and I know nothing about you. Tell me, are you a secret agent?'

His smouldering features grew puzzled. 'What is Secret Agent?'

I was devastated! My attempt at an amusing opening gambit lay in ruins at the gates of translation. I shook my head and laughed, then, seeing his annoyed reaction, reached across and put my hand on his.

'Forgive me, Mateo, what I meant to say is: what do you do for work?'

To my relief, his frown gave way to a grin, 'Ah, Sí. agente secreto like James Bond.' He turned my hand over and held it lightly in his long, sensitive fingers, smiling into my soul with those gorgeous eyes. 'You are funny girl, Rosie. I like you.'

'And I like you, Mateo. *Me gustas mucha.*'

He chuckled, then sat up straight as I gently extricated my hand; the moment gone, for now.

'So,' he said, 'I am *cirujano veterinaria*, in English, I think you say, veterinary surgeon.'

I stared at him, then rolled my eyes, laughing.

'Is funny?'

'I thought that's where you lived. It's on your card, *Cirujano Veterinaria*. I assumed it was a street name.'

'You think it—?' He spluttered, and we laughed together.

More wine came, and yet more tapas. It seemed like we'd been eating and drinking forever. The place was thinning out – it was well after midnight.

'Is your clinic here in the town?' I asked him.

'No, I have no clinic,' he said but didn't elaborate.

'So— you make house calls?' It was like pulling teeth.

He smiled, reached over and took my hand. I didn't resist when his fingers stroked my palm. A queasy warmth spread into my deepest regions, a sensation I hadn't felt in a long time.

'In the morning I show you where I work,' he said, cryptically, 'you will like it very much, I am sure.'

I froze. Was Mateo suggesting spending the night together?

'Mateo, there's something I—'

He hushed me with a finger to my lips, and then he cupped the side of my face, his hand so warm and gentle I might even have leaned into it a little.

'I will walk with you to the marina, and then I will go home. I will come for you at 9-o-clock in the morning in my car, and we will go to my work.'

4/4

Caballos Pasa Fino

Waking bright and early again the next morning, I stretched luxuriously on my freshly-laundered bedsheet and thought about Mateo. We hadn't spoken much on the walk back to the marina. We just strolled along the empty, tree-lined streets in companionable silence, apart from the occasional inane comment from me about how quiet it was and how clean the roads were.

  I had wondered what was in store for me this morning but hadn't pressed him further on the matter, content to let him surprise me. Despite my doubts about the guy, I was quite excited and saw no problem in having my long-overdue fling, however brief. At the security gate he'd predictably done that three-cheek kiss again, but then unpredictably planted a fourth one smack on the lips. I'm sure it was supposed to have been a chaste peck, but the wine took charge, and I turned it into a full-blown snog. Embarrassing, what was I thinking? I walked back to the boat, feeling like a silly teenager. Still, he hadn't seemed to mind.

As instructed, I pulled on a pair of jeans, socks and trainers. I supposed we would be headed out to the country. Maybe he was a farm vet. With no specifics as to the top, I donned a sports bra and t-shirt, and packed shorts and flip-flops, spare underwear and a lightweight fleece pullover into my backpack – he'd told me I might need something warm.

I'd been expecting him to be driving a sporty number and was surprised when he pitched up at the marina in a big Nissan 4x4.

'Buena Dias,' I chirped, climbing in and throwing my bag over onto the back seat.

'Bueno Dias, Rosie,' he replied with his usual bright grin. '*Cómo estás?'*

'Good, thanks. Looking forward to my mysterious day out.'

He looked out at the clear blue sky, '*El día es perfecto para eso.* You understand?'

'The day he is perfect for it?'

'Sí, the day he is perfect for it,' he grinned. '*Muy Bueno!'*

We drove northwest along the city's coastal road, making fast progress as this was Sunday and the streets were relatively clear of traffic. Reaching the end of the conurbation, we crossed an intersection. Electricity pylons now ran alongside on which white storks had built their nests. There were hundreds of them, watching us haughtily as, mile after mile, we passed beneath their roosts. Leaving the colony behind we began to climb, heading north up to the small hillside town of San Roque.

Skirting the town, Mateo took a narrow winding lane that led up into the higher hills beyond. The scenery became rugged and rocky. Solitary cows and herds of goats grazed among the scrubby bushes and stunted trees – deep *arroyos* wound their haphazard way through gullies and troughs in the hillsides.

'You work up here?' I asked him.

He turned and grinned but said nothing.

We continued our winding climb for another half hour or so, Mateo shifting expertly up and down the gears, slowing for hairpin bends. Switchbacks opened spectacular views onto the glistening blue waters of Algeciras Bay, the Rock of Gibraltar, and the hazy Moroccan mountains across the Strait. Between labouring climbs, we powered along the straight and level sections to gain momentum for the next one. The road flattened out, and we cruised on the high plateau for several kilometres before descending once more. Another series of tight switchbacks led down into a wooded valley where the vegetation turned lush and overhanging boughs obscured the sky above. After another couple of kilometres or so, we slowed, then turned left onto a sandy track that led arrow-straight up to a white-painted wooden archway with a three-bar gate. Big golden letters emblazoned above the entrance named the place:

PREMAGNIFICO
granja de caballos andaluces

I turned to Mateo and laughed. 'Horses? Of course! You're a horse-doctor?'

'Not just horses,' he said, opening his door, 'the World's greatest horses, *Pura Raza Espanola* – Andalusian Pure Breds.'

He stepped down, walked to the side of the gate, and pressed a button on an intercom box. A voice squawked, and Mateo bent to speak into it. The gate swung slowly open behind him as he walked back to the truck.

Beyond the gate, the track continued straight, lined by small cultivated trees. Mateo pointed out orange, lime, lemon, and avocado as we passed them – behind which ran a white-painted wooden fence. I began to glimpse horses and more fenced-off paddocks and more horses. And then horses were everywhere, as far as the eye could see it was wall to wall horses.

And what colours! Dark chestnut horses, pure white and pure black, piebald and skewbald, and splendid greys with bright silver whorls. Some stood alone with heads held high and proud. Others galloped playfully, their movements lithe and graceful. One or two pranced about in that showy high-step they do in dressage, while others stood in pairs with heads close, seemingly in conversation.

I'd never been what you'd call a horsey girl. Still, even I could tell these were extraordinary creatures, tall and rangy, rippling with muscle, and beautifully groomed.

'Wow!' I said. 'And you're the vet for all these animals?'

He laughed. 'We have more than three-hundred horses here – for one person would be impossible.

There are six in my team – is full-time work. Even today, Sunday, there are two veterinarios on duty.'

'Not you though?'

'No, not me.' He turned to me and smiled. 'Today I am yours.'

The track suddenly opened out into a cobblestone courtyard, fronted on one side by a big old house: broad steps tapering up to a marble-columned portico. Two other sides of the square led off to row upon row of stables, some with horses looking out over the half-doors. A dozen or so stable-hands milled about at their work; several looked up and waved as we entered the courtyard. Mateo drove up to the house and parked.

'What happens now?' I asked.

He grinned at me. 'You did not guess?'

'Let's just say I'm reigning in my curiosity.' I wasn't surprised he didn't get it.

I didn't have a clue why I was here, but willing to go along with whatever he had in mind. Well, almost.

'Now, we get out and walk,' he said. 'And bring your bag.'

He took his backpack from the back of the truck and led the way past one of the stable blocks; the stink of horse shit, faintly with us up the drive, now became overpowering.

Mateo said, 'In half an hour you will not notice it.'

At the end of the block stood a lofty barn with a small paddock alongside it. I followed Mateo inside, then stopped and stared, suddenly realising what he had in mind for my surprise. For there, in the centre of the sawdust-floored barn, stood two beautiful horses.

Two *enormous,* beautiful horses.

One, a brown and white skewbald, was already saddled up, the other, a dappled grey, was in progress of being so.

Mateo, seeing my unease, came back and took me by the hand. 'Come, come. These are gentle animals, come.'

'You expect me to ride one of these? They're giants!'

He laughed again, led me up to the skewbald, and patted her neck. 'This is Abril, she is *Pasa Fino*, and she will take good care of you, don't worry.'

The person who'd been preparing the other horse now sidled over, a short, stocky woman in blue coveralls and riding boots, grey hair tied back in a loose ponytail.

'You ever ride Pasa Fino, Honey?' American accent, her voice deep and gravelly; a fifty-a-day voice.

'I've never ridden a horse.' I said, gingerly stroking the mare's muzzle, 'and I'm not sure I can, not without— you know, training? Have you got something smaller, a pony, maybe?'

She snorted, 'Phooey, any child can ride a Pasa.'

She took the reins and led Abril over to a mounting block. I stayed put.

'Come over here, Honey.'

Reluctantly I let Mateo lead me over by the hand.

'Now, just step up on the block,' the woman instructed, 'and put your left foot into this here stirrup, Mateo'll help ya.'

Abril stood like a rock while I mounted – oh, but it was a long way to the ground. Give me a boat in roughers any day.

'See, that worn't so bad, was it?' she offered up her hand, 'Name's Bonny bah the way.'

'Rosie,' I said. Her hand was compact and calloused.

'Now, there's two ways to make her go forward, yer kin snick yer tongue in yer cheek to start her off slow or squeeze her gently with yer heels to make her go faster. Every time yer squeeze her, she'll go a little faster. Not hard, mind. Pasa's don't need no kickin'.

'When ya'll want her to stop or slow down, just ease back on the reins. When you wanna go left, ease back on the left rein, and same on t'other side. Now, I'm gonna walk ya around the paddock out there till you feel comfortable, then we'll see how ya do on yer own. Ready?'

I'd fully expected to be holding on for dear life while the horse bucked and bounced beneath me. But this was amazing. Abril's legs moved in an odd kind of fast trot, and she snorted a lot, but the ride was no worse than a pushbike on a cobbled street. And once I'd got used to using the command signals, I began to enjoy myself.

By the time Mateo's mount was ready I felt confident enough to go further afield.

4/5

Black Rice & Wet Hair

Sitting in the 4x4 after our ride, I leaned over to Mateo, hooked my arm around his neck and gave him a big wet kiss on the cheek.

'Thank you,' I said, 'that was a lovely surprise and a fabulous day.'

'It is not over yet,' he said. 'Now we go to my house, and I cook dinner.'

'Oh, really?' I said, piqued but also faintly amused by his presumption. 'And what if I had other plans for tonight?'

His grin faded, 'I am sorry. Okay, I take you back to La Linea.'

Well, that backfired.

'No, no, I don't have plans, I was just saying— you know?'

He turned to me with a solemn expression, 'Rosie, do you want to come to my house for dinner?'

'Yes, Mateo,' I replied meekly, 'that would be lovely.'

'*Bueno,* we go.' He pushed back out of the courtyard.

Teach me to be a smartarse.

Was this to be it then – the moment of truth? As the craggy scenery whizzed past, I felt my anxiety rising once more. There had been no attempt at intimacy between us during the day, Mateo had acted the perfect gentleman. There had been ample opportunity during our lunch-stop – by a river in a secluded spinney – for things to have got quite steamy. But he'd barely moved from his grassy mound, back against a solitary rock, while I sat on the bank dangling my feet in the cold rush of water. And while the horses grazed contentedly nearby, we ate sandwiches and talked.

I told him about my childhood, growing up in England, and stories from my time in the navy. He told me about his past and his work at the ranchero. At one point he became quite animated on the history of the Andalusian pure-breds. But that's as passionate as it got.

Even if I'd had the nerve to move things on a bit, I suspect it wouldn't have gone down well. It was becoming clear to me Mateo was a guy who compartmentalised his life; everything in its time and place.

Okay, that's cool.

Still, I was nervous about the next part.

His house.

I'd discovered that Mateo was thirty-six, was originally from Cadiz, and had studied at Madrid University. He had then returned home to work in a small veterinary practice. He had moved here five years ago when he received an offer the manage the Stud Farm's veterinary team.

'You live alone, then?' I ventured further, almost dreading the answer.

'Sí, my house has two bedrooms, but I use one for office. I prefer live alone.'

He paused, and turning, grinned brightly, 'Maybe one day I will feel different, eh?'

At San Roque we turned into the town's main thoroughfare – not much there: a small supermarket, a couple of shops, a taverna, all closed on Sundays – and came out into a residential sprawl; houses festooned all around with colourful flowering trees and shrubs, and a couple of nondescript low-rise apartments. Leaving these behind the road narrowed and began to descend, and there once more spread below, the grand sweep of Algeciras Bay.

Presently we pulled up at a pair of iron gates, which Mateo opened with the click of a fob.

The house was too square and modern to be called beautiful. But it was spaciously luxurious and had a view from its extensive patio to die for; a stunning panorama with the Rock at centre-stage.

After my wander around, I found Mateo busy in the large kitchen, at a sink with a knife and some kind of dead creature.

'What's for dinner?' I said, peering over his shoulder.

He spoke without looking up from what I now saw was a cuttlefish.

'Zarangollo, paella negra, y Escabeche de conejo,'

'I haven't a clue what you just said, except I did catch the word paella in there somewhere.'

'Sí, black paella.'

'What makes it black?'

'Ink.' He looked up, saw my wrinkled-up nose, and gave me a cheeky grin, 'from calamar, squid.'

'Oh, how— nice.'

He ran his hands under the tap and picked up a towel.

'You like my house?'

'Yes, roomy and all the mod cons— er, modern conveniences – great views too. Mateo, I need a shower, do you mind?'

'Yes, please use the shower – everything you need is there.'

I picked at my damp top. 'Er, you haven't got a t-shirt I could borrow by any chance?'

'Can I help with anything?' I said, returning from my shower.

'No, everything is under control.' Mateo said, then turned from what he was doing, 'it is almost—' he stopped and gaped.

'What?'

'You look— can I say, sexy?'

I laughed. I'd put on shorts and the Barcelona tee-shirt he'd given me, which was far too big and hung on me like a marquee. I was barefoot, and my hair was still wet from the shower.

'Yes, you can say it, but I think we need to talk about your— huh? Mateo … mmm.'

I was stunned by how suddenly it happened. One moment Mateo was feet away, the next, his lips were locked on mine in open-mouthed urgency, one hand cupping my wet head. At the same time, the other caressed the naked small of my back under the t-shirt.

His spontaneity thrilled me, and I melted into his embrace. Our tongues explored.

I laced my fingers into his thick mane of hair. A thrilling warmth spread into my lower regions, making me shudder, generating involuntary squeaks and moans in my throat. I pressed harder into him.

But amid my wild abandon, another urgency nagged for attention. If I gave myself to Mateo, I should at least warn him of possible consequences. I pulled my face back from his and looked him in the eye. A slight frown grew on his brow. I kissed him again for reassurance.

'Mateo,' I whispered, 'whatever happens to me, you're not to worry, okay?'

He gave me a puzzled look. I kissed him again and lowered my hand to his inner thigh, ran my fingers up his jeans and found the bulge, drawing a loud groan from deep within him.

'Whatever happens to me, it's only temporary, remember that.'

I found his lips again, kissing him deeply, passionately. His hands went around my waist and lifted me, so I wrapped my thighs and arms around him, our kissing unabated as he walked us through the house and into his bedroom.

'You are awake?'

Mateo's face came into focus above me, a lustful expression. I felt his gentle hand caressing one of my breasts.

I blinked.

'Are you okay, Rosie?'

His hand glided across to my other breast, ran his palm lightly over the hard nipple.

I blinked.

'Is okay to touch you?'

His hand was now cupping my cheek, his fingers touching my ears, softly stroking.

I blinked.

'And—' his hand moved onto my belly, then slid slowly downwards, 'down here?'

I blinked. I wouldn't have moved now, even if I could.

'You like I touch you, Rosie,' almost a whisper, his eyes half-closed.

I blinked.

His face descended, kissed my slack lips. I felt my right thigh lifted, bending at the knee, lowered gently outwards, slowly with exceptional care for my comfort, the sole of my foot resting on my left calf. His hand stroked upwards from my foot to my thigh, then came to rest, soft fingertips brushing.

'And here?'

I blinked.

We showered together, soaping one another down, playful, laughing, careful not to arouse ourselves again. Afterwards, Mateo resumed cooking while I fixed us gin and tonics. I took mine out on the patio to watch the sunset. And to think about what just happened. Weird. Passive sex, who knew? I was getting aroused again just thinking about it.

Over dinner, Mateo asked me about the sleep paralysis thing.

'It's called Hypnagogic Hallucinatory Narcolepsy,' I told him, 'HHN for short.'

He looked surprised. 'You Hallucinate?'

'Oh yeah, like you wouldn't believe,' I twirled a finger by my temple, 'all sorts of weird stuff going on up here. The black rice is lovely, by the way.'

'Thank you. Doesn't it frighten you when it happens?'

'A bit, sometimes. I'm getting used to it, I suppose. And sometimes it's quite nice, you know, like an amazing dream you don't want to wake up from.'

'And this happens only with sex?'

I laughed and shook my head. 'I wasn't sure it would until today. It only started happening to me a few months ago. No, it's whenever I get overemotional about something that happens. I try to keep cool about stuff, and that sometimes works, sometimes not.'

I reached over and stroked his face, grinning, 'You can make me lose my head anytime you like.'

'You like it when you cannot move?'

'Mateo, it's the best orgasm ever. Well, you know, not—'

'I like it too, with you helpless. It is very, how you say?'

'Erotic?'

'Sí, erotica, is same in Spanish.'

I nodded down at his empty plate. 'You finished.'

'Yes, I finished. You want—'

'Good. Let's go to bed.'

4/6

A Step Too Far

The next morning Mateo asked me if I wanted to stay at the house for a few days. He would be at work during the day. Still, there was a selection of DVD movies, some in English, and would you believe it, a swimming pool at the back of the house, shared with a neighbour who also worked during the day.

I told Mateo yes but not today. Would he drop me at the marina to get some things, then he could pick me up after work?

As much as I loved *Pasha,* the opportunity to live in comfort for a few days was not one to be missed. And there was Mateo; my god, I was getting addicted to submissive sex – I could see now what the turn-on was with bondage.

But first I wanted my toiletries and a few changes of clothes. Oh, and my Kindle – laddish DVD's weren't my thing. When I got back on-board, I changed into running gear and went for a long jog up the eastern seafront to Santa Margarita. It was a round trip of eight miles; I needed to clear my head and punish my body. It was another hot day, and I came back with my shirt and shorts clinging wet, tingling and revitalised. After my shower, I took my laptop up to the bar and wrote a long email to Doc, telling her about meeting up with Mateo again. I knew she'd be impressed, and maybe just a smidgen envious, but in a good way. Of course, I didn't go into detail about the intimate details, that would just freak her out, but I left her in no doubt that I'd shared his bed and would be spending the next few nights with him.

There was also a reply from Julie at the hospital, sent yesterday afternoon.

> Hi Rosie,
> Thanks for your email.
> I'm delighted to say I've got
> some positive news about
> your Dad. While I was reading
> your message to him this
> morning, his blood pressure
> rose slightly, as did his heart
> rate. This has never
> happened before and is a
> good indication he is fully
> aware, and his brain is
> undamaged, which is also
> borne out by his latest scan.
> Mr Murchison says we're still
> a long way from any kind of
> moto-neural recovery. Still,
> the signs are for an eventual
> positive outcome.
> Stay safe

Best regards
Julie Myers
Senior Staff Nurse

Mateo came by at six, and we stopped at a nearby beach bar for a drink. I shared my good news about Dad, and he said he couldn't wait to get me into bed. We gulped down our drinks and made haste to the car. He drove home as a man possessed.

I spent the next three days sitting quietly by the pool reading, and the next three nights in a haze of sex, mad hallucinations, and being sexually manhandled and shagged to a quivering orgasm. All while incapacitated.

I finally came to my senses when Mateo took things a little too far and scared me. He began by straddling me and stroking my breasts then slid his hands up to my face, putting his fingers in my mouth and playing with my ears, which I loved. Then his hands were around my throat, gently at first, as a few times before when I'd enjoyed the vulnerability of it, the potential danger. But then a strange look came into his eyes, and he began to squeeze, increasing the pressure little by little as if experimenting with how far he could go. My choke reflex didn't work in paralysis, and I felt my breathing starting to labour. Fear gripped me, and I blinked rapidly to let him know. Even then, it was a terrifying moment more before he released his grip.

'I am sorry, Rosie,' he whispered, then climbed off me and out of my vision. I heard him leave the room, closing the door behind him. A few minutes later, I recovered and began to gather my things together. With my bag packed, I went in search of

Mateo and found him out on the patio, just sitting, staring out across the bay.

'Take me back to the marina, please,' I said coldly.

We drove back in tortured silence.

Mateo phoned me the following morning, apologising for his behaviour, but offering no explanation.

'When I said you could do anything, it didn't include killing me. What were you thinking?'

'I just— I don't know what happened, but I promise it will not happen again.'

'Damn right it w—'

'I love you, Rosie, come back to my house, we talk about it, not make love, okay?'

I hesitated, almost caved, but then relived the fear I'd felt, how close I'd come to being strangled.

'I can't, Mateo, not now. I've got some important jobs to do here on the boat. But listen, I'll call you at the weekend. We can talk then, give us both time to cool off a bit, eh?'

A long pause.

'Okay, Rosie, you call on Saturday, I wait.'

I ended the call.

In your dreams, Mateo. There was no way I was seeing that latent necrophile again. Fun while it lasted, but now it was over.

On Friday morning, I went to Morrison's in Gibraltar with my wheely shopping bag to provision up for my trip south. Leaving the supermarket, I crossed the car park to Waterport Road with my heavy load in tow. It was when I stopped at the curb, preparing to cross the busy road, that I saw –

emerging from a small crowd of shoppers – a tall figure I thought I recognised. He could not have noticed I'd stopped, for just at that moment he looked up and saw me – our eyes locked. Shit! Without breaking step, Range Rover Man turned sharp right and disappeared behind Rooke's Monument. As I watched, he came back into view behind the statue walking briskly away across the car park. I stood there watching, stunned – trying to draw meaning from the startling discovery that my stalker was here in Gibraltar. I wanted to run over and confront him, but my shopping hampered me – there was no way I'd be able to catch him.

What, with Mateo thinking he was still in the frame, and now my persistent stalker following me from the UK, the sooner I got away from here, the better. I planned to sail early the next morning. Destination: Lanzarote. But first tonight I was having a farewell drink with Kate and Bill.

4/7

Dolphins

Monday 25th March
0800: 34 10N 11 20W Co 220 Sp 5
Trip Log: 273 miles
Wind NW 11kts Sea 0.5m with slight swell from the
west.

Inexplicably, I lost my sea legs during that week in La Linea (probably not helped by that boozy last night with Kate and Bill). Consequently, I had spent most of the previous two days huddled up, wishing I were under a tree. Huh, seasickness, the worst feeling in the world.

Saturday was the worst. Not weather-wise – that had remained fair and reasonably calm – but the density of shipping in the Strait had kept me on the lookout when all I wanted to do was curl up and die. So it was a relief on Sunday when I was over a hundred miles from land and did precisely that, popping my head out just once an hour for a quick recce.

Now I was up feeling fresh and revived. To celebrate my recovery and build up the lost calories I cooked egg, sausage, bacon, fried bread, baked beans, the works – dad-style; all in the same pan to save washing up.

After breakfast, I stripped off and settled down in the cockpit to read. A gorgeous morning: azure sky with a scattering of fluffy cumulus clouds scudding towards Africa on the warm westering breeze, with the sun rising over the lee quarter to give maximum shade from the bimini.

Around noon we were accosted by a pod of dolphins; just one or two at first, leaping up beside the cockpit then streaking along underfoot and playing in the bow wave. Then suddenly there were dozens of them. I could hear their clicks and squeaks above the sea and boat sounds. Joyfully, they surfed the short waves in formations of three or more, leaping exuberantly alongside and generally having a load of fun. I hitched up onto the counter and called to them – mad nonsense.

'Hey, how's the water?'

'Want me to join you down there? Sorry, no can do—'

—

But why not?

The sea was calm enough.

Something on everyone's bucket list isn't it?

Would they hang around if I stopped the boat?

There was only one way to find out. The anticipation of doing something so outrageously beautiful and dangerous thrilled and almost overwhelmed me.

Then it *did* overwhelm me.

I took the wheel in hand and turned upwind, sheeting-in the main as I went, watching to make sure the dolphins stayed with us. They did, so I continued through and when the headsail backed, reversed the helm. *Pasha* hove-to gracefully as always.

Without another thought, I climbed onto the counter and dived over the stern rail. I gasped as I surfaced, the water colder than I'd expected, but my body quickly adjusted. I looked around for my new friends. Then, a nudge in my back. I turned around, and there, not an arms-length away, a grinning head upright in the water. I reached out to touch it, and it was gone. Something brushed by my legs, and another one, or perhaps the same one, surfaced next to me, moved its shiny flank close into my shoulder. I reached up, stroked its sleek back, its head rose and gave a squeak, rows of tiny teeth lined its grinning mouth. Another brushed by, going quite fast, spinning me in its wake.

Another nudged up to me, its snout digging softly into my breast. I moved around to the side of the beast and laid a hand just behind the blowhole, then ran it slowly back towards the dorsal fin. The animal hung as calm and still as a pasa fino horse. I took hold of the dorsal fin, and suddenly we were off, not too quickly, but I had to hold on with both hands. In the thrill of that ride, I had no thought for my safety: alone in the open ocean with a wild animal and out of physical contact with my boat. I was in the moment, and oh, the joyful abandon of it!

I felt a ripple down the dolphin's flank, its head rose, then began to dip, I managed a deep breath, and then we were under, going down, down. All around us dolphins streaked to and fro, some at tremendous speeds, leaving a matrix of turbulence trails hanging in the clear water. The noise was remarkable: a cacophony of clicks and pops, squeaks and squeals, an all-consuming crescendo that penetrated beyond mere hearing. But we were still descending; my lungs were starting to deflate under pressure – I was losing buoyancy. I prepared to let go and claw my way back to the surface. But then, as if aware of my human limitations, the animal's back arched, and we headed for the wobbly sun above. Relief as I felt my lungs inflating, then bursting from the water with such force that I lost my grip, falling backwards with an ungainly splash. When I surfaced again, I found myself within a few yards of *Pasha*'s stern. My ride rose in front of me, an open-mouthed grin, eyes sapient and friendly, making that odd squeaking noise, almost like laughter. Perhaps it was.

'Thank you,' I called, 'thank you, my friend.'

Then suddenly, as if by signal, they all turned away, and were gone, leaving me feeling strangely empty.

Come back soon, guys, we'll do it again.

I came-to lying sideways on the banquette, hot from lying too long in direct sunlight. *Pasha* was sailing on as if nothing had happened – indeed, nothing had, except in my head. The dolphins were gone. I wondered what I would have done had I not had a seizure in the very throes of reckless impulse. Would I have taken the risk? A scary thought.

4/8

Port of Refuge

Wednesday 27th March
1243: 32 01N 11 34W Co 180 Sp 9
Trip Log: 401 miles
Wind WSW 28kts+ Sea 4m with a heavy westerly swell.
Main fully reefed, 1/3 genoa

'*Oh dear. There goes dinner.*'
　　'Oh, Fuck off.'

I suppose there *was* a funny side to seeing my lovingly-prepared beef stew swishing across the galley sole boards. But right now, I just couldn't appreciate it. The saucepan had been held on the gas hob by roll-clamps. Fair enough, you would have thought. But that would be reckoning without a humungous wave smashing into your weather side, lurching the boat onto her beam ends. There comes the point where gravity wins, no matter what.

I staggered aft from hand-hold to hand-hold and made it to the head. Wedging myself into the small compartment with a foot up on the bulkhead, I opened a locker and dragged out a bucket, a dustpan, and a large cloth. Struggling back to the galley-sink, I half-filled the bucket with seawater and soaked the mopping-up cloth. Just then, a violent lurch threw me sideways – I skidded in the slippery goo, lost my grip and fell on my bum, warm gravy soaking into my shorts. Boohooing in frustration I hitched up and peeled a squashed dumpling off my leg then grabbed the empty saucepan as it slid down towards me. For just a moment, I hung my head between my knees and despaired. But the stink of stew and the motion of the boat were starting to sicken me. With a renewed effort, I began to shovel up the odorous avalanche of meat, gravy and veg and slop it back into the saucepan.

An hour later, with my ruined dinner flushed down the loo. I stripped off my stinking clothing and collapsed onto the lee banquette, utterly spent. In weather like this, the simplest tasks become exhausting.

I had a decision to make, and after a while, heaved myself up and got to work. First, I checked the wind: a little north of west at 28 knots, gusting 33. I checked the chart plotter; we were well to the east of track, nearer to Morocco than Lanzarote. I plotted our position on the paper chart and considered my options. Maintaining our current course wasn't one of them because I would overshoot by many miles. I could heave to and wait for the gale to abate, or, the more prudent, run downwind and take refuge in Agadir, where I could remain at leisure for better wind. I realised I'd never been to Morocco.

'We're going to Agadir. No arguments, okay?'

'You're the boss.'

I donned my lifejacket and harness and went up to adjust the sails and wind vane for a downwind run.

Eighteen hours later, we entered the port where Marina Control directed me to a finger-pontoon in the sparsely populated marina. Once tied up I grabbed my documents, a floppy sun hat and shades, and made my way quickly along the line of floating-pontoons and up the gangway – steep because the tide was low – to the quay. I headed for the lighthouse at the end which, according to the Pilot Guidebook, was the co-located offices of marina reception, customs and immigration. I should have also read the section marked 'Guidance for Visitors'.

A few people were already out and about, browsing the high-fashion shops along the quay and taking morning coffee outside the several café's. I began to get a bad feeling about the hostile stares from head-scarfed women, some pointing and whispering to one another. Men scowled at me as I hurried along – I wondered if I'd grown a second head or something. A young woman of European looks crossed from a cafe and intercepted me.

'Excuse me,' she said politely, her accent Germanic, 'are you checking in?'

She was about my age, slim and pretty, and wore a white cotton shirt with long sleeves and blue calf-length pedal-pushers with flip-flops, blonde hair tucked into a white baseball cap.

'Yes, why?'

'I do not mean to be rude, but if you go in there dressed as you are, they may refuse to process you. You must cover your arms and legs. Do you have something more suitable?'

I shook my head, 'Only some winter clothes. What's wrong with shorts and tee-shirt? It's not indecent or anything.'

She laughed. 'This is a Muslim country, and here in Agadir, they are quite conservative. Come with me. I have something on-board I can lend you.'

I followed her back down to the boats, bemused and mildly shocked by this novel development. Of course, I knew about niqabs, bourkas and headscarves worn by some Muslim women. You saw them everywhere. And though I was aware their culture had a thing about showing naked flesh, in all my travels in the navy I'd never had to conform to another country's dress code. But then, when I thought about it, I'd never visited a Muslim country. We live and learn.

Helga was another single-hander. Her boat – a 40-foot aluminium sloop – I thought rather ugly-looking compared to *Pasha*'s more traditional lines, but she was roomy and comfortable below.

I sat in the saloon while she went to find some clothes.

'Where did you sail from?' she called from the large quarter-berth.

'La Linea. You?'

'Funchal was my last port, and before that, Horta, in the Azores.'

She came back into the saloon carrying a pair of lightweight boat-trousers in one hand, and a shirt like the one she was wearing in the other.

'These will suit you, I think, try them on.'

When I had changed, Helga gave me the critical once over and declared me fit to venture out in public.

'Be sure to keep your hat on when you are out,' she added, eyeing my shoulder-length hair, 'and tuck your hair up inside.'

'Thanks,' I said, 'I'll bring your clothes back when I've bought some stuff.'

She waved a dismissive hand. 'Ach, there is no rush, I am here for another week,' she hesitated a moment, appraising me, then smiled brightly. 'If you like, I will show you where to shop. Come to me this afternoon, and we can go to the town.'

How sweet, to help a stranger like that? I was discovering among the boating community a more considerate world, where mutual support and easy friendship seemed a given.

4/9

Helga

Our shopping trip ended in torrential rain: we reached Helga's boat laughing like drains and helped each other aboard, clambered below and dashed around closing hatches.

Helga spread a big towel on the banquette, and we both slumped down, still giggling.

She suddenly turned to me, a look of concern, 'Are your hatches closed?'

I tensed for a moment, then relaxed. 'I didn't open my hatches,' I said, 'and my washboards are up.'

I watched her take off her baseball cap and shake out her long blonde hair, which was still mostly dry, unlike mine which lay wet and sculpted to my scalp and neck.

'Don't you find long hair a nuisance on a boat?' I said.

'It is difficult,' she said, flipping hers into a ponytail, 'but short hair does not suit me, so I suffer.' She looked at me and touched my wet locks,

'But your hair is quite long, and now it is slicked down so, I see it would suit you better short.'

'Mm,' I agreed. 'You're probably right, but can you find a hairdresser when you want one?'

She got up and went to the head, came back with another towel which she handed me.

'I am hairdresser,' she suddenly announced with a gleam in her eye.

I towelled my head in silence as the rain thundered down unabated on the coach-roof. Was she offering to cut my hair? Did I even want her to cut my hair?

'At least your sole boards got a good wash,' I said, running my toes through a puddle by my feet, one of many pooling the deck, 'where do you keep your cleaning cloths? I'll help you mop up.'

'This is very unusual,' Helga said, standing up, taking the folded towel and shuffling past me. 'It never rains here – this is why they desalinated their water from the sea.'

'My fault,' I said, 'it must have followed me.'

She laughed, 'Oh, so it is English rain, that explains it.'

With the awkward moment behind us, we set to mopping the deck. Afterwards, I took my new clothes into the head to change out of Helga's damp ones. At the door, I stared goggle-eyed: walk-in shower, full-length mirror and double sink unit – and still room enough to move around comfortably. Jealous didn't cut it.

I'd bought a long-sleeved cotton smock-top, white with a colourful arabesque motif, and pink cotton trousers, loose-hanging and comfortable. I dropped my damp underwear into the bag and hung her stuff on a rail over the sink unit to dry.

Checking myself in the mirror, I paused, plucking at my hair, now all frazzled from the drubbing I'd given it. Maybe Helga had a point. I'd always worn it short in the navy, and since my discharge, only let it grow because I could. Mateo was the only person who liked my hair long, and his views no longer mattered.

Returning to the saloon, I found Helga had also changed. It had stopped raining, and she'd re-opened the hatches, letting a breeze waft through the boat. Wearing a short black kaftan, she sat cross-legged on the banquette rolling a cigarette from a cellophane bag stuffed with what looked like cannabis weed.

'I made coffee,' she said, nodding to a steaming cafetiere and two mugs on the table, 'help yourself.'

'Thanks, just what I need.' I pressed down the plunger and began filling the mugs, hiding my surprise at this unexpected revelation.

'I hope you don't mind,' she said, looking up from her makings and smiling, 'it is time for my daily fix.'

'It's your boat,' I said, 'not my place to judge you.'

'That is good, but I ask if you don't mind me smoking marijuana in your company – I don't want you to leave because it offends you.'

I snorted a laugh. 'I've smoked weed before – it doesn't offend me. Fill your boots. I might even have a toke or two if there's no tobacco in it.'

She nodded wisely, licked the paper, and rolled it up with a practised flourish. 'I would never mix it with tobacco, such an addictive substance.'

I snorted. 'Tell me about it.'

She reached over for her lighter.

'Er, Helga, before you light up, I want you to cut my hair, maybe a buzzcut?'

She dropped the spliff and lighter on the table and gave me a devilish grin.

'Take off your clothes,' she said, untucking her legs and jumping up, 'I will get my clippers and comb.'

She set up her improvised salon in the bathroom; a folding chair facing the mirror, a plastic sheet covering the deck, and me sitting with a proper hairdresser's cape Velcro-ed around my neck. All very professional. Except I was naked under the plastic, which felt kind of odd.

'It is too damp for the clippers,' she said, raking my hair with her fingers, 'I will need to dry it first.'

She switched on a blow dryer and began training it back and forth while teasing out strands of my hair with her fingers. The ambience in the bathroom became sultry, and as sweat trickled under the cape, I was thankful I'd taken off my new clothes. When the drying was finished Helga plugged in a portable fan to cool things down, then picked up the electric clippers.

'Number three, I think, okay?'

'Perfect,' I said.

'Now, Rosie,' she said, poised with the machine, like an executioner, 'last chance to change your mind.'

I laughed. 'Go for it, Girl.'

She worked with expert efficiency, great clumps of hair falling in my lap and around me, her fingers gently roving along the furry furrows where the clippers had been. Every so often she would stop and stroke the new stubble against the grain with her palm, which was incredibly cathartic, erotic, almost.

When our eyes met in the mirror, her smile suggested she sensed my pleasure. When she began working around my ears, I could have sworn she knew how sensitive they were to touch, for she continually brushed them with her fingers.

Pull yourself together, Rosie!

I couldn't believe I was fantasising over another woman - one who was probably straight as a die and behaving quite innocently. When she was satisfied by the evenness of the cut, she removed the attachment and shaved off the hanging hairs at the back of my neck, then swept around my face and neck with a soft brush.

'There, all finished.'

Her fingers swept gently across my newly mown scalp, then her hands landed either side of my head, open fingers straddling my ears. I watched her in the mirror. She removed her hands.

'What do you think?'

'Amazing, Helga. Thank you.'

And I didn't just mean for the haircut – it was only a buzzcut after all – it was the sensuality of the process that was amazing. But I wasn't going to tell Helga that. God, how embarrassing would that be? Smiling broadly, she unfastened the cape from my throat. She gently shook it loose, spilling the remaining tresses onto the deck covering.

'Now, into the shower with you,' she said, 'I will clean up here.'

4/10

Attraction

I came into a saloon pungent with the haze of
marijuana. Helga sat in the same place as before,
again cross-legged, smoking dreamily on her joint.
Two glasses and a wine bottle on the table in front of
her. She was unclothed and unselfconscious about it.

I sank on the opposite banquette, not knowing
where to look, feeling a little out of my depth. I had
a towel wrapped around me and wanted the security
of my clothes, but they were over there on the
banquette, next to my naked new friend.

'The nightlife in this town is a little difficult for
unattached women,' Helga said, 'I thought you
might like to join me in a glass of wine.'

She handed the joint across the table, 'Here, take
some of this.'

I eased it from her fingers and took a cautious drag
while she filled our glasses with wine. Red, I was
pleased to note. Okay, she's a hippie throwback
from the sixties, that's cool, just go with it.

With that thought, I took a drag deep into my lungs, gasped at the searing cut of the smoke, and suppressed an almost overwhelming urge to cough. With watering eyes, I handed it back to Helga and took a slurp of wine.

She chuckled, 'I think you have not smoked in a long time, Rosie.'

'No,' I said hoarsely, 'not since Uni—' I inhaled noisily, 'seven years ago.'

'Well catch your breath and then try again, but not so deep this time.' She patted the seat beside her, 'Here, come sit by me.'

She saw my hesitation. 'My nakedness makes you uncomfortable?'

'No, well, yes, I suppose it does.'

'But I have seen you naked. Why are you embarrassed to see me so?'

'Well, because you're just sitting there— I mean— ' I giggled, 'Oh hell, I don't know what I mean.'

I felt suddenly liberated, my inhibitions wafting away into the ether with the marijuana smoke. I stood – somewhat unsteadily as if we were at sea – and shuffled around the table to Helga. I threw my clothes carelessly over to where I'd been sitting and flopped down next to her.

'Sorry.' I said.

I took the spliff from her and toked, not so deep this time, kept it down, then breathed out slowly, watching the heady smoke drift around me.

'You would feel less self-conscious,' she said softly, reaching across me and untucking the towel from my chest, 'if you were naked as well.'

Heat rushed into my face. Hardly aware of what I was doing I eased up my bottom to let Helga pull the towel away.

'There, that is better,' she murmured, 'you have a beautiful body, such a shame to hide it.'

Was she trying to seduce me? How I would I react if she tried it on? I took another suck on the weed and told myself to relax. She's not gay, just liberated. I passed her the joint and looked at her properly for the first time.

Like me, she had small, tight breasts with well-formed nipples. Her straight-backed posture showed off her stomach muscle-tone to perfection. Shapely hips without a hint of cellulite curved down to beautiful thighs, attractive legs lying comfortably across one another, and feet so cute and perfect they could never have seen a high heel. With her flowing blonde hair and even, all-over tan, she could have been a goddess. I suddenly realised she'd been watching me watching her, an open-mouthed smile and an eager gleam in her dark emerald eyes.

I gave her a lazy smile. 'You've got a better one,' I slurred. I was feeling most peculiar and slightly dizzy. I reached over and picked up my glass, brought it up to my lips and put it down again. I turned to find Helga looking at me strangely. I realised her hand was stroking the nape of my neck.

'Are you okay, Rosie?' concern in her voice.

'Have you got some water?' I croaked.

'Of course.'

In a moment she was back with a glass of water. I gulped it down, then took a deep breath. I felt sick.

'I think I need to lie down for a while,' I murmured. I swivelled my bum on the seat and threw my legs up along the length of the banquette. 'If that's okay,' I added.

As I slumped back, hardly aware of what I was doing, Helga eased my head down into her lap.

Into her lap!

But I was too stoned to care. Helga's long fingers caressed my brow, and she was cooing softly. 'It is fine, Rosie, it is okay. You have a whitey now, but you will feel better soon.'

Her breasts, inches from my face, shimmered goldenly – above them, her beautiful face gazed down, smiling kindly. I reached up to touch a perfect nipple, dropped my hand again. Too stoned to care. She picked up my hand, placed it back over her breast. 'You want to touch me,' she murmured, 'it's okay.'

I cupped her small breast, felt her nipple come erect, tickling my palm, and I giggled.

'That feels nice,' I said. I giggled again, stroking Helga's breasts, first one, then the other. Too stoned to analyse what was happening. Her fingers slid down over my ears.

'You like your ears caressed,' she whispered, 'I knew it, earlier when I cut your hair.'

Butterfly fingertips caressed my ears, around and around. So gentle, so sensual. I wanted it never to stop. I was in heaven. Her other hand settled onto my right breast, gently tweaked the nipple as she gazed down into my eyes. 'I know you are not gay, Rosie,' she whispered, 'but sometimes it can be nice with a woman as well.'

'So I'm finding out,' I said, smiling back up at her. I was coming out of my stupor, but my libido was running wild and undiminished – for a girl!

That was the enigma I wasn't yet ready to analyse.

'Are you gay, Helga?'

She nodded.

'Do you think we could, you know— I'd like to, kind of try it, with you, now?'

Her smile widened, and smoky love came into her eyes. Her hand travelled down my belly, bringing with it a flood of hot anticipation that spread deliciously into my loins.

'Helga, there's something you need to know.'

'What?' she whispered huskily, as her hand crept between my thighs,

'Oh, nothing—'

By morning the wind had eased and shifted into the southeast, bringing with it a haze of Saharan sand that layered the boats in the marina with a fine layer of ochre. Helga made us breakfast, and we said our goodbyes; she had to stay and suffer the dust while waiting for delivery of a part for her engine. But I just wanted out of that filthy cloud before it stained my teak deck and clogged up the sail tracks. The online forecast was perfect for a fast crossing to Lanzarote, so by the time the sun peaked over the desert hills, I was motoring past Helga's boat.

'Bon Voyage, and fair winds,' she called, waving madly.

'And to you,' I replied. 'I hope your part comes soon.'

She grinned and waved again.

Gosh! Who knew?

What was also interesting was that, despite multiple orgasms, I had not succumbed to a seizure. I could only guess it was the weed, and that was a compelling theory on which I would need to work.

4/11

Lanzarote

Sunday 31st March
0930: Berthed alongside at Marina Lanzarote, Arrecife
Trip Log: 773 miles

Fast passage of two days. No trauma, no incidents, just enjoyable, exhilarating sailing. And to cap our success, I got a cheap deal on a six-month pre-paid berth with water and electricity included.

When my phone connected to the local network, I had fourteen missed calls from Mateo. And one text message, saying simply.

    You bitch!

I deleted it and blocked his number.

The marina served WIFI to the moorings, so I wasted no time logging in and catching up on my emails. One was waiting from Doc.

Hi Sweetie,
Great news about your
meeting up with your Spanish
beau. Horse riding, eh? Now
there's a euphemism if ever I
heard one. Big fancy house
too – chance to get spliced
and flog that old tub of yours?
Aaargh! I can hear you from
here.

Apart from that, how's Gib?

And more importantly, how's
your Dad?

So, right now we're anchored
in a bay on St Vincent for a
week, and tomorrow I'm
booked on a trip to see an
active volcano, how cool is
that? Well, no, not cool
exactly, but hey, you know
what I mean.

I take it you're still determined
to cross the big pond to visit
this mysterious aunt? (Still
don't get why you don't just fly
over.) Shame I never got the
chance to meet her, she
sounds a lovely woman.

More news soon, stay safe on
that boat and give that hunk

of yours a big wet shnozzer
on the mouth from me.
Much love
Doc. Xx

I took a deep breath, then rattled off a reply.

Hey Doc,
Silly bint! So, just to bring you
up to date, my Beau, as you
call him, is history. I won't go
into detail, but there's a dark
side to him that scared me.
Anyway, I've left La Lins and
am now in Lanzarote.

Think I might be getting over
my seizures, haven't had one
for quite some time now.

Good-ish news on the Dad
front: he's responding to my
emails the nurses read to him
– his vital signs jump, you
know? Still a way to go, they
reckon, but hey, that's
something, eh?

Yeah, the trans-At's still on for
the end of the year. I know
you don't get sailing. But then
you can't unless you've got
the bug. For me, it feels like
the life I always should have
had.

Going to stay in the Canaries
for six months, so if you want
to come out and join me
during your summer leave,
you are of course welcome –
the accommodation's a little
cramped, but free. And if you
want, I'll take you out sailing,
though I can guess your
response to that suggestion
lol.

Anyway, I'm online for the
duration now, so email
anytime. We can even Skype
if you fancy a tete a tete.
Love Rosie x

Next, I emailed Aunt Georgie and made up a story
about being in Cartagena; only because I went there
once and knew the port well enough to make it
plausible.

And finally, Julie at the hospital, with a few more
lines for Dad.

The remainder of my day was dedicated to *Pasha*,
hosing off the Saharan muck I'd accumulated in
Agadir and on passage across. The trouble was,
while the wind was in the east that corrosive and
cloying red dust continued to plague our boats, even
this far out, so I was thankful not to be on metered
water.

I wondered what exactly I was going to do for six
months on a small volcanic island. Over the next
days, it became apparent I would need to spend

some of that time improving my Spanish. Arrecife was not a holiday town, and apart from the waiters and staff in the marina, few of the locals spoke English. By the end of that first week, I'd downloaded a Spanish Course and joined a language club that met every Tuesday in one of the town's bars. Here you paired up with a Spaniard who wanted to improve their English. I was pleased to learn that most of the English-speakers were fellow yachties; an opportunity perhaps to gather friends.

And I reassembled my bike and gave it a blitz of maintenance ready to begin exploring the island. With no more seizures since the dolphins, I began to believe Rosie was getting her act together.

And then, suddenly, she wasn't.

It happened one hot afternoon as I was walking back from the supermarket with my weekly provisions. The motorbike came roaring out of a side alley and slewed the corner into the road that ran parallel to the cobbled quay. There was nothing unusual about that, motorbikes were popular with the young men of the town, and they just loved to show off.

But as the rider accelerated past me, the scene changed to night time on an urban highway. A horrible and familiar tableau began to unfold under sodium streetlights as the motorcycle skidded sideways and its rider lost control. I screamed as the bike barrelled over and over with a slim female body impaled on its frame. Abruptly, the scene froze, everything stopped. Cigarette cartons hung in the air and littered the road. And then, as inevitable as night and day, a severed foot strapped into a beaded sandal landed with a thump amongst the debris. My knees gave way as flashing blue lights, and helmeted police officers arrived on the scene.

Lots of voices, urgent, shrill. Spanish gabble.

I opened my eyes. My cheek lay pressed against hot cobblestones. A face appeared, inches away, a young man with dark stubble and eyes sharp with alarm. It was only then I realised I had fallen.

'Señora, can you hear me?'

I blinked at him. I was on my left side, the palm of my right hand rested on the hot cobbles – the *very* hot cobbles – my legs bent at the knees, one in front of the other. Coma position: someone knew first aid. Except that my left leg and face were on fire – not so smart.

Please, somebody, get me off these fucking stones.

The man failed to notice my rapid blinking and moved out of sight. There was more Spanish chatter, too fast for my un-practised ear. Then at last, as if answering my call, unseen hands rolled me carefully onto my back. The same man's face came into view, wearing a worried frown.

'We are going to lift you now, Señora.'

He moved back, and three men and a woman, all in green outfits, bent down over me, then:

'Listo? —uno— dos— tres.'

I was airborne, moved sideways, and lowered onto what felt like a canvass stretcher. My face and leg felt numb and tingly from the heat of the cobbles. My leg twitched even before they'd closed the ambulance doors, and seconds later my motor function returned.

'I'm okay,' I said, sitting up and swinging my legs over the side of the gurney, 'I'm fine now.'

I looked at my watch, twenty minutes, tops. I forced a grin at the four paramedics looking at me with stunned expressions. 'Thank you, really I'm fine now,' I scissored my legs – livid red blotches on my left one from the cobbles. 'See? Good to go.'

My bag of groceries was on the floor of the ambulance. I stood and picked it up.

'Señora,' said the woman, 'we should take you for a checkup in hospital,'

'No, honestly, I'm okay now.' I jumped down and turned back to them; they still looked shell-shocked. *'Gracias, mucho gracias.* Sorry to cause you so much trouble.'

I looked over to where I'd seen the accident. The road was quiet, people going about their business, no sign of any recent kerfuffle. I'd hallucinated the whole thing.

Ignoring the bystanders looking on open-mouthed, I smiled again at the medics. *'Siento tu molestia,'* I apologised. *'Adios amigos.'* With that clumsy farewell, I turned and legged it quickly back towards the marina.

4/12

Learning Spanish

'Good evening, Rosie, how are you?'
'Buenas tardes, Enrico, er— esta muy bien, gracias. Y cómo estás?'

Enrico was my partner in the language club. He was around twenty, bright and handsome. This session was my second with the group, and already – because of my perfect recall – I was reasonably competent in the language; in speaking it, at least.

Enrico thought so, anyway, 'Your Spanish is coming along very well. Have you practised him— it?'

The audio lessons were helpful, but you couldn't beat the real thing. My partner's English was much better than my Spanish, but then he'd learned it as part of his school curriculum. He'd told me he was brushing up to get a job as a waiter in the resorts down south.

I thought a moment, and replied, 'Sí, he practicada en el supermercado.'

'Very good,' he smiled, 'you remembered the gender conjunctive. You can also say "*sí, lo he practicada—*" this means "I have practised it" — for better precision.'

Our conversing continued thus for the next hour or so. Enrico was unusually patient for a guy his age and spoke his Spanish slowly enough for me to understand. It was apparent I was getting more out of the exchange than he was.

Throughout that evening's session, I had been framing a delicate question in my head. Finally, I asked the young Spaniard: *'Sabes dónde pueda comprar marihuana?'*

To my surprise, he didn't bat an eyelid. Just chuckled and said, 'Yes, of course. It is quite easy to buy weed in most Spanish territories, including Lanzarote. But maybe not so easy for not Spanish people. Would you like me to get some for you?'

'Non-Spanish,' I said.

'Que? Er— I'm sorry?'

'You said "not Spanish". It's "non-Spanish".'

He reddened. 'Oh, yes, of course.'

Incredible. The young man was far more embarrassed by his minor slip than talking about supplying weed.

'And—' I lowered my voice again, 'Sí, por favor, podría conseguirme un poco?'

He grinned and nodded. 'Luego. Ahora hablaremos nuestro propio idioma.'

I sighed and smiled my thanks – job done. Though I wasn't sure of the temporal significance of 'later' – this was Spain, after all.

We went on with the session in our native languages, learning to listen rather than speak, which for me was more challenging.

Enrico came through for me later that evening after a brief errand to a nearby corner shop. I walked back to my boat, nervous of another episode. I worried what would happen if someone discovered my hundred grams of the illicit herb during my incapacity. After so many attacks, I was becoming accustomed to the episodes themselves. It was just so fucking embarrassing.

That night I tumbled into bed and dreamt narcotic dreams of bizarre encounters with people from my past interspersed with meaningless snatches of Spanish conversation.

At the top of the steep rise, I dismounted and leaned my bike against the rock wall that bounded one side of the road. On the other, a steel barrier – undergrown thickly with aloe and cactus – guarded a near-vertical drop, overlooking a huddle of white, boxlike buildings. Beyond these, the barren slopes levelled out; a steady stream of cars glinting in the harsh morning sunshine delineated the motorways and intersections, like a shining river with many tributaries. A vast complex of industrial and commercial enterprises encircled the airport runway and control tower. Beyond, lay the candy-coloured holiday homes of Playa Honda, its ivory beaches leading around the sweep of the bay to the storied hotels and resorts of Los Pocillos and Bocaina.

All this manufactured leisure lay dwarfed against the broad expanse of a windblown ocean. Ivory flecks of scudding waves and the tiny white triangles of sails lay upon a vast tableau of startling blue stretching away to endlessly-deepening violet.

A pinpoint light at eye-level betrayed the approach of yet another planeload of early holidaymakers. And another landing-light beyond that. And there, yet another—

Still gasping from the exertion of the climb, I opened my backpack and dragged out a towel to wipe my face, then took a long swig of water.

Revived, I mounted up and continued pedalling up the steep, narrow road, occasional cars and small trucks passing or coming down, giving me a wide berth. After half an hour, the lane levelled and passed a small village – with, inevitably, a cute little church – and then began to descend. A panorama of desolate lava flow opened before me, leading down to the western shore and the dark expanse of ocean beyond. I stopped pedalling and let the bike gain momentum as the downhill slope steepened.

Faster and faster, I went, thrilling to the freedom of speed with no effort. I leaned into bends and sat-up on the straight sections to let the refreshing wind-rush blast my face and dry my clothes. There was a scary moment when an oncoming car appeared from around a bend. I had taken the corner a little too wide, and the bike gave an uncertain wobble as I adjusted trajectory. For a nanosecond, I thought I'd lost it. But then the danger was past. I blew out my cheeks in relief. I laughed when an angry car horn sounded behind me, more in response to adrenalin rush than at the driver I'd just pissed off. Ahead of me lay my destination, something called a Geopark

with a mysterious cave, an unusual feature I'd
spotted on the map. I began lightly breaking.

An hour later I was riding again, this time along the
cycle path beside the broad straight highway leading
south, through twenty drab kilometres of ejected
magma – nothing to please the eye, nothing but
twisted basalt and pumice ash – and down to the
resort town of Playa Blanca.

I don't know what I'd expected from the Geopark,
but it certainly wasn't what I found. I guess I
thought I'd be visiting a managed tourist attraction
with stalactites and a tour guide. Instead, I found a
featureless, hollowed-out tube running beneath a
desolate lava flow. The only concession to visitors, a
faded sign that told me the cave was over two
kilometres long and had formed less than three-
hundred years ago.

Not that I went far inside; there was no lighting,
and I hadn't brought a torch. I found it all quite
dreary and stayed only long enough to eat my
sandwiches, sitting on the cave's roof and
contemplating the ocean. And the prospect of six
months on an island with little to offer but extinct
volcanoes and countless acres of ash. There was not
a soul in sight anywhere – some attraction.

Ninety minutes after leaving that dreadful place, I
locked the bike onto a parking rack in Playa Blanca.
I walked along the crowded promenade, eying with
dismay the noisy, wall-to-wall humanity that
festooned the beach below me. Eventually, though,
the crowds thinned, and then, joy of joys, I found
what I'd hardly dared hope for. A secluded and

child-free beach, a handful of basking adults, some wearing nothing but shades and sunhats. I hurried down, dropped my bag on the sand, stripped down to my skin and ran into the sea.

Gasping at the first invigorating splashes on my overheated body, I plunged headlong into the water. I struck out in an energetic crawl for a hundred metres or more, enjoying the primal thrill of swimming naked after the dust and heat of my ride through the lava fields.

I rolled over onto my back and just floated, heaving gently on the slight swell and dreaming into the deep blue sky. I wondered what would happen if I had one of my seizures right now – I'd probably drown. Oddly, the thought didn't frighten me. Besides, I'd been taking my fix of weed every night so that it wouldn't happen. *Maybe* it wouldn't happen.

I switched my thoughts to my aunt. She hadn't replied to any of my recent emails, and that worried me. Pushing the maudlin mood aside, I turned and struck for the shore.

I took a different route back to Arrecife, joining the coastal highway, a more direct way of some thirty kilometres along a well-maintained cycle track. It took me a shade over two hours.

I'd been back on-board half an hour and was preparing tonight's dinner, cold chicken with salad when the knock came on the hull.

4/13

Aunt Georgina?

'Hello? Boat ahoy! *Pasha*, anyone aboard?'
I froze, Surely not?

I stepped up the companionway ladder and poked my head out. And saw Aunt Georgina standing there, wearing a stylish, summer dress and a broad-brimmed sun hat.

'Hello, Rosie, thought I'd surprise you.'

'Georgie? How— what the f—?' I pulled myself together and stepped up into the cockpit. 'What a wonderful surprise. Come aboard.'

Georgie kicked off her sandals, and I helped her over the guardrail. We hugged in the cockpit. 'You look fantastic,' I told her, still unable to believe she was here, 'that dress suits you.'

'Thanks, Sweetie,'

And then, something peculiar. It suddenly seemed perfectly natural that my aunt should be here. It was as if my disbelief just suspended itself. Why shouldn't she be here?

I relaxed and said, 'I was just getting some dinner ready, you hungry?'

'Famished!' she said, following me down the ladder. 'Didn't have time to eat in Madrid.'

She slid onto the banquette and threw her bag into the corner – the most natural thing in the world, immediately at home. Nothing odd about her being here. It didn't even occur to me to ask how she'd found me.

Instead, I just went over and gave her another hug, 'It's good to see you, Georgie.'

'Good to see you too, Honey. Thought you were doing the Med. Don't want to worry you, Sweetie, but you missed.'

'I— I wasn't sure you'd approve, you know, about sailing out here in the Atlantic. If you thought I was cruising the Med—'

'—that I'd know my niece was safely close to land. Okay, I get it. But—'

'Yeah, I know it was a stupid idea. Sorry.'

She gave me a long, searching look, then smiled. 'Well, at least you got here in one piece. Say, any danger of a coffee around here?'

I jumped up to boil the kettle. 'So, when did you land? Did you fly direct? No, you said you changed at Madrid, sorry, I'm all in a tizz at seeing you.'

'Landed around eleven this morning,' she said. 'Been hanging around here most of the day waiting for you to show up.'

A sudden thought struck me. 'I'll need to clear some stuff out of the v-berth for you, or better still, you can have my cabin, and I'll bed down here in the saloon.'

Georgie grinned, 'Don't worry, dear, I'm too accustomed to my comforts these days to be sleeping on boats. I've already checked into that big hotel at the end of town.'

I spooned instant coffee into a mug and poured in boiling water from the kettle. I was secretly relieved. It would have been pretty cramped with the two of us living on-board, and I didn't want to give up my cabin, even if only for—?

'How long are you staying?'

'Oh, a few days. I got an open return.'

I added some milk from the fridge and put the coffee down in front of her. There was a strange look in Georgie's eyes, staring up at me, silent, sorrowful, and something else.

'I'll just skip to the loo,' I said.

I closed the head door behind me and sat down on the toilet lid. Without warning, my eyes filled and a great sob welled up and spluttered out in a stream of saliva. Suddenly my body was convulsing uncontrollably. Globs of snotty tears dripped off my chin in a tsunami of inexplicable sorrow.

I came out of the bathroom and surveyed the saloon, feeling bewildered. I shivered – someone walking over my grave? I shook my head and shrugged, then went over and picked up my coffee from the saloon table, then moved with it around to the galley area, placed it on the worktop. I paused again, trying to think about what just happened. Funny, I didn't remember making myself a coffee – and now it was cold. I picked up the grater and the carrot I'd been preparing for the salad. I hesitated a moment, wrinkled my nose as a vague notion niggled again at the edge of my consciousness, and continued grating the carrot. I began humming to myself.

After dinner, I fired up the laptop and checked my emails – still no reply from Georgie, strange. I rattled off another, just saying, 'Please reply, I'm worried.' and hit send. I then went to check my dwindling bank account.

4/14

Graciosa

s/y Pasha Passage Log
Crew: Rosie Winterbourne (solo)
Thursday 2nd May 2013
1025: Departed Arrecife Marina
Destination: Graciosa Island
Wind SSE 8kts Sea 0.2m.

Yes, *Pasha* and I were out on the green and crinkly once more. Our destination, the tiny island of Graciosa, less than a mile off Lanzarote's northwest shore and a half-day's sail from Arrecife.

Last week I'd taken advantage of a ridiculously cheap flight and gone home for a few days, gave the house and my jeep an airing, and went to see Dad. Julie had seemed overjoyed to see me and gave me a big hug; everyone was thrilled with the bottle of wine and a giant box of chocolates I'd bought them from the airport duty-free. It had been heart-warming to see Dad's vital signs reacting to my voice, incredibly lively when I held his big hand in both of mine. His unmoving eyes still gave me the heebie-jeebies, and I avoided looking at them. Encouraged by his responses on the monitor, I told him everything that had happened in the past two months. Well, not quite *everything*. But our unplanned diversion to Morocco and my faux pas with clothing. I liked to imagine it caused Dad an internal guffaw. I told him of my success at Spanish, the biking adventures, and other trivial stuff I reckoned might interest him. But most of all, I told him how I felt about my upcoming transAt in December. The leg from Cape Verde to Antigua was what I wanted most, but also what I most feared.

'You told me once, Dad, about when you first crossed. The Big Blue, do you remember? You said it was the sheer magic of running before the sea. Well, now I want to know what that's like, to do it on my own, to run before the sea.'

When I got back to Lanzarote and *Pasha*, I was astonished to see Range Rover Man up on the marina concourse. I was unlocking the washboards when I happened to look up, and there he stood, above me looking down with his hands on the guardrail. I stepped off the boat and called up to him, 'Hey, who are you and why are you following me?'

He stared at me a moment longer, then turned and walked briskly towards the marina shopping centre.

'Hey!' I called after him, running along towards the gangway. 'Hey, stop, I want to talk to you.'

I pressed the button to open the gate, and as soon as the gap was big enough, I squeezed through and broke into a sprint in the direction my stalker had taken. But I lost him. I checked all the boutiques, the bars, the coffee shops, even the male toilets – but to no avail, nothing. The man was starting to get on my nerves. I wasn't scared. I'd reasoned that if he were going to try anything he'd had plenty of opportunities. Besides, does a stalker follow someone this far from home? The flights alone must be costing a fortune. No, something peculiar was going on here.

I had decided to go island hopping to broaden my horizons and find some new scenery. And to shake Range Rover Man off my tail. I was reasonably sure he wouldn't have a boat. Before leaving, I told the marina to hold my berth, that I'd be back in a week or so.

Reaching the island quite late that evening, I treated myself to a meal in the local fish restaurant at Caleta del Sebo overlooking the tiny marina where I'd docked. I would probably not have noticed the American couple, had it not been for the guy's icy stare that locked on to me as I entered the restaurant.

The woman was busy with her phone, presumably unaware that her old man was ogling me. The trouble was, the only free table was right next to theirs, and as I made my way towards it, I felt those curious eyes tracking me. It made my skin crawl. For a moment, I considered abandoning my plan to eat out and settle instead for a cheese sandwich on-board, followed by my usual joint and an early night.

But no, fuck that! No way was I going to be intimidated by some old fart who's missus found her phone more interesting than him. They were in their sixties, I guessed. Both had the walnut complexions of long-term liveaboards, so a yachtswoman coming to eat alone could hardly have been novel, especially in a marina bar.

Apart from that, the place was charmingly alluring. Half the seating under a starry sky, tantalising aromas from the kitchen, softly lit tables, a beautiful view of the boats bobbing in the marina, all to the mating-thrum of a thousand cicadas. What was not to love?

The old guy was still watching me as I studied the menu. I looked up, met his gaze.

'Hi,' I tried, 'I'm Rosie,' which I'd learned was usually enough to break the ice with yachties. He kept staring, but thankfully the woman looked up and gave me a wrinkled smile.

'Hi, Honey,' she said, smoothly taking charge. 'I'm Joanie, and this here's Jim. We're the clipper, a couple down from yours.'

Jim kept on staring as if his partner's introductions didn't concern him. I ignored him and scanned the line of boats near *Pasha*. 'The blue-hulled ketch?' I ventured.

Her gawping partner chose now to chime in. 'She ain't no ketch, lady. She's a fuckin' yawl.'

'Oh I—' Stumped by his rudeness, I tried to smile away my ignorance.

'Excuse my husband,' Joanie said. 'Jim! Stop staring and say hi.'

I took an immediate liking to her. Jim stuck up a big calloused hand in a half-hearted acknowledgement.

Emboldened to match his vulgarity, I said, 'So go on then, Popeye, what's the difference between a ketch and a fucking-yawl?'.

Joanie guffawed into her wine glass, and, I wasn't sure if it was my question or my brash riposte. Still, Jim's craggy face illuminated like I'd touched an erogenous nerve. There was something like grudging respect when he said, 'Why don't you slide on over here an' I'll tell ya'll 'bout the Nantucket Clipper, best goddam sailboat ever built.'

'We saw you come alongside,' Joanie said, as I took my beer and joined them, 'pretty neat.'

I preened. It had been a tight squeeze getting into the marina, especially with nobody around to take my lines. With a rare brilliance of judgement, I managed to stop her dead in the water just as the fenders touched. I then stepped casually ashore – like an old sea gypsy – with both lines in hand and tied her up. I didn't always judge it right, but even Dad would have been proud of that one.

Before taking to a life at sea, the couple hailed from Cambridge, Massachusetts.

'We'd always said we'd like to sail away one day,' Joanie explained, 'so as soon as our boy moved out, we sold our business and moved aboard. That was thirteen years ago, and we ain't never looked back.'

'Ain't never goin' back, neither,' Jim said, 'not now they legalised fuckin' cannabis in Massachusetts.'

Which epithet had me shifting uncomfortably in my seat?

'Our son got hooked on crack cocaine,' Joanie explained. 'It nearly killed him.'

'Ah woulda killed him meself if he wouldna went to rehab,' added Jim.

I was grateful when the conversation moved on to their trip through the Gulf of Aden and cautionary tales of yacht hi-jackings off Somalia.

After food and more beers, I accepted Jim and Joanie's invitation to visit their boat for a tot of rum and finished up swapping sea-stories into the small hours. Jim was a delight; not at all grumpy – just didn't give a shit about politeness – and once I got used to his dry Bostonian humour, quite hilarious.

After breakfast, I assembled my bike and set off for a leisurely tour of the island. It was as I passed through the tiny fishing village I realised I'd missed my marijuana fix last night. Too late now. Just don't get too excited – keep those serotonin levels down.

I was passing a row of shops when:

'Señora, Señora!'

I braked to let the boy catch up.

'*¿Qué pasa?*' I said. He was young, barely out of his teens, red t-shirt splashed with the logo 'Trail Blazers'.

'Mi Papa,' he gasped, 'me envió para advertirte.'

'Warn me of what?' I returned in Spanish, looking suspiciously at his shirt logo.

'Your bicycle, she is not suitable for the trails,' he eyed my naked legs and then looked up at my Henri Lloyd cap. 'And you must wear protection. For ten euro you can hire very good mountain bike, including pads and helmet.'

A group of cyclists passed us on the street – all togged up for serious trekking. I looked down at my hybrid tyres – maybe the guy had a point.

'Ten Euros, huh?' I said.

He nodded vigorously.

'Okay, my friend, deal. Lead on.'

Safely bubble-wrapped and equipped with the kind of bike I usually sneer at, I followed another group of riders out of the village and onto a sandy trail. The ground was flat and uninspiring; the only greenery, a few scattered aloes and milk-bush shrubs growing low and dust-laden on the volcanic cinders. There was a stink of marine flora, stale and acidic. Visible all around the small island, the ocean heaved dark and sullen under an overcast sky. The only high ground was out ahead – a table-top whose flanks rose in steep, fluted ridges like a giant sponge flan.

Apart from the occasional rough patch of stones, the going was easy; I shifted up to the highest gear and put on a spurt, overtaking all but one of the bikes in front. When that rider ahead veered off the main trail I followed, weaving among shrubbery and loose rubble until we came to a line of rocks that marked the shoreline. Wavelets lapped a kelp-strewn beach a few metres below. We'd come to the foot of the plateau. I thought we would stop here – end of the trail – but my unknown leader had other ideas. He spun the bike to his right and without hesitation, stood up on the pedals and shot up a steep gully.

Okay, Amigo, anything you can do.

Shifting down to low gear, I powered the bike into the climb, scree and cinders flying out from under the tyres. Up, up we went, the guy ahead drawing away as I puffed and strained and skidded and bounced just to keep moving up that murderous incline. At last, it began to level off, the trail a little smoother with hard-packed sand and ash, until finally, gasping, I reached the top. The rider in front had stopped and half-turned, a white-toothed grin, breathing heavily but looking far less exhausted than I. He nodded once, then pedalled off without a word.

I followed, slowly at first, catching my breath, then powered through the gears to catch him up. It was biker's playground, with unexpected twists and turns, flying rises and accelerating drops and sudden challenging obstacles. As I gained confidence, I got faster and more daring. Then I was behind the guy again, matching his lightening manoeuvres with increasing skill – watch me fly, girl and machine as one. Other riders crisscrossed our path, some making breathtakingly high leaps from the ridges.

We were reaching the end of the plateau; beyond the next rise was the ocean, stretching away grey and leaden. The guy ahead swerved sideways and halted just short of the ridge. Flushed with excitement, I prepared to do the same, took up the slack on the brakes, gently squeezed—

But nothing happened! I careered on helplessly, pumping the useless brakes, moving too fast to turn, too stupefied by terror to jump off. I hit the ridge and took off, flying, with only the sea far, far below. I opened my mouth to scream, but no sound came, just the wind rushing past my ears. As my trajectory curved downwards, I gripped hard onto the bike as if it might save me. The blue-grey waves rushed up, and cold twilight washed over me. Down, down I sank, my bike was gone. I struck for the surface but to no avail, my desperate strokes no more effective than those brakes on the bicycle. Darkness closed in, and my world was cold, so cold—

My hands were shaking as I raised the water bottle to my lips. I drank deeply. José was still staring at me, freaked out by what had just happened – he'd freak out even more if he knew what I'd *imagined* happening.

It had all seemed so real at the time – as it always does – and I'd been momentarily bewildered to wake and find myself on dry land. More so with this stranger's helmeted face looking down at me. I hadn't been able to move, of course. I couldn't speak either, not for a few minutes – sleep paralysis, like in a dream; trying to run away from some nebulous terror but your limbs won't work.

I handed him back his water bottle and grinned my thanks.

He still looked shaken. 'Pensé que tenías un ataque al corazón,' he said, 'llamé al helicóptero de ambulancia aérea'

'Heart attack?' I replied in Spanish, laughing, 'do I look like I'd have a heart attack. No, my friend, you'd better cancel that air ambulance, I'm okay now.'

'Are you sure you are okay?' he said. 'When you fell into that big clump of euphorbia—' he laughed then, despite his obvious shock, 'you bounced out of it like a rag doll, and then just, kind of flopped, face down. It would have been hilarious if I had not been so scared.'

'I can imagine. So sorry to give you such a fright. Now, about that helicopter—'

'I am not so sure, Rosie, maybe you should let them take you to the hospital to get you checked.'

'Please, José, I cannot leave my boat on this island, I have nowhere else to live. Please, just call them?'

He shook his head despairingly but took out his phone. While he made the call, I jumped up and dusted myself down, grateful now for the knee and elbow pads that had probably saved me a few nasty grazes.

'There, he is cancelled,' José said, dropping his phone into his backpack. He watched me fumbling to fasten my helmet.

'Here, let me,' he said, stepping forward.

I dropped my hands and lifted my chin to let him clip me up. Close up he was no Leonardo di Caprio but had a friendly face, sweet smile.

'Take it easy going back,' he said, handing me my backpack, 'I will stay close behind you.'

I took it easy as directed, mulling over this latest surreal event. I'd evaded José's interrogation about what had happened. Because of the late night with Jim and Joanie, I'd missed my customary joint before bed.

I parted company with José at the hire shop, thanked him with a triple-cheeker, and wheeled my bike back to the marina. Jim and Joanie's boat was gone, along with most of the others; *Pasha* was one of only two visitors left in the marina.

I would also sail this evening – take advantage of this northerly breeze and head west. But first, there was one thing I had to do; after lunch, I sat down and rolled one.

Oh, I forgot to mention: the difference between a ketch and a yawl is the position of the mizzen mast relative to the rudder post. Who knew?

4/15

Big Fish

Friday 3rd May 2013
1730: Departed Graciosa
Dest: Santacruz, La Palma
Wind N 12kts Sea 0.5m.

With the wind strengthening from the north, I slipped from the marina and headed west on a two-day passage to La Palma, the most westerly of the major islands. The deadening clouds of this morning had cleared away, leaving just a few wisps of high cirrus. Dolphins joined us just a few hours into the trip. They hung around until midnight, swishing and leaping alongside me and lighting up the sea with streaks of green phosphorescence.

The following morning I assembled Dad's boat rod, not used for several years but still in good condition. The multiplier reel span free but the line on it was no good – I reeled on a new one. When it was all good to go, I attached a big red jelly-lure that I'd bought in Arrecife – armed with two vicious-looking hooks

– and let out a long trawl over the stern. I left the line out all day, and practically forgot it was there.

It was approaching sunset, and I was below, making tea when I heard the fishing rig give a short zip. I froze. The reel zipped again, then stopped, then zipped once more. I held my breath, the teabag suspended over the cup. Suddenly the line was singing off the reel.

Squealing like a schoolgirl, I legged it up into the cockpit and heaved the rod out of its holder. The line was flying out at tremendous speed, but I didn't want to strike dead for fear of losing my fish. Slowly I moved forward the drag lever until the line slowed. Then it stopped, so I locked the reel and struck tentatively. The response was immediate and violent, almost ripping the rod out of my grip.

'Fuckfuckfuckfuck!' I held on tight, bracing my thighs against the counter edge. I'd only ever caught dogfish in the Channel – this was a whole new ballgame.

I tried to pump and wind – but the fish answered every strike with a stronger one of its own.

'Shit!' I said, through gritted teeth, 'Come— on.' The line wouldn't slacken enough for me to wind any in – whatever was on the hook was too fast and too powerful. Suddenly the line went slack, and I reeled in frantically. When it tightened again the fish had shot out to starboard. I went back to playing it, trying to force my quarry back to the stern.

And then I saw what I was up against, and my heart sank. Out of the water flew a beautiful, magnificent animal – and one I knew I would never be able to land. Not alone, not from *Pasha's* counter, not without a game-fishing rig.

The big fish convulsed furiously through the air as it struggled to break loose, proud dorsal sail rippling along its back, long bill waving like a conductor's baton. And then it was gone. My blue marlin, the first I'd ever seen in the wild, let alone hooked. As I reeled-in, I reflected how privileged I'd been, and how fortunate to have lost the fight.

And I'd only wanted a little bonito for my supper.

4/16

The Volcano

Sunday 5th May 2013
1223: 28 48.3N 16 18.1W
Co: 260 Sp 6.5kts
Wind SSE 18kts Sea 1.5m. Swell: E. Heavy.

The dolphins returned this morning, so I didn't trawl the line. The wind had gradually increased, forcing me to shorten sail. But we were going as fast as I wanted; no point in reaching Santacruz before first light tomorrow. The sea was now quite rough and uncomfortable; a long swell from ahead clashing with the wind-fetch from the north.

I spent most of the day reading under the bimini until a freak wave during late afternoon washed into the cockpit and nearly drowned my poor Kindle. I went below and dried it off, then myself, glad I wasn't wearing clothes. I set the collision alarm and lay down in the saloon to get a couple of hours before dark. We were now within a hundred miles of land, and there were likely to be tuna boats around overnight. It was going to be a long, sleepless night. At least I could look forward to my evening joint.

Dawn found me bleary-eyed in the cockpit, huddled in my foully and eying a pair of fishing boats manoeuvring a couple of miles off the starboard bow. Eight miles ahead, the twinkling lights of Santacruz were beginning to fade as the sky lightened from astern, and I could make out the jagged volcanic skyline high above the town. I shivered in the morning air and stirred myself. It was time for a nice cuppa.

Two gigantic cruise ships lay alongside the quay, towering over me as I transited the length of the commercial harbour to reach the marina lock entrance. Depressing to think I'd be spending my first day in town with hundreds of rubber-necking cruise passengers crowding the streets and cafes. Still, at least they'd be gone this evening. I decided I'd just grab a shower after breakfast and get my head down until then.

I found Santacruz a universe away from Arrecife's provincial modernity; pretty, Italianate facades, complete with green, slatted window-shutters and wrought-iron balconies. The dimly-lit cobbled streets opened onto delightful little plazas with whimsical public art and trickling water features. There were orange trees laden with ripe fruit, and leafy planes under which white-shirted waiters flitted between chintz-covered tables. Sounds of clinking cutlery and the amiable chatter of diners filled the air, and from somewhere drifted the sweet sounds of an accordion playing a Moorish melody. Smells of freshly baked bread from late-night *panaderías*, and delicious spicy aromas from the restaurants wafted on the warm Atlantic breeze. Rickety tables spilled out from tavernas onto the basalt cobblestones like estuaries.

And this was only Monday, I thought, weaving among sauntering family groups with their frisking youngsters, what would it be like at the weekends? Not that I would find out; I planned to leave on Wednesday.

I dined *al aire libre* at a pasta house. The restaurant overlooked a square commanded by the statue of a rather tubby sea captain: O'Brien's dissolute hero, Jack Aubrey sprang to mind. Beyond the figure stood a life-size replica of a sixteenth-century caravel. After finishing my Chicken Alfredo, I got chatting to a trio of Chinese girls who were flying to London tomorrow and wanted to brush up their English. They looked puzzled when I told them their English was already better than most of London's inhabitants.

At 1500 metres above sea level I brought the bike to a halt. Panting like an overheated dog, I took in my stunning surroundings. *El Cumbre Vieja*, the volcano that towered over and dominated the whole island – in truth, it was the island. On my right side, the clouds swirling on the vertiginous slopes far below, and on my left, the dark, igneous wall of the caldera's outer rim, raw and spectacular, towering near-vertical to its jagged lip hundreds of feet above me. It had last erupted in 1971, and I could well imagine it doing so again at any moment.

I checked my watch. Five hours! So pleased I'd left at first light. A gruelling slog up the winding road from Santacruz, around the northern slope of the volcano; higher than Ben Nevis; the highest I'd ever been while still in contact with the Earth. And I'd cycled it. Well, most of it, anyway. There'd been sections I'd had to walk due to sheer steepness.

I drank down the last of my water and watched the wisps of clouds creep up the mountainside and burgeon at eye-level. Through them poked the pale green domes of two mountain observatories. There, I knew from my map, was one of the caldera's many visitor centres where I could buy more water, maybe even a coffee. Beyond that the road continued upwards, winding around the rim-wall where a steel crash-barrier defended an almost vertical drop into misty treetops far, far below. The verticality was dizzying.

I moved aside as a car ground up the hill behind me. When it had passed, I pedalled off after it, presently taking a slip road left down towards the visitor centre. At the car park, I dismounted and locked the bike to a railing, then stretched and shook out my burning, tingling leg muscles. They would be stiff and aching tomorrow and for days to come.

Sitting on a wall outside the small kiosk sipping my coffee, I found myself looking longingly at a guy lighting a cigarette. The craving could hit at the most inappropriate times.

He saw me looking and tapped his cigarette box.

'You would like one?' he said in English.

I am always perplexed as to how we Brits are so easily identified by Spaniards. How do they know?

'Mataría por uno,' I said, smiling ruefully, 'pero no, gracias.'

'Ah, you have given up recently,' he said, reverting to Spanish.

'Not recently,' I said, 'but the urge to smoke is always there, such an addiction, yes, such an addiction.'

He smiled then. 'Your Spanish is excellent. It is unusual for English to use everyday speech like that.'

'Thank you,' I said, flushing slightly. I'd been giving the guy an 'up yours' for his presumption. But now I felt oddly moved to have had Enrico's efforts recognised: the young man had coached me relentlessly in colloquial idioms.

'I have a good teacher,' I added, getting up and dropping my empty cup into a wastebasket.

I left him and took a walk along a paved footpath leading through a gap in the rim, where I sat and ate my lunch gazing down into the heart of the caldera. Small trees and shrubs festooned the inside of the volcano, clinging precariously to the naked rock. Further down, among hanging folds of vapour, more prominent, denser forestation as arboreal nature reclaimed the tortured remains of ossified magma. And far below that – where the volcano collapsed into the sea – lies a town. For six centuries Tazacorte has lain in the volcano's ruins on the margin of a glittering ocean that stretches westwards uninterrupted for two-thousand miles.

EPISODE FIVE

The Crossing

5/1

'Oops!'

s/y Pasha Passage Log
Crew: Rosie Winterbourne (solo)
Wednesday 2nd October 2013
1140: Departed Arrecife
Dest: Mindelo, Sao Vincente, C. Verdes
Wind ENE 12kts Sea 1m. Swell: Negligible.

We were 180 miles south of Gran Canaria when I noticed the barometric pressure falling quickly, too quickly: three millibars in the past hour. Four months alongside in Arrecife had once again robbed me of my sea-legs, so a storm coming only two days into the 800-mile passage south was the last thing I needed.

Yesterday was my birthday – my twenty-seventh, and the most miserable birthday ever. I toasted myself after dinner with a small vodka and coke and promptly threw up and then started bawling. Oh, the lonely tears. Pathetic really.

Okay, the trip down from the UK had been just as long, but these were not peaceful European waters. I was acutely aware that the land a hundred miles to the east was just a vast empty desert. It might just as well have been another ocean for all the help I could expect if the worst happened.

I know – I was just a wuss. But for the first time since setting out from the UK, I felt exposed and vulnerable. Which wasn't helped by the battalions of black clouds now towering up from astern, and the lowering sun only an hour from setting,

'Snap out of it, Rosemary. There's work to do.'

I still wasn't sure if the voice was real or in my head. But it was true. I needed to secure the boat for a rough night.

'When Depression calls, action is the key!' I declared aloud. 'See what I did there?'

'Ooh, droll.'

As I worked feverishly at the mast to hook on the reef toggles, I felt my mojo returning. *Pasha* was a sturdy sea-boat, after all, and I rated myself a reasonably competent skipper.

'What can go wrong?'

'Only Everything.'

'Oh, shut up, it's cool.'

It was with that complacent thought that I missed one necessary precaution. I gave little thought to what the approaching gale might bring: a dramatic wind shift - something a *truly* competent skipper would not have missed.

In short order I had all three mainsail reefs in, the bimini folded and lashed, and the genoa furled-in to the size of a docker's hanky. It was almost dark, and we were bumping nicely along on a beam reach in a strengthening Force Six. I now disabled the wind vane and engaged the autopilot to make taking the wheel in hand easier if it became necessary.

I took a last look around on deck and cockpit to see all was lashed or stowed, then swung below to secure everything that could move and put some clothes on. Feeling revitalised by the rush of activity, I heated a bowl of stew and wolfed it down straight from the saucepan.

And so to my final tasks: nav lights on, instrument lighting to dim.

'There. Bring it on.'

'Careful what you wish for.'

The wind came suddenly, a dull roar and a rush of power into the sails, heeling us hard over. I fastened my lifejacket over my foully and climbed the ladder to the cockpit, where a stinging lash of spray greeted me. Closing the hatch and slotting home the washboards to keep water out of the saloon, I plonked down with my back to the wind and pulled up my hood.

I watched the anemometer display; the wind had backed ten degrees and strengthened past 25 knots. I eased out the mainsheet a few inches, then likewise on the genoa.

The stern was beginning to buck and slew on a rising, quartering sea that was worsening by the minute. The autopilot was working too hard: overcompensating. I heaved myself up to the control box and reduced the rudder gain.

'Better.'

A few minutes later the anemometer read 32 knots, but *Pasha* was holding well. The wind backed another 15 degrees, and I let out more mainsail, left the genoa where it was. Letting out more would put it in the lee of the main. The wind backed further, just fifteen degrees off dead-astern now. It was then I realised what I hadn't done. I hadn't put the preventer on the boom to stop an accidental gybe.

'How fucking amateurish!'

'Yup. Too late now.'

To get a preventer on I would need to crawl along the lee side with the rope's end, with the sea breaking over me while I threaded it through a block on the forward deck cleat and dragged it back to the cockpit. Even with a harness, the thought was terrifying. And then I would need to haul in the boom to reach the end of it to tie on the rope. Single-handed it was all a bit too hairy.

'Shit shit shit!'

I pressed the button on the Autopilot for ten degrees port, then another ten to be on the safe side, and hauled in the main as she turned.

We were on a broad reach, safe for now, I reckoned, from an accidental gybe, but heading way off course. Oh well, it was not the end of the world. I would just have to ride it out and hope it didn't last days. By now, despite my foul-weather gear, I was soaked to the skin from waves breaking over the counter, the cockpit continually filling and draining. It was time once more for a cuppa.

I was waiting for the kettle to boil when it happened. The deck heaved up dizzyingly beneath me, then a dreadful graunch above from the labouring autopilot, and we began to come upright. In a cold dread, I turned off the gas and hurried back up to the cockpit to prevent a gybe.

Too late. The boom flashed over my head like lightning, snapping taut the mainsheets with the sound of a cannon shot, sending sickening shockwaves through the boat.

I quickly disengaged the autopilot and took the wheel. As we turned upwind, I applied full starboard rudder. *Pasha* heeled over to port as the gale leaned hard against the backed genoa, pushing the lee rail deep underwater. At the same time, furious waves battered the upturned weather-side of the hull.

Time to check the damage.

I hauled in the mainsheet and watched the gooseneck (the swivel attaching the boom to the mast) for signs of misalignment. I noticed one of the mainsheet block shackles had contorted; I'd need to change that. I looked up at the sail. I couldn't see much in the darkness, but I could see something was wrong; the mains'l should have been bellied out tight to the wind, not rippling like yak's fanny, as my Dad would say. I pulled the torch out of its pocket and shone it upwards.

'Oops.'

'Yeah, oops.' I breathed.

A big rip from luff to leach grinned down at me like a malicious demon.

In that buffeting wind and precipitous heel to leeward, it took an exhausting hour to get the ruined sail down and zipped up in its lazy-bag. Afterwards, I just went below and flopped into my bunk, content to remain hove-to till morning. I was in no hurry, after all.

5/2

Mahi Mahi

Friday 4th October 2013
0635: 24 51N 17 43W
Hove-to
Wind NE 12kts Sea 0.5m. Swell: Easterly mod.

After breakfast, I went up to empty my organic waste box: a few stale bread crusts, fruit and veg peelings, cooked chicken bones and skin. The gale had subsided, and it was a bright sunny morning with a warm, moderate breeze from the northeast. The sea still heaved a little but looked set to quieten down over the next few hours.

I threw the waste overboard and turned to go back below. A frantic splashing made me turn around, curious. Where I'd ditched the garbage, the water seethed and churned. I stepped over to the rail and drew a sharp breath. For there, beneath the surface of the crystal water, a frenzy of iridescence as a dozen big fish gobbled up my slowly sinking throwaways. I looked up as another leapt from the sea, proudly-raised dorsal sail, flank flashing multi-hued in the sunlight. Then I saw more of them, jumping and dancing all around my stationary boat.

'Mahi-mahi for dinner tonight?'

'Ooh, yummy.'

My stomach tightened with excitement as I lifted the rod out of its holder and swung the line out over the transom. I flicked the rod and dropped the lure a few metres out, and immediately three fish arrowed in towards it.

I whooped as the smallest of the trio took the shiny hook, while the two bigger ones snapped in frustration at the lure hanging from of its closed jaws. I pulled back on the rod with both hands, and my fish came on with little resistance. I reeled in rapidly then swung it quickly up and over into the cockpit sole, where it flipped and flapped around in frantic indignation.

'Get in!' I hissed, punching the air.

Gingerly I took hold of the shredded lure and inched my fingers to the shank of the hook protruding from the gaping mouth. Then, avoiding the rows of small but sharp-looking teeth, managed to twist it free.

Aside from the ugly, bulbous head, it was a beautiful animal; two feet long, a pelagic predator, a sleek torpedo of shimmering blue-green. It seemed a shame to kill it. Should I throw it back?

'Nah, sorry. You're dinner, my friend.'

I reached for the winch handle to despatch the creature, hefted it, then paused. I got a sudden vision of Gary with blood pouring down his face, glowering dangerously at me across the cockpit. I shivered and dropped the handle back into its pocket. Would it be cruel just to let it suffocate?

'Try alcohol, Rosemary.'

'Hey, yeah!'

Something Dad had shown me years ago with a ling we both landed. I dived below and retrieved the vodka bottle from the drinks locker. Gingerly, because it was still flapping sporadically, I poured a little of the spirit into the fish's panting gill. The effect was instant; the animal stiffened, convulsed a few times, then lay still. Within seconds its iridescence had faded to dull green.

'Yup, that worked.'

5/3

Cap'n Ahab

Tuesday 8th October 2013
0947: 16 59N 24 58W
Co 250 Sp5
Sailing (headsail only)
Wind E 16kts Sea 0.2m. Swell: NE Slight

I sipped my breakfast tea and gazed out at the unrelieved starkness of the rust-red volcanic ranges rising to port, and in sharp contrast, the lush, verdant heights of the island to starboard.

We'd been fortunate to make such good time. Without our mainsail, any wind from ahead of the beam would have given us problems. Still, the gods had smiled upon us and kept it blowing conveniently between northeast and southeast, and with enough strength to average a comfortable six knots.

Now, seven days after leaving Lanzarote, our destination was in sight at last. Two miles ahead stood the perfectly conical rock called *Ilhéu dos Pássaros*. Beyond this lay the harbour and town of

Mindelo, its low-storied frontages tinged pale pink in the morning sunlight.

As I approached the marina, an ebony wraith in a small RIB came out to meet me and led me to a pontoon berth. The two crew of an adjacent boat jumped down to take my lines, grinning hugely to show they knew the visceral joy of Safe Arrival. It was a universal language of yachts-people everywhere.

'Here, let me give you a hand.'

I stood up from the untidy heap that was my unrigged mainsail.

'Thanks,' I said, palming sweat from my brow, 'I could do with one.'

He was American, forty-something, clean-shaven and handsome, with light brown hair tied in a ponytail. His most striking feature though was the shiny metalwork extending from his left knee to a canvas boat-shoe.

Cautioning myself not to stare, I stooped and gathered up two arms full of the stiff laminate sailcloth and manoeuvred it over the guardrail to his waiting hands. Together we managed to feed it all over onto the pontoon.

'Ooh! Nasty,' my new friend exclaimed as we spread out the sail and the two-metre-long tear showed itself, 'what happened?'

I looked glumly down at the two halves of my sail, held together only by the line bonded into the luff and the reinforced hem at the leach.

'Don't ask,' I said.

'Shit happens, eh?' he grinned with a knowing twinkle.

We folded and bagged the sail then heaved it onto the flatbed trolley I'd wheeled down earlier. I'd noticed while we worked how unhampered the guy was by his prosthetic, and how unselfconscious, too. I recalled watching the London Paralympics last summer, and in the darkness of my unshared grief, had drawn comfort and inspiration from that same stoic, go-get-em attitude. I also reflected on the dismembered Afghan veterans I'd met at RCDM still coming to terms with their mechanical appendages. I wanted to think that they too had by now found purpose and inspiring challenge in their lives.

My friend glanced at his watch. 'Hey, sorry, I gotta run, damn chandlery closes for lunch soon, and I need to buy stuff.'

'S'okay,' I said, 'thanks for your help.'

I watched him walk briskly and very ably along the swaying line of pontoons, and then I stooped to pick up the handle of the trolley and wheeled along after him.

I gaped disbelievingly at the African guy in the sailmaker's shop.

'Three weeks?'

He sucked his teeth, grimaced apologetically and waved a hand at the rows of stacked sails behind him.

'Got all dees before de ARC sail. When dey gone, we can do it, no before.'

He handed me a canvas tag and a marker-pen. 'Write down name of boat and berth number. I bring sail down to you when it ready, okay?'

'Can you give me a rough estimate of cost?' I asked as I wrote.

'Where de tear, and how long?'

'Above the second baton,' I told him. 'About six feet straight across.'

'Is on de seam?'

I shook my head. 'No.'

He frowned and began tapping figures into his calculator. Finally, he looked up with a careless shrug.

'Maybe, two hundred.'

'Okay, *tchau* for now,' I chirped.

I breezed out of the shop, leaving my sail on the trolley for him to take inside. 200 Euros was about £170, not as bad as I'd feared but still a good chunk out of my dwindling resources. I shuffled my way into the crowded floating bar. I ordered a beer then hitched up onto a stool and watched the bustle of activity along the pontoons. It was the annual gathering of the ARC Rally; the marina was already aflutter with their ostentatious blue and white flags, and more boats were arriving by the hour.

'Hey, it's the pretty girl with the busted sail,' drawled a familiar voice.

I looked round to see my erstwhile helper at a table with a mixed crowd of other yachties. I threw him a smile, raised my glass to him, and turned back to the bar.

'Say, why don't you shimmy on over here and join us, lonely girl? We won't bite, you know.'

I flushed, and turned on my stool, bristling. But before I could find a witty retort, the American kicked out a spare chair from under the table, nodded sideways to it, and disarmed me with a cheery grin.

'Yeah, c'mon over, honey,' urged a feisty, frazzle-haired woman with a deep neckline showing off her more-than-adequate cleavage.

With a grin of defeat, I picked up my drink and sauntered over.

'Alone, isn't lonely,' I told my one-legged admirer. 'There's a difference.'

Which sparked off a general discussion around the table about other single-handers they knew, and which quickly strayed into lamp-swinging anecdotes and ribald badinage. Being among yachties, I realised, was not much different from being with matelots. I guess it's the sea that binds us.

'Name's Dirk,' my American friend said, holding out a hand.

'Rosie,' I said, shaking briefly. 'And thanks again for your help earlier.'

When the chatter died down Dirk stood up.

'Everyone, this here English Rose, is, believe it or not,' he paused for dramatic effect, 'Rosie!'

When the polite giggles died down, he went around the table. Of course, being me I remembered every name, but I would soon consign most of them to the trash. The Welsh couple, Terry and Karen were an exception. And then there was the big Swedish guy with flowing blonde locks and pale blue eyes, whom Dirk introduced as Erik the Viking. The thing was, Erik the Viking held onto my hand just a little longer than necessary, and I know this is a cliché, but really, a spark seemed to jump between us. Which I knew Dirk noticed because of the quizzical glance he gave me.

It was Terry though, the gregarious Welshman, who quickly enlisted my attention. His tale of starting up from nothing to build a chain of outdoor shops across Wales was astonishing enough. But the idea of starting in their seventies on a circumnavigation in a 32-foot cutter almost blew my mind. They were heading, not across the Big Pond like me, but south, to St Helena, and thence around the Cape and into the Indian Ocean.

Dirk, I discovered, was the full-time Captain of a 60-foot ketch whose owners would not join the vessel until they reached Martinique.

'Cap'n Ahab, that's me,' he declared, knocking on his prosthetic leg.

The other Americans around the table, including the Bet Midler lookalike, were some of his crew and groaned at the oft-heard trope.

5/4

Motorman

Making my spliff that night I noticed my stash was running worryingly low and wondered how I might go about getting some more. I'd had a few suspicious wafts this morning while walking across town to the laundrette. Still, I hadn't noticed any likely dealers hanging about.

And if I had, would I have had the nerve to approach them? Sao Vincente was not Lanzarote, and I had no idea of the rules here. Except I knew from the Pilot Guide, the police had a reputation for intolerance and brutality with local people caught dealing.

Next morning, I dug out my wheelie shopping-bag and set out for the markets. My first stop was the fish market where I picked up a couple of excellent tuna steaks for the pan, and a wahu-tail for a fish stew I was planning. I found a vast indoor fruit & veg market. Here I bought sweet potatoes, plantains, onions, carrots, an aubergine, and a weird-looking root vegetable whose name I couldn't pronounce. I thought it might make an exotic addition to my stew.

Aunt Georgie would be proud of me.

I also paid fifty cents for a huge bunch of green bananas that I planned to hang on *Pasha*'s stern-gantry to ripen. The rest of my staples, eggs, bread, milk, beer etc., I picked up at a little supermarket near the marina.

I was wheeling my overloaded trolley along the quayside when an emaciated Rastafarian, all hung about with colourful craft jewellery, crossed the street and intercepted me.

'You wan' buy, Missy?' he said, holding up a rather attractive beaded leather wrist-thong, 'it suit you good.'

'No thank you,' I said politely and walked on.

'Aww, c'mon, Missy,' he urged, hurrying alongside, 'you pretty lady, dis look fine on you, look.' He flipped the thong over my wrist and tried to fasten it, but I pulled away and walked faster, making for the marina gate, where I knew the security guard would shoo him away.

'Only two-hundred escudo, Missy, I know you like.'

I slowed my pace. That was what, less than two Euros? But I'd had another thought. I stopped and turned to him.

He grinned a brown-toothed grin, 'You like, Missy, here, try on.'

As I took the bracelet, I got a whiff of him and tried not to recoil. I swear I saw things moving in his dreads. I made a show of studying the thong. It was very nicely crafted and probably wouldn't fall apart in a few days.

'I'll give you one Euro,' I said.

'Aww, no Missy, you pay me two Euro, I got wife, little childra, you pay me two for beautiful bracelet.'

'What's your name?' I said.

'My name? My name Motorman. You pay me now?'

I moved close and tried not to breathe in. 'I'll pay two Euro' I said, lowering my voice, 'if you can get me some marihuana.' I moved back and watched his face grow shifty. He peered at me through bloodshot eyes.

'Pay me now, fifty Euro,' he said quietly, 'I get for you tonight.'

I blew out, 'Fifty Euros for how much?'

'Ten gram, best weed in all Cabo Verde, Missy.'

I grinned mirthlessly and shook my head. 'No deal, my friend. I need one hundred grams, and for that, I'll pay you fifty.'

He snorted, then paused, saw I was serious.

'Okay, you pay me now, I bring tonight.'

'No way, Motorman,' I said, feeling quite the streetwise buyer, 'you meet me tonight with the weed and then I'll pay you.'

Motorman went away disgruntled but promised to be back there at 7-o-clock to do the deal. I admired my new wrist-ornament, pleased with my performance at dealing with the local low-life. And more to the point, it looked like I'd scored my weed.

Silly bint that I was.

5/5

Fish Stew

Back on-board, I stowed my provisions and got started straight away on my stew while the fish was still fresh. First, I hauled out my pressure-cooker and set some coarse-chopped onions simmering in olive oil in the open pan. Meanwhile, I peeled two sweet potatoes, four large carrots, and my new root (which, eaten raw, tasted like a tangy turnip), and cut them into thick slices.

Next, I prepared the liquor. I poured a little boiling water into a jug containing a vegetable stock cube, ground cumin, and a little madras curry powder. I then stirred it all into a brown goo, which I then diluted with more water, white wine, lemon juice, and a splash of balsamic vinegar. By now, the onions were golden, and I added the vegetables to the pan, a shake of salt, a tablespoon of chopped garlic from a jar, and poured over the liquor. I secured the lid and set the valve to full pressure.

Now I skinned the wahu tail and stripped the thick white flesh away from the spine, cutting it into sizable chunks. These I placed in a polythene bag with a little seasoned flour, blew into the bag to inflate it like a balloon, and gave it a shake to dust all the fish chunks. Finally, I washed the aubergine and cut it into thin slices. By now, a glorious spicy aroma had filled the saloon. When the pressure-valve tripped, I turned off the gas and let it continue cooking until the pressure equalised. I then added the raw fish, a can of chickpeas from my tinned supplies, and some dried pulses that I'd soaked overnight. The last touch was to layer the sliced aubergines over the stew. I then resealed the lid and lit the hob. When the valve tripped a second time, I turned off the gas and went for a shower.

The stew filled ten portion-sized plastic pots, which I sealed hot and left to vacuum-cool. They would later go in the bottom of the fridge to feed me over the coming weeks. What I left in the saucepan would be tonight's dinner.

As I washed up and seven-o-clock approached, I began to get nervous about my illicit rendezvous. I pulled on jeans, socks and trainers, and my least alluring top. I took ashore with me fifty Euros, my marina key-card, and nothing else.

'Missy, missy, you come now.' Motorman, beckoning from the corner of a building. He was late; I'd been waiting there for twenty minutes and had been about to give up. Pedestrians passed on the sidewalk behind him, so I felt it safe to go over.

'Have you got it, Motorman?'

'Yeah man, but not here,' he cast around theatrically, 'Police, yanoo. You come.'

He stepped away and began across the empty street, where the buildings and alleys opposite looked dark and deserted. He saw me hang back and returned to my side.

'Just up dere, Missy, not too far.'

Where he pointed, on the street leading up the hill, I could see lights spilling from windows and a couple of bars, people milling about.

'Okay, lead on.' I said, with returning confidence. If I wanted to score here, I'd better stop being such a wuss.

A little way up the hill just a few yards short of the first bar, Motorman stopped by a dark, narrow side-alley, and I felt the small hairs spring up on the back of my neck.

'Dis man,' he murmured, as a tall figure moved out of the shadows, 'he got you stuff, you pay him.' And then Motorman was gone, shimmying quickly back down the street, leaving me alone with a stranger. My mouth went dry as fight shuffled with flight.

'Fifty Euro, right?' murmured the stranger. I still couldn't see his face in the shadows, just the tall, lean shape of him. I took out the rolled-up ten and two twenties from my pocket but kept it tightly folded in my hand.

'Er— yes, have you got—'

'Here,' he said, 'you come in here, Police, dey everywhere, you done know.'

I took a tentative step into the alley, ready to flee at the slightest sign of trouble. The stranger in the shadows handed a polythene bag towards me. I reached for it, but he pulled it back and waved a finger 'De money, first.'

I held out the cash and reached with my other hand for the weed. Suddenly the notes were snatched out of my hand, and the bag dropped to the ground, it's un-weed-like contents spilling across the pavement.

'Hey!' I shouted as he pushed past me out of the alley. I foolishly grabbed at his collar, swinging him back to face me. A dark face, angry, then a sickening thud to my temple dimmed the lights.

Dazed, I flopped to my hands and knees, but then staggered back to my feet to see a double image of my attacker weaving between duplicated drinkers outside the bar. I wobbled after him for a few steps, but overcome with dizziness, sank again, my back to the wall, feeling sick but vaguely aware of some commotion up the street.

As I sat there in a semi-swoon, cursing myself for an idiot, I heard heavy footfalls. A giant shadow appeared in front of me, legs, slightly apart, silhouetted against the light from the streetlamps. I drew up my knees and clamped my arms around them.

5/6

Erik the Viking

The big man paused on the ladder and peered down into the saloon. 'Mm, I can see this is a lady's boat – it is too tidy for a guy.'

'It was a guy that taught me to keep the boat clean and uncluttered,' I told my saviour, handing him a beer as he stepped down. 'But then he was ex-navy, and it was in his DNA.'

'I am guessing that was your father?'

I raised my beer bottle. 'Yup, good old Dad. Taught me everything I know, excuse the cliché.'

The big man's bulk seemed to fill half the saloon; I had to drop the leaf of the table on his side so he could squeeze his massive legs in. He'd scrunched his blonde hair into a ponytail, which made him look even more Viking.

We clinked bottles and drank to Dad.

'It looks like he taught you domestic economy too,' he said, eyeing my pots of stew lined up on the fridge lid.

Erik was a professional delivery skipper, here on a brand-new twenty-two-metre cutter on its way to its proud owner in the Virgin Islands.

'I should have away yesterday,' he told me. 'But my two crew for the final leg have been delayed. And now I also have to wait for a new rudder.'

'What happened to the rudder.' I said, 'or shouldn't I ask?'

'Something hit it, maybe a whale. Nobody saw it happen; we only felt it. Whatever it was, it buckled the rudder post. I thought we could get away with it until St Barts, but the owner wants it repaired before we get there. They are sending an engineer and a diver down with it.'

I puffed out my cheeks, 'Expensive, who's paying for that?'

'Ach, probably the builders, or their insurers. It's not my business to ask. So long as they pay me, I am happy.'

I suddenly felt hungry, and Erik didn't look about to leave, so I asked him, 'Do you fancy some fish stew? It's freshly made – my very own recipe. I'd be pleased to hear your verdict.'

And I was pleased with his verdict. He couldn't praise my stew enough. Afterwards, over coffee, he asked me what I'd been doing going out alone in town at night.

After a pause, I said, 'I have a bit of an issue with blackouts, random, you know. They don't happen often, but when they do, it scares me. I found, by happy circumstance really, that a little smoke of cannabis at night stops it from happening.'

'Ah, now I understand, you were trying to buy weed. And instead, you bought a broken face.'

I felt gingerly at the side of my head. It was still swollen, but an ibuprofen pill had magicked the pain away.

'Don't worry, that guy went down real quick when I punched him. But you shouldn't be—'

'Yeah, stupid, I know. Thanks again for getting my money back, cash is pretty tight right now.'

He beamed sympathy. 'I know what it's like. I used to cruise before I found a better way of sailing the world – when somebody else pays. When you own your boat, there is never enough money.'

'Unless you're rich,' I said.

'Ya,' he nodded wisely, 'then it is a different story.'

He looked thoughtful for a moment, then said, 'Come to my boat, a nightcap. I have some good vodka. And maybe something else you would like.'

I flushed. 'Erik, I don't—'

'No, nothing like that. I am not trying to seduce you,' Erik laughed, 'you have the word of a Viking.'

Mildly ashamed of my presumption and perversely unsure I wanted the word of this Viking, I looked at the clock. Nine-thirty, early yet.

'Okay,' I said, jumping up, 'I'll just wash the dishes, then I'm ready.'

The boat under Erik's charge blew me away. From her clean, classic lines and beautiful teak deck to her ingenious control arrangements, *Thorfinn* was a yachtie's dream. Stepping down to the saloon, I let out a long, low whistle at the spacious, luxurious interior. Reluctant envy vied with the guilt of disloyalty to *Pasha*. Erik lumbered down after me and went straight to his freezer, lifting out a frosted bottle of Karlsson's Gold and two equally frosty shot glasses.

'Please, take a seat,' he said, filling the glasses, 'you want a beer as well?'

'Mm, why not,' I said, sliding along the banquette on cushions still wearing their shiny plastic covers.

'Pretty tidy boat for a guy,' I observed slyly.

He cracked open two beers from the fridge and joined me on the seat opposite, sliding my beer and shot across the table.

'Ach, they keep sending potential customers to view her, the company use her as a showboat.' he said. He raised his glass. 'Skal.'

'Skal,' I responded, and we sank our shots together in one.

I gasped, and he laughed.

'Tomorrow I go to Santo Antao,' he suddenly announced, 'because I heard it is unbelievably beautiful. Do you want to come?'

'What, you're sailing over there?'

'No, no, we take the ferry, then a minibus tour, there will be other people. It is only a few hours.'

'Okay,' I said, 'sounds like fun.'

We chatted for an hour, more shots, and nursed our beers. Erik told me he had until recently paired up on deliveries with his girlfriend. But they'd split up, and she was now working out of Greece as head chef on a superyacht.

'Do you miss her?' I asked.

'I miss her cooking,' he replied with a rueful grin.

When I got up to leave, he said, 'Wait a moment,' and disappeared into the after cabin. Returning, he handed me a bulging polythene bag and said, 'Something to help your blackouts and save you from another punch on the head.'

Gobsmacked, I gaped up at him. 'Wow, Erik, are you sure?'

'Sure, I'm sure. Take it. I can get more.'

I weighed the bag in my hand; about 100 grams, I reckoned.

'Can I at least pay you something for it?'

'Ach, I don't need the money. I will come to your boat tomorrow at 8-o-clock.'

I tippy-toed and kissed his cheek. 'You're a star, Erik the Viking.'

I left him blushing.

Our minibus laboured up the steep incline at a crawl.

'You think we'll make it?' Erik said, leaning over me and grinning.

'No, don't say that?' came a startled woman's voice from the seat behind us.

To our right was a vertical drop with no crash barriers. From my seat by the window, I looked down on neat, cultivated terraces carved out of the volcanic rock and planted with produce. Out beyond the valley, rising majestically and fading into forever stood jagged mountain peaks. Between them, we caught tantalising glimpses of the glittering ocean.

'Don't scare the tourists, Erik!' came the jocular voice of Dirk, aka Cap'n Ahab, from the back of the bus. He'd come over on the ferry with us, along with his busty First Mate, Sarah. The remainder of the passengers were a mix of British and American holidaymakers staying at a beach resort on the south side of Sao Vincente.

I gave Erik a nudge, and he turned and smiled reassurance at the unnerved woman, 'Don't worry, I am sure our driver has done this before—' We slowed some more. The gears crunched heart-stoppingly before picking up again. 'Maybe,' he added, grinning hugely.

The poor woman looked ready to arrest.

I'd almost bottled it this morning, feeling self-conscious about my bruise. Still, my mood had lightened after pulling off what I considered a diplomatic triumph.

'Jesus, what happened to you, Rosie?' Dirk had called over as we waited to board the ferry.

Having thus had their attention drawn to it, some of our fellow passengers now eyed my contused temple. The bruising had turned a livid purple overnight. They began casting suspicious glances at my large companion. A story of falling down the companionway clearly wouldn't do.

'Oh, just some drunk local guy in a bar last night,' I told Dirk, loud enough for all to hear. 'Luckily, Erik here came to my rescue,' I had then gripped his big arm and gazed up at him fondly. 'My Hero.'

The mountain road levelled out, and we pulled up on a narrow ridge crossing between two peaks – a precipitous causeway in the sky – where another minibus was reloading its passengers. Everyone piled out and began snapping away with phones and cameras at the stunning vistas on either side and taking selfies against the extraordinary backdrop.

After two hours or so traversing the mountains, we descended the steep and winding road down to the sea. We passed women carrying enormous bundles on their heads and men driving sad-looking burros that plodded unsteadily under precariously-loaded baskets of farm produce. We stopped at a fishing village where our driver herded us into an open-air restaurant. Spicy aromas from the cooking range reminded us how hungry we were. We helped ourselves from groaning trestle tables, then joined other diners, from other buses, at long benches. At the same time, a guitarist sang songs in Portuguese and waiters came around with endless supplies of cheap local wine.

'Are you happy you came?' Erik asked as I prepared to tuck into my grilled grouper and salad. Unsurprisingly, he'd chosen something meaty, and smothered it in a rich, gooey pea gravy.

'Of course.' I picked up my beer and clinked it against his. 'Thanks for inviting me.'

'Thank you for coming. It is much better with a friend than alone.'

I glanced across at Dirk, currently in deep conversation with Sarah, their food untouched. From their body language, I guessed she was a 'Mate' in both senses of the word. No, Erik wouldn't have had much company from that quarter.

I said, 'That was a bus ride to die for.'

He grinned cruelly and said quietly, 'That's what the American lady behind us thought,' then levered a large, juicy chunk of meat into his mouth.

I watched him chew thoughtfully. A glob of gravy appeared on his lower lip, his pale blue eyes widening in delight, nodding his head slowly as the flavours hit his taste buds. The untethered expressiveness of his face struck me then; such an open, honest countenance that reminded me of that first electric encounter at the marina bar.

After lunch, the bus took us to a rum distillery, where, following a guided tour along troughs of boiling molasses, we sampled the wares. We gasped as the fiery spirit evaporated our lungs. One of the tourists - who couldn't decide which species of the rocket-propellant to take home to Granny - delayed our departure. Our driver had to risk life and limb to get us back before the ferry left.

That night, after dinner, vodkas after coffee, and a shared joint in *Thorfinn's* cockpit, I told my oversized Viking he needn't keep his word. And to please be gentle.

He was.

5/7

The Big Blue

s/y Pasha Passage Log
Crew: Rosie Winterbourne (solo)
Wednesday 13th November 2013
0940: Depart Mindelo
Dest: Antigua
Wind SE 16kts

It was mid-afternoon when I could no longer see the distant peaks of Santo Antao astern – when that familiar feeling of utter aloneness crept over me. This was it, the Big One! Everything from now on was down to me, and me alone. Soon I would be out of VHF range – maybe I already was – my last link with the rest of humanity.

'Alone,' I murmured, staring out at the breaking rollers. 'Just me and the great big ocean.'

'Not quite alone, Rosemary.'

Oh, of course, there was my ghostly guide, my guardian angel.

'Hardly that.'

'Why do I only hear you at sea?'

No response.

Erik had left two weeks ago. The second member of his new crew had finally arrived only a day before sailing. They were probably within sight of the Antilles by now.

We went back to Santa Antao, Erik and I, walking this time, walking on roads unsuited to motor vehicles, but well suited to us. We took sleeping bags and food, stayed overnight in the lush mountains, and made love and slept under the stars. Perhaps we'd meet up again someday, me and my Viking man-mountain. It was a small world in yachting circles.

I looked out and snorted; the world didn't look so small right now.

Saturday 16th November 2013
0830: 14 51N 31 19W
Co: 260 Sp 7
Trip Log: 394 miles
Wind: ENE 14 kts
Sea: 1m Swell: mod. Westerly

Day four. After breakfast, I brought my tea up to the cockpit. I watched the formidable rollers amassing behind us, heaving the stern upwards before washing beneath with a sucking roar, the wind vane powering up to compensate as she tried to slew to windward. Oh yes, I well knew now what it was to run before the sea.

The wind was almost dead astern; the genoa poled out to port and the newly-repaired mains'l flying slightly by the lee to starboard. Goosewinged, or Wing-and-Wing as Americans preferred to call it. Since setting course from Cape Verde, I hadn't once had to touch the sheets or adjust the steering. Over the first three days, we'd averaged 130 miles a day, not a bad start. I was firmly in the 'groove' now.

In cruising mode, something strange happens to your temporal perception. One changeless day follows another so that time becomes meaningless – especially when you transit a timezone every few days. Time is an abstract figure you write in the log every four hours. You time your meals by the solar cycle: sunrise, meridian, and sunset. Each day after breakfast, I would haul up a bucket of seawater, tip it over my head, and soap down. I would then rinse off with a miserly squirt of precious freshwater from the deck-shower. During daylight, I read in the cockpit. After the sunset meal, I would push back the bimini and smoke a joint. Lying on my back on the cockpit cushions, I would gaze up at the stars: at the thick band of brilliant light that is the Milky Way. The stars are so tightly packed they seem like a solid, diamond-encrusted belt shining with such intensity it makes my eyes water. Even in the relatively sparse skies, either side of our galactic disc, the background of billions of distant galaxies is always astonishing and frequently overwhelming.

In contrast, the planets look close and friendly, scattered like coins spilled from a drunken pocket. There's Venus, aloof but somehow one of us. And there shines warm and cheery Mars. Now jolly

Jupiter has just risen with her skittering chattering girls sparkling brightly around her. Harder to spot is silvery Saturn with just a hint of the ovality of rings that you can only see clearly through binoculars. And out here, away from the spoiling lights of cities and population, the shooting stars are magnificent. One passes over every few minutes, streaking across the sky with breath-taking velocity. Some pass so near you imagine you can hear them crackling through the ether.

Eventually, the waves slapping the hull, the clink of rigging, and the susurration of the wind, haul me reluctantly out of my trance. I sit up and scan the horizon for other vessels. I check our track on the chartplotter. I nip below to make myself a cup of tea. And when tiredness calls, I slip down to my cabin and sleep till morning.

5/8

Squalls

Tuesday 19th November 2013
0800: 14 23N 36 38W
Co: 250 Sp 4.5
Trip Log: 704 miles
Wind: NE 12 kts
Sea: 1m Swell: mod. Westerly – Squalls sighted.

We made 140 miles yesterday, the wind gusting 20 knots or more. Not so good this morning, barely twelve knots of wind and we were crawling along at a dogged four to five knots. Worse still, dark clouds were piling up to starboard, converging with our course, slanted columns of rain beneath them.

'Happy with your sail-plan, Rosemary?'

'I wish you wouldn't call me that – it's Rosie.'

I looked at the poled-out genoa. Maybe I should furl it away. Dad used to say, 'If you think something might go wrong, it probably will.'

I watched the approaching squall. Might it miss us?

Shit, I was growing lazy again. Other yachties had warned me about the danger of Atlantic Squalls and how unpredictable they are. Shaking my head in disgust, I jumped up and adjusted the wind vane to take us further to windward, and sheeted in the main as she came up until the genoa began to flog and rattle the pole. I took all but one of the turns off the sheet winch and paid out the sheet while hauling in on the furling line. Thankfully, there wasn't too much wind, and it came in quickly.

I looked at the bare pole, standing out to port like a left turn signal, and judged it safe enough – without the wind force of the sail – to leave there. Next, I came further up to windward, to a close reach, and took in two reefs on the mains'l. I hauled up the wind vane paddle and engaged the autopilot, sheeted in the main and turned downwind. Thus gybed onto the port tack, the pole would be on the weather side and not in danger of dipping in the water.

'Good thinking, Rosemary.'

First came the wind, sudden and furious. The anemometer shot up to thirty-five as it veered wildly southwards. I took the wheel in hand and fought to steer to the ever-shifting wind, regardless of our compass heading – that was now irrelevant. The sea all around us seethed chaotically as the wind ripped the wavetops into shards of stinging spindrift.

And then came the rain. And such rain. Great torrents hurled down to flatten the sea and render visibility to zero. Not that I needed to see far, only to the dial showing wind direction. The deluge swept under the bimini, so cold on my naked skin that goose-bumps sprang up like little volcanoes. I wished I'd put some clothes on while I'd had a chance; even a t-shirt would have helped.

Friday 22nd November 2013
0805: 13 58N 43 51W
Co: 265 Sp 7
Trip Log: 1126 miles
Wind: NNE 16 kts
Sea: 1.5m Swell: mod. Westerly

There had been a series of those miniature storms over the past three days, some only minutes apart. It was as if the wild ocean were taking a breath before raging again with increased fury as I fought to control the boat.

Now we sailed under clear skies once more. The more northerly wind had forced me to unrig the genoa-pole and sail a Beam Reach. That way, I could hug the Great Circle that would sweep us up to Antigua.

Yesterday afternoon, as the last of the squalls disappeared into the southwest, I was astonished to see a trio of egrets flying low around the boat. Why were they so far from land? I wondered. Egrets are not known for oceanic foraging; they're not even seabirds.

As I watched them, I realised they were trying to land on the boat. But there was no safe landing spot for them. The spinning wind-turbine precluded any attempt on the gantry, and the deck was sloping too sharply to afford traction for their webbed feet. One even tried to land on the sea but aborted at the last moment. They looked tired and desperate, and I could only assume that they were migrators that had somehow lost their way. After a few more aborted attempts to land, they flapped off miserably to the north, where the nearest landfall would be many thousands of miles away. I felt so sad for them, I wept. Wild Nature can be so cruel.

Today's visitors had been more uplifting: a pod of bottle-nosed dolphins. They arrived just as I settled down with my morning cuppa, forming up on either side, close to the cockpit: big animals, these, serene and stately. They watched me each time their heads broke the surface and paced my seven knots with consummate ease. After an hour, the mammals scattered. Each leapt joyously out of the water and shot off into the blue.

5/9

Cetaceans

Monday 25th November 2013
0803: 14 42N 49 33W
Co: 275 Sp 2
Trip Log: 1228 miles
Wind: E 4 kts
Sea: 0.5m Swell: slight. Westerly

Calm. If the wind dropped any more, I'd need the engine. I calculated with my spare fuel I could motor for 400 miles if necessary, but that was the last resort. And I still had over 600 miles to go. At least the current was with us, pushing us along at around two knots. Patience, Girl, patience.

We lolled around all day and overnight in that maddening calm. I furled the genoa away to stop its lazy walloping. The boom creaked to-and-fro as the mains'l struggled to fill with what little breeze was on offer.

But on Tuesday morning the Trades returned; a southeaster sprang up that steadily strengthened over the following two days. I'd poled out the genoa once more, and we were goose-winging on the home stretch with around 350 miles to go.

Thursday 28th November 2013
0800: 16 25N 55 12W
Co: 280 Sp 6
Trip Log: 1593 miles
Wind: ESE 15 kts
Sea: 1.5m Swell: mod. Westerly

I was about to go below to make my midday sandwich when something caught my attention on the port bow, a large object in the water. At first, I thought it must be a cargo container some ship had lost overboard, but then I saw the spout of water. A whale! And a big one at that. I'd seen whale plumes before in the distance, but never one this close. And I was going to pass it close, too close, perhaps. I tweaked the wind vane to take us a point to starboard. As I watched the whale draw closer cold fingers began to crawl up my spine. Sailing too close to large cetaceans was notoriously dangerous. And this one, I now recognised from its angular head, was a sperm whale. The most notorious of them all: Cap'n Ahab's whale, I noted and pictured my American friend Dirk in the bows brandishing a harpoon.

Suddenly, the creature's head dipped, and its massive flukes lifted out of the water, so close now the slosh from its rising tail almost reached our bow. And then it was gone, a patch of swirling froth marking its departure. I realised I'd been holding my breath, and now breathed out in a long sigh of relief at danger averted.

'Er, Rosemary—'

The whale to port had so transfixed me I hadn't considered the animal might not be alone. Just as the Voice spoke my name, another large set of flukes rose before my eyes, mere feet away to port. It was just a brief glimpse before a ton of water poured over me, and then I was hanging on to the wheel and gasping for air as *Pasha* beam-ended.

When she righted herself, I sat stunned in a cockpit full of water. I couldn't believe what had just happened.

'Er— oops.'

'Oh, fuck off! You could have warned me sooner.'

While the cockpit drained, I checked for damage. The rig looked fine. *Pasha* had picked up the wind and sailed along entirely unaffected by the near catastrophe. Two of the starboard guardrail stanchions had stove inwards, cracked at the bases so would need replacing. That was no big deal.

Down below was not so good. The washboards had been out when the whale struck, and a deluge had poured into the saloon. I could hear the bilge pump whirring away under the sole-boards, but it wasn't enough. Instead of lunch, I would spend the next hour baling out.

Sunday 1st December 2013
0801: 17 10N 61 25W
Co: 270 Sp 6

Trip Log: 1957 miles
Wind: ESE 15 kts

This morning there were birds. Oh, there'd been a few ocean wanderers around during the crossing, the odd albatross, a few petrels, and of course those poor egrets. But now I saw an abundance of near-coast dwellers. Flocks of boobies and terns dived for fish while a pair of frigate birds hovered above for a chance to rob some poor bugger of their catch. A solitary tropicbird took a fancy to my wind turbine.

By noon, a faint black line painted the horizon to port – Guadeloupe, which meant Antigua would soon be in sight.

The following morning, I took a marina berth in Jolly Harbour, on the western side of the island. I took on water and provisions, got a metalwork guy from the boatyard to do a temporary repair of *Pasha*'s cracked guardrail stanchions. I completed my ESTA online for entry into the US and got drunk as a skunk at the marina bar with a bunch of up-for-it yachties. I sailed the next day for the Bahamas and the Florida Keys.

EPISODE SIX

The Revelations

6/1

Key Largo

Thursday 12th December 2013
0930 Anchored in Garden Cove, Key Largo, Florida.

'Hey, Lady, how long ya'll planning stayin' here.'

The man had motored over in a dingy from ashore as soon as my anchor chain rattled down.

'Oh, till after Christmas if that's okay.'

'It's okay by me, but ah'll tell ya, holding's not great here, you might wanna think about takin' a ball, especially if you ain't planning to stay aboard.'

'How much?' I asked.

'Five bucks a day, you can pay when ya check out.'

'Okay,' I said, 'can you give me a hand to pick up the buoy?'

'Sure, no problem.'

Within the hour, I was motoring ashore in the dinghy with my passport, ESTA printout, and boat documents. The small customs and immigration office processed me surprisingly quickly, and the girl at the marina office was helpful with my queries, in particular, the cheapest way to get to Miami.

'Well, ma'am, the cheapest is by bus, but ya'll need to change twice to get to Downtown, and it'll take you more'n six hours.'

'Do you know where French Country Village is?'

'Sure, that's easy. You'll need an Uber from here to 98, there you get the Scooper to West Palm Drive, from there you walk to Park and Ride and get the 38 Max to Dadeland South. But you don't ride to Dadeland, you get off at University, and from there it's a ten-minute walk to French Country.'

She smiled proudly at her mastery of geography and the public transport system, but then saw my look of bewilderment and frowned. Remembering everything she said was not the same as understanding it.

'Ma'am, do you have Google Maps on your cell?'

I motored back to *Pasha* and went to bed. I'd been at sea a week since leaving Antigua and the last few days transiting the Bahamas sandbanks had been gruelling.

I woke up mid-afternoon, starving. I showered in the cockpit, then took the dingy back to shore and looked for a decent eatery. A man with straggly unkempt hair and matching beard accosted me on the boardwalk.

'Ma'am, can you spare an outa-work sailor a few dollars? I promise not to spend any of it on food.'

I guffawed at his audacity and told him I didn't have any US Dollars. He wished me a beautiful evening and wandered off. I grinned. Even the poor and penniless here were polite.

I found a busy waterfront restaurant and chose a table on decking built over the water. I ordered a beer, a shrimp starter followed by gator-burger and fries and a side order of Waldorf salad.

'I guess you're hungry, huh?' came a voice from the next table as the waiter left with my order. He was thirtyish. His friendly smile and attractive green eyes were somewhat let down by the shaved head and ginger goatee.

'Famished,' I said, then turned away to look out over the water, where *Pasha* sat, still and restful at her mooring on the tranquil lagoon.

'Nice boat,' the man persisted, despite my 'not interested' signal. 'Saw you come in.'

I turned back to him, gave him a disengaged smile, 'Thanks. *Pasha's* old and a bit cranky, but she takes care of me.'

'You sail alone, then?'

I nodded and looked away again.

'Gee, that's risky,' he persisted, 'for a purdy young thing like you. Doncha get scared?'

I paused, put my chin in my hand, and gave him my patient face, 'Are you always so rude?'

His face went beetroot, but he rallied quickly, 'Are you always so stand-offish, or is that normal British arrogance?'

'Everything okay here, ma'am?' the waiter asked, placing a tall flute of beer in front of me then glancing at the man.

'Yeah,' I told him, 'we're all good, thanks.'

The waiter hesitated a microsecond, then left.

I took a long drink and wiped the foam from my mouth, then said, 'Look, I've had a long exhausting trip here, and I'm hungry, and not the best company right now, so can we just leave it, okay?'

'Okay, okay, no problem, Ma'am,' he said, 'I apologise for any offence.' He gave an obsequious nod of his bald pate, then turned to gaze out over the water, fingers drumming silently on the table.

I grinned to myself, then took out my Kindle and began reading.

Halfway through eating, another beer arrived, unordered, to replace my empty one. I lifted an eyebrow at the waiter.

'Courtesy of the gentleman at the next table, ma'am.'

I looked across at my ginger stalker, who was staring up into space with pursed lips, looking vaguely apprehensive. Despite myself, I snorted a laugh.

'Thanks,' I said, 'that's very kind.'

He looked at me, and I gave him an apologetic smile. 'Sorry I was a bit grumpy earlier.'

He grinned sheepishly, 'Gee, you were running low on glucose, and I behaved like a dick. So why don't we just rewind to before I opened my big mouth?'

I raised my glass to him, 'Cheers.'

He raised his beer, and we drank a silent toast to our new-found geniality. He left me to eat my meal in peace, then asked if he could join me. I pulled out a chair for him.

'I'm Chuck,' he said, sitting down, 'Chuck Masefield.'

'Rosie Winterbourne,' I said, shaking hands, 'but I'm afraid I can't stay long, I've got an early start in the morning.'

'Me too,' he said, 'got to be on the road by seven. So, Rosie, where is ya sailing to next?'

'Oh, I'm not sailing anywhere just yet. I've got an early bus ride up to Miami.'

'Wow, that's some journey, ya gonna be all day on buses. Where ya headed, exactly?'

'French Country Village, it's where my aunt lives.'

'And can't this aunt come an' get yer, or don't she drive?'

'Oh, I'm sure she has a car, but she doesn't know I'm here. I want to surprise her, you know? Just show up on her doorstep unannounced and shout, "Merry Christmas!"'

'Well, that'll do it, alright. But how d'ya know your aunt's not away on vacation for the holiday? A lot of Miami folks head out when the snowbirds hit town, the white folks, anyways.'

That Georgie and Anna wouldn't be home for Christmas? I'd made some pretty broad assumptions about their lifestyle here.

'Hadn't thought o that, huh?' Chuck said.

'Er— no, I hadn't. But I'm in no rush to leave. If they're not home, I'll just hang on here till they get back.'

'Hey, listen up. I'm driving up to Miami tomorrow, what say I give ya'll a ride up there, French Country's not far outa my way. Take ya two hours instead of five.'

'Really? That would be fantastic.'

'My pleasure,' he drained his glass, 'now, let's have one more at the bar, then I'm outa here.'

6/2

Chuck

S o, this aunt of yours, you must be quite fond of her to want to sail from England just to give her a Christmas surprise, tell me about her.'

I gazed out at our speeding progress along the smooth Overseas Highway. Beyond the flashing barrier posts of the causeway, a brilliant turquoise sea shone yellow where shallow sandbanks rose, alternating with bright sandy inlets and golden beaches. Small fishing boats left crisscrossed trails of wake on the pristine inshore waters. Further out, sailboats and motor-cruisers scudded the deeper seas.

'Rosie?'

'Oh, sorry, miles away. Yes, Aunt Georgina, she prefers just Georgie. She's my mother's twin. I didn't even know she existed until Mum died last year.'

'Oh, I'm so sorry for your loss.'

The car smelled of newness; a Toyota-something in metallic green. And the aircon worked rather too well; goosebumps raised on my arms in the cold air from the vent.

'Do you mind if I open my window?' I asked.

'Oh, sure,' he said, switching off the aircon, 'go ahead. Thought you might be unused to the Florida heat.'

'Very thoughtful, Chuck,' I laughed, sliding down my window to let the warmer air from outside caress my face, 'but I've been in the tropics for months, I think I'm acclimatised by now.'

'Yeah, I guess. So, you've got me intrigued. How come you didn't know your mother had a twin?'

'I'm not sure. Georgie won't talk to me about it, and I can't ask my Dad, because—'

I sucked back a great sob. I had no idea why it hit me just then. I couldn't trust myself to go on.

'Oh, I'm sorry, I hit on something, huh? You wanna talk about something else?'

I took a breath and gave a forceful sigh. 'No, no, not your fault, just me being a wuss. My Dad's been in the hospital for the past 18 months with Locked-in Syndrome. You know what that is?'

'Huh-huh, it's when they're fully aware, but can't move or respond, right?'

I nodded. 'A fully functioning brain inside a body that doesn't work, cut off in every way from interaction with others, can you imagine?'

'No, I can't, it sounds terrifying, and extremely upsetting for you, clearly.'

'Well, in Dad's case at least, there's a hopeful prognosis, there's a definite sign that he can see and hear, I witnessed it myself last time I spoke to him. And Julie, that's the nurse in charge of his ward, tells me his cognitive functions are improving week on week. His consultant says it's just a matter of months now before he's back with us.'

'Well, that's good news. And, Rosie, I hope when you get back to England, your Daddy's going to be there, smiling and waiting to give his daughter a humongous hug. That'll be some homecoming.'

I looked out again and let the wind dry my eyes. 'Thanks,' I said, when I'd got it together, 'I hope so too.'

We sped on in silence, the engineered paradise of the Keys gradually giving way to wilder, less managed places. Swampland greenery swept out to our left, burgeoning into dense mangrove and more prominent, long-established forestry.

'The Everglades,' Chuck supplied. 'Gator country.'

I nodded.

After another few silent miles zipped past, Chuck said, 'So, back to your Aunt, does she work, retired?'

'She's probably due for retirement, she's 66, but no, she still works. Runs a software business with her partner, Anna.'

'That's 'partner' as in— she's gay, right?'

'Yup, I suppose there's no denying it, a partner in both senses.'

He glanced across at me. 'Hey, you're blushing, Rosie. Don't you know this is the Gay Capital of the World? Hell, I'm a part of it.'

I stared at him. He flashed me a sideways grin.

'You're gay?'

He nodded, 'You thought I was hittin' on ya'll last night, right? Well forget it, my preference is strictly male.'

I burst into laughter. 'I'm sorry,' I said, 'I'm not laughing at you, just the comic situation.'

'I know,' he said, grinning hugely, 'I had a good laugh about it last night in my room.'

'Like a TV sitcom.' I burst out.

'Yeah, Big Bang Theory, do you watch that? Like when that girl thinks Sheldon's coming on to him and slaps his face.'

'Sheldon just cracks me up.'

I sighed, and a few moments later, so did Chuck.

'So, what business are they in, Georgie and Anna?'

'They run a software company, outsourcing for big banks, I think. Something to do with online security.'

'Well here's a coincidence, that's my line of work too. Commercial, City Bank, that kind of thing?'

'Yes, I think so.'

He suddenly snapped his fingers. 'Wait a minute. Anna. Originates from Scandinavia somewhere?'

I stared at him. 'Finland. You know her?'

'Anna Koskinen? Is that your aunt's partner?'

I shook my head. 'Georgie never mentioned her surname. How do you know her?'

'Anna Koskinen? Everyone in my industry knows Anna. She used to be the big cheese in banking security systems.'

I went cold. 'Used to be?'

'She was called up to Washington two years back, works for the CIA at Langley, last I heard.'

I relaxed. 'Ah, that can't be Georgina's Anna, then. She still works in Miami.'

'Yeah, you're probably right,' he said, 'Anna's a pretty common name, and Finnish software people are all over America; Silicon Valley's crawling with 'em.'

6/3

Georgina & Anna

'Here you go, 1284 Seville Avenue,' Chuck said, pulling over to the kerb. 'Whoa! That's some place!'

The two-story house, painted in bright coral-pink with an orange pantile roof, was partially obscured by a profusion of tropical shrubs. Many were in brilliant bloom. The house stood back beyond well-tended lawns that had several sprinklers on the go. A concrete footpath led up between two great spreading palm trees to a glass door set in an open porticoed porch beneath a classical style architrave. A sweeping gravel driveway separated a double garage from the main house, and a tall hedgerow leading out from the rear suggested an extensive private back garden.

'Looks like somebody might be home,' Chuck said, nodding towards a silver Volvo S60 in front of the garage doors.

I'd been getting increasingly anxious as we'd driven through the Village looking for the address. Now my nerves were stretched to breaking point.

'Want me to wait?' Chuck said.

'If it's not going to make you late, I wouldn't mind,' I said, 'then if there's nobody in you can drop me at the nearest bus stop to get me back to my boat.'

'Can do better than that,' he said, 'I'm only in Downtown for a two-hour meet with a client, then I'm driving home for the weekend. Did I mention I live in Key West?'

'Oh, that's great. And you don't mind, I mean if all this goes pear-shaped?'

He snorted, 'I will mind if ya stall much longer.'

I took a deep breath and swung open my door.

'Wait a moment,' chuck said, 'I don't mean to worry you, Rosie, but did you notice the name on the mailbox?'

I turned and looked at the mailbox on a post at the end of the footpath.

Koskinen

I frowned back at Chuck, then shrugged. 'Only one way to find out – I'm here now.'

He reached into the glove box, 'Here's my card, just in case, you know—'

I walked determinedly up the drive to the sound of crickets buzzing in the shrubbery. Somewhere nearby the harsh chit-chit of a grackle echoed among the buildings. As I neared the house and its exotic shrubs, the air grew pungent with floral perfumes.

I rang the bell. A distant ding-dong sounded, then a small dog began yapping. A yellow shape approached through the frosted glass of the door, a wagging tail at near floor-level. The door opened, and a little Yorkie ran out and began sniffing excitedly around my ankles.

'Hello, how can I—' the woman I recognised as Anna broke off and simply stared at me. 'Georgie?'

'Yes,' I replied, smiling broadly. 'I'm Rosie. And you're Anna?'

Anna ignored my outstretched hand. Instead, her mouth fell open, and her face paled. She staggered back a pace and put a hand to her chest.

'I'm sorry,' I said, unnerved by her reaction. 'Has something happened?'

She began shaking her head, then said, 'I'm having a nightmare. Who *are* you?'

'I'm Rosie. Look, Anna, I don't understand, whatever's the matter?'

She appeared to get herself together, took a breath, then said. 'I don't know any Rosie. If this is some kind of—' Her face grew hard, 'Okay lady, show me some ID or I'm calling the police right now.'

The little dog at my feet backed away and began growling.

Bewildered and growing tearful, I opened my bag and took out my passport. Without a word, I handed it to Anna. She flicked through to the back page, looked at me, and then the photo, and a look of slow realisation dawned.

'Rosemary Winterbourne!' she almost whispered it, 'Rosemary Winterbourne. My god! You're Margie's daughter.'

I grinned, nodding vigorously.

'Oh, I'm so sorry, Rosemary, so rude of me, come in, come in.'

The dog was wagging its tail again.

I turned and gave Chuck the thumbs up as Anna ushered me in. Inside the door, I stopped, realising that Anna should have known who I was, from Georgie. Bemused, I shook my head and followed into the hall. Maybe Anna wasn't as well as she seemed.

'Go on inside, take a seat.' said Anna, now the bubbly hostess, 'I just made some lemonade, you want some?'

The house felt pleasantly cool after the humid air outside. There was a faint smell of sandalwood which intensified as I entered the spacious lounge: stylish, practical furniture, lots of pale woodwork, and a large potted plant in the high-arched fireplace, a dining table to one side. A glass partition looked onto an indoor swimming pool in a bright conservatory and beyond that an extensive garden dominated by a bigger, outdoor pool.

I took a seat on an ivory leather settee, and the little dog jumped up and began fussing me. I gave it a scratch behind the ears, which seemed to satisfy it, and it jumped down and curled up by my feet.

Anna came into the room with two glasses of cloudy lemonade. 'And how is your mother? God, it's been how long? Almost twenty-seven years now.' She set the lemonade down on the small coffee table and sat down next to me.

'But I thought you knew,' I said, 'Mum died last year.'

She stared at me, 'Say that again?'

'I don't understand. Aunt Georgina must have told you – I *know* she did.'

Anna's face suddenly crumpled. 'Oh my, oh my— excuse me a moment.' She ran from the room gushing, the little dog following with its tail down.

I sat bewildered. What on earth was going on here? And where was Georgie? Had they split?

Anna returned, blowing her nose on a tissue, her eyes red-rimmed. As she sat down, I looked at her, hoping for answers but not wanting to upset her further. She sniffed, then turned to me.

'I don't know your aunt,' she said, 'I never met her. I guess she must be on Peter's side of the family because Margie was an only child. So you see, Rosemary, I had no idea your mother had died.'

'Er— Anna—'

'I assume you know we were once— you know, together? I did wonder why I didn't get a card last Christmas. She never missed one before.'

'You and Mum? I don't understand. It was you and Georgina, surely—'

'You're confused, Honey. Georgie was my pet name for Margie. What, you thought you had a long lost aunt?'

I sat back, staring at nothing, trying to come to terms with what I was hearing. There was no Aunt Georgina?

'But— this can't be right, Anna.'

I couldn't stay sitting; frustration forced me to my feet. I paced the room; tears welled so I could barely see.

'Are you telling me,' I cried, 'that the woman who came to find me, the woman who told me she was Mum's twin sister and lived with you in Florida, that she— that she never— ?'

The voice of John Hardy echoed, gently chiding: Aunt Georgina is in your mind, Rosie. Nobody else sees her. Your mother never had a sister.

Anna stood and hugged me while I blubbed on her shoulder. She spoke to me soothingly, 'Give yourself a break, Honey. I don't know what's happened to you or what's going on here. So come and sit down, and maybe we can make some sense outa this.'

I sat down with her and picked up my bag from the floor. 'I want to show you something,' I said, pulling out my laptop.

'When I saw you at the door just now,' she said while I was waiting for my machine to boot up, 'I thought I saw my Georgie, aka Margaret, your mother. Because you look just like she did when I last saw her, a little younger sure, and a darn sight taller, but as like in looks as makes no difference. Of course, I knew that couldn't be right because she would have aged, but honestly, my brain did a hoopla when I clapped eyes on you.'

She watched me as I opened my email, knowing perhaps I'd only been half-listening. I went to my Inbox, then stared at the screen. The last email from Doc was there, and one from the hospital. I scrolled down. Nothing, nothing from Georgie, nothing in Sent from me to her either.

'I don't understand,' I muttered, 'she *must* be here.'

I went to my Contacts but couldn't find her there either. Confused and panicky, I looked at Anna, who was watching me with a concerned frown.

'She's not here. I know we've exchanged emails, but she's not—' my head was buzzing. I was suddenly hot, despite the cool of the room. Feverishly, I pulled out my phone and went to Contacts. Again, nothing.

Your mother never had a sister.

I stared at Anna again, 'But how—'

'shh shh,' she patted my hand, 'let me give you the whole nine yards, then questions, okay?'

I sniffed and nodded.

'So Margaret and I met in 1980, at a weekend regatta at Chichester. She was sailing her father's boat *Spectre* and was one short in her crew. I was there just to help on the marina, and I stepped in. After that, she asked me a few more times, and we found the two of us got along pretty well. Eventually, we fell in love, but this was the eighties, and it was England before the 'enlightenment' if you know what I—'

I put my hand up, bells were ringing in my head, 'wait, just stop there a minute— I *know* all this, I thought from Georgie, but it wasn't was it? It couldn't have been.'

'No, it—'

'Wait, Anna, just give me a minute.'

I leaned back and closed my eyes.

6/4

Recollections

I'm five years old, Mum has been teaching me to read, and I'm so pleased with myself. I read anything I can get my hands on – not just children's stuff. I read Mum's classics, newspapers, Dad's Navy News and Readers Digests. That's when I first realise I'm different from other kids – I never forget what I've read. Reading has become an obsession. One day, I'm in Mum's study looking through her wardrobe. I find a book in a box, handwritten, which I find challenging - some of the words mean nothing. But it's another feed for my reading addiction. I sneak the book into my room and read a little more each day. Much of it makes little sense to a five-year-old, but that doesn't matter, reading's such fun.

I opened my eyes. 'It must have stuck,' I said, 'what I read, you know, in my subconscious.'
'Excuse me?'

'Mum's diary, I read it when I was little. It meant nothing then, but you know, it must have stayed in my head, am I making sense?'

'So you think maybe—'

'Could explain a lot about— never mind, please go on.'

She gave me a blank look, then continued.

'So, Margie and I decided to live on-board *Spectre*, so we could be together, you know, without raising suspicion. I mean it wasn't a problem for me, I'm from Finland originally – the petty prejudices of the English didn't bother me. But Margaret's parents were, shall we say, more than a little conservative – especially her Irish mother – and devout churchgoers. It was essential for her to keep our relationship in the closet.

'In '84 Margaret's father died and left her *Spectre* in his will, and a big chunk of cash in a covenant to keep her living with her mother in that big ole house, 'My Golden Handcuff' she called it.'

That tugged another memory, but I parked it for now, fascinated with all this stuff coming to light at last.

'Life for us was a little more difficult, but we managed. We still had every weekend and some weekday nights together. In '85, Margaret sold Spectre and bought a new boat we called *Pasha*—'

'What gay Floridians call their adopted kids.'

'Hey, yeah, that's right. Anyhow, *Pasha* was brand-new and more comfortable as a live-aboard. Life was good, Rosie, believe me, we were so happy.'

She was welling up again. I pressed my hand on hers, 'I know.' I murmured. Something was happening to me while I listened, I couldn't fathom it, but it felt good – as if I were growing lighter.

'It was about then Peter, your Dad, started crewing for us at races and regattas. He always had a soft spot for Margaret, probably in love with her even then – but knew about us and always kept his distance. A very honourable and liberal-minded man, your Dad.

'Then, two days before Christmas '85, we were both supposed to go to the Yacht Club Christmas Party in Mullhaven. I was working for a software company in Reading at the time. I would have to work late to finish some urgent work before the holiday, so Margaret and I decided to meet at the Club and sleep on *Pasha* overnight. Georgie did go, but I was kept late at work, missed the party entirely. It was after 2 am when I got to the marina, and I went straight down to the boat.'

She paused to dab her eyes with a tissue.

'I knew something was wrong as soon as I stepped aboard. I heard voices down below, not speaking, but, well you know, kinda moaning. Margie and a guy.'

'She was having an affair?'

Anna nodded. 'I went straight back up to my apartment in Reading – I never told her that I knew, hoped it was just a one-night-stand after a drunk party.'

'And was it?'

'I thought so, for a while. But then, when I came back from a business trip to Singapore I found some guy's stuff on the boat; a pair of sneakers, socks, a dirty shirt. I asked her about it, maybe expecting her to say it was Peter's. But no. She could never have lied directly, your Mum, not to me.'

'She admitted it?'

Anna nodded, 'Straight out, no hesitation. His name was Lionel, and they'd been seeing each other for months. He also had a boat in the marina, so it was easy for them to keep it quiet. Margaret said she still loved me and didn't want us to break up. But she was conflicted over Lionel.

'I tried to keep us going, but every time I went down to Mullhaven, I'd look for his SUV in the car park – if I saw it there I'd head right on back to Reading. We kinda drifted apart, the two of us, like a slow train wreck. If I'd known how he was— if I'd known it started just with Margie trying to help a guy, I woulda tried harder to accept him, but how could I have known? Margaret never told me that stuff.'

'Whoa, wait a minute, you've lost me.'

'Lionel was sick, Rosie. He was what they now call bipolar, a manic depressive. And he had this thing with his memory – he couldn't forget anything, and it drove him crazy in the end.'

I was stunned by this new revelation, and from the look Anna gave me, it must have shown in my face. 'Lionel had *hyperthymesia?*'

'Yeah, that's right— *Christ,* Rosie, you too?'

I grinned, 'Not so bad once you get used to it – I had it all explained to me by a specialist.'

'Well, for Lionel, it *was* a big deal. He was on meds, but he didn't always take 'em. Margie was trying to make him better – she couldn't resist a hopeless case. But it wasn't enough, because one night he drove his SUV up to Beachy Head—'

'Jesus!'

'Mm, quite. The Coastguard found the wreckage down on the shoreline next morning, and Lionel, what was left of him, floating face down in the waves.'

6/5

Paternity

I did not know what to say – Lionel's was the story of a stranger, sad, but disconnected from me. Nevertheless, the revelation of Mum's lover moved me almost to tears and at the same time brought me some kind of closure I couldn't yet take in.

'Margie was shattered, of course,' Anna continued. 'But funnily enough, things between us got better after Lionel's passing. It was when Margie found out she was pregnant— ' she paused, watching for my reaction, then, 'Er, why don't you look surprised?'

I told her about my blood group discovery. No, I wasn't surprised to learn that Lionel was my father – it explained everything. And the notion that I seemed to have inherited Lionel's memory traits, though in his case, it was a curse.

Anna gave a wry chuckle, 'Your Grandma was furious. You remember your Granny Bee?'

I nodded. 'Granny Bee died when I was twelve— um 16th May 1999, a Sunday. In hospital – she was ninety-two and had dementia.'

'Gosh, well remembered, Rosie. How did you—?'

'Never mind, carry on.'

She gave me a funny stare, then continued, 'Margie's family brought her up in that strict Catholic tradition of the Irish. Not only was she not allowed a termination, but she had to marry before the baby— before you were born.'

'So, in stepped my Dad.' I supplied, my voice quivering.

She nodded. 'So, in stepped Peter. He'd always loved your mother, and even though she didn't feel quite the same about him, he was more than ready to accept you as his child. And I believe from her occasional letters they had a happy marriage.'

'They did. M & D were quite sweet together.'

'I was devastated, of course, and I know she was as well. We'd always talked about coming to Florida together someday, both for its liberal attitudes and opportunities. We were going to start a business together. But with your mother, and especially your grandmother, family propriety came first. But don't get me wrong, Margie was strong-willed in her own right and always followed her notions of what was right.'

There was a long pause while we held each other's eyes. I felt a curious sense of peace settling over me. So many questions answered – questions I'd not dared to think about for most of my life. Questions that had been bubbling away inside, begging for answers. And the vexed question of my paternity was settled. It occurred to me that in a different setting – different circumstances – I might have been raised by two women – now *there* was an intriguing thought. Without Dad's influence, the navy would hardly have won a place in my life – Wow! I'd have been a sailing liveaboard with my two mothers.

I dragged myself back to what had happened and felt a wave of sympathy. 'Anna, that's so sad, you abandoned your happiness and came here alone, lost the love of your life because of Granny Bee's rigid dogma.'

With brimming eyes, Anna bore up heroically, 'Not just Granny Bee, remember. I don't want you to think of Margie as some shrinking violet back then – she was never that as I'm sure you discovered. Yeah, I felt abandoned and betrayed for years. But now, looking at you dear, I think the sacrifice was worth it.'

'Aww—' I blubbed. We hugged again, Anna patting my back like Mum used to when I was upset.

'And you've made quite a name for yourself,' I said to lighten the mood, 'so I heard today.'

She pulled back and looked at me. 'Oh?'

'The guy that brought me here this morning, cybersecurity?'

She sniffed and nodded, 'Small world, huh?'

We both laughed – the tension gone.

While Anna made sandwiches and coffee, I called Chuck, and he agreed to pick me up on his way home. While we ate, I told Anne more about my extraordinary delusions of Aunt Georgina. The drive to Worcestershire to escape the paparazzi, walking the Malvern hills together, even going to see a play. Then—

'Hey, I just had a thought: Georgie bought you a jade necklace and matching earrings in Malvern—what?'

Anna's face was shining. 'I have them, Georgie sent them over for my Fiftieth.'

Another misplaced memory clicked into place: 14th of June, 1997, a gorgeous summer Saturday. We drove to Malvern, the three of us. The theatre was showing The Medea. I asked if we could see it, but Mum said I was too young for Greek Tragedy (it wasn't until years later at Uni that I got to see the play). And yes, I remember Mum showing me the jade jewellery she'd bought for a 'friend's' Fiftieth Birthday. Dad had been looking on, and I remembered his knowing smile. On Sunday we walked the Malvern Hills in the rain – M & D in their matching waterproofs.

And my escape there last year with my imaginary aunt? I wasn't sure now if I even made that trip; I hoped not – the very thought of being seen chatting away to myself like some broken junkie was sphincter-clenching. If Prof Hardy had discovered just how deep my psychosis ran he'd have had no hesitation in sectioning me, I was sure. I was suddenly reminded of Georgie that day in court, sitting all alone in the public gallery, watching me. The image no longer felt real – a ghostly figure, barely there at all.

'When I think about it now,' I told Anna, 'nobody ever acknowledged her, even when she came out with her funny remarks – it was only me who laughed. At the time it all seemed, you know,

normal behaviour, but I suppose that was just my
screwed-up mind playing tricks.'

Anna took it all philosophically. It had been an
understandable reaction to stress and loss, she said –
reminding me of Prof Hardy – and that it would all
probably stop now I knew the truth. I thought so too;
I felt different as if I'd walked out into the light, like
the Hebrew Slaves in Nabucco – Mum's favourite
Opera.

We talked about our very different lives. Anna had
never met anyone else she could live with after Mum
but had thrown herself into a rewarding career and
now worked for the Federal Government.

We talked about Dad – the man I thought of as
Dad. I told her how he'd got me into sailing from an
early age, about that memorable first time out on
Pasha: the terrifying heel-over to the first filling
sails, transported into a world of pure terror and
delight: the swish of the sea rushing past the hull, the
spray in my face, the salty taste on my tongue.

'Mum claimed to hate sailing,' I said. 'Never once
came out with us – now I know why: too many
painful memories. So when I joined the navy, Dad
lost his crew – then, as he turned sixty, he lost his
appetite for sailing as well and left poor *Pasha* to rot
in the boatyard.'

'Until you rescued her – I'm so glad you did.
Listen, there's so much more for us to talk about –
are you sure you won't stay for the holiday?'

'Thanks, Anna, I'm tempted. It would be better to
wait till Spring, I know, but I want to get back to
Dad. I want to be there when he wakes up.'

When Chuck tooted his horn outside, I asked the question I'd been holding back: 'This Lionel, did you ever meet him?'

She nodded, 'Sure, but just the one time. Lionel was tall and big-boned – a bit like you. You'd never have thought to look at him— wait, I have a picture of him and Margie, you wanna see it?'

'Do I want to see a picture of my birth father? Are you kidding me?'

She was back in a moment, flicking through an album. 'Ah, here we are.' She turned the page towards me. It was the kind of small polaroid shot popular in the day. Mum was in shorts and vest, laughing and looking lovely, with her hair carelessly tied with an Alice band. I'd never seen her looking so carefree, so happy. With her was a tall, handsome man, athletic-looking, also in shorts.

'She never forgot him, you know?' Anna said. 'Every year she put a single white lily on his gravestone. I don't think Lionel had any family – it was only Margie, Peter and me at the cremation. So I guess he'll get forgotten now Margie's gone.'

The couple was standing in front of a green Range Rover, the registration readable: L205 NPP. And of course, I recognised the man in the picture right away. My biological father was Range Rover Man.

EPISODE SEVEN

Homeward Bound

7/1

Reconciled

Chuck had been a sweetie – so liberating to be able to tell the whole astonishing tale to someone I knew I would never see again. He suggested I needed a break – 'Something wild and off the books to get you out of yourself—'.

I wanted to be in Bermuda for Christmas – no particular reason other than the notion of spending the day where there were people, even if they were strangers. I couldn't bear the thought of being all alone with my Christmas memories. But I had a few days in hand, so instead of dropping me at Key Largo, Chuck took me down to his home in Key West.

He and Kenny, his partner, were fabulous hosts and had a bunch of eccentric friends who liked nothing better than to party the night away. We breakfasted on Champaign cocktails to the aurora of the Atlantic sunrise. We ate lobster in the glow of a magnificent sunset on the Gulf of Mexico. We danced to rock bands and drank Strawberry Margaritas at a bar you had to swim to, got drunk on the atmosphere and stoned on the weed. I counted the five-toed cats in Hemingway's house, swam with manatees and ate carpaccio of blue marlin. I spoke with poets and philosophers and songwriters. I kicked up my legs in a fair impression of Britney Spears in a karaoke bar (which took me back to my student days in Bristol). Key West is the ultimate 'anything goes' place, and for me, finally able to bury my demons, everything went.

The sail north from Key Largo – within sight of Florida's coastal playground – was close to perfect. A fair southerly breeze meant that I could pole out the genoa and pass the whole day detoxing in the cockpit with my Kindle. The occasional pleasure boat was all that disturbed me. Noisy day-trippers who thought a day on the water involved letting everyone know what a good time they were having.

Tuesday 17 December 2013
1148 27.41.8N 079 32.2W Co 040 Sp 6.1

At noon on Tuesday, having cleared the Grand Bahama Bank, I dismantled the pole and turned northeast into the open ocean on a broad reach. 760 miles to Bermuda. The ocean remained unusually kind to me that afternoon – just a long gentle swell from astern and a breeze sufficient to glide us along at six knots without stirring up a sea. Kind and – now we were in deep water and many miles from land – empty. After lunch, I stripped off, hauled up a bucket of water and cooled myself off then rinsed off under the deck-shower. I then crashed out, alternating between reading and dozing under the bimini.

Everything felt different now. I was no longer making stupid errors, no longer letting laziness get in the way of prudence. It had only taken me a year and 7000 miles, but finally, I was getting the hang of this sailing malarkey.

My seizures also seemed a thing of the past. I was reconciled to my imaginary aunt being precisely that, even though I still felt she had been real at the time – when I had needed a friend. Such a palpable and persistent phantom had me questioning other aspects of my life—for example, my father (as distinct from my Dad), Range Rover Man. Long dead of course, so what had been stalking me – a ghost? Or another misty memory from reading Mum's diary. What about Erik the Viking? Now there was a candidate for a paranoid fancy. A thought struck me. I pulled my phone out of my rucksack and found it – the picture I'd taken on a mountain top in Santo Antao.

Yes, Erik the Viking was real, thank God!

I kind of missed *Pasha's* Voice though. I had put that mysterious guru down to my subliminal instincts telling me when I was getting things wrong. I supposed I didn't need it anymore. Well, okay. But

I missed the Voice – a crew without a physical form to annoy me was the ideal company.

There was still something of a presence, though. Mostly, it happened when I catnapped in the day: a feeling that I was not alone. It came over me in that not-quite-awake state, the strange notion that I was rude to sleep when this person wanted to talk.

All that aside, it had been a lovely sailing week, the best of the whole trip since leaving Gosport almost a year ago. The calm, balmy days had given me the space to sort out the loose ends, to rummage around the paperwork in the back office of my mind and tidy everything into its rightful place.

The so the days floated by and time drifted as light and fluffy as the clouds.

Until, that is, just after supper on the evening of Sunday the 22nd of December. The evening the VHF Radio exploded into life.

7/2

Bermuda

I sat there for a moment – startled by the intrusion on my solitude. I stood up and checked the chartplotter; the little archipelago was still 40-odd miles away. They called again.

> *'Sailing Yacht Pasha, Sailing Yacht Pasha this is Bermuda Radio, Bermuda Radio, how do you read. Over?'*

Okay, okay. Hold your horses. I swung down into the saloon, slid my supper things into the sink, and unclipped the radio mic, reducing the volume before responding.

> 'Bermuda Radio this is *Pasha*, Good Evening. You're loud and clear. Over.'

> *'Pasha this is Bermuda Radio, Good Evening. I hold you forty*

miles to the west, do you intend
to call at Bermuda? Over.'

Ah, the wonders of technology! They'd picked up my AIS signal.

'This is *Pasha*, affirmative. My
ETA at St Georges is 0600
tomorrow, Over.'

After I'd answered a shedload of their questions, Bermuda Radio ordered me to call in the morning when I reached St George's Ship Channel and 'await clearance to enter'. Like a plane on approach to Heathrow, but in slow motion.

Monday 23rd December 2013
1045 Anchored in St Georges Harbour, Bermuda

The small yacht anchorage was tight with visiting yachts up from the Caribbean, waiting for the Trade Winds for the passage to Europe. I too should be hanging on here until at least March when the flotillas began their crossings. But my last email from Julie said Dad was showing early signs of coming round, and I wanted to be there when he did. Crossing in December/January was high risk, but smaller boats than mine had done it.

After dropping anchor, I sat watching until I was sure I wasn't going to drift into anyone. Then I climbed into the dinghy with my documents and motored ashore to clear customs.

That first day at anchor, I spent cleaning and doing a few minor repairs – things are always breaking on a boat. I then got a good night's sleep. It was when I went to buy a few things from the local supermarket, that I got my first shock, paying $20 for four chicken breasts and a bag of potatoes. Who can afford to live here?

That's what I asked the eccentric old geezer calling himself Hayward whom I met in a bar on Christmas Eve, having just paid $7 for a bottle of beer.

'Simple economics, m'dear,' he proclaimed – eyes like tiny sapphires twinkling from deep laughter lines. 'The money floats into Bermuda like the Sargasso weed, the more you sweep it away, the thicker it flows back. Prices go up, driving wages up. The residents get well paid, and the rich are happy because they don't get tourists coming fucking up their cosy paradise.'

Hayward's eloquence was at striking odds with his appearance: from his profusion of straw-coloured hair to his crusty toenails, he had the look of the shipwrecked mariner.

'Reminds me of when I built my second boat over by the dockyard,' he continued, 'back in the sixties that was. Stole the wood from an old dismantled church, y' see, ninety-year-old pitch pine imported from Canada in the reign of Queen Victoria—'

After a short while, Hayward began to draw a crowd at the bar – he simply gathered them in and spoke louder, warming to his theme and his audience. It was hard to tell the bullshit from what one might believe, but then I realised nobody cared.

Turning to retrieve my drink from the bar, I noticed a freshly opened bottle had appeared alongside it.

'Excuse me,' I called to the barman, 'I didn't order another beer.'

He smiled and walked over, leaned in towards me. 'The lady over there,' he nodded towards a woman at the end of the bar. 'She bought it for you.'

7/3

Erin

She was looking my way my way, a half-smile as if unsure how I'd react to her gesture. She was an attractive forty-something, straight black hair worn in a loose, shoulder-length bob. She hadn't been here when I'd walked in half an hour ago – I certainly wouldn't have missed her. I smiled back, which seemed to reassure her – she had dazzling white teeth, eye-catching against her deep olive skin.

I wondered if this was a pickup.

Still, at these prices, it doesn't do to be impolite when somebody buys you a drink. I finished my beer and grabbed the gifted bottle. Leaving Hayward to his rapt audience, I sidled past the other drinkers at the bar.

She wore a cream shirt buttoned up modestly, blue pedal-pushers. She sat on a barstool with her white sandals resting on the crossbar. Not cross-legged, not provocative. A businesswoman maybe – not a regular here, or the barman would have said, would probably have named her for me. I relaxed a little.

'Hello,' I held up the beer. 'Thanks for this, but can I be rude and ask why?'

'Look around,' she said. 'We're the only women in the place, right? Thought you could use some moral support.'

Or *you* could, more likely, I thought but returned her smile anyway.

'Cheers.' She clinked my bottle with hers, and we drank cordially, then introduced ourselves.

Erin's handshake was firm; her hands were strong but smooth, not calloused like mine. She wore a simple wedding ring. And a neat little black wristwatch – on her right wrist, I noticed. Her honey-coloured eyes were frank and guileless; no agenda, just here to chill out on Christmas Eve. She had a mildly northern accent, Yorkshire maybe.

I liked her immediately.

She told me she was a civil servant with the Foreign & Commonwealth Office and had flown in last week for a departmental review with the Governor General's Staff. Her work now finished, she had decided to stay for Christmas and fly home on Friday.

'So you're staying in Hamilton?'

She shook her head. 'Was. I checked out of my hotel this morning.'

'Won't your family miss you?'

She laughed and shook her head but didn't answer. Instead, she volleyed it back, 'What about you, Rosie, won't yours miss you?' A teasing glint in her eye.

Another stranger to pour my heart out to – another friend I'd never see again. Why not? I left out the crazy stuff – didn't want to scare her off. I told her about the Accident, losing Mum, and Dad's coma. I told Erin about leaving the navy (voluntarily – it seemed best to say) and my Big Adventure to go to see 'aunt' Anna in Florida. I fabricated outrageously, but it all came out as a connected train of events that managed to lead credibly to my being in a bar in Bermuda on Christmas Eve. At least Erin seemed credulous enough.

'So where are you staying?' I asked, after several more beers, which Erin – bless her – insisted on putting on her tab. I suspected the British taxpayer would ultimately pay for it.

'Tonight I'm at the St Georges Club,' she told me. 'Courtesy of the Bermuda Government.'

I nodded. I'd walked up there earlier while exploring the town. It stunk of money and colonial largesse.

'And tomorrow?' I asked. 'How are you getting around, by the way?'

'I've hired a car. The GG wanted to give me a car and driver, but I told him no, I wanted to do it alone. Have you been anywhere out of St Georges yet?'

I shook my head.

'You should. The buses are rather good, apparently – aircon, the works. Did you know there are 138 islands, and the biggest eight – the ones that are populated – are all connected by bridges and causeways?'

'So that's your plan,' I said, 'drive around until it's time to fly home for New Year with the family?'

She grinned and brushed a fist softly against my chin. 'You're fishing again, Sailor?'

I shrugged. 'Just curious, but if—'

'Okay, so here's my itinerary, which by the way was organised by my hosts. Tomorrow I'll drive around to Tuckers Town to buy presents. A tour of Portuguese Rock, lunch with the Park Rangers at Spittal Pond, finishing at Government House for an evening reception followed by Christmas Dinner, and I'll stay there overnight. Boxing Day I'll drive round to Summerset Village, more shops, and a tour of the Naval Dockyard, and be back at the Airport Hilton in time for my flight the next morning.'

'Phew, that's quite a—'

'Then on Friday night, I'll be home in Harrogate with my husband, Philip, and our three children: Sara, Frances and Henry. And yes, I'm missing them terribly because there wasn't a flight that could have got me there before Santa. That's a part Daddy will be performing—' she checked her watch, 'about now because it's 1.15 at home. I called them earlier, and they're all looking forward to their presents, except Philip who wishes it was Friday.' Her eyes had pooled.

'Erin, I—'

She waved an index finger. 'Shh, no more. Now, let's move onto the gin, shall we? And then you can cut the bullshit and tell me about the *real* you.'

7/4

Wild Ocean

Christmas morning with a throbbing head: I reached over to open my cabin door and squinted at the ship's clock. Five-past-eleven. I let the door swing shut and winced at the crash it made. I opened my cabin window to let in some air. I laid back down, pressing my hands to my head and watching the sunlight's watery angles reflected on the deckhead. Gradually, fragments of last night came back to me.

What I couldn't remember was coming back in the dinghy. In a blind panic, I rolled out of bed and legged it up to the cockpit. And there my dinghy was, bobbing gently three metres astern. I sat down there in the cockpit and went back to remembering last night.

Erin and I were being chatted up by two guys wearing Santa hats. Erin had been in the middle of pronouncing on some vital issue and gave them their marching orders. More recollections filtered in, disjointed, hazy. Erin was asking me about my past.

Jesus! And she said I was nosy. That woman was like the inquisition. Like she was testing me or something. I remember thinking she's nowhere near as pissed as me. Ah! Another fragment. Later, when the place was almost empty, Erin asked me to close my eyes and describe as many people as I could recall among the earlier crowd. I think I got most of them. Why had she made me do that?

And I still didn't remember coming back on-board. I'd got myself into my dinghy, started the engine, untied myself, and motored three-hundred yards in a dark, unfamiliar harbour, and somehow found *Pasha* amongst a flotilla of anchored boats. Then, as if that wasn't hard enough to believe, I'd managed to secure the dinghy and climb aboard, presumably without falling in.

I remembered I wanted to be away today. I'd stocked up with more bottled water yesterday and had over a month's supply of food. I would need to Clear Out this afternoon and pick up the latest Atlantic weather chart – the office was open for two hours only, because of the holiday.

At midday, I upped anchor and motored in to berth alongside the office. While I was waiting for them to open, I hoisted the dinghy up onto the jetty where I could dismantle and deflate it. I then bagged it up and stowed it with my bike in the starboard lazarette.

The guy at the Harbour Office gave me a grilling. Boy, he didn't want me to go. But in the end, he couldn't stop me – he stamped my forms, shaking his head in despair.

'You got Single Side Band?' he asked as if trying for another reason for me not to go.

I shook my head. He was referring to HF Radio for Worldwide communications. It was expensive, and you needed a licence to get a callsign. Besides, my EPIRB via satellite would get me a quicker response in an emergency. I couldn't see the problem. There were no Hurricanes this time of year, the Winter cyclones generally stayed in the far north, and if one did stray south, the worst one should expect were gale force winds and maybe the odd snowstorm.

I would stay on the southerly track to avoid that as far as possible and stay south of the Gulf Stream and its notorious freak waves. It was going to be a lot livelier than my East to West crossing, but doable, I thought. As an extra precaution, I had taken down the genoa and replaced it with my smaller storm gib. I also took down the canvas bimini and stowed it – a stiff gale would make short work of ripping that away otherwise. With three reefs in the mains'l, I was as ready as I could be for whatever the winter Atlantic had in store for me.

Or so I thought.

The first week of the crossing was rough, progress slow with one or two days of unfavourable headwinds. But otherwise, the passage was unremarkable.

On New Years Day, the weather turned on us like a maddened tiger.

7/5

Storm

Wednesday 1 January 2014
1030 34 29.6N 43 36.1W
Course 075 Sp 9 knots
Wind NNW Sp 32 Px 1001 (falling)

Woohoo! A Beam Reach in a full gale.
It came out of nowhere while I was asleep.
When I turned in at two, we were close hauled into
18 knots of wind. Three-metre waves from the north
battled it out with the westerly swell; in other words,
a lively sail and a bit bouncy, but nothing I hadn't
been in before. Wedged in my bunk between a
bunch of pillows, I had slept reasonably well.

  By eight-o-clock when I awoke the wind had
backed into the north, forcing the boat to turn
northeast. It had also strengthened significantly,
whipping up four to five-metre waves that were
punishing us mercilessly. The barometer had
dropped another three millibars, so it looked like
there was worse to come.

Before doing anything else, I needed to get us back on course. So I suited up in full foulies, life jacket and harness, and let myself out into the dark, wind-torn day. The waves were charging in and hitting us like battering rams, the wind took my breath, and for the first time in a year, I felt cold. Almost immediately a solid sheet of water thrown up over the bow thumped down on my hood. And then again, and again. I snapped my harness on and moved gingerly aft, hanging on tight as *Pasha* lurched and battered into the oncoming sea.

First I let out the mainsheets until the sail was on the point of losing the wind, letting the gib blow us off, then struggled to adjust the vane's course setting with one hand, needing the other to hold on to the stern rail. Slowly she came round to starboard, and I trimmed the sails as she went. She steadied up still well short of east, so I repeated the process twice more until she was yawing twenty degrees either side of 075. That was the best I could do. Even with the sails fully shortened we were sluicing over the waves at a gut-heaving nine knots, the starboard rail just about clear of the water. The motion was dizzying and quite terrifying.

Friday 3 January 2014
0650 36 24.3N 038 51.7W
Wind NNE Sp 30 Px 997 (falling)
Course 080 Sp 9

Here's the thing about winter gales; once they get going, they just go on and on. And because of the sustained wind direction, the waves just pile up bigger and bigger. Somewhere up to the northeast, I seemed to have pissed off a humongous depression.

For two more days that hooley continued unabated. And then it just got worse.

Monday 6 January 2014
0138 37 06.5N 033 05.4W
Wind ENE Sp 45 gusting 50 Px 976
Hove-to

There was nothing else for it. By midnight on Sunday, the wind had ramped up – Severe Gale to Storm Ten, which in yachting terms, is Survival Conditions.

With the wind screaming in the rigging and threatening to blow away the mains'l, the rain and spray smashing into me like bullets, I made the only decision possible. I dropped the main and lashed it tight, then tacked to port until the gib whipped across to the other side. I wheeled over to starboard and tied the wheel off to hold it there. Thus, with the gib backed against the wind to stop her turning, *Pasha* was hove-to. To all intents stationary and in a stable list to port. And safe. That was the theory, anyway.

With a final look around to make sure everything was as secure as I could make it, I lurched down into the companionway and slotted in the washboards behind me. I would stay here battened down until the storm abated, no matter how long that took – survival Conditions.

That monstrous wind was terrifying. Demolition waves smashed against the upturned windward hull sending tons of water thundering against the coach roof. I began to understand how fragile my life was - out here in nature's wildest onslaught.

Wedging myself in on the weather side of the saloon, I began to secure the heavy books that were threatening to spill out of their shelves. That's what I was doing when a thunderous wave sent me flying across the saloon onto the lee banquette. There was the crack of a wooden slat breaking, and the library clattered down over me. An avalanche of books: heavy almanacs, hard-backed pilotage guides, thick tomes of Sight Reduction Tables, pages fluttering, like a flock of gannets landing. And there I remained, head protected, wedged into the upturned cushions, half stupefied by the noise and violence, feeling helpless and scared.

And then, with wind and waves doing their best to break us apart, it just got worse.

Pasha heeled over entirely to the storm until she was all but beam ended; blasted flat to the sea by that tremendous wind. I turned to face the saloon's headlining so that the back cushions became my seat, and the seating became my backrest. Detritus was still falling out of the shelves and stowages now almost directly above me. Water began pouring in through the ventilation grills in the washboards as the waves crashed over us. My insides heaved as we were tossed on the crests and floated dizzyingly in freefall when we plunged into the troughs. And through my fear – like a forlorn beacon of hope – I hung on to one reassuring fact: in the 1979 Fastnet

Disaster, not a single boat that hove-to was lost. Damn! Hold that thought.

Oddly, while I lay there frozen in terror, I thought about Dad, and what he'd be saying to me now. In a way – as I'd come to realise since leaving Florida – this trip had been all about him. In his diminished state, I was living the life for him, taking all the risks and rewards on his behalf. And when looked at that way, I felt at last able to forgive myself – like taking Confession but without the priest. I just hoped he would feel the same if I ever I saw him again.

And at last, in all that noise and terror, my mind did the only thing it could. It shut down to minimum processing, to standby, a dreamlike state, and I felt disembodied, contemplating imminent death with a tremendous presence of mind. It was then I felt once more that strange sense of not being alone; that in that semi-wakefulness of shock and dread, I felt the presence of my nebulous friend.

I was staring numbly at the water pouring into the companionway when it happened. There was a premonition - a fleeting sense of something falling - before the heavy wooden box struck my left temple, knocking me senseless. I knew that my injury was terrible, perhaps fatal, as I slipped down into the darkness.

7/6

Concussion

I came-to some hours later with a throbbing head, my face glued to the cushions in a sticky pool of congealed blood. I carefully unstuck myself and sat up.

I noticed the wind seemed to have lost its ferocity of earlier. However, it was still wild and dangerous, *Pasha* still bouncing and bucking horribly in the chaotic sea – but her heel-over was less acute.

Gingerly I explored my head where it hurt most, pleased to feel that the blood had almost completely dried. Under the matted hair, I could feel the lip of a big open wound at my temple hairline, and here the pooled blood was still sticky.

I felt suddenly nauseous and woozy. I wanted to go to the head where I kept the medical kit, but it was still far too boisterous to risk climbing up the tilting deck. Anyway, the way I felt I would probably pass out trying. So I turned over the soiled cushion and lay back down. After a time, I slept.

It was morning when I next woke – the worst of the storm had passed, leaving only the residual fetch of the sea – the waves still formidable.

And the damage to my head.

Apart from the headache, I was feeling much better. While I worked out a plan, I picked up Dad's sextant and slotted it back in its box, reflecting that it was probably the first time that old instrument had seen the light of day in years, probably not used since Dad taught me astronavigation when I was around ten. Now I only kept it in case of emergencies – ironic.

I climbed the sloping deck to the head, where I kept my medical kit. First, a cocktail of analgesics: two paracetamol, two ibuprofen and two co-codamol - to get through the coming hours. I washed and sanitized my head-wound, carefully replacing the flap of skin that the sextant box had opened, and taped a light dressing over it. It needed stitches, but I wasn't going to try suturing in this sea.

The automatic bilge pump was whirring away all that water we'd shipped. The mess in the saloon could wait. The time had come to open up and survey the damage.

Monday 6 January 2014
1214 38 36.4N 032 25.1W
Wind NW Sp 25 Px 998
Co 085 Sp 7.5
Storm Damage Report:
Wind Turbine – 5 Blades sheared off –
unserviceable & tied off

Radar Head – Broken off – cut cable and jettisoned.
Wind Anemometer – spinner broken off – Wind
Direction only
Steering vane – vane broken off – improvised
replacement seems to work.
Sprayhood – torn from its fittings – temporary repair
with gaffer tape.
Spare Danforth Anchor – lost overboard
Lifebuoy, light & lifeline – lost overboard
Spinnaker Pole – lost overboard

Sailing her off had been no problem – I simply
unlashed the wheel and let the wind blow us round
in a full circle, steadying up close-hauled on the port
tack. Getting the damaged wind vane to hold us
there so I could hoist the mains'l was another matter.
It was chicken and egg – without the mainsail's
stabilising influence, *Pasha* refused to hold course
long enough to hoist the mainsail. In the end, I had
to enlist the aid of the engine and the electric
autopilot.

Despite all the damage and lost equipment, my
beautiful, brave, sturdy *Pasha* had seen us through
the worst storm imaginable. And having survived all
that, how did I feel? Grateful for my good fortune,
humbled by my human frailty, and strangely, a
soaring sense of happiness and well-being.

7/7

Rescue

Tuesday 7 January 2014
0600 39 07.4N 031 12.1W
Wind N Sp 15 Px 1003
Co 095 Sp 6.5

I had an almost sleepless night – listless, nauseous, catnapping in the cockpit because we were within a hundred miles of land. I'd seen the lights of several tuna boats during the night, and many more were registering on AIS. Hence, it was not safe to sleep below, though I desperately wanted to. For the last two hours, the loom of the lighthouse on Flores had been strobing the northern horizon. It was only 120 miles to Horta, a day's passage, and my visual sighting of that outlying Azorean island should have lifted my spirits. But I'd been throwing up all night, hadn't been able to keep any food down, and my headache was getting worse.

I sat in a blue haze until sunrise, then stood up to go below, intending to try some breakfast. I stepped onto the ladder – a wave of sickness came over me, dizzy and tired, so, so tired. I realised in a half-dream I was falling down the companionway, dimly aware of my body bouncing off the steps and landing flat on my back on the saloon boards. Then, nothing more.

At some distant time later came fuzzy awareness. Everything was moving – watery sounds. In there somewhere was a noise I should have recognised, an urgent sound but it made no sense. I opened my eyes. Nothing I could see made sense; it was an alien, terrifying world. My head was splitting. I was thirsty. The sound came again, a man's voice. Thick foreign accent. A sliver of sensibility returned – the voice came over the VHF:

> *'Halloo sailing vessel, this is fishing boat Sao Teresa. I am on your starboard side. Halloo sailing vessel—'*

The darkness welcomed me back.

Someone is lifting me, hands under me, voices around me. I open my eyes, see a man's face, dark, hairy. He speaks, but I don't understand. Terrified, I struggle feebly against those carrying me, but my head, oh my head. I close my eyes, feel myself laid on something soft. Foreign voices again as blessed darkness returns.

The next time I became aware it was to a saner world. A soft pillow, thin bedcover – a world that felt weird because it wasn't moving, and I knew instantly, and with a stab of panic, that I was no longer at sea. There was a soft, regular beeping noise, a heart monitor – my heartbeat. I could feel it pounding in my ears in time to the beeping. Okay, I was in a hospital somewhere. Safe, at least. Where, and how I got here would come later. My first concern was that I couldn't seem to open my eyes. I lifted my hand to feel my face. A bandage – my eyes were bandaged over! My head too.

'Hello, can anybody hear me?'

Squeaky footsteps were approaching. 'It is okay, don't worry.' A warm, latex-gloved hand took hold of mine. 'You are in the hospital. You are safe now.' A woman's voice, gentle, caring, foreign accent. I must surely be in the Azores – Portuguese then.

I asked the question uppermost. 'What happened to my boat?'

'Shh, you must rest now. The doctor will come to see you soon. Then we will give you something to help you sleep?'

'Where is my boat – I was on my boat. Who brought me here?'

'You come on the ambulância aérea, the helicóptero, from Ponta Delgado. I think your ship she is in marina, yes?'

'What's wrong with my eyes?'

'Do not worry. You have operation for— coágulo sanguíneo – how you say in English? With the blood in your brain?'

'Blood clot?'

'Sim, blood clot. The doctor has removed. Your eye cover is for protection only, from bright light, they will be sensitive. You want I take off?'

Most of what happened to me during that lost week remains hazy to this day. The doctor in charge of my care knew little about how I'd come to be here. He could only tell me that I'd arrived by air ambulance. Following diagnosis and a brain-scan, I had been taken into emergency surgery to remove a blood clot. After that, they kept me in an induced coma for three days. I awoke on the morning of Wednesday the 15th of January.

The rest I learned later from the woman the British Consulate had sent to visit me. According to what she knew and what I could interpolate, here is what happened. Sometime after 6 am on the 7th of January, I collapsed into the saloon while climbing down the ladder. Here I remained, unconscious for three days, while *Pasha* continued sailing southeast. Help came when, forty miles west of Sao Miguel island, we ploughed through a flotilla of tuna boats, almost colliding with one of them. Getting no reply to his calls on VHF, the fisherman called it in to the Coastguard, who dispatched a cutter to investigate. Boarding *Pasha*, they discovered me unconscious and barely breathing in the saloon. They called the air ambulance to winch me off to the hospital. Someone – I never found out who – sailed *Pasha* into the harbour at Ponta Delgada.

On the following day, I had another visitor to my bedside. Someone so unexpected, I thought I was hallucinating again.

7/8

Opportunity

Her distinctive white smile entered the ward slightly ahead of her as if seeking prior reassurance. This time her dress was more formal; a light blue business suit with trousers that swayed gracefully about her ankles as she walked. It was an outfit modest enough to tone down her striking beauty without dulling her femininity.

With Erin's arrival, huge memory-blanks suddenly made themselves known to me as if they'd been hiding in some boozy corner of my brain.

'Remember me?' she said, pulling up a chair.

'Of course, but what the fuck are you doing here? You stalking me, or something?'

She shook her head, smiling sadly, 'You didn't show for our meeting, did you forget?'

That was one of those blanks that were now waving at me from the bar in St Georges. 'Huh, you said you'd be back there at 4 pm on Boxing Day. I didn't know it was supposed to be a big deal – you should have said.'

'Sweetie, I would have if I'd known you were going to sneak off like a thief in the night.'

'It was broad daylight. So, what was so important? And how did you know I was here?'

Erin returned a scornful smile, 'Same way I knew you were in Bermuda, Sweetie – did you also forget who I work for.'

I stared at her – this was getting creepy. 'So the Consulate told you about my accident. But why would that matter to you— Oh, Jesus! You haven't come to drag me back to get me Sectioned?'

She shook her head, 'No, nothing like that – judicial matters are not my area. Besides, the Crown Court lost interest when you left the country – there's no such thing as extradition on mental health grounds.

'No, I merely wanted to offer you a job, subject of course to a psychiatric examination by one of our own. Would you be interested?'

7/9

Homecoming

s/y Pasha Passage Log
Tuesday 4th February 2014
0955: 50 55N 01 28W Course 085 Sp 6
Wind SW 14kts
Sea: 1m Swell E moderate

I shivered, despite the two fleeces I was wearing under my full foul-weather gear. It would take a while to acclimatise to the British Winter.

I was nearly home. St Catherine's Point lay on the port beam with the chalk cliffs of the Isle of Wight sloping away each side. Spit Bank Fort was visible ahead.

The crossing from the Azores had been fast and furious, further winter gales boosting us along our north-easterly trajectory in little more than a week. I would have stayed longer, but I had had the fantastic news from Julie that Dad had opened his eyes unaided and was now talking. So, I was determined to press on home without further delay. Now, I was nearly home and struggling to curb my excitement.

Erin had given me three months to consider her proposal. Somehow my name had come up in a Civil Service trawl of military records for particular skill sets and attributes. I suspected Professor Hardy had been instrumental in Erin coming after me – nobody else in official circles knew me that well. I met the criteria that made me particularly suitable for a specific undercover role. The civil servant made it quite clear it was me *and* my boat they wanted to hire – one without the other wouldn't work. For security reasons, I could not know the details until, and unless, I signed up.

1425: Passed entrance to Mullhaven Marina
Trip Log: 4241 miles

As we approached the marina, I saw a familiar figure standing motionless on the pontoon and let out a great splutter of unrestrained joy. As soon as the lines were on, I stepped ashore, and we stood for a moment, grinning achingly at one another.

'You look great,' I said, meaning it.

'Quite the little navigator, I hear.'

'Oh, Dad!' I gushed.

And ran into his arms.

EPILOGUE

Random clumps of snowdrops and crocuses had sprung up beneath the two yew trees. Already the daffodils lining the cobblestone footpath were in bud, ready to burst out any day. It was an unusually warm day for February. Still, this morning only two people had ventured into the little churchyard of Cobbingden.

'Nice choice of headstone,' remarked Peter Winterbourne. 'She would have wanted black marble, like Granny Bee and your Grandad's grave in Guildford.'

'Brenton family tradition,' nodded the woman by his side.

'How did—?'

She turned to him, 'Lester told me.'

'Not the white lilies, though,' his voice cracking.

Rosie hugged his arm closer. 'No,' she agreed. 'But they were Mum's favourite flowers. Aren't they just perfect there? Like swans sleeping in the night.'

She'd never seen Dad cry before the Accident, but since he'd woken up, he'd been doing it often. Mr Murchison had told her it was a natural response after a prolonged coma and would pass eventually. Meanwhile, he'd advised, best not to make a fuss.

'Why did you decide to bury her here,' he asked after his trembling had stopped, 'and not in Guildford?'

Rosie was silent for a long moment, quietly contemplating the headstone and wondering how much to tell him. Then she decided – it was time.'

'You know why, Dad. It was the same reason Mum chose to live in Cobbingden when you sold Granny Bee's house. It was where *he* lived.'

She walked to the headstone and picked out a single white lily, then turned to him.

'Come on, Dad, have a little faith in me,' she said, taking his hand and leading him along the line of older graves. She stopped at a small grey plaque marking an interred cremation casket.

'Oh,' said Peter. 'So you do know about him.'

'Lester told me everything. The real reason you sold Granny Bee's house – when Lionel's old tenants moved out of Juniper Cottage in 2005. He left the place to Mum in his will.'

'We didn't know how to tell you—'

'I know, Dad, and I understand.' She squeezed his arm again, then knelt and brushed away a thin layer of moss, revealing the simple inscription:

RIP
Lionel Kilbride
d. 17th February 1986
Aged 36

Rosie laid the white lily across the plaque and stood, wiping a single tear from each eye. Feeling another presence nearby, she looked up towards the yew trees and saw two figures. They were smiling, but spectral, barely there at all. Mum looked radiant, all in white. But there was a certain set to her expression, a worldly-wise look that the Mum she knew had never owned – a look that was all Georgie. Range Rover Man stood by her, tall and handsome but strangely insubstantial, fading in and out of vision as if unsure he belonged. Rosie pictured Anna, and a younger M & D – unmarried then, of course, just good friends – paying their respects all those years ago at this very spot.

Dad was standing on the footpath, head bowed. 'Your Mum came here every year about this time,' he murmured. 'A single white lily—'

She went to him and laid her arms on his shoulders and touched her brow against his.

'Hey,' she said gently. 'I never said, but thank you so much for coming back to me, because you know what? There's only ever been one Dad in my life.'

s/y Pasha Log
Wednesday 19th February 2014
Hauled out at Mullhaven Boatyard
(Repairs and Hull Maintenance)
We'll be back soon

Thank you for reading *To Run Before the Sea*, the first in the Rosie Winterbourne Series. I hope you loved Rosie as much as I enjoyed writing her story.

But, whatever your experience, please remember to post your review on Amazon.

Amazon ratings, based on reader reviews, are the only way independent authors can break into the commercial market. To write a review on Amazon:

https://www.amazon.co.uk/dp/B08FFRJF4F

and scroll down until you see the Write a review button.

I hope you continue to follow Rosie's adventures. Happy Reading

Glossary of Nautical Terms

Autopilot: an electronic device to steer the boat via an electric servo motor attached to the wheel (which I affectionately refer to as *Georgina*).

Azores High: the seasonal high-pressure system prevailing over that part of the Atlantic during late Spring and Summer. Its centre is renowned for its lack of wind and can delay sailboats for many days.

Beam Ends: heeled over on the side so that the deck is almost vertical.

Blocks: the working parts of a pulley system through which a rope is fed.

Broach: to swerve sharply and dangerously in a following sea, so as to be broadside to the waves.

Broad Reach: sailing with the wind on the beam, i.e. at 90° to the bow.

Chainplates: brackets embedded in the deck and anchored inside the hull, to which the shrouds are attached.

Close-hauled: sailing upwind, within 45° of the wind direction; in order to achieve this the sails must be hauled in close.

EPIRB: Emergency Position Indicating Radio Beacon; used to alert search and rescue services in the event of an emergency. In *Island Spirit* the EPIRB is attached to a bulkhead in the saloon, only to be removed for testing or when in actual distress.

Forestay: a wire rope stretched from the bow to the top of the mast; used to hold up the mast and on which the foremost sail (the genoa) is attached.

Genoa: a large, triangular sail attached to the forestay and the masthead.

Hove-to: heaving to (to heave-to and to be hove-to) is a way of slowing a sailboat's forward progress, as well as fixing the helm and sail positions so that the boat does not have to be steered.

Knot: unit of velocity used at sea; equal to one nautical mile per hour. (5 knots = 5.75 mph)

Lee, Leeward: the downwind, or sheltered, side of a vessel. Its opposite is 'windward' or 'weather' side.

NM: Nautical Mile i.e. 1852 metres or 1.15 statute miles. All references to 'miles' in the narrative can be assumed to refer to nautical miles.

Rig: a collective term for the mast, boom and all associated rigging.

Sheet: a rope attached to a sail or boom, used to control the angle of the sail to the wind.

Shrouds: wire ropes supporting the mast on either side of the boat. *Island Spirit* has three shrouds on either side.

Starboard Tack: to be sailing with the wind coming from the starboard side of the boat i.e. the sails are on the port side.

Tack: a verb which means to turn the bow through the wind, causing the sails to switch to the opposite side.

THE TRAVEL AGENT

Rosie Winterbourne Book 2

Rosie is back in an exciting new role.

Employed as a part-time Intelligence Officer while studying Arabic at University, Rosie finds herself headhunted by the secretive Firegate organisation, to be trained in surveillance and self-defence, and sent to Gibraltar in her yacht, *Pasha*, to investigate rumours of defeated Daesh fighters attempting to return home via the Rock.

A fast-moving sequel packed with action and intrigue. *The Travel Agent* is available on Amazon

Coming Next:
The Conflicted Bride: Rosie Winterbourne Book 3

I

About Michael Rothery

I divide my time between working at my home in Elgin, cycling around the Highlands, and cruising the Atlantic/Caribbean islands in my yacht, *Island Spirit*. In past lives, I served twenty-five years in the Royal Navy and then another twenty as Director of a computer software company in the Midlands. Although I have written several novels since retirement, I consider *To Run Before the Sea* my first quality work. I am currently (Oct '20) completing the sequel, The Travel Agent, to be released in December 2020. Several more Rosie Winterbourne stories will follow.

When people ask me what I do, my reply is always, 'I am a novelist'.

Weatherdeck Books